LIZ CARLYLE

Wicked
All Day

POCKET BOOKS

NEW YORK LONDON TORONTO SYDNEY

Pocket Books
A Division of Simon & Schuster, Inc.
1230 Avenue of the Americas
New York, NY 10020

This book is a work of fiction. Names, characters, places, and incidents either are products of the author's imagination or are used fictitiously. Any resemblance to actual events or locales or persons, living or dead, is entirely coincidental.

First Pocket Books paperback edition October 2009

POCKET and colophon are registered trademarks of Simon & Schuster, Inc.

For information about special discounts for bulk purchases, please contact Simon & Schuster Special Sales at 1-866-506-1949 or business@simonandschuster.com.

The Simon & Schuster Speakers Bureau can bring authors to your live event. For more information or to book an event contact the Simon & Schuster Speakers Bureau at 1-866-248-3049 or visit our website at www.simonspeakers.com.

Designed by Julie Schroeder

Cover photography by Pixelworks Studio Inc. Hand lettering by Dave Gatti

Manufactured in the United States of America

10 9 8 7 6 5 4 3 2 1

ISBN 978-1-4165-9492-5
ISBN 978-1-4391-0097-4 (ebook)

Prologue

IN WHICH THE DRASTIC
AND SHOCKING EVENTS COMMENCE.

Even as a small child, she knew that she was different. In a world of the well-born and the other—those far, far beneath—the girl had the misfortune to be neither high nor low. She lived on the outside looking in, her nose pressed to a cold pane of glass which walled her away with whispers, and with glances cut askance.

In her earliest dreams, the girl became not a princess, but a downstairs maid in a gray serge gown with a snowy white apron and a stiffly starched cap. She took tea and toast at the kitchen table, elbow to elbow with everyone else, laughing at the coachman's card tricks. She exchanged hair ribbons and gossip with the chambermaids, and walked out on her half-day with the footman. She became the other. She became someone who *belonged*.

But by the time the girl had grown tall enough to peek over her windowsill at the greater world beyond, it was decided that she should learn to read, and in this way, she came to understand that dreams did not often come true. That unless something drastic and shocking happened—which it never did—she would dwell forever in that oblivion which the world had seemingly destined for no one else. Guarded by her gorgon of a governess, she would live out her days in an empty house devoid of light or warmth, save for those rare occasions when she was driven to Town, or her father came home to dandle her on his knee before vanishing again into the stews and hells of London.

And so it was that the girl began to harden her heart at an age when she scarcely knew she had one. She learned to bear the whispers—and sometimes, even, to laugh at them. But on beautiful days like today, when the clouds scuttled high in a clear blue sky and there was a rolling expanse of green grass to be played upon, she simply vowed not to think of them.

"Poor child. 'Tis said the mother never wanted her."

As usual, the words—benign enough on their face— were spoken in a self-righteous undertone that carried on the breeze, then seemingly hovered, like a mosquito in search of a place to strike blood.

She shut out the voices, tucked her sharp little chin, and tried to look smaller than she already was—which was very small indeed. Forcing her attention to the red-coated infantrymen that her cousin Robin had so assiduously set up across their blanket, she selected the next, and set him in place.

"French, wasn't she? The mistress?"

"And a bit Italian, Cook said. A vile temper to match, too."

"So the chit got it honestly, eh?"

A titter of feminine laughter followed.

Her cousin, of course, was oblivious to the gossip. "Not there, you goose," Robin complained, moving her infantryman to the other side. "The formation is called a square for a reason, Zoë."

She blinked against the hot rush of tears. "But these

two soldiers have made friends," she protested, her bottom lip coming out. "Like us. They should never be separated."

Propped on his elbows, Robin looked up, his hair ruffling in the breeze. "This is war, Zoë, not a doll's tea party."

"Courting a bride now, the black-hearted devil"

"Rannoch? You cannot mean it!"

"They say she's bringing children. Won't want his by-blow, I daresay."

Zoë tried not to look at the servants. "Fine, Robin!" she huffed. "Let's just go back to Brook Street and play with Arabella's dolls."

"Zoë, shush!" Robin cast an anxious look toward his elder brother. The young Marquess of Mercer was knocking around a cricket ball with a pair of older lads, his long legs carrying him gracefully over the grass. Robin returned his gaze to the blanket. "Zoë," he whispered darkly, "if you *ever* tell him about the dolls, I swear—"

"Oh, I shan't tell, you big baby!" Zoë burst out. "I promised, didn't I?"

"Miss Armstrong!" Miss Smith's tone was sharp as she half rose from the park bench. "If the two of you mean to quarrel again, we shall go."

Zoë ignored her. "Sometimes, Robin, you are just mean," she muttered, throwing her arms across her chest.

"Oh, I'm not, and you know it." Robin dumped another bag of soldiers onto the blanket with a clatter. The summer sun shone brilliantly across the flat expanse of Green Park, casting his dark hair with a mahogany sheen. "Here," he said conciliatorily. "Form your next square, goose. No—put back the Green Jacket. This is the 28th Gloucestershire Foot, Zoë. Look, I'll help you sort 'em."

As he began to pluck the green soldiers from the red, Miss Smith harrumphed, and sat back down by her sister. Once a fortnight for the last several months, Miss Smith and Zoë had journeyed from Richmond across the river to London, ostensibly to shop and to become better acquainted with Zoë's cousins. But the truth was, Miss Smith came to meet her sister, Mrs. Ogle, so that they might revile their respective employers, and complain about their circumstances.

As Robin began the next square, the whispers resumed.

"At least he took the chit in. Give the devil his due."

"Still, a wife . . . Mark me, Jane. This is drastic!"

"And shocking!"

"Aye. Things will change—and not for the good."

Almost against her will, Zoë's fists exploded. The 28th Gloucestershire Foot went flying—into the grass, across the blanket, one even striking Miss Smith's spectacles, knocking them askew.

"Zoë, that is quite enough! Up with you, miss!" The governess jerked to her feet and frog-marched her off the blanket. "I've had quite enough of your insolence."

"Ow, stop!" Pain shot through Zoë's shoulder. "It hurts!"

"Zoë?" His voice sharp, Lord Mercer came toward them, swinging his cricket bat almost menacingly.

Immediately, Miss Smith released her arm and crossed the blanket. "Lord Robert," she snapped, cutting a chary glance at Mercer, "gather your toys. Miss Armstrong must go home and learn to govern her wayward temper."

Calmly, Mercer swept up the offending soldier from the grass, then crossed to Zoë and knelt. "Here, Powder Keg," he said, affectionately tapping her nose with it. "Ladies don't hurl toys about. But you knew that, didn't you?"

Lowering her gaze, she took the soldier with a shrug, her bottom lip coming out.

Mercer tipped her chin back up with one finger, his solemn gaze holding hers. "Just try to be good, minx," he murmured. "And I shall ask Papa about . . . things." He shot a glance at Miss Smith. "Can you do that for me? Just for a little while?"

Shyly, Zoë nodded. She never knew what to say to Robin's brother. He seemed so much older. And bigger. But as Mercer withdrew, an even taller shadow fell across the blanket.

"Here now!" said a deep, gentle voice. "What's all this?"

Zoë looked up at the handsome, broad-shouldered gentleman who wore the stiff collar and unrelieved black of a priest, yet carried himself with the unmistakable bearing of a military man.

"Mr. Amherst." Miss Smith curtsied low. "It's just Zoë again. She threw Lord Robert's toys."

"Ah, then he likely provoked it," said Robin's stepfather evenly. He smiled, and bent down to tweak Zoë's chin, his thick, gold hair lifting lightly on the breeze. "My dear child, did I tell you that you grow prettier by the day? Another few years, and you'll be breaking hearts, I'll wager." When he straightened up, he set a hand atop Robin's head. "Now pack up, my boy. We're wanted home for tea, and Zoë has a long drive."

Reluctantly, Lord Robert finished bagging up his soldiers and took his stepfather's hand. After saying one last round of good-byes, they set off in the direction of Mercer, who still observed Zoë with a steady, watchful eye. Almost reluctantly, he hefted his cricket bat onto one shoulder, lifted a hand in Zoë's direction, then fell into formation beside his stepfather.

Zoë watched with envy, and thought of their mother in Brook Street, who likely awaited them with scones and biscuits and warm hugs all around.

Zoë, if she was lucky, would take tea with MacLeod, the butler. Her papa, the Marquess of Rannoch, was never at home. And now—if Miss Smith had the right of it—Papa might get married. Then Zoë would have that most dreaded of creatures, a stepmother, which would likely be worse, even, than having Miss Smith as a governess. Her lip still protruding, she turned to see the two sisters shaking the grass from the blanket.

"When I grow up," she announced to no one in particular, "I shall marry Mercer and go to live in Brook Street."

Mrs. Ogle gave a sharp laugh. "Oh, I doubt that, Miss Armstrong," she said, snapping the last wrinkle from the blanket. "For all that they are your distant relations, Lord Mercer and Lord Robert are . . . well, rather differently placed in society."

"Yes, *quite* different," said Miss Smith coldly. "Your cousins shall marry ladies of rank and proper breeding.

Do not embarrass yourself, child, by assuming that family feels anything for you save Christian charity."

Zoë watched as the two women stuffed the blanket back into its wicker basket, and felt the old, familiar resentment boiling up inside her. She *hated* Miss Smith and Mrs. Oglethorpe. Hated them for the way they made her feel—and for the truth they spoke whilst doing it.

They were referring, she knew, to what Miss Smith called *"the unfortunate circumstances of her birth."* Zoë wasn't perfectly sure what that meant, but she knew it wasn't good. That *she* wasn't good. And it was slowly dawning on Zoë that if one couldn't be good no matter how hard one tried . . . well, perhaps one might as well revel in being bad?

Drastic and shocking indeed!

Chapter One

The utter silence that hung expectantly over the card table was broken only by the distant *clack!-clackity!-clack!* of a roulette wheel somewhere in the depths of what had once been an elegant ballroom. But the merchant who had built the brick mansion two decades past had long since bankrupted himself on—ironically—a turn of the cards. And now, in the smoke-hazed gaming hell, over the merchant's former dinner table, a collective gasp held sway.

The swell of her ivory breasts shifting beneath her plunging bodice, Lufton's dealer leaned over the polished mahogany. The last card fell as if through water, sent floating from Mrs. Wingate's slender fingers like an autumn leaf seeking the rot and ruin of an earthly end.

The ace of hearts.

The collective gasp burst into exhalation, then into reluctant applause.

"Well played, my lord!" For the fifth time in as many hands, Mrs. Wingate pushed a pile of ill-got gains toward the Marquess of Mercer. "Will you try your luck again?"

With a stiff nod, the marquess relaxed into his chair, his silver cheroot case glittering in the lamplight as he withdrew it. Standing behind him, Mercer's mistress settled a hand anxiously upon his shoulder. He ignored it, lit a cheroot, and kept his eye on the man who sat opposite, for the scent of feverish desperation was growing thick in the air. He had been driving Thurburn relentlessly these past three hours, and now, as dawn neared, the signs of strain were telling.

Mrs. Wingate finished her deal. Mercer drew middling cards, and decided to leave well enough alone, blowing out a long plume of smoke as the other three gentlemen drew again. He watched assessingly the small bead of sweat which trickled south, catching in the fine hair of Thurburn's left eyebrow. Mrs. Wingate turned up a queen, and the gentleman fell back into his chair with a groan. "I'm out."

"Oh, your luck's what's out, old chap!" Beside Thurburn, Colonel Andrews grinned. "Got to come back soon, what? Probability, and all that rot."

In the end, the remaining players drew hands no better than Mercer's. Mrs. Wingate smiled almost beatifically. The house held a pair of nines and a deuce. Mercer inclined his head. "Madam, we congratulate you."

Suddenly, the strain broke. Thurburn tossed back what was left of Lufton's very fine cognac and pushed away. "The hour grows late," he murmured, only the faintest tremble of his hand betraying him. "Gentlemen, I bid you good night."

The late hour, of course, had nothing to do with it. Thurburn and his coterie were regulars at Lufton's, and nothing but desperation drove them from their gaming tables before dawn. The man was edging near insolvency—which suited Mercer's purposes very well indeed.

Amongst the hoots and derision of Thurburn's companions, Mercer lifted one finger. The insults died away, and Thurburn's eyes lit with hope. "Yes?"

"You are on your way out, I realize," said Mercer quietly. "But I wonder . . . could you perhaps be persuaded to a small private wager before you go?"

His gaze suspicious, Thurburn hesitated. "What did you have in mind, Mercer?"

The marquess feigned a look of utter boredom, a skill well honed. "You have in your possession, I believe, a certain trinket belonging to the Vicomtesse de Chéraute? One which you won from her earlier in the evening?"

Behind him, Claire gave Mercer's shoulder a faint squeeze. Something like fear flitted behind Thurburn's eyes. "The hand was fairly played, sir."

"To be sure," said the marquess coolly.

Thurburn's gaze flicked up at Claire, a faint, sour smile curving his mouth. "Ah, wants it back, does she?"

Mercer crooked one dark eyebrow, and turned to look over his shoulder. "Madam, your wish?"

Claire shrugged. *"Alors la,* 'tis but a trifle," she said with Gallic disdain. "But *oui,* if you should like to play for it, why not?"

If he should like to play for it?

Mercer resisted the urge to shove her hand from his shoulder. Claire's desperate missive, sent round to his Mayfair house near midnight, had been spotted with her tears and sealed with her kiss. The whole of it reminded him yet again of her inherent guile—and her incurable fondness for gaming.

He managed to smile up at her. "One hates to see you deprived of so much as a bauble, my dear," he said. "What do you say, Thurburn? A quarter of my night's winnings against the necklace? Of course, if you win, your companions will no doubt implore you to remain at the table—tiresome, to be sure."

Thurburn licked his lips avariciously. He was more prideful, Mercer knew, than his cohorts, and perhaps hesitant to stake plunder so recently won, thereby all but admitting to an empty purse. But Mercer—helped along by the competent Mrs. Wingate—had been systematically stripping the man of cash, and in this poor light, flushed with a copious amount of brandy, Thurburn could not be entirely confident of the necklace's worth.

"*Half* your winnings, my lord," Thurburn proposed, drawing his chair back to the table with an ominous scrape. "What do you say?"

With a smile, Mercer reached up, and patted Claire's hand. "I'm a fool, I daresay, for I have a fondness for the trinket, even if the vicomtesse does not," he said. "As I often remind her, that little ruby drop in the center quite puts me in mind of—"

"My *lord*!" Claire snapped out her fan and began to ply it vigorously.

Mercer lifted one shoulder, then nudged half his winnings forward. Thurburn rummaged in his pocket, extracted the strand of perfectly matched rubies, and laid it upon the table with a faint clatter.

Mercer looked at Mrs. Wingate. "Madam, will you oblige us?"

The woman nodded and extracted a fresh pack. "The dealer abstains," she said, cutting it cleanly. "This *once*."

Her message was clear. Lufton's made no money on a private wager. Good clients were to be indulged from time to time, but if they wished to continue, they must go elsewhere. It little mattered, for Mercer meant to finish this business now.

Mrs. Wingate dealt the first two passes, the initial cards down. Thurburn drew a deuce, Mercer a three. An unpromising start. Mercer tipped up the corner of his first card and felt Claire's nails dig into his shoulder.

Mrs. Wingate cocked a brow in Thurburn's direction. The gentleman smiled confidently, and touched the back of his card. Mercer followed suit. A six of clubs and a four of hearts fell, respectively. Mercer cursed inwardly.

"Small fish, sir, small fish!" warned Colonel Andrews, who sat nearby.

Again, the dealer offered. Thurburn nodded. Mrs. Wingate laid a ten of diamonds before him. The crowd groaned. She turned her gaze on Mercer, a hint of warning in her eyes. A fourth card, he knew, was most dangerous. But there was something—something in Thurburn's face. Yes, that faint twitch at one corner of his mouth. It was telling, for Mercer had been closely observing the bastard all night.

Swiftly, he ran through the odds—admittedly bad—then cast one last look at Thurburn's hand. A respectable eighteen. And still he sat, unmoved. Knowing it was at once sheer folly and yet his only alternative, Mercer nodded.

The four of diamonds fell.

The crowd about the table bent expectantly nearer. With a satisfied smile, Thurburn flipped his first card, another deuce. Colonel Andrews patted a heavy hand upon Mercer's shoulder. "Bad luck, eh?"

Mercer softly exhaled, then, with the corner of the four, flipped his first card.

The jack of spades.

"Mon Dieu!" Claire cried.

The applause broke out yet again as Mrs. Wingate's eyes widened. "Your luck is indeed prodigious, my lord," she murmured.

Claire seized his hand and drew him from the table, Mercer sweeping up the tangle of rubies as he went.

Moments later, Lord Mercer and his mistress stood but inches apart in one of Lufton's private chambers, rooms that were set aside for patrons who were too inebriated to make their way home, or who found themselves otherwise in need of a firm mattress. The fact that the gaming hell kept a carriage harnessed and a list of London's best prostitutes to hand was certainly not lost on their customers. Anything to keep a pigeon from flying Lufton's finely feathered nest.

Claire circled around Mercer, drawing her long, clever fingers across his back as she went. *"La, monsieur,* once again you have rescued your damsel in distress," she murmured. "How, I wonder, am I to show my appreciation tonight?"

"By promising to never again wager your husband's family jewels," he snapped.

But Claire was too intoxicated on gaming and champagne to sense the seething anger inside Mercer. She trailed her fingertips across the breadth of his chest, then twirled about like a ballerina, rubies dripping from one hand. *"Mon Dieu,* my lord, you sound like my husband— and what is the pleasure in that, I ask?"

"Pray stop twirling about, Claire, and sit," he ordered. "I wish to speak with you."

Claire's bottom lip formed a perfect moue as she

paused, lowering her gaze with a sweep of dark lashes. "No, you wish to chide me," she corrected. *"Alors,* I have it!" She glanced up, her blue eyes alight with mischief, her clever fingers going at once to the fall of his trousers.

"Claire," he said warningly.

But she had already sunk down onto her knees, the pale pink silk of her gown puddling about his shoes. *"Oui,* I will reward you with this—my special skill, which you like very much, *n'est-ce pas?"*

Mercer fisted one hand in her hair, intent upon dragging Claire to her feet. But in the end—being a man of strong appetites and less discernment than was wise— the marquess accepted her gesture of gratitude in the spirit in which it had been offered. Out of greed, and out of desperation. Theirs had long been a symbiotic relationship.

When the spasms had ceased to wrack his body and given way to a mild, emotionless sort of enervation— Mercer could not quite call it satisfaction—he drew Claire gently to her feet, and began to restore his clothing to order.

"Do you remember, Claire, the night we met?" he asked, stabbing in his shirttails.

Claire had extracted a small mirror from her reticule and was leaning over the bedside lamp, studying her lips as if for damage. *"Mais oui,* at Lady Bleckton's winter masque." She paused to dab something red onto her lips with her pinkie. "How dashing you were, my lord, in your sweeping black cloak—and that is *all* I can remember."

"Indeed? It was the night your husband left you."

Claire trilled with laughter. *"Oui,* but who has got the

better of that bargain? He has his draughty old château, whilst I have his jewels. And you, *mon chéri*. I have you."

When he turned to merely stare at her, Claire snapped the mirror shut, and came tripping across the room, her face fixed in that sly, suggestive smile which no longer had the power to make his groin tighten and his stomach bottom out.

"You have the *use* of his jewels, my dear," he warned her. "They are not yours to wager."

Setting her small, white hands against his chest, she leaned into him, washing him in the familiar, almost sickening scent of lilies and anise. "A mere technicality, my lord," she murmured. "And do you not confess that *le vicomte*'s loss has been your gain?"

He felt his mouth curve with a faint smile. "I never confess to anything, Claire. You know that."

Her pout returned. But this time, as he stared down his chest and watched her lips—lips that mere moments ago had been slick and wet on his feverish body—it was as if he watched from a great distance, through pane after pane of wavering glass which somehow distorted her beauty and made it hard to remember why he had once thought himself so taken with her.

A feeling of cold resolve flooded over him, and with it came something darker. Stronger. It was shame, he thought. Shame and the wish to flee this farce of his own making. How had he not seen it? Even his own mother, who never interfered in anyone's business, had warned him it would come to this.

Oh, he had kept women of skill and experience before, when it had been mutually beneficial to both parties. And God knew Claire was tempting, with her pale, ethereal beauty, and that eternal need to be rescued from *something*. A bullying husband. A broken fingernail. Debt. Any disaster, large or small, could engender tears which, on any other woman, would have reddened the nose and swollen the eyes, but on Claire merely clung to the tips of her impossibly long lashes and left her looking even more fragile and dewy-eyed than before.

Mercer stepped away, and finished hitching up his trouser buttons. Claire shot him a suspicious, assessing look, that plump bottom lip snared in her teeth now. He could almost hear the cogs and wheels inside her head spinning as she calculated. Suddenly she turned and, casting one last glance over her shoulder, swished her way toward the bed, and began to draw down the covers, smoothing the wrinkles from the sheets in long, inviting motions, knowing all the while that he watched her.

Mercer remained silent.

"You are displeased with me," she eventually said, feigning contrition. "I should not have intruded upon your privacy tonight. Come to bed, my lord, and I shall make it all worth your while, *oui?*"

But he went instead to the window and stared down into the late night traffic of St. James's, one hand at his waist, the other rubbing pensively at the back of his neck, where a dull ache was setting in. Carefully, and with a measure of reluctance, he chose his words.

"I am not going to bed with you again, Claire," he finally answered. "It is over. It has been over for some time. I think we both of us know that."

"Mercer?" Her voice was sharp, her silk skirts rustling as she hastened toward him. "Whatever do you mean?"

He lifted his gaze to the window, observing her

approach in the watery reflection. "We are just using one another, Claire," he said quietly. "As I used you just now. As you used me tonight in the gaming room. This—*us*— it is over, my dear."

Her breath seized. *"Mais non!"* she whispered, setting a tremulous hand between his shoulder blades. "You— You cannot mean this! Why, there is nothing for me but you. What will become of me? Where shall I go?"

"Oh, such drama, Claire." His voice was hollow. "You shall go home. To the house in Fitzrovia for now. But home to Auvergne—to your husband—would be even better."

"Non!" she cried, recoiling. "Chéraute, he . . . why, he hates me. And he is old. He smells of camphor and of onions and—oh, *how* can you say such a vile thing to me in that cold, cold voice of yours?"

At that, Mercer turned abruptly, fixing her with his stare. It was not the first time he'd been accused of being cold. "Chéraute does not hate you, Claire," he replied. "Indeed, I begin to think he never did. He simply cannot afford you—and neither can I."

"Oh! Do you think me such a fool as all that?" All pretense of seduction gone, Claire narrowed her eyes to glittering slits. "You are likely the richest man in all London. You could afford me ten times over."

He seized her firmly but gently by her upper arms. "I choose *not* to afford you," he corrected. "However much money I have, I can no longer afford this . . . this *madness* in my life. The not knowing where you will be from one night to the next, nor how much you will lose. Claire, you shed your notes of hand like my dogs shed hair, and I must follow you all over town, sweeping up the mess."

"Then you mean to leave me with nothing—not even my pride?" Her visage darkened. "Your heart is like ice, *mon chéri.* Chéraute does not want me. You heard him say as much all those months ago."

Mercer gave her a gentle shake. "*Make* him want you, Claire," he answered. "That is what you are so very good at. Ply those 'special skills' upon your husband for a change."

He saw the hand rise to strike him, and did not wince from it. The backhanded blow caught him square across the cheekbone, her ruby ring stinging like a blade beneath his eye. When it was over, he still stood unflinching before her, almost savoring the pain. It was probably less than he deserved.

"Go back to France, my dear." He kept his voice steady. "You are a beautiful young woman. Go to Chéraute and mend your fences. Change your ways. We are both of us better than this."

But Claire was still trembling with indignation. "I will not be sent away like a child! I will not go to France. You will not avoid me like this."

"I am not trying to avoid you, Claire. I am telling you what is so. We are done."

A mélange of hatred and resignation sketched across her face. "*Très bien,* my lord," she retorted, drawing back one step. "But know this: I will not hide myself. I will not make this easy for you. Indeed, I have a card to Lady Kildermore's soiree in a week's time. Do you imagine I will not go?"

Mercer let go of her arms, and gave one last, bitter smile. "If my mother invited you, Claire, then by all means, go," he answered. "I do not think our grief is such that either of us is apt to burst into tears at the sight of the other, do you? Certainly mine is not."

It was not, apparently, a question Claire wished to ponder. *"Espèce de salaud!"* she hissed—just before she tried to slap him again.

Chapter Two

IN WHICH OUR VALIANT
HEROINE IS RESCUED.

*L*ord Robert Rowland propped one heel upon the ballroom wall and reclined, absently nibbling at the sweets he'd plucked off one of his mother's elegant candied centerpieces, and pondering his imminent death from sheer and utter boredom.

"Here lies Robin," he muttered to himself, *"choked to death on tedium and sugarplums."*

It was, at least, a beautiful sort of tedium. Lady Kildermore's little soiree—for Robin's mother refused to think of it as a ball—had gradually grown into the celebrated grand finale of London's social season. Beneath the glow of two hundred candles, half of Mayfair seemed to promenade and twirl to the sound of London's finest orchestra. Tables covered with food and footmen laden with drinks dotted every public room in the house, while the library had been given over to cards, with half a dozen tables filled.

Lady Kildermore, however, had forbidden her second son the solace of cards, and ordered him to remain in the ballroom where he was to converse with all the wallflowers. Instead, to amuse himself, Robin had been drinking a trifle deep, and letting his eyes trail over the crowd, methodically dividing the women into three categories:

bedable, unbearable, and already bedded. He was just settling his eye on a quite bedable widow in a red dress, and wondering at his odds, when his elder brother, Lord Mercer, materialized from the throng.

"Kindly take your foot off the wall." Mercer looked as cool and detached as ever. "Your heel is marring Mamma's new wallpaper."

"Umgh." Robin would have told Mercer to go bugger himself—good-naturedly, of course—but his tongue was occupied with a bit of sugared goo wedged against his upper molars.

Unlike Robin, who preferred brighter colors, the marquess looked starkly resplendent tonight in black with a silver waistcoat and a flowing, flawless cravat. Elegant, but plain as a pikestaff. That was old Stuart.

"At least we've a crush tonight," Mercer murmured, his gaze sweeping across the ballroom. "I hope Mamma is pleased."

"Mamma does not give a damn." The goo finally dislodged, Robin tossed the last sugarplum into the air and caught it expertly in his mouth.

"Indeed?" His brother merely crooked one eyebrow.

"She does this only because it is expected," Robin continued, speaking around the sweet. "As soon as you do your duty and marry your marchioness, Mamma will flee to Cambridgeshire to live out her life in Papa's poky old vicarage."

"You used to like Elmwood." Mercer was still scanning the crowd as if he were an officer of the deck searching the horizon for enemy warships.

"Still, it *is* poky," said Robin, swallowing. "And old. But then, I like Scotland, so what does that say of my taste? By the way, where the devil have you been this last hour?"

"Working the back rooms," he murmured, "and averting various catastrophes whilst Mamma and Papa finish receiving."

Robin gave another noncommittal grunt and began to dust the sugar from his hands. Strictly speaking, Mercer should have been receiving, for the house in Brook Street was his, the estate having come to him upon their father's death almost two decades past. But their mother and her second husband, the Venerable Mr. Cole Amherst, still resided there when in town, along with Robin and their four sisters, all of whom were still in the schoolroom.

For his part, Robin had often contemplated removing to a bachelor's accommodation, but he was a man who loved life's comforts, and had grown overfond of the many little luxuries life in Brook Street had to offer—and, truth be told, he was passing fond of his family, odd lot though they were.

"Any catastrophes thus far?" he asked Mercer as the widow in red came twirling past.

His brother jerked his head toward the grand entrance hall. "To commence the evening's festivities, Freya slipped out of bed to peek over the balustrade, then dropped her stuffed octopus onto Princess Lieven's head. Sent the poor woman shrieking back into the street."

Robin winced. "Thus dooming her chance at Almack's at the tender age of nine?"

"With Freya, it was merely a matter of time." Mercer lifted one shoulder. "At least she wasn't drunk in the card room. That's where I found Sir Stephen, accusing Mrs. Henry of having an ace down her bodice."

"Noxious old sot." Robin tried to follow the lady in red as she wove through the crowd. "What did you do?"

"Put him downstairs in Charlie's sitting room to sleep it off," said his brother, extracting a slender silver case from his coat pocket. "Now I mean to go light a much-deserved cheroot on the terrace, and pray that Mamma does not notice. Join me?"

But Lord Robert had other plans. A man, he reminded himself, should never become too attached to any one female. That was how accidents like marriage happened. "No, but thanks," he said distractedly. "I think I ought to kindle another sort of flame. That lady in red just there, Stu—I cannot quite recall her name."

"Ah, the infamous Mrs. Field!" murmured Mercer with a mocking bow. "Good luck, Brother. May you find her easily plowed."

Robin groaned, but at that very instant, the violins drew their last, tremulous strains. The notes hung in the air for an expectant moment, then the dancers fell away from their partners, smiling and laughing, Mrs. Field but a few paces distant.

Surrendering Robin to his fate, Lord Mercer set a course directly across the ballroom. The remaining dancers parted like the Red Sea before him. At his approach, a few of the more practiced ladies snapped open fans and plied them rather too vigorously, their gazes dropping with feigned modesty as he passed. Mercer was not fooled; he knew precisely what such women offered—and had he not, these last few months with his mistress would most certainly have enlightened him.

No, he was far more intrigued by the slender, waif-like creature he had just espied strolling deeper into the gardens. His cousin Zoë, God's most diligent mischief maker. And she was hanging upon the arm of one of her more salacious suitors. Mercer sensed another catastrophe in the making.

At the French windows, he hesitated, taking a surreptitious look round to see who might be observing his departure. Zoë's father, Lord Rannoch, was nowhere to be seen, and the musicians had just struck the first notes of a popular country dance. Everyone seemed to be surging toward the dance floor.

Tucking his silver case away, Mercer stepped out onto the terrace. Here, the garden lanterns swayed in the faint summer breeze, casting eerie, flickering shadows across the flagstone and into the garden's lush foliage. Mercer went down the steps, not entirely sure why he did so. Indeed, he was never certain of anything where Zoë was concerned. He knew only that she was apt to get herself into trouble, and that he would drag her kicking and screaming out of it. Then, undoubtedly, she would rail at him after the fact whilst he held his tongue and his temper.

A telltale flash of shimmering gold—Zoë's shawl— led him down the garden path and round the faintly gurgling fountain. Frustrated, he picked up his pace. In the deepening gloom, his every sense heightened. The sound of the crickets. The smell of the Thames far below. And still lingering in the air, unless he imagined it, the fragrance Zoë had long favored; an exotic combination of citrus and jasmine which always made him think of her. All these things came to him as Mercer's feet fell softly on the winding flagstone, and something vaguely sickening—dread or regret, perhaps—began to churn in his stomach.

He had no doubt that he would find the pair—the garden was not large—and little doubt of what he would see once he did so. A rake and a rotter to his very core, Randall Brent was forever on the doorstep of Insolvent Debtor's Court. Such a man had but one reason for escorting Zoë so deep into the greenery, and Zoë was a fool to have gone. Perhaps, he grimly considered, it would serve the heedless chit right to find herself married off to the bastard. But that notion served to make him more frustrated still.

Just then, Mercer turned a corner near the very edge of the lamplight's reach. Zoë's back was to him, her gossamer gold shawl hanging carelessly from her elbow, one end trailing the ground. Her gaze was locked with Brent's. The scoundrel towered over her slender form, his hand grasping her upper arm. Clearly they did not hear his approach, for though their voices were low, both spoke with an urgency Mercer did not like.

Suddenly, everything happened at once. Brent seized Zoë's other arm, yanking her nearer. But not near enough. In a flash, Zoë lifted one knee. She stamped her foot hard, ramming her heel into the top of Brent's arch. On a yelp, Brent let go, and hopped back on one foot, careening sideways into Mercer's path.

Mercer caught him by the shoulder, and jerked him up sharp. "Brent, you will excuse yourself from my home, sir," he said tightly.

Brent's eyes widened. "But she—she—" Here, he cut

Zoë a nasty glance. "You minx!" he hissed. "You came out here with me willingly. Tell him, damn you."

"La, sir," said Zoë, calmly drawing up her shawl, "I agreed to stroll with you, not to be dragged into the shrubbery like some threepenny strumpet."

"Zoë, be silent," Mercer commanded. He thrust out his arm in the direction of the back gate. "Now get off my property, Brent. I don't give a bloody damn what you thought she intended."

The man sidled away, still hobbling on one foot. "The little jade was *willing*," he hissed. "She came out with me alone into the dark—and I shan't hesitate to say so."

"You weren't in the dark," said Mercer coolly. "Moreover, I have been your escort the whole time, as I am sure Miss Armstrong is aware. You realized, Zoë, did you not, that I was but a few steps behind?"

Zoë lowered her sweeping black lashes in mock contrition. "Yes, my lord. Of course."

Mercer smiled tightly at her. "Well, that affair is settled," he said, returning to his former guest. "As to you, Brent, should another vulgar allegation pass your lips with regard to my cousin, you'll be settling *your* affairs. I trust I needn't strip off a glove to make my point?"

A look which might have been fear flared behind his eyes, then Brent turned and slowly melted into the darkness. Mercer watched him go, raw hatred seething in his gut.

But why? Brent was the same scoundrel he had ever been. And Zoë—well, she was the same rash little coquette, and too damned beautiful for her own good. Mercer wanted, suddenly, to rail at her. To shake her until her teeth rattled and her hair came tumbling down. To turn her over his knee and—

Ah, God. What a fool he was.

Abruptly, he turned. "Take my arm," he gritted, offering it. "I shall see you safely inside."

Zoë looked at him hesitantly.

"*Take* it," he snapped.

Something in his gaze convinced her. Abruptly, she seized it, stepping out in some haste to keep pace with his longer strides. Mercer did not slow, but instead more or less dragged Zoë back up the garden path, stopping only when they were well within view of the ballroom.

On the flagstone terrace, she paused some distance from the doors, lifted her skirts a fraction, and gave a perfunctory curtsey. "You are very kind, Mercer," she said. "I thank you."

He gave a humorless laugh, and drew his silver case from his pocket again. "Oh, I doubt it," he said. "As usual, Zoë, you think you had matters under control."

Her lips formed a perfect little moue. "Good heavens, Mercer, it was just a flirtation," she said. "I daresay you mean to rip up at me now."

He watched her intently across the terrace as he extracted a cheroot. Sometimes it felt as if she *wished* to torment him. But the urge to rattle her teeth had receded, thank God, displaced by his usual cool distance. "It is hardly my job to lecture you," he returned. "But it *is* Rannoch's—and in my opinion, the man's a coward for not giving you a good caning eons ago."

Zoë gave an impudent swish of her skirts as she stepped an inch nearer. "Why, you look rather as if you might like to do the job for him," she whispered, her voice pitched as if to send a shiver down his spine. "And I swear, Mercer, that scowl quite ruins your good looks."

Somehow he managed to look unfazed. "Why Zoë," he drawled, "I didn't know you cared."

She tossed her head, the lamplight catching the emerald drops that swung from her plump earlobes. "Well, I don't, I daresay," she retorted. "Just be careful it doesn't freeze like that and stick your haughty eyebrows together. Your pretty vicomtesse mightn't find you so appealing in bed."

Despite himself, Mercer gave a bark of laughter. The chit really was quite unrepentant. After shaking his head, he set the cheroot to his lips. "I would ask your indulgence, Zoë," he said, thumbing open his vesta box, "but I know you aren't much bothered by smoke."

A familiar, deeply mischievous smile tugged at her mouth. "Very little," she agreed, lifting her chin as if to show off her pale, swanlike neck. "I don't suppose you'd care to share?"

"Absolutely *not*." Mercer lit the cheroot, still eyeing her warily. "Now, tell me, Zoë, what would you have done had Rannoch caught you hiding out here with Brent? Do you never consider such things?"

"Dash it, I wasn't *hiding* with Brent." She exhaled on an exasperated huff. "I was hiding *from* Papa, if you must know, because Sir Edgar told me Papa was looking for me, and those two circumstances taken together never spell good news for me, if you know what I mean."

"I'm not sure I do," he replied.

"Oh, never mind!" Zoë threw up her hands. "In any case, Brent merely caught up with me on the terrace, and asked me to stroll. It seemed as good a diversion as any. After all, that's half the battle, isn't it?"

"What?"

"Diversion," she answered impatiently.

"Diversion from what, pray?"

She swallowed, the muscles of her throat sinuous as silk. "Well, from . . . from life's tribulations."

"Life's tribulations, eh?"

Pondering this, Mercer puffed for a time in an attempt to coax the tobacco fully to life, his wary gaze never leaving Zoë's face. He had never understood her, this dark, dangerous vixen who had somehow grown from a solemn, mop-haired child to an effervescent, giggling pain in his arse, and then into—well, into something that could cause even a sensible man to lose sleep at night, were he fool enough to let it. And no one had ever called Mercer a fool.

"Do you know what Brent is, Zoë?" he finally asked.

"Oh, for pity's sake, I cut my teeth on men like Randall Brent." She marched two steps nearer, defiance flashing in her oddly colored eyes. "The man's an arrant womanizer, yes. On the other hand, so are you—and yet here I stand, perfectly safe."

He exhaled slowly, sending a long stream of gray smoke into the darkness. "Yes," he said quietly. "But I am a womanizer of a different sort altogether, my dear."

"Well, it hardly matters, does it?" She leaned into him, her small, gloved hands still set high on her hipbones. "Indeed, I sometimes think you wouldn't try to kiss me again, Mercer, if I begged for it."

"How astute of you," Mercer murmured, wishing to God she'd step back, and stop reminding him what a fool he was. Wishing to the devil that warm, sensual scent of jasmine and spice didn't waft up on the heat from her skin. "No, I do not trifle with unmarried ladies, and—"

"You did once," she persisted, her voice a dusky whisper. "A long time ago. Do you remember, Mercer? I do."

Did he remember?

Dear God. He remembered every time he saw her— but if ever he laid a hand on Zoë Armstrong again, he likely would not stop at a kiss. Mercer, however, was schooled in self-discipline, so he hid the heated frustration that was ratcheting up inside him. Instead, he merely lifted one brow and forged on.

"Brent is not just a womanizer, Zoë," he continued. "He's a rake. He'd ruin you just for the pleasure of it."

"My, are we changing the subject?" Zoë stepped another inch closer, charging the air with electricity as her voice warmed him. "Are you really so unlike me, Mercer? Do you . . . do you never think about . . . well, about that one time?"

For an instant, his breath seized, then, "Oh, no, don't try your wiles on me, my girl," he gritted. "I don't for a moment think you serious. Now, I believe we were discussing Randall Brent?"

The charge in the air quieted abruptly, and Zoë's mischievous smile returned. "Hoo!" she said dismissively. "You think I can't handle his sort?"

"That's half the trouble, Zoë," he answered, pensively tapping off his ash. "I'm relatively confident you can."

At that, her dark, arching eyebrows snapped together. "Then I do not understand why you must be so churlish over a meaningless flirtation."

Inexplicably, her sangfroid angered him. "And what I do not understand," he snapped, "is why you cannot see that you deserve something better."

Her gaze widened.

"And what I cannot understand," he continued, both his tongue and temper slipping, "is why you throw yourself away on men like Brent. Why you break men's hearts for sport. Or why you waste an obviously fine mind in frivolous pursuits and pointless flirtations. That, Zoë, is what I do not understand. So, would you like to argue about those things? Would you care to explain to me why you prefer something meaningless to something— or *someone*—who is real?"

At that, she dropped her hands, still fisted, her glower melting into a look of dumbstruck stupefaction. Her mouth opened, then closed again.

"No," he said quietly, "I thought not."

Then Mercer drew one last puff on his cheroot, and hurled it into the darkened depths of the side garden. He had lost his taste for it. Moreover, he'd lost his taste for this conversation. And he certainly did not need his impetuous young cousin reminding him of his own folly, however long ago it might have been.

With one last nod to her, he turned on one heel and reentered the ballroom, his face as emotionless as when he'd left it. But he scarcely saw his mother's guests, nodding to them mechanically as he tried to figure out just when it was that Zoë had begun to enrage him so thoroughly.

Was it when she had challenged him to a carriage race in front of the Prime Minister? When she had held her nose and pretended to drown in Elmwood's millpond, costing him his brand new pocket watch? Or perhaps it was when she'd announced her secret plan to seduce his stepfather's curate, and proceeded to charm the poor man into a state of utter discombobulation in the middle of Lent.

The list of possibilities had grown as long as his temper was short by the time he ran into his brother. Robin's face held a sheepish grin which jolted him at once from his sullen mood. Somehow, Mercer managed to greet him with a hearty slap on the back, and together they turned to cross the ballroom.

"Any luck with Mrs. Field?"

Robin shrugged. "I don't think the lady cared for my waistcoat," he confessed. "I am unaccountably cast down."

"As I see." A wry smile twitched at Mercer's mouth. "Lord knows you've delicate sensibilities."

Robin laughed. "Perhaps my heart just wasn't in it."

They made the rounds together for perhaps another quarter hour, greeting friends and family, and occasionally pausing long enough to pencil their names onto a lady's dance card. "Doing the pretty," Robin called it, and although he made fun of the process, he set about it with good grace. He had no choice. Their mother would have cheerfully flogged him otherwise.

Mercer did not bother to tell his brother about Zoë. Too often, Robin was Zoë's partner in crime—though admittedly less so now that Robin's heart had been engaged, however inconstantly, by another. But his mistress aside, Robin would just defend Zoë's antics as he always did. Taken together, Mercer sometimes thought, the pair of them wouldn't add up to one sensible person.

At last he and Robin paused long enough to snatch two glasses of champagne from a passing footman. "Well, I'm glad that's over," said Robin, surveying the crowd over his glass. "I think I have made idle chitchat with each of Mamma's designated wallflowers."

Suddenly, a motion by the orchestra dais caught Mercer's eye. "God's teeth," he swore.

Robin's head swiveled round. "What now?"

"Rannoch," Mercer whispered. "He's dragging Zoë from the ballroom."

"Gad, that's becoming a regular ritual," muttered Robin. "Wonder what old Powder Keg's done this time?"

Mercer was rather afraid he knew. "He is not quite dragging, perhaps," he amended, as they watched Rannoch, looking dark as Hades, urge his daughter into the servants' passageway. "But I had better go and intervene. Trouble's afoot."

"Then you're a braver man than I," said his brother. "Rannoch is . . . oh, hell and damnation—!"

"What?" Mercer looked back to see Robin's gaze had shifted.

"If you think trouble's afoot, Brother," said Robin quietly, "just turn to your left. Looks as though your mistress is about to swoon headfirst into Mamma's punch bowl."

Mercer followed his gaze, and felt his face heat. "Oh, God," he gritted. "Look here, Rob, are you sober enough to deal with Rannoch?"

"Well . . . yes, I daresay."

Mercer left him with little choice. "Then go and extract Zoë from whatever crisis she has got herself into," he said, setting off toward the punch bowl. "And whatever you do, keep Rannoch from throttling the chit. You may trust that *I* will take care of Claire."

Chapter Three

AN UNFORTUNATE TURN
OF EVENTS.

*T*he Marquess of Mercer was not the only person whose hackles were raised by the sight of Lord Rannoch and his eldest daughter departing the ballroom. Lady Rannoch, too, watched in disapprobation as the marquess propelled Zoë past the orchestra dais and through the rear doors toward the servants' stairs.

This was perhaps a fortunate observation, for Lord Robert's progress across the ballroom was impeded by a gauntlet of otherwise well-intentioned guests—"Cards on Monday at Wentworth's, old boy?" then, "Gawd, that a lavender waistcoat, Rob?" and "Tatt's is auctioning that bay tomorrow. Fetch you at nine?"—until Robin felt rather like a salmon laboring upstream. A popular and slightly pickled salmon, mind, for unlike his elder brother, Robin was ever known for being approachable, fond of good drink, and up for most any manner of lark.

Lady Rannoch, however, whilst well liked, was not inebriated, and far less subject to distraction, particularly when one of her cubs was at risk. She crossed the room in an instant to find the quarrel—spoken in hushed, hortatory tones but a quarrel nonetheless—already under way.

She reached her husband's side, and set a reproachful hand upon her husband's arm. "Elliot!" she whispered in her faint Flemish accent. "What is this about? Sir Edgar, I presume?"

Zoë Armstrong looked back and forth between her father and stepmother, the latter's words not quite registering through her fury. Her head was awhirl from too much flirting and dancing, her temper still raw from Mercer's cold criticism. And now—well, it really was too humiliating to be bullied about by one's papa—and this time, she feared, even her stepmamma mightn't save her.

Sir Edgar Haverfield was a fate she had thought she'd long ago escaped, but like her past, the man kept returning to haunt her. Zoë felt the hot, urgent press of tears behind her eyes, and felt her temper about to slip. "So I'm to have no choice in this?" Her words were cold and quiet. "Really, Papa, how can you have agreed to such a thing? Without even asking me?"

"Aye, and what good would it do to ask?" Rannoch's faint burr was thickening from temper. The corners of his mouth had gone tight—a sure sign of impending doom—and the heat of his black gaze was boring into her. Some believed Rannoch akin to the devil himself. Tonight, his eldest daughter was inclined to agree.

"Zoë, darling," her stepmother murmured, laying a cool hand upon her arm. "It is just for tea."

"And then?" Zoë's head snapped round, her gaze locking with Lady Rannoch's. For an instant, it was as if she could not get her breath. As if she were trapped in some dark and airless place—which she very nearly was. "Tea shan't be the end of it, Evie," she managed. "Pray do not pretend it will be."

Faint color suffused her stepmother's cheeks. "And

then Sir Edgar wishes a moment to speak with you privately."

"*Sir Edgar,*" said Zoë tightly, "has already had *half a dozen* moments alone in which to speak with me privately. Indeed, he's already buried one wife in between his moments."

"Zoë, *hush*!" Lady Rannoch dropped her voice. "The gentleman is still enamored of you. What is the insult in that?"

"Sir Edgar is enamored of my dowry." Zoë stopped herself, and gulped down cool air lest she begin to cry in earnest. "Oh, why must everyone be so cruel to me tonight? I tell you, I shan't have him, Papa. I've told him—over and over—and now I'm telling you. You never should have agreed to it."

"I've agreed to naught," he rasped. "That is the very reason, lass, we're having this discussion. But I highly suggest you listen to the man. You could do worse."

Humiliatingly, Zoë's mouth began to quiver. "I—I *cannot*," she whispered. "Please, Papa. Oh, *please* don't make me. Please give me another choice. His mother—she hates me."

Lady Rannoch circled an arm around Zoë's shoulders. "Zoë, darling, Lady Haverfield knows you will make an eminently suitable bride," she said gently. "Sir Edgar is handsome and kind. You are lovely, and, as you say, you have a large dowry. It is no bad match."

Rannoch set a finger beneath Zoë's chin, and turned her face to his. "Evie has the right of it, lass," he said, his tone gentler. "The rest of it—the things you fret over—Lady Haverfield can ill afford to concern herself with such just now."

"Why?" Zoë looked at him incredulously. "Because she is *poor*?"

"She's not precisely poor," said Rannoch impatiently. "Her late husband was overfond of horses and brandy, that's all. Haverfield's estate requires an injection of capital."

"So Lady Haverfield must grit her teeth and bear me?" Zoë's eyes flashed with fire—much like her father's, did she but know it. But her temper had long ago become her most stalwart shield against fear. "Is it too much to ask, Papa, that just once, some decent man might wish to marry me for who I am? And not in spite of it?"

"Zoë." Her father reached out to touch her arm, but she pulled away. "Zoë, is there someone, lass? Someone who has your heart?"

For a moment, she hesitated, then shook her head. "No," she said sharply. "There is no one."

Lady Rannoch flashed a sympathetic smile. "You know, my dear, that Lady Hauxton married late, and look how well that has turned out," she murmured. "Almost three years of wedded bliss, and two lovely children—three, counting Priss. And Frederica—why, she did not wish to marry Bentley at all, yet they now live in one another's pockets."

"But I am nothing like Freddie or Phaedra," Zoë returned. "If you cannot see that, I shan't waste my breath." Just then, a waiter appeared at the top of the service stairs. Zoë snatched a glass of wine from his freshly laden tray.

Lady Rannoch set a gentle hand on her shoulder. "Should you, my dear?"

"This conversation has parched me," she said irritably.

"No, never mind. Here, take it." She pressed the wine-glass into her stepmother's hand. "Drink it. I see Robin wading through the ballroom. I promised him this dance."

Her stepmother exhaled slowly. "Go, then," she answered. "We cannot very well stand here squabbling any longer."

Just then, the music ended and the crowd fell away from the dance floor. "Hell and damnation," said the marquess, pinching hard at the bridge of his aristocratic nose as his eldest vanished into the surging tide of dancers. "I've tried to do everything right. Tried to make amends. Does the chit know no gratitude?"

"Oh, Elliot, it's not that," his wife whispered. "I do feel for her. She is not entirely wrong, you know. Lady Haverford is a bitter pill—and altogether too high in the instep, if you ask me."

"Don't undermine me in this, Evangeline," he warned darkly. "The lass cannot go on as she is, dancing on the edge of ruin. She's but one step away from being thought fast and given her situation . . . well, it will be the end of her in polite society. No, I fear it must be marriage or . . . the other."

"Oh, Elliot!" His wife's face nearly crumpled. "You *cannot* send her to Scotland. Zoë is like a rare, hothouse blossom. Alone, deprived of all she has grown accustomed to, she will but wither and die."

"If the girl would just fall in love, Evie, I swear I'd let her wed the butcher's boy and settle them with a fortune." He crossed his arms over his chest. "But this is her fifth season, and there's no one left to meet."

"What she wants, I think, is for the butcher's boy to

love her without the fortune," said Evangeline quietly. "Can you not see that? Zoë has learned to laugh in the face of society, yes—but there's little humor in it."

But Lord Rannoch's temper would not be so easily assuaged this time. "The girl was dealt a bad hand, aye, and the blame is mine," he said, his arms falling. "I know that, and I'm sorry for it. But instead of helping herself, and behaving with a little decorum, the chit's run mad."

"And who, I wonder," said Lady Rannoch quietly, "did she get that from?"

To Robin's relief, Zoë espied him through the ballroom doors, making his way in her direction. While he had never been called a coward, he'd no wish to beard Rannoch, even in someone else's den.

Zoë had apparently survived whatever tongue lashing her sire had laid out, and had come away with nothing more than a brilliant blush high on her cheeks, and a glittering rage in her eyes. Only someone who knew her as well as he would have suspected the color came not from excitement, but from the barely banked emotions which so often threatened to consume her.

Tonight Zoë wore a deep shade of green with tiny emerald teardrops dangling from her ears and a gossamer gold shawl hanging off her elbows. Her mass of unruly dark curls had been tamed into a sleek, classic arrangement entwined with gold cord, and a dozen appreciative male gazes followed her as she strode with unladylike haste across the ballroom.

Zoë cast Robin an exasperated look and said not a word, but instead merely hooked her arm through his, and spun him around in the other direction. Robin felt his lips quirk with amusement. "Powder Keg," he murmured. "Where to?"

"Out," she snapped, propelling him onward. "Upstairs. Anywhere. Just get me out of here."

"The lady's wish is my command."

At the front of the ballroom they passed into the grand entrance hall where both the front and rear doors stood open to the night, but crowds were gathered at either end, fanning themselves in the July heat.

"Follow me," he said, turning up the marble staircase.

Chambers on the first floor were being used for the guests' retiring rooms, so Robin passed them by and continued up another flight to the relative silence of the family's private quarters. Here guests would not normally have been invited, but he felt only the faintest qualm in taking Zoë, for she was family—or something near it—and had been through every room in the house from cellars to attics over the years.

"Where are we going?" she asked, peering down the passageway.

"Mercer's study," he answered, turning to push open the next door. "No one to bother you there."

Inside, a lone lamp burned upon the desk. Robin went at once to the rear of the room, which overlooked the gardens, and threw open the French windows which gave onto a narrow balconet. Here, the night air stirred, while the lamps along the rear veranda cast up a faint, pleasant glow. Even the strains of the orchestra seemed clearer here as it drifted up through the darkness from the ballroom two floors below.

Zoë stepped onto the threshold, her arm brushing his. She set both hands upon the railing, and as was her habit in most things, leaned recklessly over the edge. "It's so peaceful up here," she said, her voice wistful. "It's as if all those people below have just faded away, leaving only the music."

Robin propped himself against the window frame and cut her a sidelong glance. "Who are you looking for on the terrace?"

"Oh, no one." She leaned back from the railing. "It's just that Mercer and I had another quarrel tonight. I think sometimes, Robin, that he hates me. He used to be so kind—but now he's more like Papa. So full of *should* and *ought*. So . . . disapproving."

Robin didn't know what to say. Stuart *had* distanced himself from Zoë, and Robin wasn't sure why. He changed the subject. "Glad the season's over, old thing?"

She lifted her narrow shoulders. "I think I've finally grown weary of gaiety, Robin," she mused, drawing her shawl up as if chilled. "There must be something more to life than all this. Mustn't there? But I'll never find out, for now Papa says . . ."

There was no need to finish the sentence. Zoë was two-and-twenty, or thereabout, and her father's patience was wearing thin.

"Do you want a drink?" Robin asked, fracturing the awkward silence. "Stuart might have some Madeira up here."

Fleetingly, she hesitated. "A little brandy, Rob, if you won't think too ill of me?"

Robin had never been able to deny Zoë anything.

Against his better judgment, he went to the sideboard and poured one for each of them, splashing a generous dose of water into both as an afterthought. He did not like the look of her tonight. Zoë seemed different. More brittle—and brittle, to his way of thinking, was but another word for fragile. This had been a hard season for the old girl. Rannoch had pressed her to the breaking point, laying down ugly ultimatums about marriage and Scotland.

But in his more sober moments, Robin could admit that Rannoch deserved a little sympathy, too. Even a scoundrel could see that Zoë was pushing the boundaries of polite society, out of frustration and perhaps even a little self-loathing. She had frittered away five seasons flirting, dancing, breaking hearts and eliciting marriage offers—and even a few less honorable proposals—all of them from scoundrels, aging roués, impecunious widowers, or gentlemen otherwise pressed by circumstance to marry for money. Zoë was Rannoch's illegitimate daughter, and to society's best families, she simply would not do, no matter how desperately their young scions might fall for her beauty. Beauty which was, admittedly, beyond compare.

As he crossed the room, two brandies in hand, Robin watched her at the balconet, the gossamer gold shawl billowing faintly in the breeze, her lithe arm propped wearily against the window frame. Zoë was small and dark, scarcely five feet tall, but her ebullience and charm more than made up for whatever she lacked in stature. Now, however, Zoë's shoulders were uncharacteristically slumped, her long, swanlike neck bowed. She looked frail and almost ethereally lovely, like a damsel in distress, peering down into the night as if in search of her knight in shining armor.

Regrettably, that was not a role for him. Though for Zoë, he considered, he could almost be tempted to try. He was dashed fond of the girl—had sometimes even lusted after her—and it tore at his heart to see her unhappy. Though they were but distant cousins, he had known her all her life, and they shared a strong vein of stubborn Scots' blood from a great-grandmother neither had known.

Zoë heard his return over the music and turned in the gloom, a smile curving her face. She looked up at him from beneath a sweep of coal-black lashes when he pressed the glass into her hand. "Have you anything to smoke round here?"

He flashed his most wicked grin. "Does Pan have horns?"

Stepping back into the room Robin took the precaution of snapping the lock in the door, then pilfered one of Mercer's best Turkish cheroots from the cedarwood box on his desk. In a moment he and Zoë stood shoulder to shoulder in the faint breeze, passing it back and forth between them in quiet companionship.

Though a few elderly ladies were still known to take stuff, smoking was primarily the provender of courtesans and actresses. For a girl of Zoë's situation, it was not thought at all the thing. Still, Robin had begun to permit her to smoke when both of them were very young and a good deal too daring. And as with most of Zoë's high jinks, there was no getting the horse back into the barn.

Robin pinched the cheroot between two fingers and

exhaled a stream of white smoke into the darkness. "So, what's the trouble, my girl?" he asked lightly. "Rannoch husband hunting again?"

Zoë drank a little too deeply of her brandy. "How did you guess?"

For a heartbeat, he hesitated, then, "Betting book at Boodle's," he confessed. "Wentworth claims Sir Edgar means to propose again now his wife's dead. Wagered twenty pounds you'd capitulate. But I know better—laid a monkey you wouldn't."

"What?" Fleetingly, she was outraged. "You *bet* on me?"

Robin pulled a chagrined face. "Seemed a sure thing," he said, lifting one shoulder. "If you've turned him down twice, no reason to agree now, right? Tell you what, Zoë, just say *no*, and we'll split the take."

She turned her face to the darkened gardens, then tossed back the rest of the brandy in a reckless motion. "Shall I say *no*, Rob, and live out my days in Perthshire?" Her voice was suddenly husky, her slender fingers going white as she clutched the glass. "Or shall I say *yes,* and watch Lady Haverfield hold her nose through the wedding ceremony?"

"Oh, Scotland's a bonnie place, my dear, but it's not for the likes of you." Robin plucked the glass from her hand lest she shatter it. He set both glasses away, then touched her lightly on the shoulder. "Not for the rest of your life, at any rate. Surely, Zoë, Rannoch isn't serious?"

She turned round, her eyes welling with tears. "I think this time he is," she whispered. "He fears I mean to ruin myself. And I know, Robin, that I've not been a pattern of rectitude—I know I've flirted and been perhaps too gay—but do I really deserve to be saddled with Lady Haverfield as a mother-in-law? The woman despises me."

"Zoë," he softly chided. "Why do you think that?"

Zoë would not hold his gaze. "She once said as much," she confessed, her voice almost inaudible. "It was during my second season. At her sister's garden party in Hampstead. Some of us we were playing hide-and-seek, and I had climbed up into the rafters of Mrs. Holt's belvedere."

"Good Lord, Zoë! That must be twenty feet!"

Zoë gave a bitter laugh. "I sometimes wish I had fallen," she replied, "for what I got, ultimately, was worse than a conk on the sconce. Whilst everyone else was darting about in the shrubbery, Lady Haverfield drew Mrs. Holt up the steps, you see, and told her that she was horrified Edgar meant to offer for me. That she blamed her dead husband for leaving Edgar in a position that he *'must take an opera dancer's bastard to wife just for money.'* "

"Malicious bitch." In disgust, Robin hurled what was left of the cheroot into the dark. "So you refused Edgar, then. Serves the pantywaist right."

"B-But I didn't want to refuse him!" Zoë whispered. "Indeed, I had begun to quite fancy myself a little taken with Edgar. I never dreamed . . . oh, Robin, to have such a thing said of me! I was just struck all of a heap. And that's when I realized that what Miss Smith used to say—that no one would ever want me—was true. That I would never be good enough, no matter how much Evie and Papa loved me."

Robin felt his face twist with grief. "But that's why

Rannoch fired Miss Smith all those years ago," he countered, raising one hand to lightly cup her cheek. "Because it's all balderdash. Indeed, you are all that is beautiful and kind—and monstrous good fun into the bargain."

"But being kind and beautiful and fun isn't enough, Rob." Despite his touch, Zoë was still staring at a point deep in the gardens. "You know it isn't. Pray don't try to cozen me just to be polite."

Robin weighed how to answer that one. But there had never been anything save honesty between him and Zoë. "I'm sorry," he said softly. "I only meant—"

"I know what you meant," she cut in, lifting her gaze to his. To his shock, tears were actually leaking from her eyes now and her bottom lip was wobbling in a way it had not done since they were children squabbling over draughts. "Oh, Robin, it's all so frightful! What am I to do?"

Robin hesitated but an instant. "Come here, old thing," he murmured, throwing open his arms. "That's what you're to do, and bugger old Lady Haverfield."

"Oh, Robin!" At that, Zoë dove into his embrace, and set her cheek to his lavender waistcoat, sobbing in earnest now. "Papa—is—is—going *to send me away!* Banished forever to his estate in Scotland. Just me—and two thousand *sh-sheep!*"

Robin set his lips atop her head. Zoë smelled like spicy fruit and warm flowers as he held her tight and wished to the devil he could somehow make things right for her. "Zoë, I think you should tell Rannoch what Lady Haverford said. Surely he'd understand?"

But that seemed merely to make Zoë sob harder. "Oh, Robin, don't you see?" she cried. "That w-would just cut

Papa to the quick. Since he married Evie, he has tried so hard to be good—indeed, he has been a perfect pillar of society. He persists in believing if he tries hard enough—if I am good enough—society will forgive my birth."

"Oh, Rannoch's hardly naïve," he answered. "Society will always have its high sticklers, I reckon, but I think a chap ought to account himself fortunate to have you, Zoë."

She looked up, blinking her damp, dark lashes and looking remarkably vulnerable—a rarity for Zoë. Suddenly, Robin was struck by a deep and chivalrous desire to kiss her, and, as with most of his baser impulses, he gave in to it. With just a twinge of guilt and not a whit of forethought, he tilted his head and slowly lowered his lips to hers.

It was not their first stolen kiss, by any means. Since the age of fourteen, Zoë had been a temptation he'd occasionally given in to, but it wasn't serious, and never had been. But this time, as their lips molded softly together, it was as if she swayed in his embrace, leaving him with the notion that for once it fell to him—instead of to his elder brother—to shore her up and be her strength. That it was both a masculine and noble calling to prove to Zoë how infinitely desirable she was.

Zoë sensed his response, and curled her hands into the lapels of his coat, clinging to him in a way she never had before, leaving him with no alternative, it seemed, but to deepen the kiss. Lightly he stroked the seam of her lips, urging her to open beneath him. When she did, on a little sigh of pleasure, Robin stroked tenderly, twining his tongue sinuously with hers, and leaving himself dizzy with desire.

It was Zoë who broke the embrace, her eyes wide and knowing. "Oh, Robin!" she whispered. "I am so tired. So tired of having my virginity haggled over like a pound of good wool. I should just give it to you and be done with it."

He kissed her again, setting his mouth lightly to the corner of hers. "Zoë, love, we've talked about that," he murmured. "You'll just end up married to me."

He felt her lashes flutter, and realized she was blinking back tears. "Would that be so terribly bad?" she asked. "You don't mind my bloodlines, Robin—do you?"

"Zoë, you know I don't." He brushed his lips over one of her perfect, inky eyebrows and pondered her tempting suggestion. "But you don't love me—not like that."

"No," she whispered, "but you are handsome, and so very kind."

"That's not enough," he said. "And marriage, Zoë—it just isn't for me. Not right now."

And not with you, said his heart.

But his heart, alas, was not in charge, such matters having already been referred to his nether regions. And his mind—hazy with brandy and deprived of blood flow—was imagining what Zoë would look like with her clothes off and her legs wrapped round his waist.

She gave a pitiful little laugh. "Then just kiss me again, Robin," she managed, dashing a hand at her tears. "Kiss me and make me feel beautiful and help me forget all the Lady Haverfords out there who think I'm not fit for their sons to trod upon."

It seemed such a simple, harmless request. Zoë shivered in his embrace, and impulsively, he drew her closer. She felt warm and delicate against him, her head barely reaching his chin. Her high, round breasts pressed against his chest and her delightfully feminine scent began to mix with the brandy and his vague notions of chivalry until it became a dangerous, dizzying miasma. Before Robin knew it, he had drawn her to the long, leather sofa by the fire and pulled her into his lap.

Later, when the heat and the heedlessness had turned to a cold, damning reality, Robin wondered if he'd been a little mad instead of just a trifle sotted. But in that moment—faced with her sobs and her tears and the unfairness of it all—Robin knew only that someone he cared for was alone and in pain, so he held her. In his weakened condition, however, holding her wasn't the half of it, and he'd never been the sort of fellow who denied his baser appetites.

It was this confluence of unfortunate circumstances—combined with the feel of Zoë's breast in his hand—which Robin later blamed for the fact that matters got so quickly out of hand. Before he knew it, he'd lost his coat and his waistcoat over the side of the sofa, tossed Zoë's shawl atop the heap, and eased the bodice of her gown half off.

Zoë threw herself into the passion with an almost feverish urgency, as if the heat might keep the truth at bay, her hands skating up his chest to tug at his neckcloth as she kissed her way down his throat as if asking for more. And how could a chap deny her? It would have been ungentlemanly.

Beneath her kisses, Robin tore at the neckcloth, trying to yank the long strip of linen free. As if to help him, Zoë lifted herself away and the cravat slithered from his shirt collar. She looked so damned beautiful, on impulse,

Robin draped it round her neck. His gaze holding hers, silently urging her tears away, he wrapped it round once, then fisting his hand in the linen, drew her back, closed his eyes, and deepened the kiss.

Robin felt his body flood with desire. Tenderness turned to passion as he speared his fingers into her hair. Again and again, he slanted his mouth over her, his kisses hungry. One sleeve slithered to her elbow. A piece of the gold cording came free, and half her unruly dark curls came spilling over one shoulder, further enticing him.

Oh, he'd seen Zoë's hair tumbling down before— tomboy that she was, it had often been unavoidable. But tonight, with her exotic scent surrounding him, her cheeks damp with tears, and the soft, evocative strains of the orchestra below, he longed suddenly to draw the pins from it in the way a man might take down his lover's hair.

And yet, beneath all the passion, something nagged at him. Fleetingly Robin considered stopping, but at that very moment, Zoë wriggled slightly in his lap, causing her dress to shift, baring one small, perfect breast. A curl of dark hair teased at her nipple, causing it to peak into a sweet, tempting bud.

And that was the end of it. "Zoë," he muttered against his mouth. "Zoë. Let me."

Zoë didn't answer, but nor did she stop kissing him. Before he knew what he was about, Robin had the fall of his trousers undone, and Zoë astraddle him, her skirts drawn up to reveal a pair of slender, milky thighs encircled by the most unique—and erotic—garters he'd ever seen; ruched satin of emerald green fringed with dainty gold beads that swayed as she moved.

He plunged his fingers into her hair again and kissed her deeply. Good God, he wanted her. Wanted her, perhaps, badly enough to pay the price. At long last, he was going to make love to Zoë—no turning back.

And no more Maria.

Ever.

The insight cut into his consciousness like a newly honed kitchen knife.

Zoë sensed it the moment Robin stiffened beneath her. Well, he'd been stiff for quite some time—which, Zoë had on excellent authority, was a good thing. But this was a stiffening of another sort altogether. A physical jolt that cut through the sensual heat. She set her palms flat to his chest and lifted herself up to look him straight in the eyes.

For a long moment, their gazes held, locked in a long and silent question as if words were no longer necessary. And suddenly, she knew. Oh, she knew. This was a dreadful mistake. He sensed it as surely as she. And it was just the sort of thing—ten times magnified—she kept doing when she let temper and pain get the best of her. The very reason Papa was so mad at her.

No longer able to look at him, she dropped her gaze, only to be horror-stricken.

She was fully astraddle him, her skirts hiked up to her hips, her décolletage in utter disarray, and one breast bared. Robin still had one hand on her arse. Still, it wasn't embarrassment she felt. It was shame—shame she'd let her temper bring her to this, something she did not want, the taste bitter as blood in her mouth.

"Oh, Robin," she whispered. "I—we—we simply cannot . . ."

"—do this?" he finished, relief flooding over his features.

She nodded, then fell against him, eviscerated, her forehead lightly resting on his.

On a nervous laugh, he took his hand from her arse, and settled it at the small of her back. "Dashed sorry, old thing. Got out of hand."

Zoë squeezed her eyes shut. "It's my fault," she choked. "All my fault. Just promise me, Robin, that we will *never, ever* speak of this ag—"

Suddenly the light in the lamp wavered as if caught in a draft. Precariously positioned, Zoë jerked upright in alarm. But Robin did likewise, almost tumbling her onto the floor. Zoë clutched at both Robin and her bodice, fighting for balance.

A harsh voice cut through the gloom. *"Robin—?"*

Zoë turned in horror. Lord Mercer stood upon the threshold, his face a mask of rage. Beneath her, Robin uttered a vulgar curse.

"Robin?" Mercer choked. "And—*good God* . . . !" He spun about at once as if to shield them from view.

Too late. A slight, feminine form slipped past him. The Vicomtesse de Chéraute's gaze swept over the frozen tableau, her eyes alight with an unholy glee.

"Nom de Dieu, Miss Armstrong!" she said on a spurt of laughter. "You really *must* give me the name of your modiste. I should love above all things to have a pair of those green and gold garters."

It took a moment for the full horror to register in Zoë's brain. Then Mercer slowly turned around again, his cold eyes sweeping over her, his mouth twisted with what looked like disgust.

Mercer. Again. And this time—oh, this time he had every right to hate her!

On an agonizing sob, Zoë leapt from the sofa and bolted, one hand over her mouth, Robin's cravat still wrapped about her throat, streaming behind her as she ran.

Chapter Four

Robin sat in stupefied silence as his brother dragged the vicomtesse from his study. He seemed unable to rise, or to utter even the vaguest of apologies as Claire's skirts swished round the door. The woman vanished into the gloom, her laughter still pealing down the passageway.

Robin's respite lasted but seconds. Slamming the door as he came, Mercer stalked back into the study. "Robin!" he uttered, his face twisted with black rage. "What in hell's name—?"

"I . . . I don't know," Robin muttered. "Look, Stu, I—I'm sorry."

"*You don't know?*" Mercer cursed again, dragged both hands through his hair, and began pacing before the cold hearth. "You are sorry—? *Bloody, bloody hell, Robin!* One is sorry for spilling one's wine at dinner! And Zoë! God's truth, have you any idea what you've done to her? To *yourself*?"

Did he? Robin was still sitting on the sofa, his shirt open to the throat, staring at his elder brother. Mercer looked worse than angry. He looked like the wrath of God incarnate—as if he might reach across the room and rip Robin's head from his shoulders. He was perfectly capable of doing it, too.

"Stuart, I—I . . ." He swallowed hard, his mind in a knot. Reason escaped him. There was only the music, still wafting up from the ballroom below as if nothing had happened, and the ominous *tock, tock, tock* of the mantel clock deep in the shadows of the room. The sense of dread and doom, sucking him down like a quagmire.

"Just get dressed," Mercer snarled. "Get dressed, damn you, then go downstairs and speak to her father."

At first, Robin did not catch the implication in his brother's words. "But Stuart, she was crying," he finally said. "Rannoch's trying to marry her off to Haverfield again. You . . . You told me to help."

Mercer stalked across the carpet, seized Robin's shirt-front, and dragged him to his feet. "No, what I told you to do was *keep Rannoch from throttling the chit!*" he roared, his nose but an inch from Robin's. "Instead, you've all but ensured it. And now, you are goddamned well going to marry her!"

"M-Marry . . . *Zoë?*" Robin whispered. "Stuart, what in God's name is wrong with you? I—I can't get married! Marry her yourself if you're suddenly so hell-bent on it!"

At that, Mercer drew back one arm as if he might backhand him. Then, before Robin could feint, dodge, or make sense of it all, Mercer's wrath seemingly collapsed inward. Something raw and agonizing sketched across his face and on a harsh, almost choking sound, his brother thrust him away and stalked back to the hearth, his shoulders hunched as if suffering some physical pain.

On a long, shuddering breath, Robin turned to stare at the door through which Zoë had just vanished. He began mechanically to hitch up his trouser buttons, the dark shroud of reality settling inexorably over him. Life as he knew it was imploding. Mercer looked like a madman. And only God knew the damage being done to Zoë two floors below. Somehow, he had to put it all to rights—and yet his mind was still scrabbling for a way out.

"Stuart, I didn't mean what I said," he whispered. "I—I *am* worried about Zoë."

"You had damned well better be," said his brother.

"Look, where did she go?" he rasped. "Claire, I mean?"

"I put her in the family parlor." Mercer stood in profile now, edged by the flickering lamplight as he pinched hard at the bridge of his nose. He seemed stripped bare, his voice hollow. "I told her to wait there, Robin. But she likely won't, so we can let go that tenuous thread of hope."

Robin hissed through his teeth. "Blister it, Stuart, can't you shut her up?"

"No, Robin." His voice was a harsh whisper. "No. I cannot. You and Zoë have finally got yourselves into something I cannot fix."

Robin held out both hands, palms up. "Look, Stuart, I wanted only to cheer Zoë up."

Mercer whirled about. "So you decided to bed her?" he roared. "Oh, it wasn't the first time, I daresay—but I'll tell you, my boy, you must be losing your edge, for she didn't look too damned cheerful tonight."

"Oh, go bugger yourself, you arrogant ass!" Robin growled. Then his shoulders fell. "Look, Stu, *it was Zoë.* You know how she is—"

"*Zoë?*" he said, incredulous. "Zoë is a calamity—a heedless little hellion—a walking whirlwind in satin slippers. But you *knew* all that, Robin. And yet you took her clothes off!"

"I didn't quite take any off," Robin clarified, bending over to snatch up his waistcoat. "Not—Not completely. Nothing happened. Well, not much."

"Not *much*?" Mercer's voice was almost lethally quiet. "When did that signify? You had your trousers laid open, Zoë was astride you with her skirts hitched half up her arse—oh, no, Robin—*not much* is meaningless. Hell, I don't even believe it. I know you—and I know Zoë—too bloody well."

"Believe what you want then, damn you," Robin snapped, shoving his arms into his waistcoat.

"What does it matter what I want?" Mercer looked bitter, his eyes hard and his voice cold. "What has it ever mattered? You comprehend what must be done."

"I—I don't . . ." Robin set his fingers to his temple. "I don't know." Good God, but his head was pounding! "Stuart, what about Maria?" he whispered. "How am I ever to explain this?"

"I don't give a damn," Mercer snapped. "She's your mistress. Deal with her as best you can."

"Maria isn't my mistress," Robin challenged. "She . . . She isn't like that, Stuart. And I—why, I love her."

"You love her." His brother's mouth twisted with disgust. "I'm sure she'll find that comforting when she reads your announcement in the *Times*."

Robin's shoulders fell. The *Times*? Oh, Maria was good and kind—tolerant, even, of his ways. But this?

This would take a vast deal of persuasion. And jewelry. Possibly even an annuity . . .

Mercer stood in front of him now, better than six feet of barely-leashed wrath, his evening coat pushed back by broad hands that were set almost threateningly upon his hipbones. "Stop!" he ordered. "Do not even think what you are thinking. Do *not*."

"Oh, no." Robin lifted one hand. "No, Stuart, you'll not tell me how—"

Abruptly, he found himself snatched and yanked into Mercer's face again. "You brought an unwed girl up here alone," he rasped, tightening his fist in Robin's collar. "*Our* cousin. And by God, now you are going to marry her. And you are going to spend the rest of your life making her deliriously happy, or I will kill you with my bare hands. Do you understand me?"

"Christ, Stu, it was just Zoë." Somehow, he shoved his brother away and stepped back. "N-Not that I don't respect her. I . . . I love her, too, in a way. But it's just that she's been up here a hundred times."

"Not when all the household was downstairs! And half of the *ton* with them. You have ruined her, Robin—and to drive the nails in this coffin of your own making, the ruination was witnessed by hell's most vindictive, vicious-tongued—"

"Aye, *your* mistress," Robin snapped. "And who brought *her* up here?"

Mercer held up an implacable hand, the brass key glittering between two fingers. "Recall if you will that this is my study," he said tightly. "And that Claire is no innocent miss."

"That's rather an understatement," said Robin snidely.

"I grow weary of your tone, Robert," Mercer answered. "Claire and I had unpleasant business to discuss, and I wished to do it in private. Moreover, she is not my mistress. I ended it a week past—hence my use of the term *vindictive*."

"Well, you'll pay dearly for that," said Robin darkly. "That ice-blond she-devil will gut you faster than a Billingsgate fishwife." He'd had enough, he decided, of his brother's high-handed temper. After all, Zoë was nothing to Mercer; hell, he'd been halfway avoiding the girl for years.

"No, Robin, *you* will pay for it," his brother answered. "Claire will gladly wound you to punish me. Indeed, the noose of matrimony is already tightening round your ballocks, and now we all of us must live with it." At that, Mercer bent down to snatch up Robin's coat. "Here. Tidy yourself, for pity's sake."

Robin opened his mouth to tell Mercer to go to the devil, but the words faded on his lips. Try as he might, he could not quite maintain his ire. Slowly, he finished dressing. The hell of it was, Mercer was not wholly wrong, he inwardly admitted as he shrugged his coat on. Resigned, he turned around, methodically yanking his cuffs into place.

"Look, Stuart, I'm sorry," he said quietly. "I'll make this right. I swear it."

"Yes, by God. You will."

Robin exhaled slowly. "Fine. What must I do to protect her?"

Fleetingly, his brother seemed to hesitate. Then, "Go to your room and ring for your valet," he coldly suggested. "You are in want of a cravat. When you've made yourself presentable, take your arse downstairs and beg Rannoch for his daughter's hand whilst you pray I've been able to stall Claire. And you will make it sound convincing, even if it kills you."

"Convincing—?" Robin echoed witheringly.

Mercer smiled, but there was a dark and abiding sadness beneath it. "Yes, for this is to be a love match," he said, fisting his hands at his sides. "You were overcome with passion, you see, at the thought of losing Zoë to another. You . . . You have loved her, perhaps, all your life. But you realized it just tonight."

Robin winced doubtfully. "Rather a load of balderdash, ain't it?"

Mercer's smile faded. "One might think so," he said quietly. "But I daresay it could happen, were a man not . . . not expecting it. In any case, you will make them believe it, Rob. For it is the only way."

"The only way?"

"The only way to keep Rannoch from punishing Zoë." Mercer's voice had gone hollow. "Do you understand me? Do you want her life to be a living hell? If not, go—and for God's sake, Robin, give the performance of your life."

Slumped over the dressing table in the ladies' retiring room, Zoë was still sniveling and dabbing ineffectually at her swollen eyes when Jonet, Lady Kildermore, found her there but a few minutes later—summoned, no doubt, by the rather alarmed chambermaid who'd slipped out after Zoë burst in with Robin's cravat still wrapped round her neck.

"Zoë, my dear?"

Zoë lifted her head, catching Jonet's worried gaze in the mirror. Her cousin came forward and laid a cool hand upon Zoë's shoulder. With her raven hair and fine-boned face, Jonet was as beautiful and as serenely confident as Zoë felt awkward. She was afraid to speak; afraid of what Robin's mother might already know. Afraid she might otherwise betray herself by bursting into a full flood of tears.

But there was only concern in Jonet's eyes as she settled onto the bench beside her. "My dear, is something amiss?" she asked, tucking a strand of Zoë's hair back into place. "You look . . . unwell."

Unwell. It was as good an excuse as any. "I've the most frightful headache," Zoë lied. "Please, Jonet, will you send Evie to me? I wish quite desperately to go home."

"Ah." Jonet nodded, but her lips thinned knowingly. "I shall have your father's carriage brought round at once." Then, to Zoë's shame, Jonet bent down and picked up the cravat she had thrown so hastily beneath the dressing table.

For a few seconds, Jonet drew the cloth almost pensively through her hands. "Perhaps you might prefer, my dear, to leave from the mews?" she finally said.

Zoë exhaled on a tremulous sigh. "Oh, yes, Jonet, if you please!" she whispered, dashing her hand beneath her eyes. "I—I am so sorry. I look a fright, do I not?"

"No, you look unhappy, child."

Zoë watched as Jonet carefully refolded the wrinkled length of snowy linen, her gaze flicking up only once. It looked, of course, like any gentleman's white cravat, but it had no business in a ladies' retiring room. What excuse might she give? Zoë could think of nothing—nothing save the humiliating truth—and so she sat mutely by, feeling more miserable by the instant.

When she had smoothed the last wrinkle away, Jonet laid the neckcloth aside and turned to face Zoë on the bench. "Do not despair, my dear," she said, her smile muted as she tucked another wayward curl behind Zoë's ear. "Whatever is done can be made right again. There is always a way."

There had been a way, perhaps. Before the Vicomtesse de Chéraute had barged in.

But that was not precisely fair, was it? Zoë had ruined her own life. Indeed, she had been on a path to destruction for some years now. She had only herself to blame.

"Oh, Jonet!" The words exploded on a sob. "Oh, you shall never forgive me for this!"

To her shock, Jonet merely set an arm around her shoulders. "I am quite sure, Zoë, that is not true," she said, giving her a swift hug. "Now come, let me repin your hair. Then we shall go down and find Evie, all right?"

Lord Rannoch was at the edge of the gardens just beyond the ballroom doors, and wondering what had become of his eldest daughter when he felt a presence hesitating in the gloom behind him. He did not turn, but merely spoke over his shoulder. "Come!" he said imperiously.

One of Jonet's sons—the youngest—stepped into the faint light that spilled from the ballroom. Tonight Lord Robert Rowland wore a pale purple waistcoat and a nauseous expression—though whether the two were related the marquess was not perfectly certain. The waistcoat was indisputably hideous.

Rannoch tossed back the rest of his claret. "What do you want?"

The young man edged nearer. "Moment of your time, sir?" he said hesitantly. "Been meaning to ask, you know—a-about Zoë, I mean?"

The marquess felt his dark brows draw together. "About *Zoë*?" he asked, trying not to sound impatient— a failing for which his wife was forever chiding him. "What the devil do you mean?"

Lord Robert cleared this throat a little awkwardly. "Well, the thing is, sir—er, Haverford, you see—not quite the thing. As things stand, that is. With Zoë. And me."

"No, Robert," said Rannoch, wondering how many times a man could use *thing* in a sentence. "I don't see."

Lord Robert made a wincing expression, as if he'd been struck full in the face by a beam of bright light. "A good chap, of course," the lad went on. "Sober—paragon of rectitude—all that rot. Mother's a bit of a harpy, to be sure. Still, not a'tall the thing—the thing for . . ."

"For what, Robert?" Rannoch pressed. "For God's sake, man! Speak up!"

"For Zoë," Lord Robert finally uttered. His face was bloodless now. "Offering for her, you see."

For a long moment, the marquess stared down at his young cousin—rather far down, too, for although Robin was not a small fellow, Lord Rannoch was downright hulking.

"Haverford has already offered for Zoë," he said tightly. "Not that it's any business of yours."

Lord Robert scratched his head. "No, no, what I mean, sir—*I'd* like to offer for Zoë."

Rannoch fell back a step. "You?" he barked. *"You* would like to offer for Zoë?"

"Y-Yes, sir." If Lord Robert had held a cap, he'd have been wringing it right now. "Been in love with her, you know, all my life," he stumbled on. "Madly. Passionately. Just came to me, you see. When I heard about Haverford. Can't have it—her married off to him. More than my heart could bear."

"Why, that's utter balderdash." Rannoch leaned over the young man and sniffed. "Have you been at Charlie's good whisky again?"

"No, sir," he said swiftly. "Sober as a country curate, sir. I should like above anything to marry Zoë."

Just then, a passing shadow caught Rannoch's eye. The marquess turned. "Charlie!" he bellowed, motioning the butler from the ballroom. "Kindly send one of your flunkies to fetch my wife and daughter, and bring round my carriage. There's something strange afoot here."

Charles Donaldson stepped through the French windows and bowed stiffly at the neck. "At the back gate, sir," he said in a stout Scottish burr. "I collect Lady Rannoch and Miss Zoë already await."

Rannoch returned the bow. "You're a prince among men, Charlie," he said. Then he returned his attention to Robert. "As for you, sir, you must be quite mad. Now I'm off to have a long talk with my daughter. Do you think I'll hear this same crackbrained, lovelorn tale from her?"

"I—I couldn't say, sir." Lord Robert winced again. "Possibly . . . I daresay . . . you might."

"Aye," said Rannoch snidely. "Possibly I daresay I might, too—and then, my boy, *I* shall be a good deal more suspicious than I am just now."

Chapter Five

IN WHICH LORD MERCER
LAYS DOWN THE LAW.

*E*vangeline, Lady Rannoch, entered her husband's private library at Strath House the next morning with a sinking sense of having lived through this day once before. To her relief, she found the room still empty.

She felt rather a coward, she inwardly admitted, crossing the room to the wide bank of windows that looked out across their long, immaculately landscaped lawns to the River Thames below. During the many years of her marriage, she had never been afraid of her husband. But afraid *for* him—oh, yes. That she had been, and too many times, for Rannoch's temper was legendary.

To steady herself, Evangeline set her hands flat upon the massive, eight-foot sideboard which was the centerpiece of her husband's bastion of masculinity. Within the confines of its doors and drawers could be found a vast array of masculine contrivances; tobacco in its every form, a score of different whiskys, a dozen sets of ivory dice, cards unaccountable, and wedged behind it, a well-worn faro board, still much used. When they had married, her husband had been far from a saint, and Evangeline had done herself the favor of never expecting he would become one. A man, she believed, could change but so much before he became a caricature of himself.

And so his temper must once again be dealt with. Drawing in a long, steadying breath laced with the scent of stale cigar smoke and the woody cologne her husband favored, Evangeline turned from the window and let her eyes take in the opulently decorated room. The heavy velvet drapes. The thick Turkish carpet that had cost a king's ransom. The wide mahogany desk cluttered with ledgers, quills, and inkstands. Her husband's domain, and a room she rarely entered.

But not too many years ago she had come here on just such a morning, and on just such an errand as today's. Her husband's reaction then had been to seize a porcelain bust of George II from the sideboard and hurl it through the window beyond, shattering glass and splintering wood in the process. Then he had called for his horse—and his horsewhip.

Evangeline squeezed shut her eyes. Oh, she really did not wish her husband to take a horsewhip to Lord Robert Rowland! She was quite desperately fond of the handsome young scapegrace.

On the other hand, she had not cared one whit for Mr. Bentley Rutledge, who had compromised their ward Frederica. But look how that had turned out! Rutledge, a dangerous, devil-may-care sort of fellow who had dressed like a disheveled, disreputable coachman and who had frequented the lowest manner of hells and taverns imaginable, had turned out to be quite rich and perfectly sensible—and utterly devoted to his wife. Now, after a few short years of marriage, with the twins on his knee, little Henry clambering up his boot, and baby Francisca nestled in the crook of his arm, Rutledge looked more doting than dangerous.

What, she wondered, should one take from that? Would Lord Robert disappoint her? Surely not? Unlike Rutledge, Robin had been raised by two stern and loving parents who had never flinched in the face of discipline. Indeed, his stepfather was now an important archdeacon in the Church of England, a man known far and wide for his many good works. Their mother was a Scottish countess in her own right, with vast estates which she deftly managed. Robin had been brought up a gentleman, in the most altruistic sense of the word. Despite a somewhat misspent youth, there was no reason for him to fail her—or the wife he was soon to have.

As Lady Rannoch reassured herself of this fact for what must have been the tenth or twelfth time in as many hours, she became acutely aware of her husband's presence. It was the strengthening of his scent, perhaps, or the subtle sound of his breathing. Whatever it was, she opened her eyes to find him mere inches away, his dark, slashing brows drawn sharply together, his gray eyes still glittering with anger.

"Ready to talk now, are we?" he said. "McLeod found me in the stables. Looking for my horsewhip."

"Your . . . horsewhip?"

"Aye, I've a notion I'll be needing it," he muttered, dragging a hand through his dark hair, now touched with silver at the temples.

Evangeline took her husband by the arm, and drew him to the chairs before the hearth. She had forestalled his curiosity last night, and bought herself enough time to persuade Zoë to explain herself. The poor girl's story had not come as much of a surprise; Evangeline had long suspected there was more than a childhood friendship between her stepdaughter and Lord Robert.

Rannoch flung himself into a chair, dwarfing it with his length and breadth. With his flashing eyes, strong jaw, and square, stubborn chin, he would have proven daunting in a temper, did she not know him well. "I'll have the whole of it now, Evie," he said sternly. "I know you'll do anything to spare Zoë, but not this time. Do you understand me?"

A little wearily, she nodded. "The good news, I suppose, is that we won't need to see Sir Edgar for tea this afternoon," she answered.

"Aye, I thought not." Her husband's mouth twisted wryly. "And the bad?"

"Yes, well, the bad. I fear the bad news is that Zoë was caught—er, *kissing* Lord Robert last night. They were alone, unfortunately, in Lord Mercer's study. It was improper, of course, even for friends and distant cousins. They have grown entirely too familiar over the years."

"Kissing, eh?" Rannoch gave a grunt of disgust. "That would explain his crackbrained marriage proposal, then. It is, of course, out of the question."

"A marriage proposal?" Evangeline sat up a little straighter in her chair.

Her husband cast her a chary, sidelong look. "Aye, and I would have told you, too, but you were to busy fretting over Zoë. What was it Jonet whispered in your ear last night?"

Evangeline had the good grace to blush. "Merely her suspicions." She let her words falter, uncertain how to go on.

"Evie," he said warningly. "Out with it, woman."

Fleetingly, Evangeline considered not telling him the whole of it. But she did not keep secrets from her husband. No, not even for Zoë. "It was, I fear, a little more than kissing," she finally said.

Rannoch's right hand fisted on the chair arm. "More?" he growled. "What, then? What did Jonet see, exactly?"

Evangeline could not hold his gaze. "It . . . it was not Jonet who saw," she answered, her eyes focused somewhere near his feet.

"Hell and damnation," Rannoch uttered. "Who, then?"

"The Vicomtesse de Chéraute," Evangeline whispered.

"The who?" Rannoch's black brows drew tighter still. "Who the devil is the Vicomtesse de Chéraute?"

"Mercer's mistress," she answered.

"What, that backbiting French harlot?" Rannoch looked affronted. "I thought he turned her off?"

Evangeline's gaze jerked up. "Oh, dear, I hope he did not!"

Rannoch gave a dismissive grunt. "Aye, well, the woman caused a nasty scene last night by Jonet's punch bowl," he answered. "Nattering on about how she was feeling faint, one hand on her belly, and all but claiming to be carrying Mercer's chi—"

They both came to the same conclusion at precisely the same instant. Rannoch's knuckles, still fisted, began to turn white. "Oh, dear," said Evie again. "She will have no mercy, will she? She will vilify poor Zoë just to embarrass Mercer's family."

Rannoch drew a long, put-upon breath. "Evangeline," he said in barely restrained fury, *"what did she see?"*

One elbow propped upon her chair arm, Evangeline let her face fall into her hand. "Oh, dear!" she murmured. "They were in a . . . a slight state of dishabille, I fear. And Zoé—well, she might have been a little . . ."

"Aye—?"

"Well, somewhat . . . in his lap."

"In. His. Lap." Rannoch pronounced each word in the voice of doom. *"Undressed* in his lap? Is that what you mean? Hell and damnation! Well, go on! Was that the worst of it? Or were they . . . were they . . ."

Even Lord Rannoch could not say it.

It would be a hard, nearly unbearable thing, Evangeline supposed, for any father to imagine a daughter he has loved and raised in the arms of a man other than himself—and to imagine anything more intimate was a fate no father should suffer.

But they all did suffer it, eventually. Such were the lessons of human nature. Yet this . . . this was far more agonizing. This was imagining one's daughter violated, then vilified. This was imagining society's whispering their worst. This was, in truth, the very thing Rannoch had feared these last three years or more, if not the whole of Zoë's life. She was irrepressible. Passionate. She possessed her father's appetites and her mother's exotic beauty—and Rannoch had long feared the combination would doom her.

Evangeline stared into the hearth, which was swept clean this time of year. Her heart felt utterly shattered, and she was afraid—this time deeply afraid—for her stepdaughter. To her, Zoë was still the wide-eyed waif she'd taken to her heart upon her marriage. She loved Zoë as much as she loved the siblings and cousins she'd brought to the marriage, and the three children she'd borne Rannoch since. Some days, she had even loved Zoë more—because Zoë had suffered more, and in a way the others had not.

"It is very bad, Elliot, is it not?" she whispered. "Zoë and Lord Robert must be betrothed straightaway."

His face a mask of agony and anger, Rannoch jerked to his feet, turned, strode to the sideboard, and pounded his fist until the stoppers nearly leapt from the whisky decanters.

Evangeline rose and followed him. "Elliot, pray do not!" she said.

"I should have sent her to Scotland!" he gritted, pounding again. "I should have thought less of my wants, and more of her recklessness, and sent her safely away years ago. Had I done my duty, Evie, the girl would not now be ruined."

"No, she would be miserable," said Evangeline quietly.

On a low, inhuman sound, Rannoch's fist settled round the throat of a Ming dynasty vase, his knuckles going white.

Swiftly, Evangeline reached to set her hand over his. "Please, my love," she said. "Mr. Kemble went to such pains to acquire that vase. Pitching it through a window will not help Zoë. Come, sit by me. Let us think what we must do next."

"Just get her down here, damn it!" he choked, his hands set wide upon the sideboard. "There's naught else to be done."

But the words were spoken with such lethal anger, Evangeline forced her husband to turn round—and was shocked to see the tears welling up in his eyes.

"Oh, Elliot!"

His gaze held hers, and within it lay a wellspring of sorrows. Better than two decades of worry and guilt. And she knew then that his anger was for himself, and that he understood rage would resolve nothing now. The fight had drained suddenly out of him, his broad shoulders falling. Such uncharacteristic surrender worried her almost more than his temper had.

"Oh, Evie, you have tried," he whispered, his face twisting with grief. "God knows you have. But Zoë is half me, and half her mother. And all the maternal kindness on this earth could not have overcome such accursed blood."

Evangeline opened her arms, and drew him to her. "Shush, my darling," she cooed. "You are a good man. A fine man. And a wonderful father to all our children. I will not have you say such vile things of yourself—or of Zoë—do you hear me?"

But Elliot, she feared, never fully believed her, no matter how often she might say it. And she had said it—and meant it—many times throughout the years. He was all she had ever dreamed of, and both respected and loved by his children. Why could he not see that this was just Zoë reacting out of pain?

She had not long to fret about it, however. A few minutes later, Zoë was shown in, her eyes swollen from crying. Nonetheless, her diminutive height was drawn up like a duchess and the sight of her seemed to rekindle Rannoch's resolve.

"M-Marry *Robin*—?" she choked when her fate was laid out. "Oh, Papa! No!"

"*No*—?" Rannoch had begun to roam the room like a great, caged beast, his mane of dark hair tousled from having his hand dragged through it. He turned now, and stalked toward his firstborn. "What do you mean, *no*?"

Despite her tear-ravaged face, Zoë marched boldly toward him. They met somewhere near the tea table, both of them rolling onto the balls of their feet like sparring partners—and looking so very like one another, Evangeline would have laughed if she wasn't still on the edge of tears herself.

Zoë had her mother's infamous beauty, Evangeline did not doubt, but her posture, her flashing eyes, that stubborn set of her shoulders—all of it was pure, passionate Armstrong.

"Robin and I shall never suit," Zoë shouted, hands fisted at her sides. "He—He does not love me. Not like that! Besides, Papa, he doesn't *wish* to marry me."

"Wish?" snarled her father. "*Wish* has naught to do with it now, my girl! He wished well enough to paw you like some slavering beast, and to rip your clothes half off, so he can damn well wish to wed ye!"

The Scots' burr was cutting through Rannoch's speech with an intensity his wife had never before heard. To avert catastrophe, she swooped in and set her hands to either side of Zoë's shoulders. "Zoë, please!" she murmured. "Robin has offered for you, and I really think you must say—"

"*Offered* for me?" Zoë's dark eyes flew wide with alarm.

"Aye, the lad, at least, knows what's expected of him," said her father, "and assuming he wants to live to see another day, he'll do it."

Evangeline shot her husband a chiding glance. "Elliot, do hush!" she said. "Lord Robert may be a scoundrel, but he has ever been a gentleman. Now, we're to have a wedding in the family. We should all be happy."

"What, happy I've ruined Robin's life?" Zoë wailed. "Evie, next to Freddie and Phaedra, Robin is my d-dearest friend! How can I see him tied to me?"

"By being the best wife you can possibly be," said Evangeline solemnly. "And by being a lady his family can be proud of. I know Mr. Amherst and Jonet will welcome you."

"No!" Zoë's hands came up as if to shield her eyes. "Evie, please! I cannot!"

But for once, Evangeline gave her stepdaughter no quarter. "Zoë, resign yourself," she said quietly. " 'Tis done, child. If I could save you from it, I would—even your Papa would. But we cannot. And we all of us expect you to accept that with grace."

The Rowland and Amherst families sat assembled in Lord Mercer's study, the marquess seated behind his polished mahogany desk with his dogs, Mischief and Bonnie, asleep by his feet. His mother Jonet sat to his left, his stepfather Cole to his right, with the condemned prisoner seated directly between them.

Mercer stared across his desk at his brother. Robin hung his head as if beaten, his shoulders slumped, and yet Mercer could find little sympathy in his dry husk of a heart.

The lull in what had already been a strained conversation was broken by the sound of coffee being brought in. At his mother's indication, the footman set the tray upon one corner of Mercer's desk. Delicately, Jonet cleared her throat, stood, and began to pour.

Mercer watched her as if through a veil, barely seeing the delicate china cup she set down before him. He tried not to think of himself, but of his mother. One might say both her sons had disappointed her last night. Was she still outraged? Resigned?

Her soiree could scarce have been more of a debacle, Mercer brooded, tapping his new metal-nibbed pen atop the desk. His quarrel on the terrace with Zoë had rattled him, for reasons he still didn't want to think about. Then Claire had made a swooning spectacle of herself in a performance worthy of Drury Lane.

But fate had deemed all of that an insufficient punishment. He had been required to witness Zoë's ruination, too; to see her half naked in his brother's lap—a vision that was etched in his memory. Zoë astride his brother's thighs, one plump breast peeking from her plunging bodice, those luxurious curls tumbling down. With her wet, swollen lips, she had looked wild. Wanton. Indeed, she had looked just as he had always imagined she might in the throes of passion.

Disgusted with himself, Mercer closed his eyes and shoved the erotic image into the darkest, dankest recess in the cellar of his mind—for about the hundredth time. *Zoë was to be his brother's bride.* The memory of that plump, perfect breast with its pert, rosy nipple should never come to his mind again. His anger with Zoë, his ever-present frustration when he thought of her—which was too bloody often—even his concern for her welfare; all of it had to end. Those were now his brother's obligations. Mercer should have been relieved to have the burden lifted. Instead he found himself wondering if Robin was man enough for the job.

There had been no need, of course, to tell their mother what had happened in the study. She was far too shrewd. Last night, she'd dragged Robin over the coals in both directions as soon as the door thumped shut behind the last guest, and the Spanish Inquisition couldn't hold a candle to Jonet Amherst on a rampage. Robin had spit everything out in a rambling, half-coherent string of excuses and apologies until his mother at last sheathed her claws and sent him off to lick his wounds. One did not cross the Countess of Kildermore and expect to come away unbloodied.

Their stepfather, while more diplomatic, was no happier than his wife, for Zoë had long been a favorite of his. As for Mercer himself—well, he hardly knew what he felt, he decided as his mother finished passing the coffee around. There were elements of both anger and sorrow, but also an inner rage he could not explain.

"Good God, would you stop that infernal tapping!" Robin was glowering at Mercer's pen. "Marriage I can bear, I daresay—but that damned racket's got to cease!"

Mercer slammed the pen down, sending it skittering across the desk.

Their stepfather cleared his throat sharply. "Language, Robin, language!" he cautioned. "Your mother is present."

Robin tossed Jonet a chary glance. "Aye, well, it's a good thing, sir, that you didn't hear *her* rip up at me last night. It would have curled the hair in your ears."

"Though I may look old as Moses to the young and impertinent," said their stepfather, "I have not *quite* reached the age of developing ear hair." He glowered for a moment, then took up his coffee cup. "As to this marriage, Zoë is a lovely girl. Your mother and I have long loved her almost as if she were our own. Still, if we thought you miserable—"

"Cole, surely you cannot think misery matters now?" Jonet interjected. "Zoë has been dishonored, and Robin has no one to blame save himself. It's done."

"Aye," said Robin sadly. "I've only to await Rannoch's answer."

"I daresay we all know what it will be," said Mercer, "though he may horsewhip you half to death after the vows are said."

"Thank you for those words of comfort," said Robin snidely.

Mercer ignored him and took control of the conversation again. "Mamma," he said, turning to Jonet, "will you be so good as to write the announcement?"

"Certainly," she said. "We may as well have it to hand. And Cole, can you speak to the bishop?"

"Ah, yes, the special license!" murmured their stepfather.

"And then there is the choice of a church," said Mercer, "since Richmond is so far from—"

"No, wait!" Robin cut in. He glanced desperately back and forth between them. "All of you—all of this—

I need some time. I don't need a special license. I have things to do. People to . . . to see. Can we not wait a few days? Call the banns? Have a long engagement?"

A long engagement.

A prolonging of this hell for everyone.

Mercer shrugged off the dread. "As I explained at breakfast, Papa, I fear I'm needed most urgently at Greythorpe," he said. "I leave London on the morrow, regardless. But it is the end of the season. Perhaps Robin might consider going with the rest of you to Elmwood for a time? There will be less talk once everyone in Town has gone to the country."

Robin, however, looked no happier with this prospect. Leaning over, their stepfather clamped him firmly on the shoulder. "I think your brother is right, my boy."

Their mother, however, shook her head. "Engagement or no, that will look as if he is abandoning Zoë." Jonet paused to lift her coffee cup to her lips, calculation in her eyes. "Stuart," she finally said when she put it down again, "I think this year we must all go to Greythorpe—Zoë included."

Mercer drew back in his chair. This he had not expected. Indeed, it was quite the opposite of what he wanted—which was to be as far away from Zoë and Robin as possible. "It is out of the question," he said sharply. "Even if it made sense—which it does not— Shepton's letter yesterday warned we've an outbreak of smallpox nearby. I must go, and go alone."

"But we have all had Mr. Jenner's variolation," his mother countered. "Besides, the house is three miles from the village. We shall be quite safe."

"And what of Zoë?" Mercer's words came out too sharply. "Will *she* be safe? Good God, is anyone thinking of her?"

Bonnie, sensing the tension in Mercer's voice, sat up and placed a paw upon his knee, her head crooked solicitously. To reassure her, he slicked a hand down her silky black head.

"It is called *vaccination* nowadays," said Robin glumly. "And Zoë had it."

"Indeed, the whole family had it before going abroad last year," Jonet agreed, watching Bonnie absently. "So we are settled, then. A family house party to show our acceptance of Zoë, and our joy at the coming nuptials. I am sure Evangeline and the children will come. Elliot, too, if his duties permit. That will help to hush up the gossipmongers, and give Robin and Zoë time to—"

"To *what*?" Mercer cut in a little bitterly. "Get to know one another? Rather too late for that, from what I saw."

"Oh, holier than thou, now, are you?" Robin braced his hands on his chair arms as if he might spring from it.

"Gentlemen—!" said their stepfather sternly. "Sarcasm becomes neither of you. We have a family crisis before us, and regardless of how it came about, we will resolve it *as a family*. Is that understood?"

"Yes, sir." His mouth sullen, Robin settled back into his chair.

Their stepfather scrubbed a hand pensively round his jaw. "And one must admit, your mother's notion does answer well, Stuart. You are the ranking member of this family. And a family gathering would look very proper."

"I cannot entertain," said Mercer tersely. "I have a crisis to deal with. I may have to quarantine the village."

His mother leaned forward in her chair, all innocence. "But entertaining is what your mamma is for, dear boy," she murmured, "since you have not yet wed. Cole and I would invite everyone to Elmwood, but the interiors are being painted. And Kildermore Castle is too far. So it must be Greythorpe."

"Oh, Mamma!" groaned Robin. *"Must* we?"

"Yes, we must. And now I must set about writing that announcement, though perhaps we may delay it a few days to permit Robin to get his . . . well, his *affairs* in order." Jonet rose, smoothing the wrinkles from her skirts. "Cole, send word to Mr. Moseby, and tell him he must spare you for the early harvest. Robin, you will ride to Richmond, make a very pretty proposal—on one knee, if you please!—then invite Rannoch and his family to Greythorpe. Stuart, you will take Charlie down with you tomorrow. He'll know which rooms I shall want aired, and what manner of provisions I'll wish laid in."

And that was that. There was no gainsaying the Countess of Kildermore.

Mercer's stepfather cast him a sympathetic look as he left.

The door thudded shut, leaving only Robin, his expression darkening by the moment. "Summer in Sussex!" he said bitterly. "With my family and my betrothed. What more could a man ask for?"

"Yes, what more indeed?" Mercer snapped.

"Why so cynical, Stu?" Robin gave a sour smile. "Bloody hell, even you tried to get out of it."

Mercer regarded him across the expanse of desk. "I did not compromise Zoë," he coolly returned. "You did. Pay the price like a man."

"Oh, be damned to you!" Robin jerked from his chair and went to the sideboard. He yanked the stopper from Mercer's brandy with a harsh clatter, then seized a glass from the galleried tray adjacent. "I think that's half the problem, Stuart," he added over his shoulder. "I think you wish it *had* been you."

"Hush, Robin!" Mercer demanded, closing the distance between them, Bonnie on his heels.

Instead, Robin laughed. "Oh, do you think I've never seen the way you watch her?" he retorted, sloshing the glass full as his voice rose. "Others may not notice, but trust me, Stu, I know you too well. It rankles you, doesn't it, that women always prefer me—*especially* Zoë. But then, why wouldn't she? You're so bloody cold and rigid you might as well have a poker up your arse."

"Shut your mouth, you self-pitying fool!" Mercer slapped a hand over the glass of brandy. "Do you want the servants to overhear? Do you want the gossip surrounding Zoë to be uglier than it already is? Do you, Robin? Because, between the pair of you, she's already damaged. One of you must show a little sense now, and stop dragging her name through the mud to avoid utter ruin. Even Bonnie, it seems, has sense enough to know that much."

At that, Robin's face flamed with color. He dropped his chin like a chastened child.

Mercer removed the glass. "It's too bloody early for this," he ordered. "You've got to see Rannoch. You'll want all your wits about you for that."

"Aye." In disgust, Robin shoved away the brandy decanter.

For a long, tense moment, Mercer studied his brother's

profile. He was almost three years Robin's elder—though it often felt like twenty—but for all Robin's profligate ways, Robin sometimes knew him better than Mercer knew himself.

He settled a hand upon his brother's shoulder. "Look, Rob, I'm sorry," he said, forcing a conciliatory tone. "As Papa says, it's useless to quarrel now. We've both made our choices, however unconsciously, and I take no pleasure in your misery."

"Oh, you don't know the half of it." Robin's voice was hollow as he stared down at the sideboard.

Mercer tightened his grip. Something beyond Zoë, he realized, was troubling Robin. "It really is Mrs. Wilfred, isn't it?"

Robin turned from the sideboard to face him. "I've got to go and tell her, Stuart," he rasped. "Even I am not so selfish as to simply let her read it in the *Times* next week—assuming I can hold Mamma back that long. And Maria . . . well, she deserves something a little better than a fickle lover and an unexpected slap in the face."

Mercer did not know what to say. Maria Wilfred was a quiet, unassuming young widow of very little consequence and even less money. Her husband had been a cavalry lieutenant—a poor devil who'd died, not in the heat of battle, but in an ignominious fall from his horse but a fortnight after purchasing his commission. For her part, Mrs. Wilfred was merely the daughter of some Yorkshire parson, and thus possessed the merest pretensions to gentility. Nonetheless, her beauty and her grace had given her entrée into the lower ranks of polite society.

How on earth such a self-effacing creature had come to his brother's notice was beyond Lord Mercer's comprehension. How Robin had won her as a mistress a greater mystery still. Given the way of the world, one might naturally assume it was his title, his looks, and his money—the latter of which Robin possessed in abundance due to their mother's marriage settlements.

But so far as he could discern, Mrs. Wilfred had asked nothing of Robin. Mercer had quietly taken the liberty of having her thoroughly vetted once he'd realized Robin was keeping her—and *keeping* her was perhaps too strong a term. In fact, Mrs. Wilfred had been at pains to keep the relationship secret. Still, it little mattered now. Whatever had been between them was at an end.

"I am sorry for Mrs. Wilfred," he said. "I rather liked her, Rob. Will she understand?"

Robin stared into the depths of the room and lifted one shoulder beneath the fine, dark wool of his coat. "Oh, I daresay," he answered. "Maria has a calm temper and a kind heart. I just hope . . ."

"Hope what?" Mercer did not like the guarded look in his brother's eyes.

Robin just shook his head. "I . . . I don't know. I just pray I can persuade her . . ."

Suddenly, Mercer grasped where this was heading. *"No,"* he ordered, taking a ruthless grip on his brother's lapel. "We already had this discussion. You are to be married. And however ungovernable Zoë may be, she deserves a faithful husband."

Robin shrugged off his grip and stepped back. "Take your hands off me, blister it," he growled. "Yes, I'll be faithful. Did I say otherwise?"

"No," said Mercer. "But you *thought* it."

An ugly smile tugged at one corner of Robin's mouth.

"Oh, that's high talk, Stuart, for a chap who's been keeping another fellow's wife for the better part of a year," he snarled. "At least I'm not an outright adulterer yet."

His brother's blade found its mark, and struck home with a vengeance. Mercer faltered, and stepped back. Apparently satisfied, Robin turned and rammed the stopper back into the brandy decanter. "Let's just face it, old boy," he said, his voice edged with spite. "Neither of us is going to have what we want when all this is said and done—but at least I've got the ballocks to admit it."

As he watched his brother stride from the room, Mercer felt something a little sickening wash over him, like the wave of faint nausea that follows a near accident.

But why? His obsession with Claire was at an end, and the shame was his to bear. And Robin, for all his fine words, had bedded more married women that anyone cared to count. As for the rest—the fate of Mrs. Wilfred, the fidelity in Zoë's marriage—what was any of it to him?

Nothing. By God, it was nothing to him. Zoë and Robin had made their bed, and they could bloody well lie in it. Together.

At that thought, however, Mercer fleetingly closed his eyes, and braced his hands wide on the sideboard. His righteous indignation brought him no comfort. The truth was, the sight of Zoë making love to Robin had left him shaken; more shaken, even, than Claire's allegation. And that should not be.

Always, *always* it had been Zoë and Robin. Robin and Zoë. Robin had been her precious confidant. Mercer had been her personal crossing sweep, simply there to smooth the path to her next escapade, and clear away the debris and destruction left in her wake. Zoë had scarcely spared him a glance.

In truth, however, he did not for one moment imagine Zoë was any happier about this marriage than Robin, for she'd long made a near blood sport of breaking hearts. A similar and far more dangerous scene was likely playing out this minute over at Strath House.

Mercer had not long to think on it, however, before the door opened again to admit his mother. She hesitated for an instant on the threshold, a sheaf of paper held lightly between two fingers as Bonnie and Mischief surged forth to greet her, their feathery tails wagging as if they'd been parted from her for weeks instead of minutes.

"Read this," she blurted, striding in to place the paper squarely on his desk. "Though I daresay there's no need. They all say the very same thing, don't they? I can't think why I'm so troubled by it."

To appease her, Mercer returned to his desk and stood, staring down at the announcement as his mother knelt to ruffle the dogs' ears, and coo at them in turn.

The paper was his mother's personal stationery, smelling faintly of roses from her bureau drawer, and bearing the arms of the earls of Kildermore. Upon her second marriage, his mother had ceased to be Lady Mercer. But as was sometimes the case in Scottish inheritance, the earldom was hers by birth. She would bear the title of Countess of Kildermore until her death.

"Stuart?" His mother turned her attention from the dogs and settled slowly into the chair Robin had vacated. "What is it? Have I misworded something?"

Roughly, he cleared his throat. "No, sorry. Just woolgathering." He really had no wish to see the damned thing, but he sat down and read it in earnest. "No," he said when finished, passing it back with a perfectly steady hand. "No, that reads well enough. Give Robin a few days, though, won't you?"

"Yes." Jonet sighed. "Very well."

She did not immediately reach for it, however, and it was then he realized how tired his mother appeared. Though she certainly did not look her age, Jonet's raven black hair now held a thread or two of silver, and her eyes were heavy with grief. The realization shocked him. The whole of his life, his mother had been like a force of nature—to him, and to the world. For her children, she had been a lioness when necessary, and it had been very necessary in the long, bleak months following his father's murder.

Though he and Robin had been but children, Mercer remembered that terrible time with an almost luminous and painful clarity. His mother had fought valiantly to keep them safe, and when at last she had reached the breaking point, Cole had come into their lives to save them from what might have been utter destruction. And he had made a far better father than the previous Lord Mercer had ever done.

And now Robin was to put their parents—all of them, really—through hell with this misbegotten marriage?

"Stuart," she said quietly. "What is wrong?"

He relaxed into his desk chair and forced a smile. "You look tired, Mamma," he answered. "I know you must be troubled by this."

She cast him an odd, assessing look. "I should have said the same of you."

"Of course I am troubled," he answered. "I should have preferred that Robin chose his own bride."

His mother smiled faintly. "Mrs. Wilfred, perhaps?"

"Ah," he said softly. "You know of her, then?"

His mother lifted her slender shoulders beneath the dark amethyst silk of her gown. "I expect such things of Robin," she said evenly. "Of you—well, I have always counted on you to do the right thing, perhaps unfairly . . ." She let her words trail away, but her gaze was on him, knowing and unhesitant.

He looked away. *The right thing.* Sometimes he was a little slower to do it than was wise.

Abruptly, Jonet got up and offered him more coffee, pouring for herself when he declined. "Claire approached me last night," she murmured as she tipped the pot. "She hinted—and not just to me—that she might be carrying your child."

Mercer exhaled slowly. "I find I do not care for being the subject of gossip."

"Is it true?" Jonet sat and flicked a quick glance up at him.

Mercer stared at the spoon she was lazily circling in her cup. "I doubt it," he said at last. "Perhaps I say that to comfort myself. But the timing . . . it is too convenient. I have broken with her, you know."

"Have you indeed? I confess my relief, though I've tried to be civil to the woman." This time Jonet's glance caught his eyes. "What will you do, dear boy, if she is not lying?"

Faintly, he smiled, and turned his hands palm up. "The right thing, Mamma," he said quietly. "Isn't that what you just accused me of?"

"Good," she said, tucking the spoon onto her saucer with a faint *chink*. "But she will prove difficult, I fear.

Your concern and your money will not be enough to appease her. Claire will want more."

He smiled sourly. "The last I heard, France had outlawed divorce," he answered. "She most assuredly won't get one here."

His mother looked at him, and lifted both brows. "Would you marry her if you could?"

He hesitated, and pushed himself a little away from the desk, as if to find more breathing space. "I don't wish to, no," he answered. "But would I? Yes, I daresay. To give my child a name—to keep him or her from suffering as Zoë has done—yes. I would marry her."

Jonet looked fleetingly shaken. "Then I am glad, I suppose, you cannot," she confessed. "Still, society would see it a little differently, perhaps, from Zoë's situation. However much I may dislike her, Claire has noble bloodlines. And you have not thrown her in the face of the *ton*. You have been discreet."

Mercer gave a grunt of disgust. "Little good that did, given her rather public intimations last night."

"I take your point," said his mother, "but I expect Claire imagines this will reunite you."

"I have broken with her," he repeated more harshly, "and that shan't change. If there is a child, I shall give her every financial incentive to leave it with me, and return to her husband. But in either case, I will see the child properly brought up."

"Ah, you mean to buy her off." Jonet's slender shoulders seemed to sag. "It is a cold alternative, I daresay, but probably the best. I cannot see the vicomtesse as a mother."

"Mamma, I am sorry if my personal life has been a

disappointment to you," he said stiffly. "But I think you must depend upon me to handle Claire."

Jonet relaxed into her chair, the wan smile returning. "I do," she murmured. "I shall not speak of it again. You are my rock, Stuart—though that duty came to you too young, and in the most horrible of ways. Perhaps I have held you to unfairly high standards. And I have sometimes depended upon you more than I should have done."

"But you have had Papa these last few years," said Stuart quietly.

"And I thank God for him every day of my life," his mother answered. "But *you* are Lord Mercer now, as I am Lady Kildermore. I depend heavily upon you to help me unite this family. Indeed, we are more than a family, Stuart, we are a *clan*—with all the inherent responsibility that the term implies."

"What, am I to hitch up my kilt now, and sing 'Lass o' Ballochmyle'?" He appraised her wryly. "Come, Mamma, what is your point?"

"That Zoë Armstrong is a child of our clan," said Jonet. "And we have always treated her as such. Now we must all of us rally round her, despite our personal feelings regarding this marriage."

"I have been the first to make plain to Robin his duty," Mercer answered tightly. "But do you believe, Mother, that she is a proper wife for Robin?"

"Why would I not?"

He shrugged and looked away. "I had hoped Robin would settle on someone more serious," he answered. "Zoë has always been so light and gay—always flirting and charming every man around her, from the boot-boy to the bishop, none can resist her."

"Can *you* resist her?" asked Jonet. "Perhaps that is the question."

Slowly, he turned his head to stare at her. "I can't think what you mean."

"Robin has always been Zoë's partner in crime, 'tis true," said Jonet. "But you—*you* have always been the one who looked first to Zoë's welfare. The one who rescued her—and sometimes Robin, too, depending upon what sort of scrape he'd got her into."

Mercer did not like the turn of this conversation. "Zoë and I were never of an age to be playmates," he said, jerking stiffly from his chair. "I treated her as I treated Robin. Like a younger sibling."

"Oh, is that what it was?" she murmured.

"Yes, but now they have got themselves into a scrape from which none of us can rescue them."

"No, no," said his mother, "perhaps not."

He strode to the open window, and closed both fists over the balconet railing. "That, perhaps, is a part of my concern," he continued, looking across the rear gardens to the mews and houses beyond. "I see Zoë for what she is."

"You see Zoë for what she is *now*," his mother corrected. "I am not at all sure you see her for what she could be in a strong and loving marriage."

"For what she could be?" He turned to look at his mother. "No, I daresay I do not. As to Robin, aren't they . . . well, rather too much alike?"

"Perhaps. But now they must both grow up."

"But—"

His mother held up a staying hand and rose. "I know what you are saying, my dear," she said gently. "Yes, Zoë gives every impression she's full of joie de vivre, but there is a solemnity there, too. One saw it more plainly when she was a little girl. And yes, to answer your question, I've always thought Zoë would make one of my sons a most admirable wife."

"You . . . you do not frown at her bloodlines?"

Jonet flashed a dry smile. "No more than I frown on yours," she said lightly. "After all, you are half English. It would be unfair to hold that against you."

"Really, Mamma." He cocked one hip against the balconet, and propped his hands wide on the railing behind. "That is hardly what I meant."

On a light laugh, she stepped away from the desk. "My dear boy, I know it is not," she answered, sweeping across the floor toward him. "Yes, Zoë is the illegitimate child of some opera dancer—French or Italian or whatever she was—it little matters to me. Because she and Robin, did they but know it, are Scots to the very core of their souls, and no foreign blood—no illegitimate blood—can ever water down that strength and passion. You have it, too, Stuart, though 'tis true you've inherited much of your father's English reserve. Still, there is a passion running beneath it."

At last he laughed, and came away from the window. "You are right in that, Mamma, though I do my best to quash it," he agreed, catching her hands in his. "And yes, we are a clan still, and a powerful one, at that. I know Zoë is a part of it, and I'll do my duty by her. We all will, Robin included—or I shall know the reason why."

Jonet set her lips to the lean hardness of his cheek. "I never doubted it, my dear," she murmured. "You are always the ruthlessly dependable one."

Lord Robert took a quite roundabout route to Rannoch's riverside estate in Richmond. Instead of making his way across the Thames as his mother had ordered, he rode first across the parks and deep into Westminster, winding through the narrow lanes to his usual livery stable.

Around the corner in Rochester Street, he found the windows of Maria's little house already thrown open to the late morning air. Meg, the maid who'd never much liked him, was bent over sweeping the doorstep. At his approach, she gave a tight nod, lifted her stiff-bristled broom in one hand, then pushed open the door with the other.

Inside, she curtsied. "Good morning, my lord," she said, her eyes holding more than a hint of disdain. "The mistress walked o'er to Blewcoat School. Will ye wait?"

Though Robin held his hat in his hands, Meg made no move to take it. "Yes," he finally said. "In the parlor, if you please."

"Tea?" She fired the word like a bullet.

"Thank you, no."

Meg bobbed again, and abandoned him.

Robin turned into the parlor and stood before the open windows overlooking Rochester Street. The summer breeze lifted lightly at his hair and billowed the sheer ivory curtains about his shoulders, bringing with it the happy cries of children from the Westminster playground beyond. A cricket match, by the sound of it. He smiled ruefully at the memories the hubbub recalled. A pity he was not out on just such a lark today.

He turned and looked about the shabby parlor in which he'd whiled away many an evening during his courtship of Mrs. Wilfred. It had taken him all of a month on that worn leather sofa to coax his way up the stairs to her bed; far longer than he'd ever wasted in pursuit of any female.

Her servants, of course, had been casting dark, censorious glances in his direction ever since. And Maria—well, she had been embarrassed by the whole affair. It was a sad testament to her love for him, he supposed, that she'd taken him to her bed despite it. Which, to his way of thinking, was the perfect justification for properly keeping up one's mistress: better furnishings, a better address, and servants who did not dare cast disapproving looks at the source of their benefaction. But Maria would have none of that.

Just then he heard her light, quick steps coming from the back of the house. His stomach turned sickly in his gut as she neared, until at last he saw the flounce of her dark blue skirts come round the corner. And that was it. He was trapped. A dead man.

"Robin!" she cried, coming in to the room, her bonnet still in her hands. "So early. What on earth?"

"Maria." He did not sweep her into his arms and dance her round the room as he usually did. "Good morning."

"I just took a basket of currant cakes to the children, and—" She saw, then, the pallor on his face and faltered. "Robin, what . . . what is it? What has happened?"

He lifted his leaden feet and stepped into the center

of the room, the worn carpet like glue beneath his tasseled knee boots. "Maria, I have something to tell you," he said. "I . . . I wanted you to hear it from me."

"Oh . . . oh, God." The pretty bonnet fell, the ribbons trailing through her fingers as it went. Her opposite hand flew to her throat. "Robin, your mother—? The girls—?"

"All well, I thank you." Robin drew a deep breath, and wondered if he was about to disgrace himself on her carpet. "But I am getting married, Maria," he finally managed. "I wanted you to be the first to know."

For a long moment she stood, merely blinking up at him, as if he spoke a different language. It seemed, even to him, as if it might be so. The words he spoke felt foreign. Wrong, somehow.

"Married," she echoed. She managed an unsteady smile. "I . . . well, yes, I see. I wish you joy, then, my lord."

He bent down and picked up her bonnet with his empty hand. The simple straw creation with its wide blue ribbon looked incongruous next to his own expensive top hat. He could not look back up at her, and felt the unfamiliar press of tears burning behind his eyes.

"Maria," he whispered, "I am so sorry."

"What, pray, are you sorry about?" Her voice was unnaturally shrill, but her words were calm. "I understood, I daresay, from the outset that eventually you would marry someone else. I knew that your attentions toward me were not . . . were not . . ."

He lifted his gaze to hers. "Not *honorable,* Maria? Is that what you meant?"

"No, I daresay it is what *you* meant," she returned,

her tone a little bitter. "After all, you asked me time and again to be your mistress. A man does not seduce a woman he means to—"

"Maria!" he softly interjected, stepped nearer. "Maria, don't say that."

"No." The word came out tremulously. "No, indeed, I shan't say it. *Seduce* is such an ugly word, is it not? And I have none but myself to blame. I went to bed with you of my own volition."

It was, he thought, a generous interpretation of what had happened. There was no question but that he had used every weapon in his vast arsenal of charm to get what he wanted from her. And now, a better man than he would have regretted it. But he did not. He could not. For all of six months, he had bedded her almost at his pleasing. And he had enjoyed every minute of it. Now, faced with losing her, he had begun to feel not just sorrow, but desperation, too. So befuddling and unfamiliar were these emotions, Robin forgot entirely the oath he'd sworn to his brother.

Maria was still staring at the pattern in her threadbare carpet. Her shoulders were set stiffly, on the verge of shaking with grief, he knew. He had to do *something*.

Roughly, he cleared his throat. "The wedding will take place before the autumn is out, I daresay," he went on. "I must spend much of the next few weeks in Sussex with her family. But I will return to London, Maria, as soon as I may. I swear it."

Suddenly, she lifted her head and nailed him with her stare. "Indeed?" she said. "And pray what is that to me?"

He stepped another foot nearer. "Maria, love, it's not so long," he pleaded.

"I beg your pardon?" Her voice no longer shook.

"I—I'm just saying," he went on, "that . . . well, when I come back . . . perhaps we might . . . you and I—"

"Why, you—you *arrogant* scoundrel!" Maria interjected. "How *dare* you!" Without taking her eyes from his, she snatched up a brass candlestick from the adjacent table and bore down on him with it.

"Maria!" he cried. "Wait!"

"Wait?" she said, waving it over her head. "I'll give you *wait*. You are daring to suggest that I might *lie* with another woman's husband?"

"No, just suggesting—" He widened his eyes, searching for an explanation.

"That I am a *whore*?" she cried. "That I would commit *adultery*?"

"No, no!" he said. "But if I could just see you—"

"No, see *this*!" she hissed. Then Maria of the calm temper and kind heart hurled the candlestick at his head.

"Maria, wait!" Dropping both hats, he ducked.

The candlestick clanked against the oak chimneypiece.

"Get out!" she screeched. "Get out of my house, Robert Rowland! Get out and do not *ever* dare darken my door again! Do you hear me?"

"But Maria—we care for one another," he pleaded. "D-don't we?"

"No, you care nothing for me!" Pure wrath was etched across her visage now. "Oh, I knew, Robin—I *knew*—that the daughter of a plain country parson would never be good enough for you. I accepted that, eventually, I would lose you. But never, ever did I dream you would take me for a common harlot."

"No, no, sweeting, I *don't*!" He started toward her.

Maria backed into the entrance hall. "Stay away!" she cried, yanking a long black umbrella from the stand. "Do not touch me. Do not even speak to me. Just *get out*!"

She was almost screaming now, tears of rage running down her face. Robin couldn't think straight. "Maria, she is my cousin," he pleaded. "If she doesn't marry, her father will send her away. And . . . why, you don't know Zoë. She's like a delicate flower, Maria. I cannot see her exiled to Scotland. She would die. This isn't what I want, I swear to God. It is what I must do. Can you not see how this hurts me?"

"How it hurts *you*?" Maria had drawn herself flat against the opposite wall.

"Maria." He opened both hands plaintively. "Maria, I . . . I love you."

And there it was at last. That magic phrase guaranteed to turn a woman to warm pudding—and, more frighteningly, it felt like the awful truth. No, it *was* the awful truth.

But there was to be no pudding for Robin. Instead, the rage left Maria's face, only to be replaced by a sneer. "Oh, you poor, poor boy!" she said, coming away from the wall, her spine ramrod straight. She shoved the umbrella back into the stand with a vengeance that suggested she'd far rather ram it someplace else. "What a pity you did not know your own wishes so well before you compromised her. You could have saved yourself all this pain."

Robin felt his chest tighten horrifically. Dear God, he had let himself fall in love with her—and now he was losing her! "Maria, you . . . you cannot have heard that already."

"I did not need to hear," she snapped. "I *know*. You are nothing but a pretty, charming rake, Lord Robert Rowland, and everyone knows it." She marched across the narrow hall and jerked open the door. "Now get out of my house. Get out, and may God show me the one small mercy of never having to lay eyes on you again so long as I may live."

"Maria." Robin hung his head and felt the pressure well behind his eyes. "Maria, is that what you truly want?"

"That," she said tightly, "is what I really, truly want."

"I don't believe you," he protested. "Maria, I love you. I . . . I swear it. I would do anything for you. *Please* don't turn me off."

"But Robin, *I* do not love *you*." Pity sketched across her face. "Nor do you love me. Not really. If you did—if ever you felt anything even remotely akin to fondness for me—you would promise me that I shall never have to see or hear from you again. That, at the very least, is the one thing you would do for me. You would promise me."

"You will never forgive me this, will you?" he said quietly.

"No," she answered. "I will never forgive you. And I will never forgive myself, Robin, for what I have let you make of me."

His hat forgotten, Robin stepped over the threshold. "Then I promise, Maria," he said, staring down into the street below. "I swear it on my honor."

"On your honor?" she softly echoed. "Indeed! I wonder what *that* is worth!"

The door slammed shut behind him with a resounding *thump*.

Chapter Six

IN WHICH LADY HAUXTON
GIVES SAGE ADVICE.

The old adage "misery loves company" was never better served than at Strath House the following week when Zoë Armstrong took to her bed for two days of tearful pouting, coddled by Trudy, her devoted abigail, a trio of upstairs maids, and—when he could manage it—MacLeod, the butler.

On day three, her half sister Lady Valerie was allowed out of the schoolroom to bear Zoë company, and on day four, Cook began carrying up trays of Zoë's favorite tidbits. On the fifth day, the stillroom maid began to prepare an assortment of special potions and poultices—for what purpose, only God knew—so that, as the end of the week neared, half the household was dancing attendance on the girl. Zoë was nothing if not spoiled.

This was, in large part, her father's fault. When Zoë was about eight years of age, an ugly incident ensued with her upstart of a governess, and Lord Rannoch realized—albeit belatedly—that there was just a little more to seeing to a fragile child's welfare than simply hiring the best servants his money could buy. One occasionally had to sober up, stay at home, and crack a whip over their heads—and none was better at the last than Rannoch.

Miss Smith was summarily discharged without notice

or reference, and her belongings pitched into the street behind her. And ever after, the household staff was given to understand that Miss Zoë's utter happiness was paramount to their survival. Never mind that—as Zoë's stepmother was later to remind Rannoch—there had doubtless been some happy, less indulgent compromise to be found. Where his loved ones were concerned, Rannoch did nothing by half measures.

To be fair, however, this was not an alteration in circumstance which Miss Zoë exploited. Indeed, she scarce seemed aware of the power she wielded, and was genuinely liked by everyone. The boot-boy thought her a "proper good sport," the second footman claimed that she "never got above herself," and MacLeod simply thought the sun rose and set atop her head. Indeed, as her stepmother often remarked, Zoë had a very good heart. She was kind to her sister and little brother, and even tolerated with reasonable grace her middle brother, who had an unfortunate propensity to put garden snakes in her pockets.

But none of this negated the fact that Zoë *was* willful—and increasingly so. Thus when day seven arrived, and Zoë sent to London for her bosom beau, Lady Hauxton, to attend her, Zoë's stepmother was feeling, for once, quite out of charity with the girl.

"Of course you should have sent for me!" cried Lady Hauxton, sweeping across Zoë's elegant bedchamber to embrace her. "What are friends for? And what can Evangeline have said to put you in such terrible tears?"

Zoë sat up a little straighter in bed and gave a pathetic sniffle. "Something about me being monstrous selfish, and that it was nearly an hour's drive from Marylebone to here, and hot as seven hells in this frightful summer heat, and that you had a husband and three children who needed you far more than I possibly could," she answered, much of this muffled by the handkerchief she was dabbing at her nose. "At least, I think that's what she said—I really didn't attend, you know. And besides, Phae, I cannot understand why no one round here can ever think—just once—of *me*!"

So Phaedra drew a chair to the edge of the bed, cutting a swift glance at the two chambermaids who were helping Trudy pack. "Well, Agnes has taken Priss to Regent's Park, and Tristan is with the twins," she said, taking Zoë's hand between hers. "And I am *glad* to be here for you, so explain, pray, what has happened to put you in such a state—and why you are packing enough trunks for an expedition to the Punjab."

At that, Zoë drew in a shuddering breath. "No, it's an expedition to *Sussex*!" she complained. "And Phae, it gets w-worse! I am to b-be *married*!"

Lady Hauxton cut an askance look at the maids. "Dear heaven!" She leaned nearer. "To Lord Robert Rowland?"

"Y-Yes!" sobbed Zoë. "How did you know?"

Lady Hauxton gave a sympathetic smile. "Oh, Zoë, my dear, did I not recently warn you it might come to this?" she said in a low undertone. "Now do send the chambermaids away, and ring for tea."

Zoë swallowed hard, then nodded. In a moment, the maids were gone, leaving only Trudy, who had been with Zoë since childhood, and who knew more of her mistress than did Zoë herself.

Phaedra relaxed into her chair with a faintly exasperated expression. Zoë jerked the bedcovers up to her chin. "Oh, please do not cut up at me, Phae!" she said pitifully. "Not you, too!"

"I shan't, for it wouldn't do one whit of good," said Phaedra. "But you'd better tell me everything, Zoë—and no whitewash, mind."

And so Zoë did. The tea was brought in, Zoë sat up, and soon was confessing the worst in a small, pathetic voice while Phaedra poured, and Trudy looked on with what could only be called indulgent disapproval.

"Oh, Zoë!" said Phaedra, setting down her teacup at the end of it, "Oh, my poor girl! I am so very sorry."

"And Lord Mercer's mistress, of all people!" Zoë complained. "That spiteful cat!"

"Tristan says the vicomtesse is addicted to gaming," Phaedra murmured, her gaze turning inward. "Still, I can think of no way of getting out of this, short of running away to America or—"

"*America*—?" Zoë recoiled in horror. "Heavens, Phae, have you seen what they *wear*?"

Phaedra shrugged. "Well, it wouldn't matter to me, but to you . . . yes, I daresay you'd better marry Lord Robert. He won't mind so awfully, will he?"

"Oh, he says he does not." Zoë's eyes brimmed with sorrow. "Indeed, he is resigned to it, and cheerful enough, I daresay. He even got down on one knee! But what if I have cheated him, Phae, of his one chance at true happiness?"

"He had you half undressed and almost willing," said Phaedra evenly. "To some men, that *is* true happiness."

Zoë threw up her hands. "Phaedra Talbot, how *can*

you be so cynical?" she asked. "Robin has lost his chance to marry for love—and it is all my fault!"

Again, Phaedra lifted one slender shoulder. "Were he in love with someone else, Zoë, he would not have been making love to you on that sofa," she answered. "Now you must go to Greythorpe and make the best of this. And really, have you any real choice? Save for continuing to make yourself and everyone who loves you miserable?"

"Oh, bother!" Zoë threw herself against her pile of pink satin pillows, and sank back into them. "When you put it like that, I daresay I do look . . . a little childish, perhaps." Then she craned her head to look round the towering mahogany bedpost. "Tru, do you think I'm childish?"

"That would be the one way o' putting it, miss," said Trudy, her head inside one of the tall trunks. "When you were eight, you seemed past twenty, and now that you're past twenty, you sometimes seem eight."

"Oh, bother!" said Zoë again, casting a forlorn gaze up at the delicate plasterwork ceiling. "I'm going to be Lady Robert Rowland, aren't I?"

"Yes," said Trudy and Phaedra at once.

Zoë threw one of the pink satin pillows over her face. "Lud, must you two always be so horribly honest?"

At that, Phaedra rose from her chair and tossed the pillow aside. "Oh, Zoë, I wish you could marry because you are head over heels in love," she said, setting a hand round her cheek. "But do go to Sussex and try to be happy, won't you?"

Zoë gave a shuddering exhalation. "I just wish we were going to Elmwood," she said, picking absently at her coverlet. "But this is Greythorpe—one of the biggest, most imposing piles in all of England. And worse, it belongs entirely to Lord Mercer. How will I ever hold up my head in front of that arrogant man, Phae? After all, he saw my bare . . . well, he saw a good deal more of me than any gentleman ought. But there, that was my fault, wasn't it?"

"Buck up, my dear," said Phaedra, settling back into her chair. "You are more than a match for Lord Mercer, trust me. The poor man hasn't a chance."

"But he has become so grim, Phae! So . . . so dour and dark and perfect."

"Yes, Mercer does have that reputation," Phaedra acknowledged,

Indeed, one always feels such a failure round the man, it is almost easier to be naughty," said Zoë. "Sometimes I do things just to see that look of exasperation darken his face."

"Really, Zoë," Phaedra murmured. "I cannot think Lord Mercer the sort of man one would wish to antagonize, from what I hear. Moreover, he will be your host now. What of Lady Kildermore and Mr. Amherst? They like you very much, do they not?"

"Well, they *did*," Zoë muttered.

"Then they will like you still," said Phaedra. "I am quite sure of it."

At last, Zoë sat up, and turned as if she might climb from the bed. "Phae, I want to ask you something," she said, "and you must be honest. I depend upon you for that, you know—to be brutally honest when others are not."

"You just said you didn't appreciate it." Phaedra

flashed a grin. "But there, I oughtn't torment you. Ask me, Zoë. I'll tell you the truth. Always."

Zoë slid to the edge of the mattress. "Do you really think, Phae, that I can make Robin happy?"

"I . . . yes, I am quite sure of it." But Phaedra dropped her eyes to her lap.

"Phaedra?" Zoë leaned over. "Phaedra, what is it?"

Phaedra's head jerked up, her mouth shifting a little uncertainly. "I do think you can, Zoë," she repeated. "Truly."

"Phaedra," she said warningly, "what is it you aren't saying? Is there something wrong with me? Something I should try to change? I—I will, you know. Or I shall make a valiant effort, at least."

"No, no, nothing like that," said Phaedra hastily. "Besides, I daresay you already know . . ."

Zoë felt a moment of alarm. "Well, quite obviously not," she said sharply. "I don't know anything that would make you look as if you just swallowed ground glass—which you *do*."

Phaedra had begun to toy nervously with the lace on her glove. "Tristan once mentioned something in passing," she said. "But . . . it was nothing, I daresay."

"Phaedra," said Zoë warningly, "you just pledged to be honest *always*."

"Yes, I did, didn't I?" she whispered. "Well, then, Lord Robert has—or had—a mistress."

Zoë's eyes widened. *"A mistress?"*

"But he will give her up," Phaedra swiftly added. "Really, Zoë, if he hasn't already, I am quite sure he will. He must know you couldn't bear it."

"Indeed, I could not," Zoë murmured, her head suddenly swimming with something besides self-pity. "A *mistress.* Well. I never dreamt . . ."

Phaedra winced. "I am sorry," she said softly. "Ought I not have told you?"

"No, you did rightly, Phaedra. I thank you." Zoë dragged a hand through her disordered curls. "This woman—do you know her? Have you seen her? Is she . . . pretty?"

Phaedra swallowed hard. "Once," she said quietly. "At a wedding at St. James's Piccadilly. Yes, she was very fair, and quite lovely."

"Lovely! Aren't they always?" Zoë sighed and looked down. "Do you know her name?"

Fleetingly, Phaedra hesitated. "Mrs. Wilfred, I believe," she finally answered. "Maria Wilfred. She is accounted to be quite kind, and has a little house in Rochester Street. Near the charity school."

"Oh," Zoë whispered. "Does Robin own it?"

Phaedra shook her head. "Her late husband bought it," she said, wringing her hands. "He was a military man. Oh, Zoë, I am feeling quite wretched! Really, I ought not have told you."

"But you would wish to know were you in my shoes," said Zoë. "Admit it."

Phaedra's gaze fell again to her lap. "Yes," she whispered, her hands stilling. "Yes. I would."

Zoë forced a warm smile. "And I thank you," she said. "What is it to me? Most men keep lovers. At least she isn't an ice-cold witch like Mercer's mistress. And as you say, Robin will do the right thing before we are wed."

"Yes," said Phaedra, smiling. "I know he will." She stood and held out a hand to Zoë. "So come along, then.

Get out of bed and wash your face. We are going to help Trudy sort out your gowns."

At last, Zoë threw back the covers.

"Lady Robert Rowland," she repeated, this time on a sigh. "I suppose it has *something* of a ring to it."

The day after Lady Hauxton's visit to Richmond, Lord Rannoch's entourage set off on what was to be a slow journey down to Sussex, for just ten miles south of Epsom they had the ill luck to meet a driving rain which swept up from the Channel. The weather reflected Zoë's mood as she peered through the spatter at the rolling countryside beyond. Her lukewarm enthusiasm for marriage had barely survived Phaedra's departure.

The family traveled in three coaches with Rannoch and a groom as outriders. As she rocked back and forth across an assortment of cobbles, ruts, and macadam, Zoë watched the men, their cloaks pulled close about them, their hats tilted against the worst of the weather. Her father must be soaked through to the skin, she realized, her nose pressed to the glass.

At Tunbridge Wells, the journey was given up for the day, and the family stumbled into the Hare and Hounds, commanding most of the rooms. The following morning dawned bright and became miserably warm, but it was not enough to dry the roads nearer the coast. Ten miles from Lower Thorpe, the coach carrying half the servants and much of the baggage lost a wheel in the mud, requiring Rannoch to remain behind to oversee the repair, his shoulders slumped with fatigue.

He was worn utterly down by it all, she realized—and much of it was her fault. She had broken his heart.

"Papa is like to take a fever after yesterday," Zoë fretted, watching him disappear in the distance. "And I will have caused that, too."

"Nonsense," said Evangeline briskly. "Your father is tough as old shoe leather, child. He will be perfectly well." She sounded, however, as if she wished to reassure herself.

"Old shoe leather," thirteen-year-old Lady Valerie muttered into the shawl she'd wadded against the window. "You make Papa sound ugly, Mamma, when he's so very handsome." But the girl's eyes dropped shut before anyone could reply.

They rode on in silence for some miles, Valerie gently rocking as she slept, and Evangeline reading, or looking longingly through the window, as if her husband might miraculously reappear. At the next milestone to Lower Thorpe, they left the main road and rumbled down a narrower lane with a high hedgerow to one side and rolling pasture to the other. They must be drawing near the village.

Dreading their arrival, yet anxious to be out of the carriage, Zoë smoothed her hands down the bloodred silk of her carriage dress, and adjusted the tiny red plumes in her hat. She had taken care to wear her most elegant traveling ensemble, for if she was to be left to languish in the country, she wished at the very least to arrive in style. At that instant, however, the carriage rounded an especially sharp curve, then lurched hard, harnesses jingling.

"Whoa! Whoa up!" someone cried.

A tumult of more distant shouts followed. The carriage rocked to a halt.

"Lud, what now?" muttered Zoë, still clutching a

plume in one hand, and bracing against the carriage with the other.

Beside her, Evangeline stuck her head out the open window. "There's a dray in the ditch up ahead," she answered. "It appears to be stuck."

Asleep on the banquette, Valerie scarcely stirred. On a frustrated sigh, Evangeline shoved open the door and kicked down the steps. "Send Duncan up ahead," she directed Zoë. "I shall go back to look in on the children. We cannot have far to go now."

Curious, Zoë followed her stepmother down, then pinched up her red skirts as she stepped gingerly across the muddy stones. Here the air was humid with the smell of damp earth and moldering leaves, and beneath it all, the faint scent of the distant channel. Duncan, the coachman, had leapt down ahead of her and was approaching a man in a stained leather jerkin holding a team of wild-eyed shires, still in their harnesses.

"One-Two-Three-*Push*—!"

In the ditch nearer to Zoë, a lad and two broad-shouldered men were attempting to heave out the dray, which was mired to the axle and sitting at such a cock-eyed angle, Zoë wondered how they'd got the horses unhitched. Stripped to the waist save for their thin linen shirts—now soaked with sweat and filth—the three had their shoulders set hard to their task.

"On my count!" someone bellowed. "One-Two-Three-*Push*—!"

Their backs to Zoë, the men rammed their shoulders hard. The dray creaked, rolled forward a few inches, then groaned and rocked back again, splashing up water and mud.

"Bloody hell!" someone muttered.

At Duncan's approach, the man holding the horses gestured at the verge of the road. Zoë's gaze followed to see that an assortment of boxes and crates had tumbled off the dray onto the grassy verge.

"One-Two-Three-*Push*—!" came the cry as Zoë drew near.

Again the dray rolled forward, then back, this time more violently, flinging back filthy water between the men and sending it splattering across the road.

"Oh!" Zoë squeaked, leaping to one side. "My skirts!"

The man nearest Zoë turned round, his expression incredulous beneath the shock of blond hair plastered to his forehead. "I beg your pardon, miss," he said, surveying her in disapproval, "but you *are* standing too near."

"Devil take it!" The rightmost man slammed his open hand hard against the dray's gate. "There's nothing else for it, Sam. We must offload."

He stepped backward in the mud, then his head jerked round. "Ware, we'd best send for—" Lord Mercer's words fell away as he stared at Zoë, his expression stark, almost stricken. Then the look oddly shifted, and his hazel eyes flashed with irritation. *"Zoë Armstrong,"* he said, teeth nearly clenched. "I might have known."

Zoë drew herself up a notch. "Don't look daggers at me," she called down at him. "It isn't my fault your dray is in the ditch. I wish merely to pass."

Mercer flicked her a dark glance that suggested he'd happily lay the blame at her doorstep anyway, then turned and waded from the ditch. With his collar laid open well below his throat, and his sleeves rolled to his elbows, he stepped back onto the roadbed looking very large, deeply annoyed—and incredibly male.

He gave a mocking half bow. "Your pardon, Zoë," he replied. "Far be it from me to keep two such ardent lovers apart. I shall have my dray out of your path momentarily."

Zoë tossed her hand, which was gloved in fine red kidskin. "Oh, pray take your time," she said, looking pointedly at the streak of mud across his forehead. "This is vastly entertaining."

His expensive white shirt, Zoë could not but notice, was plastered wetly to the thick muscles of his chest, and sweat ran down his temples and his neck. His dark brown hair was disordered, as if he'd been raking his hand roughly through it.

"I'm glad I amuse you, Zoë." Mercer's glittering, hazel-gold gaze swept down her finery, and his irritation turned to something else. "Nonetheless, I cannot but wonder if your wardrobe is suited to a long stay in the country. I hope you brought some real clothes."

"Like yours?" she snapped, letting her gaze sweep all the way down to his knee boots, now splattered with mud up to the tassels. "How utterly diverting it must be, my lord, to play the peasant on a lark."

His eyes blazed with anger, and he opened his mouth to speak, but at that moment, the blond gentleman started toward them. Zoë looked past him to see that farther up the road, Duncan was now soothing the dray horses, the driver having limped off to sit along the hedgerow. The lad called Sam was unloading the dray.

The blond man drew up alongside Mercer. "George's

ankle is sprained." His gaze shifted to Zoë. "Ah, one of your houseguests, I collect?"

Mercer inclined his head. "Miss Armstrong, may I present the Reverend Mr. Andrew Ware," he said. "Ware is my vicar at St. Anne's."

Zoë blushed, and gave a half curtsey. "How pleased I am to meet you, sir."

Mr. Ware smiled faintly. "Alas, without my collar," he said, "or any other proper vestment of service. I am not accustomed, Miss Armstrong, to greeting my parishioners—even those who are visiting—in my shirtsleeves."

Ignoring Zoë, Mercer turned away and began to gesture instructions, the thick muscles of his back shifting beneath the damp shirt as he gave the vicar orders about the offloading.

"Blankets and clothing first?" Ware clarified. "Then the crates?"

"Aye," said Mercer, setting his hands on his narrow hips. "And best send Sam to fetch the cart."

His forearms, too, Zoë noticed, were sculpted with muscle, and dusted with soft, dark hair. Her gaze was oddly fixated, her mouth a little dry. But surely she'd seen Mercer's bare arms before? Of course she had. But she fanned her face more vigorously, the air having turned quite stifling.

As Ware set off toward the dray, Zoë watched him go with an overbright smile. "Have you bought new blankets, then?" she said to Mercer. "How welcoming. I should have thought you'd expect me to use just any old moth-eaten rag."

"*You* can use whatever Charlie drags out of the linen

press, like the rest of us," said Mercer coldly, "be they moth-eaten or no. These blankets—along with the crates of food and medicine—are being given away."

Such a caustic tone was uncharacteristic, even for Mercer.

"Given away?" she echoed.

"Yes," said Mercer tightly, "for whilst I stand here 'playing the peasant' and dancing attendance on my houseguest, villagers from here to Hastings lie ill—some deathly so—of smallpox."

"Smallpox," she said quietly. "Oh. I—I did not know."

"And why should you? It shan't affect your pleasure in the least." He bowed tightly at the neck. "Now, if you will excuse me."

Zoë mouth fell open. Her *pleasure*? Did he really think so ill of her?

But before she could think of a scathing set-down, Mercer's golden eyes shifted past her shoulder, his expression shuttering. "Lady Rannoch," he said, bowing lower this time. "Welcome to Sussex. I apologize for this delay."

"No, not at all," murmured Evangeline. She drew up beside Zoë and set a warm hand at her stepdaughter's waist. "Why don't Nanna and I take the boys for a romp in your pasture? But first, how may we assist? Might my footmen help you unload that dray?"

"Thank you," said Mercer, dragging a filthy sleeve across his forehead. "I should be most grateful for that."

Then, to Zoë's shock, he strode back through the muddy ditch, dropped the dray's gate and leapt onto it. Zoë retreated to her carriage and sat in sullen silence as Lord Mercer unloaded the crates and bundles himself, handing them down off the dry, uphill end to their footmen and the vicar.

Once the dray was emptied, it took little effort to force it from the mud with the footmen pulling on the tongue and the two men pushing from the rear. It rolled free in a surge of muddy water, and almost at once, the lad named Sam returned from the opposite direction driving a cart. Soon the two vehicles sat end to end, and still Zoë seethed—not just at Mercer, but at herself, too.

Once again, her stepmother had unwittingly shamed her. Evangeline was kind and solicitous, and with her corn-silk hair and soft blue eyes, everyone's vision of a perfect lady. Zoë was—well, perhaps she was just what Mercer thought. A self-indulgent hoyden. A better woman would have risen above Mercer's scorn. A better woman would have—

On impulse, Zoé leapt back down from the carriage.

"Where are you going?" muttered Valerie from her makeshift pillow.

Zoé whirled around. "To help," she said, stripping off her delicate red gloves and thrusting them back inside the carriage. "Here, Valerie. Hold these."

Then Zoé strode across the cobbles, never bothering to lift her skirts.

"Mamma shan't like this," called Valerie as Zoé's ruched hem went dragging through the mud. But Zoé kept marching until she reached the cart. She ignored the stares of Mercer and Mr. Ware—nothing she did ever shocked her father's footmen—then looked up at the lad who'd been hefting up blankets.

"Hullo," she said, smiling sweetly up at him. "You're Sam, are you not?"

"Aye, miss." His eyes focused on her elegant red carriage dress, the lad tugged his forelock.

"I'm Miss Armstrong." Zoé held up her hand. "Here, hand me up, won't you?"

Dumbstruck, Sam extended a rough, grubby hand. Unflinchingly, she took it, and leapt lightly onto the cart.

"Capital!" said Zoé, catching her balance. She looked down at the second footman. "Poldroy, you go help with the heavy crates. Sam here will take your place, and hand up those bundles to me."

"Aye, miss." Poldroy nodded, and walked back to the dray. Eyes still wide, Sam leapt down as she'd ordered.

Mercer apparently decided things had gone too far. "Get down, Zoé," he barked, "before you get hurt."

"Get *hurt*?" Zoé turned and shot him a quelling glance. "Recall, if you will, that I once walked the hip of Elmwood's granary roof in my bare feet. So I think I can balance on the back of a cart—even dressed in my *frivolous* clothes."

"Get down, Zoé," he gritted, "or by God, I'll—"

"Heavens, Mr. Ware!" Zoé interjected, her eyes wide. "Your parishioner has developed a vile habit of taking our Lord's name in vain. I begin to fear for his mortal soul." Then she looked down at Sam. "Don't listen to Mercer, he's just in one of his moods," she ordered sweetly. "Now, hand me up some blankets."

Sam had clearly decided Zoé was in charge. He pulled his forelock again, then set about hefting the bundles.

The blankets were made of heavy wool, no more than five to a pile, then wrapped in a sort of Holland cloth and tied with thin hemp ropes. Zoé carried each to the front of the cart and stacked them about six high.

Soon half the cart was filled, and they started on the food, which consisted primarily of bagged flour, sugar, and tea. Over and over she leaned down to heft up the boxes and bundles. Her shoulders started to ache, but in an altogether satisfactory way, she decided, as the cart filled.

Such a volume of goods could have come only from London, Zoé guessed. Bedding and belongings of those who survived smallpox—and those who did not—were often burned to control the contagion. While it was true that many people, especially amongst the upper classes, were now vaccinated, in rural areas, outbreaks were not unknown. It was likely made worse here, Sussex being a coastal county teeming with traffic from the Continent and beyond. Clearly, Mercer had prepared for the worst. In that, at least, she commended him.

Soon Sam was handing up the last sack of tea. Zoé leapt down and thanked him. Poldroy and the first footman returned to their carriages as Sam and the vicar helped the limping driver up onto the dray. Mercer said not a word to anyone, but strode to the hedgerow to snatch up his coat and waistcoat, then disappeared beyond, only to return leading a handsome, long-legged bay, still saddled.

"Gentlemen, well done!" Evangeline's light voice carried from a distance.

Zoé turned to see her stepmother returning from the pasture with her little brother Angus in tow. Mercer swung up into his saddle, and the handsome horse began to wheel anxiously. "I shall meet you at the house, Lady Rannoch," he called across the ditch, lifting one hand. "We thank you for the assistance."

At that, the dray and the cart set off. Lightly, Mercer tapped his mount's flanks and the great beast surged, leaping the ditch in one bound, then vanishing round the distant curve, throwing up mud and a clatter of stones as he went.

"Well, that was swiftly done," said Evangeline as Duncan climbed up onto the box.

"Zoé leapt up on the cart, Mamma!" Valerie tattled, leaning out of the coach. "And look—her hems are muddy now."

Evangeline glanced down. "Zoé, my dear!" she said admonishingly. "I hope you did not get in the way. Those men had work to do."

Zoé lifted her filthy skirts and bobbed a curtsey. "I know," she said, smiling sweetly. "I'm nothing but a fribble, am I?"

Chapter Seven

A LITTLE QUARREL
AMONGST FRIENDS.

*L*ady Rannoch's family passed through the village of Lower Thorpe some thirty minutes after parting company with Lord Mercer. Zoë pressed her nose to the window, watching as they went spinning past the whitewashed, half-timbered cottages dotting the outskirts, then the tidy rows of thatched shops along the high street. The village was lovely, with flower boxes hanging from most of the windows and doorsteps carefully swept. But the village green, Zoë noticed, was almost devoid of people, and at the wayside inn adjacent, no horses waited in the yard.

Near the end of the village, Duncan turned the carriage to the right, up a wide, well-manicured lane. As the village scene vanished, Zoë looked back and caught sight of billowing smoke somewhere behind the last of the cottages. Fleetingly, her heart sank at the sight. Perhaps someone was burning bedding or clothing because of the smallpox.

Or perhaps not. Perhaps it was something perfectly ordinary. Still, she turned away from the window with an ominous stillness settling over her. A moment later, however, the mood was broken when Valerie gasped.

"Zoë! Mamma! Look up!"

Zoë turned back to the window, then craned her head

upward. They were passing beneath a wide entrance, with gateposts set some twelve feet apart, and above them a gilded arch of entwined vines. In the center, set in a gold oval, was a black lion passant with a golden olive branch clutched in his upraised paw; the arms of the house of Mercer. It was an awe-inspiring sight, and one which was hard to reconcile with the worn and muddied man from whom they had just parted.

"Oh, I've never seen anything so grand!" Valerie declared, turning back to face them.

"Indeed?" Evangeline murmured, setting aside her magazine. "Then you shall quite squeal with delight when you see the actual house."

Valerie scooted forward on the banquette. "Is it immense, Mamma? Shall I get lost going from one room to another?"

"No, because Mr. Stokely or I will be with you," said her mother with mild asperity. "You must on no account wander away from the schoolroom alone, Valerie. I pray you will not disappoint me in this."

"Oh, very well." Valerie sat back, her wide blue eyes still focused expectantly on the window.

Unlike her younger sister, elegance and ostentation cowed Zoë very little, for she'd been invited to most of London's finest homes for one thing or another, and a great many elegant country estates, too. But, as she'd already confessed to Phaedra, the thought of Greythorpe *did* intimidate her. The knowledge was a little lowering. How foolish of her. It was, after all, just a house.

She had not long to wait. Three elegantly manicured miles later, the road bore sharply right again and Zoë looked across a vast, rolling parkland dotted with deer and cattle to see the house standing high upon a hill with nothing save blue sky as a backdrop. Beyond it, she guessed, lay the Channel.

"Look, Mamma! Look!" Valerie was pointing through the window. "It is *huge*. Oh, Zoë! Are you going to live there when you are married?"

"No, of course not," said her mother. "Zoë will live in London, I daresay, with Lord Robert. But she will visit here often, to be sure."

Zoë was not so confident. She was not at all sure Lord Mercer would be issuing invitations to his brother and his new bride. Today's little contretemps had proven he was still angry with her; deeply, perhaps unforgivably angry. He behaved as if she'd trapped Robin into marriage. Then it struck her. Dear God, what if he really *did* believe that?

It was entirely possible. Despite the beauty of the distant Palladian mansion, she squeezed shut her eyes. Oh, how she wished she could melt into the banquette and disappear.

But that would not do. She opened her eyes as the house came ever nearer, and forced her nerves to steady. She'd never been a coward. She would not start now. Especially not with her own cousin, whom she'd known since he was a lad. However large and arrogant and grown up—not to mention handsome—he might now be, he was still just Stuart.

She sat back against the velvet, and plastered a smile upon her face as they gazed through the carriage window. Greythorpe was a massive, elegant beast of a building, made of a reddish-tan limestone with a deep, three-storied portico that sheltered another row of entrances beneath—access to the kitchens and laundry, most likely. To either side of the great portico, two wings the size of most country houses spanned out, then turned back as if to form some sort of courtyard in the rear.

Valerie touched her fingertip to the window. "Mamma, their portico is as big as Aunt Winnie's house!" she said in an awed voice.

Evangeline leaned over her shoulder. "At least you know what to call it, my dear," she answered, pointing. "Now, can you tell me which kind that is? And what it projects from?"

"Um, Palladian, I think, owing to that pediment above?" said Valerie. "And it projects from . . . from a neoclassical façade—is that right, Mamma?"

"Just so," said Evangeline. "It appears Mr. Stokely is doing a fine job with your architectural studies."

"But I wonder how many bedchambers Greythorpe has?" Valerie's attention was clearly focused on less artistic details. "A score or better, I daresay."

"Thirty-two," said Zoë dryly, "not counting the servants' quarters. I read that somewhere."

Valerie turned, her eyes widening even further.

"The house was begun only fifty years ago by Robin's grandfather, who brought an architect from Italy to design the exteriors," Zoë went on, parroting like some dull church docent. "The interiors were done by the Adam brothers. You have studied them, too, I daresay? Mr. Stokely used to drone on and on about their ceilings, or some such thing."

"He still does," said Valerie witheringly.

But Zoë scarcely heard the rest of her sister's answer. She was focused numbly on the nearing house, feeling a little like a prisoner in a tumbrel being carted off to the guillotine. The house—and her fate—was looming larger and larger, and soon they would be sweeping round the circular carriage drive. Already she could see two small figures standing at the stone balustrade and looking down at them. The thought made her unaccountably ill.

But Robin would be there, thank God.

The sudden recollection flooded her with relief. Robin would not fail her. And with him, she could face anything—even his dour, disapproving brother. Just as he always did, Robin would take her hand, say something incredibly foolish but utterly charming, and immediately put everyone at ease.

"Look!" shrieked Valerie. "There is Arabella! And Davinia! And Fiona!"

"And you must not forget Freya," Evangeline cautioned as they drew up at the steps, "even though she is much younger than you."

Apparently noting Zoë's silence, Evangeline turned to her with a reassuring smile. "Buck up, my dear," she whispered, patting Zoë's knee. "It shan't be so very dreadful. I promise you."

As they descended from their carriage, however, Lord Robert was nowhere to be seen. Lady Kildermore and her husband, the Venerable Mr. Amherst, came down the stairs, arm in arm. Behind Jonet stood her big, brick wall of a butler, Donaldson, who almost never left her side. The butler was followed by a battery of underservants, as well as the four Amherst girls, who ranged in age from nine to almost sixteen, perfect playmates for Valerie.

Zoë made her most elegant curtsey to Jonet and her husband, then kissed the girls in turn. Soon Valerie had run squealing into their midst, and as Nanna unloaded the children, Evangeline explained the accident with the wheel, and the stuck dray.

"Yes, Stuart is upstairs dressing now," said his mother. "He begs your forgiveness for the delay."

"Well!" said Mr. Amherst brightly, "Miss Adler, our governess, has laid out a tea for the children in the schoolroom, I believe. After you've freshened up, why don't the four of us repair to the parlor for ours?"

"Thank you, sir," said Zoë. "That would be most welcome."

With that, Jonet took Evangeline's arm and started back up the steps. "I have put all the girls together in the east wing," she warned them. "Will that suit, do you think? Or are we just asking for mischief?"

Evangeline laughed, and fell into step beside their hostess.

Mr. Amherst offered Zoë his arm with a neat half bow. "You have brought Harlan Stokely with you, I hope, Zoë?" he said, smiling warmly. "I must persuade him to give me a game of chess."

Zoë laughed. "You don't object to being thrashed, I collect?" she said in the blithe voice she reserved for social banter. "Dear old Stokie has a vicious hand, I warn you."

"Indeed, your tutor has whipped me many a time," Mr. Amherst agreed, still smiling. "And what of you, Zoë? You are quite a bruising player, too, as I recollect Stuart once learned, much to his detriment."

"Yes, Mercer began refusing to play with me when I was twelve, I believe," said Zoë.

Mr. Amherst laughed. "Yes, right about the time he nicknamed you 'Powder Keg'!"

"Oh, that awful name! Robin uses it still." Zoë rolled her eyes. Then she dropped both the voice and the pretense. "Might I ask, Mr. Amherst, where is Robin?"

Even to her own ears, the question sounded pathetically wistful. Mr. Amherst cast her an odd, sidelong look, then patted her hand where it lay upon his arm. "Robert is a little under the weather, I fear," he finally said. "He has promised to join us for dinner."

For dinner? That was hours away!

"Oh . . . well." Zoë tried not to look distraught. "I hope it is nothing too serious?"

"No, no," said Mr. Amherst soothingly. "I think it is not."

Together they crossed the shadowy depths of the portico and entered the house. If the portico had been impressive, the great hall beyond was palatial, both in proportion and decoration. The ceiling was vaulted almost to the height of the exterior portico, and supported by four massive columns of marble scagliola that matched the marble floor, and were set into gilt Corinthian capitals. The ceiling far above winked down in shades of azure blue and gilt, lit by the sun that shone in from the rear courtyard. Balconied on two sides, the chamber boasted a pair of broad, serpentine staircases that wound up to the massive wings to the east and west.

"Oh, my!" said Zoë quietly. "This is . . ."

"Pretentious?" supplied Jonet as they strolled deeper into the room. "Yes, the Rowlands tended toward flamboyance, I fear. And poor Stuart is stuck with it now. One cannot very well pull down those scagliola pillars or paint the ceiling beige. Ah, here is Miss Adler. If the young ladies would kindly follow her?"

Since there was no baggage as yet, Zoë and her stepmother were shown to their rooms so that they might at least bathe away the residue of travel.

Zoë's bedchamber was in the east wing, and overlooked an orchard and woodland beyond. It was not an overly large chamber, but the subtle shades of mauve and pink on the walls and bedding were lovely, while the white marble mantelpiece and delicate French furniture appeared elegant but not ostentatious. Here, someone had clearly exercised restraint in the décor—Jonet, no doubt, during her tenure as Lady Mercer.

Yes, outwardly, everything—save for Robin's absence—was better than she'd dared hope. She wanted desperately to see him, she realized, going to the window to stare blindly into the sunshine beyond. Somehow, Robin would make all this feel right. Robin understood her, and never, ever looked down at her. Why it had always been thus, she did not know.

Perhaps it was because Robin was kindhearted. Or perhaps it was because there had been rumors about Robin's parentage, too. Though Zoë had never dared mention it, some believed Robin was not the late Lord Mercer's son at all, but the son of Jonet's lover, Lord Delacourt, a formerly hardened rogue who was very like Robin in looks and personality. Delacourt was still a dear family friend—and as close to Mr. Amherst as to his wife, which was a little odd.

But people were sometimes forgiving, and to Zoë it did not matter. He was Robin, and she loved him. Somehow, they would make this marriage work. And yet dinner was three hours away, and just now, she felt a little heartsick and lonely. Moreover, she had not considered the fact that her baggage would be some miles behind, thus requiring her to take tea with her future in-laws looking like an ill-bred ragamuffin.

After washing her face and repinning her hair, Zoë looked down at her muddied hems and sighed. Once again, she'd acted on impulse in leaping down from her carriage and onto Mercer's cart. Fortunately, she found a brush on a shelf in the dressing room, and when Lady Kildermore's maid came in to enquire if she needed help, Zoë smiled and ruefully passed it to her. Together they made short work of the worst of it, but there was no disguising the hint of grime about her hems.

She was escorted through a seemingly endless series of corridors and stairs to a room called the small parlor which was, in fact, more massive than most double drawing rooms. The long, high-ceilinged room blazed with early afternoon sun that shone through a row of half a dozen French windows, all of them thrown open to a side terrace. In the center of the room near the hearth sat her stepmother with Jonet and Mr. Amherst.

To their left, however, by the chimneypiece, stood Lord Mercer, one elbow propped upon the green marble mantelpiece, one boot heel resting on the brass fender, and looking every inch the rich, powerful lord at leisure. His two ever-present collies lay at his feet, Bonnie dozing happily.

At her approach, Mr. Amherst came swiftly to his feet. "Ah, Zoë, my dear," he said, gesturing toward a chair. "Will you take souchong? Or gunpowder?"

"Gunpowder, if you please," she said.

"Why am I not surprised?" remarked Mercer from the hearth, an enigmatic smile tugging at one corner of his mouth.

Zoë turned and made a stiff curtsey. "My lord, how do you do?"

He came away from the mantelpiece with his graceful, long-legged indolence. "Oh, pretty much just as I did an hour ago," he said. "Less the mud and filth, of course."

Faintly, she smiled. "Indeed, you look much improved," she acknowledged. "I, on the other hand—ah, well. Our luggage will come before dinner, I pray." She sat down beside her stepmother, and turned a little away from Mercer.

Jonet slowly poured, then passed a cup to Zoë. "Still nothing for you, Stuart?" She flicked an assessing gaze up at him.

"No, ma'am. I thank you." He moved toward his mother, setting a hand almost protectively upon the back of her chair. His fingers, Zoë noticed, were long and thin, and now immaculately clean. His thick, dark hair was tidy, but still damp.

"I trust your journey was uneventful, Lady Rannoch," said Mercer, "and that the rain caused you no great difficulty?"

"Not as much difficulty as it did you," she admitted, lifting her teacup from its saucer. "Our last carriage merely lost a wheel. I think we may expect them any moment now."

"Yes, we suffered a frightful storm here yesterday," said Jonet, turning to warm her husband's tea. "Charlie says we lost a little slate off the stable roof."

The conversation carried on in a similar vein—an

aimless discussion of weather and storms and mud—but Zoë let her attention fade. Her mind turned back to Robin, and to her sinking sense of disappointment at his absence. She had not perfectly understood how much she had been counting upon him to diffuse this awkward situation in which they found themselves—or how much she yearned for him to simply *be* there. To laugh, and buck her up with his silly, sideways smile. Here, all but alone with his family, she felt strangely awkward and out of place.

And now Robin was sick. Indeed, a great many people were sick—some even dying, according to Mercer. Zoë was just coming to terms with the fact that she and Robin were to be wed, and trying to convince herself that she could not live without him. It would be just like fate to play her false now.

But Robin could not have smallpox, for he'd been inoculated. Still, that did not mean he mightn't have something else quite serious. Something, perhaps, even worse. The more her mind twisted round it, the more an unfamiliar sense of panic gripped her. It was irrational, of course. But next Zoë knew, one hand had gone to her heart, and her teacup was chattering upon her saucer.

"Was Robin caught out in the rain?" she suddenly blurted, her gaze flying to Jonet's. "I mean . . . his illness . . . I do hope he is not . . . feverish? Or something quite worse? I think, perhaps, that I ought to go up to him."

Everyone turned to look pointedly at her. Evangeline cleared her throat delicately. "Zoë, my dear, we were discussing tonight's dinner," she gently prompted. "And there can be no question of your going upstairs to—"

"But of course she is concerned." Jonet's soft interjection forestalled Evangeline. "She is his affianced bride. But pray do not fret, Zoë, for Robin is perfectly well."

"But if he were perfectly well . . . why, he would be here," Zoë pressed. "I mean—*wouldn't* he?"

At that, Mercer made a slight, choking sound—temper or laughter, Zoë couldn't have said—then swiftly left his mother's chair and crossed the room as if to leave. The black-and-white dogs leapt up to follow, their claws clicking softly on the parquet floor as they trailed past the tea table. Bonnie paused long enough to nuzzle Zoë's knee as if to say hello, then dashed after her master.

Zoë's gaze followed them but an instant, then returned to Jonet's face, which had lost a little of its color.

Roughly, Mr. Amherst cleared his throat. "I fear, Zoë, that what my wife is trying to explain," he said quietly, "is that Robin is not ill, but merely suffering the after-effects of a very late night at the Rose and Crown, a circumstance for which I beg you will soundly upbraid him, as, I can assure you, we have already done."

"Do you mean to say that he . . . he is just . . ." Zoë paused, searching for the right word as her fear swelled to indignation.

"A trifle green about the gills, yes," Robin's stepfather supplied. "He will be perfectly fine by dinner, to be sure."

Zoë set down her cup with an awkward clatter, heat flooding her face. "Yes, well . . . I see," she said. "I shall hope to see him at dinner, then." Abruptly, she stood. "Will you be so good as to excuse me? I think I should like to go and admire your view."

"By all means," said Jonet swiftly. "From that most distant end of this west terrace, one can see a bit of our lake and the roof of our summerhouse. It is a very pretty prospect."

Zoë bobbed deferentially. "Thank you, ma'am."

On that, she turned and crossed to the farthest windows. Too late, she realized Lord Mercer already stood on the terrace with his dogs, his dark brown hair lifting lightly on the breeze, and one hip propped leisurely upon the stone balustrade as he surveyed the goings-on deep inside the parlor.

"Oh, well done, Zoë," he said quietly as she passed. "One would almost think you care about the old boy."

She turned on him then, her eyes wide with anger. "I *do* care—and how dare you suggest otherwise?" Her low voice trembled now. "Honestly, Mercer, what *is* wrong with you? What can I possibly have done to deserve the full brunt of your lordly disdain?"

"I beg your pardon?"

"You can beg all you wish," she whispered with barely restrained anger, "but I will tell you plain out, sir, that your attitude grows tiresome. As to your insinuations, I will not put up with them. If you have something you wish to say to me, then say it and have done."

He drew back mockingly, his eyes widening. "You think I have no right to be concerned about my brother?"

"Your brother," she gritted, "if I have the right of it, lies upstairs suffering the ill effects of too much ale. Were you concerned for him, you would be up there with a pot of strong tea, and giving him a talk on temperance. Not out here bedeviling me."

"I beg your pardon, but I believe I was on the terrace first." Something that might have been black humor lit his eyes. "One might almost say you followed me—and by the way, my dear, it certainly isn't my fault your fiancé decided to drink himself halfway to the grave last night."

Zoë set her hands on her hips and leaned deliberately into him. "Oh, why must you always be so holier-than-thou when it comes to Robin!" she snapped. "Or to me? I can't think why you feel you have that right. We are adults now. We do not need you, Mercer."

"No, no, and you never did, did you?" he shot back. "Even as children, you and Robin were peas in a pod—and it was a damned tight pod, too."

"Oh, don't come whinging to me," said Zoë with a derisive jerk of her head. "You never wanted any part of our pranks."

"I did not have the luxury, Zoë, of living the kind of carefree existence you and Robin enjoyed," he said tightly. "Not even as a child—much as I may have wished it."

"Oh, yes, I beg your pardon!" said Zoë caustically. "We were nobodies—and you were the great Lord Mercer. I forgot."

"Do not put words in my mouth, Zoë," he gritted. "You know nothing of my life."

"And you know nothing of mine," she countered. "Nor of Robin's, I begin to think."

"I know you are about to become his wife," he said coolly, "and that neither of you are particularly happy about it. That, I daresay, is one of your pranks I am glad to have missed."

Zoë could only stare at him, speechless, her right hand itching to slap the arrogance from his face. Indeed, she wondered if she had been about to do just that when the swift *click-click-click* of feminine heels approaching stopped her.

Mercer returned to his leisurely posture against the balustrade. Zoë tried to cling to her outrage with little success. In some respects, it had always been thus between them; short bursts of fireworks, and then an amicable truce. They got along best, she knew, when neither opened their mouths.

Jonet poked her head round the window. "Stuart, my dear," she said, "why do you not take Mischief and Bonnie for a walk? And perhaps Zoë might like to accompany you, since Robin is still abed."

Tightly, he smiled. "I daresay Zoë is tired, Mamma."

"No, actually, my legs could quite use a good stretch," Zoë interjected. "If Mercer does not care to go, perhaps I might take the dogs myself?"

Mercer came away from the balustrade, and uncrossed his arms. "What, and have you walk off a cliff somewhere?" he muttered. "No, I think not—not with my dogs, at any rate."

"Stuart!" his mother chided. "Bonnie loves Zoë! And you mustn't tease her any further. Now go, the two of you—and be back by six to dress for dinner."

"It isn't enough," said Mercer as they left the drawing room, "that you hefted a wagonload of blankets this afternoon? You still need to stretch your legs?"

"*I* need to get out of this house before I fly at you like a harpy and claw out your eyes," Zoë retorted, Bonnie prancing happily at her heels.

He shocked her then by laughing as he started down the staircase. "Come along, then," he said over one shoulder. "I daresay the gardeners could use a good laugh at my expense."

For their part, the dogs did not seem to care what had

motivated the walk, nor how their master felt about it. Sensing freedom at hand, they went careening down the stairs ahead of Zoë and around Mercer, skidding to a halt on the marble floor below as they turned to head toward the rear of the house.

In the back of the great hall, Mercer pushed open a door that gave onto a broad, sunlit veranda. Stone steps ran the full length of it, descending like a vast waterfall into a sunken formal courtyard nearly the size of Grosvenor Square. Zoë gasped at the sight below, her feet frozen to the top step.

"A parterre garden!" she whispered. "And—oh, my!—*that fountain!*"

Two steps below, Mercer turned and looked back. "Her Highness approves, I hope?" he asked over the faint roar of the water.

Zoë could only stare. The sunken parterre was perfectly symmetrical, each corner sharp and tidy, every hedge shaved perfectly level, and, seemingly, every peastone on every path laid precisely in its place. In the center of the four quadrants rose a gray stone fountain shooting water almost as high as the great hall itself.

Her gaze fixed upon it, Zoë went down the steps and straight through the center of the garden. Some twelve feet from the fountain, however, she was compelled by the spray of mist to stop. She stood immobile, her face lifted heavenward. Far, far above her, a Greek god rose from the water, a trident lifted triumphantly in one hand, his opposite hand seizing the bridle of a great, rearing steed. Even cut in stone, the horse's eyes could be seen shying wildly, its front hooves pawing the air as it reared up from the very center of the spray.

"It is Poseidon, god of the sea, subduing Demeter, the earth goddess," shouted Mercer over the gushing water. "My grandfather thought it appropriate, given that Greythorpe's fertile farmland stretches to meet the sea."

Zoë turned to see Mercer pointing through the courtyard, beyond the fountain. Her gaze followed, seeing nothing save the blue sky and a few scuttling clouds. "We are perched upon a clifftop!" she said, suddenly comprehending. "I remember wondering how the land lay when we drove in this afternoon."

Mercer offered his arm, and drew her round the fountain. "One does not realize it when approaching from the village," he said, stepping briskly onto one of the graveled paths. "And we are not set at the cliff's edge, by any means. But the land does fall away dramatically."

Here, the roar of the water faded as the graveled path led to a short stone staircase. Zoë looked up to see terraced lawns climbing up to the west wing, with steps leading to each. "Can one walk down to the Channel from here?" she asked, their feet crunching softly in the peastone.

"One can, yes." He turned to snap his fingers at the dogs, who had drifted off to sniff at one of the low hedges. "But it requires sturdy shoes and a good nerve."

"Oh, I should love to go!" Assuming Robin sobered up long enough to take her, she mentally added. "The view must be magnificent."

Mercer went up three short steps to the first level. "I would warn you against it," he said, turning to extend a hand down to her, "but I know from experience that would serve only to embolden you."

Eschewing the hand, Zoë picked up her skirts and set

a foot on the first stair, looking up at him. "Thank you, I shall manage," she said, stepping up to join him.

Some nameless emotion sketched over his face, but was quickly concealed. He withdrew the hand, turned, and resumed his sedate stroll, his long, booted legs requiring her to step a little briskly. "Tell me, Zoë, how do you find Greythorpe?" he asked, his voice stiffly polite.

She cut a swift glance up at him. "Fishing for compliments, Mercer?" she murmured. "I should think that beneath you."

He shrugged. "Why should I fish?" he said, sweeping his hand over the vista. "All of this came to me through little effort on my part. I did nothing to deserve it, nor earn it."

Zoë laughed a little bitterly. "Most noblemen think that the mere blood in their veins makes them deserving of life's every indulgence, and they should have to earn nothing."

"Then they are fools," said Mercer softly. "A man must earn respect. And he can take pride only in that which he has accomplished with his own mind, or his own two hands."

Zoë cut another sidelong glance at him. "So you hope merely to leave a better, more prosperous estate to your children?"

A cynical smile tugged at one corner of his mouth. "Or, perhaps, to yours."

She jerked to a halt, heat flushing up her throat. "I . . . I beg your pardon?"

He turned on the path to look at her, his glittering eyes now gold in the sunshine. "Have you not considered, Zoë, that as things now stand, your eldest son will someday inherit all this?" he said. "That is the law."

She opened her mouth to speak, then shut it again. "Well, yes, I daresay," she finally said. "But that assumes you will have no children of your own."

"No *legitimate* children," he said quietly.

She dropped her gaze. "I—yes, I beg your pardon," she replied. "I did hear that . . . that you are—"

"That I am to be a father?" he supplied, his mouth twisting sourly. "That remains to be seen, I daresay."

Zoë stiffened her spine. "You are displeased, I collect? Robin said you had quarreled with the vicomtesse."

As if they had agreed to forestall their walk, Mercer drew her to a nearby bench. Bonnie, the smaller of the two collies, followed, flopping her salt-and-pepper muzzle across Mercer's knee as soon as they were settled. The strange tension between them still thrummed in the air, though for the moment, much of the anger was gone. But Mercer, she sensed, was still on edge.

"To answer your question, Zoë, I don't know what I am," he answered, his outward calm belied by his right hand, which wrapped round the bench's seat, clenching until the knuckles whitened. "Do I want this child— assuming there is one?" he continued. "Yes, more than anything. Am I happy about the circumstances in which my child must live? No, it sobers me. Terrifies me at times."

"Mercer." On impulse, Zoë curled her hand over his. It felt warm and strong, and almost immediately, she felt his fingers relax against hers. "Mercer, there is nothing to be terrified of. Who should know that better than I?"

He laughed darkly. "Rannoch, perhaps?" he asked.

"Tell me, Zoë, how did he persuade your mother to part with you?"

It was her turn to look away. "I gather it was no great feat," said Zoë. "Miss Smith once claimed she simply rang the bell and dropped me on Papa's doorstep."

Mercer's expression paled. "Ah," he said softly. "I imagined he . . . he paid her, or some such thing."

Strangely, Zoë was reluctant to remove her hand from his—and he did not seem to expect it. "I believe he may have done later," she murmured. "After a time, I think she thought better of her decision."

"And so she demanded you back?"

Zoë shook her head. "In England, one cannot so easily take a child from its father," she said, "especially when possession is nine-tenths of the law. But in the end, Papa settled an annuity on her, and she went happily away to live in Italy with some impoverished artist. That was really all she wanted. Not me."

"Ah, I am sorry." His lordly reserve had softened a bit. "Does she live there still?"

"She is dead," said Zoë tightly. "Evangeline is my mother."

"And yet you rarely call her that."

Zoë was surprised he had noticed. "Not often," she agreed, "though Evie always said that I might. But then there was Freddie, who was her cousin. And Michael, who was her brother. Then Gus and Theo and Nico-lette—all practically cousins. They did not call her Mamma, and we all lived together. So I thought it a tri-fle unfair that I should get a mother out of the bargain, whilst they had their lives turned upside down."

"Turned upside down?"

Zoë stared out across the parterre, scarcely seeing it. "They had to leave Chatham Lodge, and come to live in Richmond with Papa and me," she said. "They had to give up their bohemian ways—well, a little—and become a part of society. Now Michael is Lord Trent, Freddie is Mrs. Rutledge, and we are all just so . . . so *boringly* normal."

"Boringly normal?" Mercer was eyeing her assessingly. "And you think they did that for you?"

"No, *because* of me." She shrugged. "But what is in a name? Evie has always been a mother to me, and that is all that matters."

"And now everyone is grown and gone, and you are left with your younger siblings," he said pensively. "That must be hard, I suppose."

It was as if he'd never considered such a thing before. And the truth was, she sometimes felt dreadfully alone. Oh, she loved Valerie and the boys. But she was of an age with Frederica and Michael, with whom she'd grown up. To Zoë, who had always hungered for a sense of belonging, it was a miracle her father's marriage had brought her a family.

Zoë realized it was that same hunger which, when she was small, had driven her to look up to Mercer, and to yearn for his attention. To fantasize about him in the way young girls dreamt of white knights on charging steeds. And it was precisely why she'd become too attached to Robin—an attachment that had only grown worse. Freddie and Michael had gone on to their own lives, while she had not. The fact that she had—in part—chosen her path scarcely lessened the loneliness of it.

But perhaps being wed to Robin would change all

that? Perhaps she simply wasn't destined to experience that kind of head-over-heels love that Phaedra and Freddie had found. Perhaps there was no such thing as a white knight at all. At least Robin did not look down on her, as most of her suitors had done.

This trip to Sussex had brought home to her the inevitability of this marriage, and she had struggled to fan the small flame of optimism that flickered in her heart. And why not? When one was up against a wall, what else was there to do save try to scale it? Perhaps Robin would be her salvation. Perhaps he would come downstairs at dinner tonight, his eyes twinkling, and everything would be put to rights again.

But these thoughts she could not share with Robin's haughty elder brother, no matter how well he was behaving at present.

"Mr. Amherst is very different from your father," she remarked, delicately shifting the subject. "Didn't your life change upon your mother's remarriage?"

He was silent for a moment, as if considering it. "Only for the good."

"But . . . but you did miss your father, did you not?" said Zoë. "I mean, I remember him, but a very little. He was so intimidating. And so frightfully elegant."

"Was he?" said Mercer absently. "Boys do not attend such things, I daresay."

"And very stern," Zoë added.

"Ah, now that part I remember."

There was an edge to his words, and Zoë did not pursue the remark. Mercer's jaw was set hard, and his eyes were closed off from the world. It was a look she knew too well.

She had first met Robin and Mercer when she was perhaps six or seven, before her father's marriage. She did not recall what had prompted that first visit to London; there had been something odd and a little strained about it all. But she knew that she had been invited at the insistence of Jonet, then Lady Mercer, to meet her children. Papa had sent the horrid Miss Smith to accompany her, for although he and Jonet had been kinsmen, they had not been close, for Papa's reputation had been very scandalous indeed.

"Mercer, why did your mother invite me?" she asked, her brow furrowed. "That first time, I mean. To Brook Street, when we were children."

He lifted his hands. "I . . . cannot say. Because you were a part of our clan, I suppose."

She turned on the bench to look at him. "I think you can say," she pressed. "I think there was a reason."

Bonnie had shifted her chin onto Zoë's knee now, her brown eyes wide and earnest. Mercer looked down, and began to stroke the dog's silky head. "My mother's mind is a complicated thing," he said evasively. "Perhaps Robin can tell you more. After you are wed."

"I think she felt sorry for me." On a sigh, Zoë flopped back against the bench. Mercer seemed to have let go some of his anger, and for now, she was willing to let his earlier disdain pass. She felt so deeply alone, and even he, for all his paternalistic arrogance, was better than no one.

The strange silence about them was broken only by birdsong, and by the sound of a distant gardener tidying one of the paths, Mischief darting about his boot tops as he raked the little stones back into place. Finally Zoë spoke again. "So when was it, Mercer, that we began to quarrel, you and I?" she asked, her voice softly musing. "We never used to as children."

"Did we not?" he murmured, his face half turned away.

"No," she said. "But you were always so frightfully solemn, and forever chiding me—as if I were a younger sister."

Slowly, he turned round, his stern face implacable, his straight, dark hair lifting softly in the breeze. "It has been a long time, Zoë," he said softly, "since I thought of you in that way."

"Has it?" She blinked her eyes in confusion.

He stood abruptly, startling the dog. "Come on, if you wish to see the lake," he said, "or they'll be serving dinner without us."

"Wait, Mercer—" she blurted, "I hope that . . ."

His solemn gold gaze returned to hers warily. "Hope what, Zoë?"

For a moment, Zoë snagged her bottom lip between her teeth. "I hope you get the chance to raise your child," she finally said, "if that is what you want."

"If there is a child," he said grimly, "then yes, that is what I want."

Zoë managed a smile, and stood. "Then perhaps you might remember one thing?"

"Aye?" He narrowed his eyes against the sun. "What might that be?"

"You must not try to make up for her illegitimacy by spoiling her as Papa did me." When he began to protest, she leaned into him, and set two fingers to his lips. "No, do not claim, Mercer, that you shan't. You will be tempted—and when you are—well, just consider what you think of me. I am, as you are overfond of saying, pampered and impetuous. A little scandalous, even."

He watched her for a time, and she could almost see the thoughts running through his mind. But in the end, he did not back down from his opinion, or try to console her with foolish platitudes. And for his honesty, at least, she respected him.

"Very well," he finally said. "I shall endeavor to remember your advice, Zoë."

Then Mercer stepped back onto the path, and almost immediately, the dogs surged around them as if eager to be off. She bent down to stroke Bonnie, who was looking up at them ardently.

"Oh, come here, Bon-Bon!" Zoë cooed, ruffling the collie's ears to break the tension. "Lud, this dog is utterly devoted to you."

Mercer's smile was muted. "She likes you well enough, too," he admitted. "Mischief was one of her pups, you know. He adores everyone. But Bonnie and I, we have rarely been apart these last twelve years or better."

The collie's graying muzzle was a testament to that; twelve was quite an age for such a dog. But the look in Mercer's eyes as he gazed down at her said that he was all too aware of that fact. Zoë had always thought Mercer the sort of man who liked his dogs better than he liked most people. Perhaps she did not blame him.

Together they strode back to the steps where she had refused his hand. "So," she said brightly as they started up to the next expanse of manicured lawn, "may I go, then? Down the cliffs to the sea?"

He turned around, hesitating on the step above her for a moment, his hands now clasped behind him, his broad shoulders blocking out the sun as his gaze drifted over her face. "You may go," he finally answered. "Provided I am always with you."

"You?" she echoed incredulously. "Not Robin?"

Something uneasy passed over his visage, then just as swiftly vanished. An edge of anger had returned, she thought. "Robin may do as he pleases," he finally answered. "But he hasn't been down those cliffs in years, and the path is treacherous. I fear you must reconcile yourself to another afternoon in my company."

Zoë sighed. "Mercer, Robin and I are not complete idiots."

"Nor did I say so," he answered tightly. "Nonetheless, you will go with me. Or you won't go at all."

But Zoë scarcely heard him, and she wasn't sure why. There was something in his posture—the wide breadth of his shoulders, or the way he held his arms, as if he did not mean to offer his hand to her ever again. And his face, cast faintly into shadow by the sun, seemed remarkably strong.

Oh, he had never been as handsome as Robin. His eyes were too bleak, his jaw too hard. And yet there was something there that made her breath oddly catch and her pulse ratchet up. It was the eyes. The stern, hard gaze had gone soft, and suddenly, she wanted to—

"Zoë?" His voice was quiet.

"Oh—yes, I beg your pardon!" Abruptly, she lifted her skirts to set off again, but in her haste, she stepped awkwardly. Her toe caught in the hem of her petticoat, tipping her forward with a frightful, ripping sound.

"Zoë!"

Mercer caught her smoothly, one arm going round

her waist, the opposite hand sliding beneath her elbow. In his arms, she swayed, and in response, he hitched her hard against him and carried her effortlessly up, their bodies molded together. His scent washed over her; fresh starch and warm tobacco and something purely, deliciously male. For a moment, they stood toe to toe on the step, her hands braced wide upon his chest, her nose reaching only to the point where his cravat fluffed from beneath his waistcoat.

Zoë's head seemed to swim, and it wasn't caused by a trip over her hems. Somehow, she caught her balance, glanced up, and drew in an unsteady breath. For a long, indescribable moment, Mercer's hard, sensual mouth hovered over hers, his eyelids heavy and half shut. Her stomach bottoming out, Zoë instinctively tilted her head.

And nothing happened.

"Zoë?" he rasped.

She blinked. "Y-Yes?"

Mercer let his arms fall, but when he spoke, his voice was thick. "Are you perfectly well?"

The warmth flooded lower as her heart thudded in her chest. "Oh. Yes, quite." She took her hands from his chest, and somehow collected her wits. "And I begin to believe, Mercer, that you might finally be right about something," she added breathlessly. "If one cannot walk safely through the garden, one ought not contemplate hiking down a cliff."

But he did not laugh. Instead, he merely regarded her in silence. And Zoë was suddenly struck with the sickening sensation of having just missed something . . . something life altering. It felt, just for an instant, as if all she'd ever wanted had been fleetingly within her grasp, and she had foolishly passed it by. Something far more than this odd, quixotic moment in the garden with the man who'd once been her hero.

No, Mercer was too real—and too supremely *male*—to be any young girl's fantasy. But the aching sense of loss was still with her, and Zoë found herself suddenly blinking back tears, and feeling utterly, girlishly silly.

It was then that something inside her seemed to shatter, and then collapse. It was the sound of her childhood dreams, perhaps, giving way at last to a cold and certain reality. And the only thing left to fight for was a little scrap of friendship.

"Oh, Mercer," she said softly. "Why do you so disapprove of me? When will you cease to see me as that impish little troublemaker?"

He managed a tight smile. "When you stop being one, I daresay."

"Why can you not wish us happy?" she whispered. "It's done, Mercer. Whether any of us likes it or not."

He looked away, into the depths of the garden. "I wish us all to be happy, Zoë. And that includes my brother."

She laid her hand lightly upon his arm. She wasn't sure when his opinion had begun to matter so much to her, but it did. "You think I cannot make him happy," she said. "But I will, Mercer. I will. I got him into this—do you think I don't know that?—and I shall make him happy if it kills me, do you hear?"

Mercer's face was a mix of emotion. His heavy eyes dropped half shut again, and oddly, Zoë's heart began to hammer. That vision, unwanted and unbidden, of Mercer's mouth upon her own flashed suddenly through her mind once again. The sensation of him clasping her body to his, and thrusting his tongue slowly and languidly inside her mouth. His had been her first kiss—a kiss just like that—and now it felt as if she'd been searching ever since for something that felt even half as earth shattering.

Good Lord, what was wrong with her?

"I will make your brother happy, Mercer." This time her words came out tremulously. "I swear it."

"Will you, then?" Abruptly, Mercer turned, and paced away. "I hope, Zoë, that you do. For all our sakes."

Zoë dropped her gaze. "Do you know," she said quietly, "I believe I am a trifle weary after all."

He stepped back incrementally. "Shall we postpone our walk to another time?" he said, sounding almost relieved.

She forced herself to look at him. "Yes, if you please," she managed. "I think I should like to rest before dinner."

He gave one of his tight half bows. "As you wish," he said. "May I show you back to your bedchamber?"

"No." She shook her head and turned to go. "No, I shall manage, thank you."

"Until dinner, then."

She heard the crunch of gravel as he turned to walk way. Heard him snap his fingers for the dogs, and watched them rush up the steps past her. The press of tears came again, and was fought down. But Zoë wished suddenly—and more than anything—that Mercer not think ill of her.

Abruptly, she turned and looked up at him. "Mercer?"

On the top step, he stopped, the fine, dark wool of his coat straining across those impossibly wide shoulders as he turned. "Yes, Zoë?"

"I did not mean to trap Robin into this marriage," she said quietly. "Tell me—tell me, Mercer, that you believe that. I may never have your good opinion, but I cannot bear your thinking something which is not true."

He regarded her solemnly. "I never said you trapped him," he finally replied. "As the two of you so often do, you just got carried away."

Lightly, she lifted one hand. "Call it what you wish," she answered, refusing to rise to the bait, "but however this has come about, Mercer, I am resolved to make this marriage a happy one."

His eyes went as flat as a hard, cold rain. "Well," he said quietly, "good luck with that, my dear. But however it all works out, I know Robin will come to terms with it."

And then he bowed once more, and turned away, the dogs still prancing about his boots.

Zoë watched him go, a cold sense of reality creeping over her as Mercer strode up the path.

Robin will come to terms with it?

Was this what her marriage had come to—and the vows not yet spoken? Robin "coming to terms" and his fiancée fantasizing about some pathetic, long-ago kiss? And had Mercer meant his words to sound so cuttingly cruel? Or was he merely softening her fall?

Mercer was arrogant, but never had he been deliberately malicious. Perhaps he was warning her. And putting into words her greatest fear. That Robin's reserve on the day he'd come to Strath House, the stiff awkwardness of his marriage proposal, the lack of so much as a letter from him last week, and now his obvious absence today—that all these little things, taken as a whole, meant something. Something dire.

Fleetingly, she closed her eyes. All of this was simply too much to grapple with, and logic was beginning to escape her. Something like panic began to twist in her belly. But Zoë managed to turn and walk from the garden at a steady pace, even as her legs pleaded with her to run until her lungs burst and she gasped for air. She would not give Mercer the satisfaction of seeing her bolt from the garden like a startled rabbit.

Still, however arrogant he might be—however angry he sometimes made her—she was not fool enough to think Mercer her enemy. His eyes had been more sad than bitter; his touch gentle. Too gentle, perhaps. Even now she could still feel his long, capable fingers at her waist, and on her skin. Could still feel the strength of his arms, and in his eyes, something that looked like regret. Always it had been like that when Mercer touched her. And to her utter disconcertion, strength and restraint— and yes, even arrogance—was beginning to hold a certain appeal.

Your fiancé decided to drink himself halfway to the grave last night, he had said.

That was not strength. It certainly wasn't restraint.

Good Lord, she needed to see Robin! She needed him to reassure her that she—that *they*—would be all right. Tears sprang to her eyes as she hastened toward the house, but were quickly blinked back. At the foot of the wide steps, Zoë darted up to the veranda, then plunged into the now shadowy great hall.

At first, she thought it empty, but her relief was short lived when Charlie Donaldson stepped from the shadows. "Miss Zoë," he said in his heavy Scots burr. "Gude day tae yee. May I be of help?"

"Mr. Donaldson." She didn't know why she prefaced a butler's name with *Mr.,* but in Donaldson's case, it always seemed appropriate. "Thank you, no. I was just going up."

His gaze swept over her face, then softened. "Verra weel," he said quietly, "but if e'er there's anything, miss—anything a'tall that troobles you—you've only tae ask for Donaldson."

Blushing, Zoë thanked him again, then bolted up the stairs toward her bedchamber. On the gallery, she turned and went down the corridors at a near run, her footfalls soft upon the thick, luxurious carpet. Then she paused at the next turn and looked about. *Her room.* Which way was it?

She turned another corner and tried the knob of a door that looked very like her own. But it was locked, and when she looked around, the paintings in the passageway were all wrong. She backtracked again, the hot, heavy weight of tears pressing behind her eyes. Zoë stifled a sob with the back of her hand. What if Robin desperately did not wish to marry her? Why did she still feel the warmth of Mercer's touch upon her arm? And why was this blasted house like a maze?

At last she found the right room, and burst in just as the tears flooded forth. She hurled herself across the bed, not even certain why she was crying. Good Lord, she'd never been a watering pot! It simply was not like her.

"You are about to become his wife," Mercer had said, *"and neither of you are happy about it."*

At that recollection, Zoë buried her face in one of the mauve velvet pillows, and sobbed like a child. The most frightful suspicions were creeping over her. That Robin would never forgive her. That Mercer hated her. And that this whole betrothal was one great, miserable quagmire from which she would never extract herself. And why, oh, why could she still smell the clean, sharp scent of Mercer's laundry starch in her nostrils?

She was not certain how long she had been lying there sobbing out her heart and feeling sorry for herself when she heard voices followed by an ominous bump in the passageway. But in an instant, the door flew open and Trudy walked in, followed by four of Mercer's footmen bearing Zoë's trunks and dressing case.

Trudy's gaze flew to hers, expectant and worried. Zoë stood and went at once to the window, her back to the servants as she dashed away her tears with the backs of her hands. As soon as the door thumped shut, however, Trudy laid a cool, soothing hand upon Zoë's shoulder. "Miss? What is wrong?"

"Oh, Trudy!" she said, her voice tremulous. "Everything! Oh, I am so glad you are here! And now I wish desperately we might leave!"

"Oh, miss!" Trudy's clever hands had already gone to the buttons at the back of her elaborate red dress. "Please don't cry. It cannot be as bad as all that."

"B-But—it—is!" she said, her words jerking with each hiccupped sob. "Mercer is j-just so cold! And Robin doesn't wish to m-marry me!"

"But you knew that, miss, did you not?" said Trudy, the buttons swiftly slipping free. "Nor do you wish to wed him."

Abruptly Zoë turned from the window. "Oh, Tru!"

she said in a small, whispery voice. "I guess I'd hoped we could at least pretend—and that pretending might make it all right. But it won't, will it?"

"There, there now," Trudy cooed, turning her back around. "As the master often says, many a misty morn will become a clear day."

"It *is* a clear day!" said Zoë. "And I still feel miserable!"

Trudy clucked. "My gracious, miss!" she chided, working the last of the buttons free. "You don't cry over men! If anything, 'tis the other way round. Now all you need is to just get out o' these filthy rags and into a nice, hot bath. Things will look better then."

"D-do you think so?" The expensive red silk went slithering onto the floor.

"Indeed, I do," said Trudy sternly. "For you are Miss Zoë Armstrong, as plucky and smart and pretty as they come—and if Lord Robert don't want you, then someone else *will*."

Mercer strode through the carriageway which cut beneath the main house and the west wing, Bonnie at his heels. Sensing that they were bound for the lake, Mischief raced on ahead and down the hill, rousting up the ducks as he circled the water's edge in some ill-fated attempt to herd them.

As the ducks went tumbling willy-nilly into the water, Mercer strode almost blindly downhill, cutting a swath through the high grass rather than keeping to the longer, manicured path. The tall blades swished about his boot tops, seeds flying. Absently, he snared a stalk and clamped it between his back teeth. He needed something to chew on—something besides his own spleen.

God's truth but Zoë Armstrong maddened him! Even when she behaved with perfect decorum—or perfect kindness—he still came away agitated and angry.

But this time, he was angry with himself.

He reached the water's edge, and stepped up into the summerhouse, which had been left open to the breeze at both ends. The front door gave onto the cottage portion, a simply furnished sitting room with a tidy kitchen and dining room off one end, and a staircase leading to the unfurnished rooms above. Mercer merely passed through it, and into the storage room, where he strode between the shadowy racks of rowboats, past Robin's expensive, newfangled shell and a moldering pile of rope, then onto the planked dock beyond. Leaning over the water, he propped his elbows upon the railing that ran around the better part of it, and stared out across the lake to the high chalk hills beyond.

Damn it, but this marriage of Robin's was becoming more of a travesty than even he had expected. Robin still lay abed after staggering in at daylight, well past last call at the Crown, so only God knew where he'd been or who he'd been with. And now Zoë looked as if marriage was a spoonful of arsenic she meant stoically to swallow. And he—bloody hell!—*he* was stuck in the middle. Because he'd put himself there. Emotionally, and in a dozen other little ways.

The truth was, Zoë did not wish to marry—not even to Robin if she could help it. The girl had made that abundantly clear these past years. Many a man she'd charmed had offered for her—scoundrels, mostly—only to find himself refused. And if she behaved in such a way to a suitor whom she gave every impression of tolerating, what chance had any man she truly disdained? The girl was just damnably perverse.

Except that today, she had shown a remarkable degree self-awareness. And in the middle of their conversation, Mercer had realized that it was the first time they had talked—truly talked—in years.

Or had they ever really talked at all? Perhaps he had been merely watching her warily from a distance for the whole of his life. It certainly felt that way.

When Zoë was eight, he'd been a lad on the verge of manhood. When Zoë had come out at seventeen, he'd been a young buck about town, a little struck on himself, and already wary of women—especially Zoë, who always left him oddly frustrated. And by the time he'd realized the sort of trouble she was in—that society looked down their noses at her, and that Zoë's antics hardly furthered her cause—she was all of nineteen, and he was just her dour, driven cousin whom she kissed teasingly on the cheek before breezing through the ballroom and onto the next heart that was soon to lie broken at her feet.

He had quickly resolved that his heart would never be amongst them.

But it would be a lie to claim he'd never thought about offering for Zoë. More than once he'd been tempted to simply approach Rannoch, and offer himself up as the family's sacrificial ram, so to speak. He told himself that Zoë needed a good husband; one who knew her well enough to keep her in check. One who could both guard his heart *and* hold the reins.

As Marchioness of Mercer, Zoë would have been sneered at by no one. With a stroke of the pen and a few spoken vows, he could have fixed many of Zoë's problems, and perhaps given rise to a great many more. He'd wanted to both possess her, and yet avoid the eternal hopelessness of loving her. Because, yes, he was a mere mortal. And like every other mortal man who saw her, he desired her—even when it had been shameful to do so.

There, he had admitted it. He burned for her even as she angered him with her madcap escapades and foolish flirtations. And yes, once he had even kissed her—the day he'd fished her, shivering, out of Elmwood's pond. Soaking wet and still shaking with the fear of almost losing her, he had drawn Zoë into his lap and plumbed the depths of her mouth with his tongue until he'd feared he might die of the pleasure. But Zoë had been just fifteen, and he had been old enough to know better.

Mercer had borne the shame of that kiss for years. Even now he still dreamed of it. Thought of it—every bloody time he looked at her mouth. The yearning had never quieted. It had seemed far safer to spend himself and his desires inside women like Claire—and even to think himself half in love with a few. He became instead, more than ever, Zoë's guardian. Her shepherd. Her unwanted moral compass.

More than once he'd drawn her aside for a mild scold or an outright rebuke. More than once he'd hauled her out a bad situation, just as he'd done with Randall Brent but a few days past. He'd done it so often that Zoë had come to resent him. To avoid him. And watching her from afar simply fueled the fires of his frustration.

She had never favored him. She had thought him too stern. Too sober-minded. It had always been his light-hearted brother whom she'd turned to. Unless she was in a pinch, and then . . . ah, then he would do well enough. Long enough, at least, to get her out of it.

He could still see her on the terrace that night in her shimmering gold shawl, her deceptively sweet, heart-shaped face turned up in the lamplight, telling him how she'd cut her teeth on rakes like Randall Brent.

He could still see those sweetly plump earlobes, and those dangling emeralds swinging with her indignation. Those small breasts swelling from the bodice of her gown, and that full bottom lip just begging to be suckled. Indeed, she had all but suggested he could—and he had damned near obliged her, too. He had very nearly shoved her against the brick and taken what that bastard Brent had so clearly wanted. He wished now that he had.

But what would that have made him? It would have made him worse than Brent.

In disgust, he yanked the stalk of grass from his mouth and hurled it into the lake. His cock was hard enough to hammer nails now—from fantasizing about his brother's wife-to-be.

On a curse of disgust, he jerked off his coat and hurled it onto the planking. His waistcoat, his boots, and everything save his drawers swiftly followed.

But it did little good. The vision of Zoë shuddering beneath him was still in etched in his brain as he smacked the icy surface of the water, and dove deep into the murky depths beyond.

Chapter Eight

IN WHICH LORD ROBERT
BEHAVES BADLY.

Zoë had cause to remember another of her father's favorite proverbs as she went down for dinner that evening. "Fools look to tomorrow; wise men use tonight."

There was no use hoping matters between she and Robin would come aright on their own. She had to make it happen. She had to make him *happy*. It was a foreign concept to Zoë, who was more accustomed to being catered to by those who adored her than the other way round. But, she consoled herself, anyone could change. So tonight, she would stop watching Robin's brother from one corner of her eye, and thinking foolish thoughts. Instead, she would flirt, she would charm, and somehow, she would make Robin glad of this misbegotten marriage.

She strolled into the parlor alone, her favorite gold shawl draped across her arm, to see that Robin stood by the windows with Jonet and her butler. Robin looked wan but startlingly handsome in an ivory waistcoat; a remarkably restrained sartorial choice, given Robin's taste.

After greeting Mr. Amherst at the door, Zoë crossed the room with a smile on her face. "Robin!" she said brightly, catching his fingers in hers. "My poor, poor boy. How do you feel?"

Robin flashed a weary grin. "Well enough, I daresay," he said, releasing her hands. "What of yourself, old thing? You look togged out to the nines, by the way."

Zoë smoothed her hands down the front of her gold satin dinner gown, which was cut just a little dramatically for a dinner in the country. But despite his light words, Robin's eyes were flat, and she saw no hint of the usual appreciation in his eyes.

"Thank you," she said just the same, then dropped her voice. "Robin, I'm ever so glad to see you. I've missed you dreadfully."

"Yes, was it a frightful drive down?" he asked. "I heard Rannoch lost a wheel."

"Indeed, in the mud," she said.

Robin smiled vaguely, and took two glasses of sherry from Donaldson, who scowled disapprovingly at him as he passed. "Dreadful thing, mud," he remarked, handing one to her. "We've had miserable weather here."

"Yes, a lot of rain, your mother said," she said, a little impatiently.

"Yes, but we needed it desperately," he replied. "Raining in Town, was it?"

"No," she said tightly. "Not until we left."

The conversation, however, did not improve, as Robin droned on about ruts and mud. He then moved on—she thought—to leaking roofs, and half a dozen other things she scarcely bothered to listen to.

Good Lord, was *this* what she had waited for all day? Yet another tiresome discussion of mud and rain? They might as well be married!

Then she remembered her vow. She wanted to attract

Robin. To make him happy. But when Zoë, the consummate flirt, wracked her brain for something coquettish to say, she could come up with nothing clever. So she leaned nearer, and gave him an ample view of her cleavage. But Robin kept shifting his weight uneasily, as if he'd far prefer to bolt from the room, and rattling on about the dullest things imaginable.

Her attention wandering, Zoë watched Donaldson move through the room, commanding the staff like a sergeant-major. Indeed, Zoë had been told eons ago that he was a former soldier who had been wounded at Vitoria. Just then, Donaldson touched Jonet lightly on the shoulder—a somewhat forward gesture—whispered in her ear, and together they left the room.

Zoë returned her attention to Robin's ramblings. She resorted to batting her lashes as seductively as she dared, and waited for Robin to draw her out onto the terrace for a kiss, or to take her hand, or at least to wink at her. But he did none of those things. Instead he kept up a constant stream of small talk, even when she glanced longingly through the French doors.

"Must have been, oh, ten sheep to an acre," Robin was saying. "Up to their hocks in mud, too. And then it began to rain."

She smiled, leaning into him so that he might draw in her perfume, then set a suggestive hand on his arm. "How fascinating!" she said, and waited for his eyes to light.

Nothing.

"Aye, fascinating," he answered. "I can't think why he didn't plant corn, but then, what do I know about farming? Other than the mud and rain, of course. Now Scotland, on the other hand, sheep are suited there. I know you don't care for it, P.K., but I like a good, green hill dotted with sheep."

Zoë wanted to scream. Robert Rowland did *not* make small talk or ignore batted eyelashes. Not with a woman of bedable age, at any rate. And *sheep*? Wasn't that how she got into this mess? To *avoid* sheep?

"Robin, my dear," she murmured when he paused for breath, "why don't we slip outside alone?"

He shrugged. "Why not?"

But just as he turned and offered her his arm, Lord Mercer came into the room looking resplendent in dark charcoal dinner attire, and a shimmering champagne-colored waistcoat that matched the flecks of gold in his hazel eyes. He hesitated just beyond the threshold, his gaze sweeping over the room with uncharacteristic intensity.

Almost at once, their gazes caught, and for an instant, Zoë went perfectly still. Robin, the hum of conversation, all of it simply fell away. Mercer, too, seemed frozen in time. Something in those eyes drew her. Commanded her.

Then Robin touched her shoulder, and the illusion shattered.

"Come on, Zoë. Let's go."

"Oh. Yes, of course." Zoë laced her hand round his elbow.

Mercer dropped his gaze, turned away, and extended a hand to Zoë's father, who had come in behind him with Evangeline on his arm.

Robin cast one last glance at his brother as they went.

"Crepehanger," he muttered, almost hauling Zoë from the room.

"What did you mean?" she asked, once they were outside. "A crepehanger is obsessed with death, and with funerals."

Robin threw himself against the balustrade and drained the rest of his sherry. "Funerals, weddings, what's the difference?" he said sullenly, setting the glass away. "Stu just enjoys the misery of others, that's all."

Zoë drew back an inch. "Misery?" she echoed. "Do you mean us? *Our* wedding?"

His brooding expression relented. "Oh, Zoë, not like that," he said. "I just grow weary of Stuart's incessant air of moral superiority, that's all."

Zoë looked at him in the falling dusk, her brows drawing together. "We have inflicted this upon ourselves, Robin," she said stridently. "Your brother is not at fault. And if you think our marriage will be akin to a funeral, then please, I beg you, cry off. For I shall assuredly survive that better than a miserable marriage of—"

"Zoë, stop!" he interjected, catching both her hands in his. "It isn't like that, and you know it."

She looked at him as if he were a stranger. *"Do* I know it, Robin?" she whispered. "I begin to wonder."

With a remorseful expression, he drew her closer. "Oh, come here, old thing!" he pleaded. "I'm sorry. Stu and I quarreled this morning, that's all. But I just didn't need him raking me over the coals again."

"For what?" she answered.

He gave a halfhearted shrug. "I had a late night," he said. "What of it? He's the one who insists on rising at dawn—an ungodly hour, by the way."

"Robin!" She looked at him chidingly.

"I know, I know." Robin sighed. "He was riding over to Fromley with the doctor or some damned thing. The pox again. But I'm not angry at you, Zoë. Not even at Stuart. Not really."

On a sigh, Zoë turned and settled herself close beside him, still holding one of his hands. Given Robin's mood, there seemed no way of making him happy. Zoë felt utterly in over her head, another novel experience. Perhaps when she had more practice at pleasing someone rather than merely charming them? Or if she simply tried harder?

Whilst she pondered it, they watched in silence as the crowd inside the parlor swelled. Both Lady Valerie and Lady Arabella were to be allowed out of the schoolroom tonight, and the Reverend Mr. Ware and his family were to join them. Soon everyone had wandered onto the terrace, and Robin was making very pretty, very proper introductions to those few people whom Zoë did not know.

But the token sense of possession in his voice now could not undo what had already been said—and what had already been implied. The panic she'd felt crossing the parterre this afternoon threatened to well up again, and it took all her will to hold it back.

She turned her attention to the newcomers, forced herself to smile hugely, and accepted the congratulations of Mrs. Ware and her two handsome sons. Then Miss Ware, a girl a little older than Arabella, approached to shyly ask questions about Zoë's bride cake and gown and flowers—all things which Zoë had not yet bothered to consider. But somehow she managed to keep the smile in place, and to poke fun at herself for having failed to properly plan.

She was deeply relieved when the bell rang for dinner, and she was taken into Greythorpe's elegant dining room on Robin's arm. Her relief strangely faltered, however, when she realized they had been placed next to one another. They were soon seated, however, and when Zoë drew the conversation back to his obvious absence that afternoon, Robin expressed effusive regret for having lain abed late and missing her family's arrival. But she could not escape the feeling that Robin's apology was perfunctory at best.

"Oh, yes, drunk as a lord!" he said breezily when she pressed him about his late night. Then Robin paused to heap his plate with mashed parsnips. "Scarce remember riding home, but I daresay I must have done—Charlie says he carried me in. Next I knew, m'brother was standing over my bed looking dark as a thunderhead. Here, parsnips?"

Zoë took the parsnips, and tried to take no offense.

And so began the first of nearly a fortnight's worth of days and dinners at Greythorpe. Mornings were given over to reading or letter writing, and each day Zoë wrote diligently to Phaedra or to Frederica. In the afternoons, they picnicked or strolled or played at battledore with the children. And each evening, a few of the local gentry were invited to dine, so that the neighbors might begin to make Zoë's acquaintance.

After the Wares on Wednesday, there was the beleaguered village doctor and his family on Thursday. Sir William and Lady Shankling, who lived on the opposite side of the village, came on Saturday, along with their son and a neighboring squire. And though the squire was a blowhard and Lady Shankling a twittering featherbrain, Zoë found them almost stimulating conversationalists in comparison to her husband-to-be, who suddenly, after years of flirtation, had nothing to say to her.

Which was not to say that Robin was inattentive to Zoë or her family. He was perfectly polite—sometimes stiffly so, at other times inappropriately ebullient. With his feverish eyes and fraught expression, he simply was not himself, and Zoë was not the only one who noticed it. She could not miss Jonet's occasional sidelong glances, or the tightness about her father's mouth as he observed Robin's demeanor. Evangeline said nothing, but Rannoch's temper was shortening with every passing day.

It wasn't as if Robin meant to be distant, Zoë thought. He looked rather as if the joie de vivre had gone out of him, to be replaced by something that seemed more like desperation. But flirt as she might, there were no late-night larks to be had, no whispered confidences, no wicked, stolen kisses—not even so much as a ribald jest to be shared between them.

Indeed, it was almost as if he took great pains never to be alone with her, or anyone else, for that matter. And when she gave up trying to make him happy, and turned instead to her usual repertoire of flirtatious banter, spreading it liberally amongst all the gentlemen guests, he seemed not to notice that, either.

Lord Mercer, however, did. He would watch her from across the room, his golden gaze gone flat. And occasionally, he would slide past her with some overbearing comment which only she could hear. Zoë refused to be baited, and merely tossed her head. She was beginning to feel quite out of charity with everyone—and, truth be told, a little desperate herself.

As the days passed, Robin slept late, barely rising before noon. He would spend his afternoons amongst them, playing the attentive fiancé, but it rang oddly false. Following dinner each evening, he would eschew his port and go directly to the parlor for coffee with the ladies, but then excuse himself for the evening as soon as could be done within the bounds of propriety.

He had become like a stranger to Zoë, and she did not know which was worse; this newfound distance between them, or the fact that everyone who cared about them both was observing it, while pretending they did not notice.

As to Lord Mercer, he was rarely at home. The outbreak of smallpox was still moving from village to village, Jonet reported, but quarantines and burning had kept it largely contained. Still, the wife of one of Greythorpe's tenant farmers had fallen ill, and better than a dozen people in the surrounding villages had now died of the dread disease.

At dinner, Mercer, too, was distant—but more from fatigue, Zoë thought, than anything else. Once, at Jonet's insistence, they played at backgammon together after dinner. Mercer was polite, though a little worn and quiet. Despite his passing remarks, on most evenings there seemed to exist between them a sort of truce; a truce made, perhaps, by their mutual affection for Robin, for Mercer, like his mother, was ever watchful where Robin was concerned.

"Really, my dear," chided Jonet one evening when

Robin pushed Bonnie away too roughly. "What has got into you?"

"She wants up on the sofa," said Robin petulantly, "and she's too big."

Glancing over his copy of *The Agricultural Quarterly,* Mercer snapped his fingers. "Bonnie, come," he said quietly.

The dog hastened across the room, leapt onto the settee beside her master, and cast Robin a scornful glance.

"I believe Robin's in a foul humor from keeping his Town hours in the country," said Mr. Amherst with an impatient snap of his newspaper. "Try to get up a little earlier, my boy, and find something useful to do. Remember, slothfulness casteth into a deep sleep."

"Really, Papa," said Robin on a sigh. "Is a biblical lecture warranted here?"

"Chasten thy son while there is hope," quoted Mr. Amherst, snapping the newspaper again for good measure, "and let not thy soul spare for his crying."

Robin put down his coffee cup, and stalked off toward the door. "On that parting shot, I shall make my exit," he said. On the threshold, he turned to give a mocking bow. "Good night, everyone. I trust you will all sleep well."

Inwardly, Zoë sighed. Such was her life as a betrothed bride.

Jonet dropped her needlework abruptly. "Wait, I have it!" she said. "Robin needs something to arise *for.* Zoë, you wished to walk down to the sea, did you not? Tomorrow would be a lovely day, and the beach is beautiful just after sunrise. Stuart, will you lead the way?"

"Down to the sea?" Mercer had laid aside his reading to stroke Bonnie, whose head now lay in his lap. "Tomorrow? Yes, I suppose."

Robin had propped himself against the doorframe. "At *sunrise,* Stu?" he said disdainfully. "That job I shall gladly leave to you." Then he turned and strode from the room.

With a sound of irritation, Mr. Amherst cast an odd look at his wife, laid down his newspaper, and rose to follow Robin. His spine was ramrod straight, and he wore his soldier's face—a sure sign of trouble to come. Zoë felt almost embarrassed on her betrothed's behalf.

"Well, it appears it will be just the two of you," Jonet remarked dryly.

Zoë shook her head. "Another time, perhaps," she said quietly.

From the settee, Mercer cast her an odd, sidelong glance.

Jonet sighed. "It has been too quiet here for you young people," she said, pausing to bite off her thread. "Perhaps we should have a long ride soon? Along the coast, perhaps?"

"That would be lovely." Her evening ruined, Zoë stood and forced a smile. "And now I think I shall follow Robin's good example. I'm going to find a book, and retire early."

Robin had already rung for his valet by the time his stepfather rapped upon his bedchamber door.

"I was just on my way out, Papa," he said when the door opened. "Can't this wait?"

"It cannot." His stepfather shut the door firmly. "I am afraid, Robert, that you and I must speak frankly."

Just then, his manservant Watts came in, Robin's freshly brushed riding coat hanging from one fingertip.

"Leave us," snapped his stepfather, his voice uncharacteristically harsh.

Eyes widening, Watts bowed, and backed his way out again. Robin watched him go, his jaw set tightly. He knew, of course, what was to come, and if he were honest, he knew he likely deserved it. But his method of coping with life nowadays had become delay, drink, and delude—the latter two being applied primarily to himself, for if he did not acknowledge what his life was swiftly coming to, he did not have to think too much about it.

So he attempted to delay. "Really, sir, I'm afraid we must talk about this tomorrow," he said stridently, already stripping off his coat. "I've promised Millard a hand of cards at the Crown tonight."

"Yes, as you did last night." Robin's stepfather had begun to pace back and forth before the cheval glass. "And better than a dozen nights before that, apparently. One might be forgiven for concluding that Millard and his cards are more important than the happiness of your affianced wife."

"What, am I now accountable to you for every damned move I make?" Robin flung his coat down, his barely tethered temper slipping. "Well, to hell with that! My God, Father, I am five-and-twenty years old!"

"And thus old enough to watch your language," snapped Cole.

"My language?" Robin choked. "My *language*? That, sir, is the least of my problems. Now if you will kindly excuse me, I am expected elsewhere."

Cole caught him lightly by the arm. "You are expected to make Zoë a good husband," he said, his voice implacable. "And thus far, son, you do not look promising."

"Good God, I shall be married to Zoë until hell freezes over!" said Robin, his hand spasmodically fisting round a brass candlestick on his night table. "Isn't the rest of my goddamned life enough? Won't *that* make her happy?" He scarcely knew what he intended until the stick went hurtling across the room. It struck his cheval glass with a resounding crack, shattering it into a spider's web of shards.

For a moment, his stepfather was speechless. He stood merely staring at the ruined glass. "Robin," he said quietly, "this simply will not do."

"Fine, then fetch your bloody parson tomorrow!" Barely restrained emotion shuddered through him. "Let's have done with this farce of a marriage!"

His stepfather whirled round, his face rigid with anger. But his words faded when he saw Robin's expression. He took a tentative step forward.

"No!" Robin lifted his hand, palm out, his voice breaking. "Just . . . *don't*."

"Oh, Robin," Cole whispered.

Robin looked at him bitterly. "Let not thy soul spare for his crying," he replied, trying to force down the pressure that welled behind his eyes. "My problems are my own, sir. Kindly go, and leave me to them. I'll do whatever you wish."

"Robin." His father's voice softened. "No one wishes you unhappy. Certainly your mother and I do not."

Robin turned away, and went to one of the chairs by the hearth. To his undying humiliation, the welling tears began to leak out—a dreadful side effect, he'd found, of sobriety.

"Tell me, son." His father edged nearer. "Tell me what is wrong."

Robin fell into the chair, and let his face fall into his hands. He was ashamed. So ashamed, and so angry. At himself. And, unfairly, at everyone else, too. He knew this, and yet was powerless to stop it.

"Robin." There was an ache in his stepfather's voice. "Don't you love Zoë at all?"

"Of course, I love Zoë!" He felt his face twist with pain, and he set the heels of his hands to his eyes. "Why must everyone keep asking? That's half the bloody problem! Zoë is dear to me."

A heavy silence held sway over the room. Finally his stepfather spoke again. "I think, Robin, that the trouble is you are trying to find a way out of this marriage."

Robin lifted his face. "There is no way out!" he choked. "I *know* that. I said I would marry her, and I shall."

"Doing it and wanting it are two quite different things. All of us—Zoë included—want what is best." His stepfather sat down, propped his elbows upon his knees and leaned forward, his fingers thoughtfully entwined. "Robin, is there . . . someone else?"

At last Robin's gaze returned to his stepfather's face. "There was someone," he whispered. "My mistress. But I have broken with her."

"Ah." His stepfather winced. "Yes, your mother said she thought you were keeping a young lady."

"I wasn't *keeping* her," he bit out. "It wasn't like that."

"Then it does not sound as if she was your mistress,

precisely," said his father gently. "But in any case, son, do you love her?"

"Yes," he cried, his hands fisting. "Desperately. But she loathes the very sight of me now. She has shut me completely out of her life—and I cannot blame her, for I've treated her abominably."

His stepfather studied his face as if trying to understand. "But why not *her,* Robin, if you loved her? Why were you with Zoë? This woman—is she married? Is she a . . . a courtesan? What?"

Lamely, he lifted both shoulders. "None of that," he whispered. "I just thought . . . that I had time to enjoy life before settling down. That she would put up with it, I suppose. I wished to have my cake and eat it, too. And I thought . . ." Here, he hung his head in shame, "I suppose I thought that people would say she was beneath me."

"And now?" His father's words held a wealth of meaning.

Robin turned away again, lest his father see his tears. "And now I realize," he choked, "that it is quite the other way round. That *I* am beneath her. And I am so ashamed. Ashamed of how I treated her. Ashamed I cannot be what Zoë deserves. Just . . . everything. Everything is bollixed up. And now Zoë is ruined, and yes, I know it is my fault. I just never dreamed a silly flirtation would come to this."

"Oh, my son." His stepfather rose, and set a warm, heavy hand upon Robin's shoulder. "Oh, I am so very sorry. And indeed, even if I could restore your beloved to you—and I can think of no way to do it—matters have simply gone too far this time."

"Good God, Papa!" he choked. "You think I don't know that?"

His stepfather did not remove his hand, for which Robin was oddly grateful. Nor did he chide him for his language. "Zoë is a good girl, and her father is your kinsman," he said instead. "I am heartbroken for you, Robin. But to shame Zoë now is utterly out of the question."

"Yes, sir. Quite." Abruptly, Robin jerked from his chair. He went to the hearth and stared into the sooty depths of the firebox, wishing he could vanish up it like so much smoke.

But he could not.

He set his jaw rigidly again, and said what he knew he must. "I will do what is right, sir, by Zoë," he finally said. "You have my word as a gentleman. Still, you would have liked her—Maria, I mean. She is a vicar's daughter, if you can believe it. And a good person. Perhaps, if I had let her—if I'd done right by her—she might have made *me* a better person. Do you think such a thing is possible?"

"I think that is precisely what a good marriage does, Robin," said his stepfather quietly. "It makes us better. And stronger."

Robin considered it. "I believe, sir, that the two of you would have had much in common."

He heard his stepfather's soft footsteps behind him. "You are a good person, son," he said, patting a warm, comforting hand between Robin's shoulder blades. "And I am very sorry I shan't have the chance to meet Maria."

"As am I," said Robin quietly.

His father gave him one last pat. "Well, go on then," he said. "Go on. You have a hand of cards to play. Zoë has gone to bed, so there is nothing else, I suppose, that can be done about any of this tonight."

Zoë moped in her room for a time, drifting from one window to another, wounded by Robin's indifference. After a time, she went to her writing table and began to pen yet another letter to Phaedra, but after a few lines, she realized she did not quite know how to explain what she was feeling—all the confusion, the bottled-up rage. Moreover, there was no need to trouble Phaedra with it, when she was enjoying the happiest time of her life.

And what was there, really, to say? How had she imagined this would all come out? With fireworks, bagpipes, and pledges of undying love?

No. No, she hadn't been fool enough to hope for that. She'd merely wanted, she supposed, just what she'd said to Trudy—that Robin would make a pretense of being happy. And in his way, he was, but Zoë was burdened by the fact that she knew far him too well to be fooled. Worse, she knew she had led him into this. How, then, to explain all this to Phaedra, who had so wisely warned her—and more than once—that she and Robin were dancing on thin ice?

Phaedra, nonetheless, would wish her happy, which was more than she could apparently hope for from her fiancé. Choked by sudden tears, Zoë cursed aloud and hurled down her pen, flicking drops of blue-black ink across the foolscap. She seized the letter on a rush of anger, crushed it, then hurled it into the cold hearth. She was ashamed of herself, truly. Never had she wallowed in self-pity, no matter how cruel the world had been.

It was time to do what she'd tried her best to delay.

To grow up. To accept that life, for her, would never be a fairy tale. Impatiently she dashed away her tears and went to the door, jerking it open. She would do just as she had said. She would go into the library, and find something edifying to read. The Book of Job, perhaps. The recitation of his many plagues might be sufficiently chastening.

Greythorpe's library was a vast room on the same floor as Zoë's bedchamber. She had seen it the day after their arrival when Jonet had given them a tour of the house. But this library was like a living, breathing thing, not some showpiece displaying row upon row of leather-matched spines and exotic works so new the ink still reeked in the air.

In Greythorpe's library, most of the books were worn, the pages even a little tatty. Journals from agricultural to zoological were piled upon tables and shelves. The furniture was well worn, too; soft leather chairs, some of them cracked with age, and a trio of large desks lined neatly down the center of the long, columned room for anyone to use as they pleased.

"Good evening, miss."

Zoë jumped. Harlan Stokely jerked to his feet at the center desk, which looked half an inch deep in his papers.

"Oh, hullo, Stokie." She kissed him lightly on the cheek as she passed. "Sit down, do."

She was deeply fond of Harlan Stokely, for he'd been tutor to Frederica and Michael, and to Evangeline's sister before that. Zoë had not been especially happy to be given over to Mr. Stokely upon her father's marriage, but he'd soon proven far smarter than the horrid Miss

Smith, and had dragged her—sometimes kicking and screaming—toward a fine classical education.

Nowadays, Zoë tended to hide the fact she spoke Latin, French, and a passable Greek, and that at geometry, she was better, even, than Michael. For a pretty girl out in society, such skills were worthless, even frowned upon, she'd quickly learned. But Zoë found that it was no harder to bat one's lashes and appear pleasantly vacuous than it was to work out a Euclidean algorithm. So she had let herself seem what society expected—then embellished it just a trifle for good measure.

Stokely was sketching something. Zoë drew a finger over the corner of his paper. "All work and no play makes Stokie a dull boy," she teased. "Lesson plans again?"

"Yes, geography," he said, pushing his spectacles up his nose with one finger. "Lady Valerie expressed an interest in the topographical characteristics of the Wealden anticline as it extends into Sussex. I was just drawing some explanatory diagrams."

"Pray do not let me disturb you." Since the light was fast fading, Zoë took a candle. "I came merely to search for a little bedside reading."

Stokely smiled up at her. "You shan't go away disappointed, miss," he said, beginning to stack up the books he'd been using. "And pray take your time. I'm off to play chess with Mr. Amherst."

Zoë let her eyes trail along the shelves, but half her attention was focused on the vast bay window in the center of the room, both sides of which were pushed wide to the fine evening air. A blue brocade chaise sat tucked inside it; an inviting nook for a rainy day. As Zoë passed, she paused to look out over Greythorpe's elegant fore-court.

She had not come solely for a book, after all, had she? No, she was a glutton, apparently, for punishment. A gudgeon. And an utter fool.

Still, one ear cocked toward the open windows, she dallied, drawing out first this book, then that, even pausing to flip blindly through a few of the pages. The many plagues of Job looked too grim, even given her present mood. Zoë moved on past the Bible, but never far from the window. She had just pulled a worn copy of *Roxana* from the shelves when the pounding of hooves drew her.

Lifting her candle high, Zoë leaned across the chaise to peer through the window. In the falling dusk, a lone rider came round the east wing, crouched low over his pommel as he set a thunderous pace toward the village.

Though the sight was perhaps not unexpected, Zoë's heart sank. The big gray horse was easily recognized—as was the rider. In an instant, however, he was gone. For a long moment, she merely stared at the spot in the trees where the rider had vanished. Soon, however, she became aware her old tutor was staring at her.

"Stokie," she said quietly, her gaze still fixed upon the forecourt, "are you here every night round this time?"

"Yes, miss. Generally speaking."

"And does Lord Robert . . . does he go out like that every night?" she asked. "Riding hell-for-leather, I mean?"

She heard Mr. Stokely push back his chair.

Zoë clutched the book to her chest and turned round. Stokely would not hold her gaze. "Yes, miss," he finally answered, standing. "He goes to the village tavern, I believe, to play at cards and to dice."

"And to drink?" Zoë added.

Stokely glanced at her, his expression rueful. "Most young men do," he said, shuffling papers into his leather folio. "It means little, I daresay."

It means he prefers gaming and drinking to my company, thought Zoë bitterly.

But that was hardly fair. She and Robin, even at their closest, had never spent any time in one another's pockets. And in truth, she did not yearn for his companionship. She just yearned for this—all of this—to feel *right.* Or at least to feel endurable. For the next thirty or forty years.

Dear God. That was a lifetime. Quite literally.

Unfortunately, Harlan Stokely was still looking at her, his reticence rapidly shifting to something more like pity. And that, most assuredly, was *not* endurable.

Zoë flashed him her brightest smile. "Yes, as you say, young men must have their leisure," she agreed, setting her candle upon his table. "Tell me, Stokie, have you read this? Shall I like it, do you think?"

"Mr. Defoe!" Stokely looked down at the book, obviously grateful for a change of subject. "Oh, yes, you shall quite like it, Zoë—though it is thought a trifle scandalous."

"Scandalous?" Her smile never dimming, Zoë walked him to the door. "Why, Stokie, that sounds just my thing, does it not?"

Stokely laughed, and drew open the door. "It does, rather," he admitted. "Good night, miss."

But Zoë did not follow him out. Her mechanical

smile fading at once, she turned round and looked assessingly at the blue brocade chaise beneath the windows. It looked wide and reasonably comfortable, with a rolled pillow that would fit—

Horrified, she realized the direction her thoughts were taking.

No, she *would not* wait up for him!

Good Lord, was she contemplating actually spying on Robin? Before they were even wed? That was gutless. And what did it matter where he had gone or how long he stayed? But the frustration she'd hidden from Mr. Stokely began to build into a full-blown temper. The fact remained that Robin had abandoned her—no, worse, he'd tried to fob her off on his brother! Everyone else likely knew where he went, too. Certainly Mercer did. The humiliation of it stung.

How had she, the consummate flirt, been brought so low?

Well, damn Robin to hell. Zoë began pacing almost frantically back to the window. Let him go play his cards and dandle his tavern wenches upon his knee. Once they were wed, he could go his way, and she would go hers. She would throw herself back into the whirl of society with a vengeance, she decided, turning round again, her skirts whipping about her ankles.

Yes, she would go back to doing precisely as she had done these last five years or more—flirting and laughing and behaving just a trifle outrageously. Heaven knew she was capable of giving as good as she got. Let Robin see how he liked being the one who was humiliated!

Having worked herself up into a frenzy of indignation, Zoë slammed the book onto the empty table with such force the candle guttered and went out. She scarcely saw it, for she was already halfway to the door. But blinded by temper, she failed to look where she was going, and on the threshold, ran smack into an immovable force.

A very warm, very solid force.

"Mercer!" she said into his cravat.

"Zoë?" Mercer's heavy hands settled lightly on her shoulders, and he pushed her a little away. "Zoë, are you all right?"

"Perfectly," she returned, backing up. "What do you want?"

He paused for a heartbeat. "I believe this is my library," he said, nudging the door shut behind him. Then he set his head to one side, studying her. "Zoë, have you been up here alone all this time?"

Good Lord, not more sympathy. And not from him.

Zoë shrugged, and paced deeper into the room. "I was looking for a book," she said, throwing her arms over her chest. "As I said after dinner, I wished something to read."

Mercer followed, watching warily. "Indeed," he murmured, flicking a quick glance at the open windows. "And yet you were leaving without one?"

She cut a sidelong gaze at his stark, handsome profile, and suddenly, she knew what he was thinking as surely as if their minds had been one. It served only to heighten her rage. She whirled around to face him.

"Yes, Mercer, I saw him leave," she ground out. "Don't look at me in that way."

"In what way?"

"All pity and self-satisfaction!" she cried. "What

did you think I imagined? That Robin spent his nights curled up with a good book and a cup of warm milk?"

His broad shoulders fell. "I'm sorry, Zoë," he said. "Robin is a scoundrel. And however this travesty came about, you deserve better. But you mistake, I think, my emotions."

"Oh, I doubt it!" she said, forcing down tears. "A part of you is pleased, I daresay, to see me get my come-uppance! I have come to a bad end, just as you always expected."

"Zoë, I never said that."

"You did not need to," she returned, her voice strident. "It has always been there. In your disapproving expression. Your hard voice."

Hugging her arms tightly about her, she turned her face away. She couldn't bear to face him; not like this. Hurt and loneliness welled up in her, making her weak. And oh, how she hated it!

"Don't say such things." To her shock, Mercer's hand slid around her cheek and forced her face back to his. "Zoë, look at me," he said. "*Look* at me. You have no idea what I think, trust me."

Tenderness she could not bear. "You think I'm a fribble and a flirt," she cried. Then her voice dropped tremulously. "You should have let Brent have his way with me in the garden that night."

Some black emotion sketched over his face. "What, now I'm to apologize for saving your reputation? So you could go upstairs and throw it away on my brother?"

"If you had not," she whispered, "then at least we'd have only my life ruined. Brent deserved to be stuck with me. Robin does not."

"Robin!" he said, his voice sharp. "Must it always, Zoë, be about Robin?"

She pushed his hand away and strode to the window. "I don't wish to discuss it."

"For once, perhaps, we should," he gritted, following.

"Kindly leave me," she said. "No, wait. This is your library. I shall go."

He caught her shoulder before she could turn. "Do you really want to know what I think, Zoë?" he rasped. "Fine. I think Robin is just another of those men you throw yourself away on because you think you don't deserve better."

"What is your point, Mercer?" she snapped. "Kindly get to it."

"My point," he said, his voice rising, "is that Robin is down at the Rose and Crown enjoying himself, whilst you are here, bored witless and picking a fight with *me*."

"*Picking* a fight?"

"Yes, and why is that, Zoë?" he snapped. "Why is he perfect, whilst I'm the enemy? I swear to God, woman, sometimes—*sometimes*—I want to shake you till your teeth rattle!"

Zoë spun about, and gave no ground. "And sometimes, Mercer, I'd like to slap the arrogance off that handsome face of yours!"

"*Me?*" he said flatly. "The fiancé you so cheerfully defend is off leering at some barmaid's arse, and you want to slap *me?*"

"I do not need—nor will I bear—your condescension." The last vestige of her self-pity had vanished, replaced by an exhilarating wish to quarrel with someone. "If you no longer wish me to be a guest in your home, then simply say so. I shall go, and gladly. I can assure you, I have no wish whatever to be here."

Abruptly, he caught both her hands, circling his fingers round her wrists. "Pax, Zoë," he said. "I did not say you were not welcome."

"Yes," she bit out, her voice climbing, "you did. And you've said it often—oh, not in so many words, perhaps, for you are far too clever for that—but you do not want me here. Admit it."

Softly, he cursed beneath his breath. "God's truth," he whispered, "but you've always been like some wild, nerved-up filly."

"Oh!" she said hotly, trying to jerk away. "Now I am a *horse*?"

"Only in that you require a husband who can manage you." He held her wrists firmly, his fingers banding about them like iron manacles. "You need a man who can manage you without trying to crush your spirit. And Robin quite obviously needs a serious wife. Nonetheless, in life we do not always get what we need. So I wish, Zoë, at the very least, that you and Robin were getting what you want. But you aren't, are you?"

At that, the rigidity left her arms, and she cut her eyes away.

"Zoë, tell me," he demanded. "Tell me the truth."

She could no longer bear to look at his piercing gaze, or at that hard, square jaw, shadowed with beard. She bit back a sob, something inside her beginning to give way.

"Are you, Zoë?" he demanded as she almost sagged against him. "Are you getting what you want? Do you want Robin?"

"I love Robin!" she cried. "I love him enough, Mercer, to do whatever I must."

"Good," he said quietly. Slowly, he released her wrists and stepped back. "I am reassured to hear it."

"But you do not wish me to marry him, do you?" Zoë found herself inexplicably trembling. "You think I am not right for him."

"You are *not* right for him," Mercer snapped. "And he is not right for you. But that, apparently, matters damned little to anyone."

"Why, how dare you?" she whispered, raising one hand dismissively.

She had not meant to strike him—at least not consciously. But Mercer apparently thought otherwise. On a whispered oath, he caught her wrist and jerked her hard against him. For a long moment, they stood toe to toe, gazes locked, nostrils flared. And then Mercer's beautiful, snarling mouth came crushing down upon hers.

For an instant, Zoë fought him, but his arm lashed about her waist, drawing her body to his. Mercer's lips slanted roughly over hers, urgent. Hungry. He didn't ask, but simply took—as if it were his lordly right.

With the strength of his body enveloping her, a torrent of emotion surged through Zoë. Anger and lust. A yearning deep within. A kiss long remembered. A sensation that unfurled, unwanted, from her belly then shot through her veins like a living thing.

Oh, God, she thought, *this cannot happen.*

But it was happening. And it felt inevitable. Towering over her, Mercer groaned against her mouth. As if it possessed a will of its own, Zoë's body molded to his. Rose to his. He had released her wrist, but she was still his captive, unable to pull way. Unable to think. His warm, heavy hand settled insistently at the small of her back, urging her against him.

"Zoë."

The word was a murmur against her flesh, but a command all the same. The brush of his lips on hers was a sensual, seductive caress, like nothing she'd ever experienced before. Mercer's straight, heavy hair fell forward like a curtain of silk as his tongue began to stroke and to coax.

Dimly, Zoë knew she should stop him. Knew this was wrong. That she belonged to another, and that Mercer had truly lost his mind. But her heart was beating a thunderous tattoo in her head, and the yearning was spiraling up and up to a dizzying height. On a soft whimper of surrender, Zoë opened beneath him.

Mercer groaned, a deep, savage sound, his tongue thrusting into her mouth, sinuous and powerful.

It was like a flash fire against her skin. Every nerve prickled with awareness. Desire surged again, stronger still. Dear heaven, this was like nothing she'd ever felt before—like nothing she'd shared with Robin. This was raw, male sensuality. Barely leashed power.

Ashamed yet unable to deny him, Zoë gave herself over to his strength. To his demands. Tentatively, she let her tongue entwine with his. He captured it, and sucked it deep, his hand sliding round the swell of her derrière, lifting her to him. Zoë answered, nestling the swollen weight of his groin against her belly.

Mercer was melting her into a puddle of incoherence. Unable to think, Zoë instead let one hand slide round his waist, then up and beneath his coat, releasing a waft of woody, masculine cologne. It settled round her like a sensuous heat, drawing her ever deeper. He thrust again, insistent and hungry, and something bumped against her calves. *The chaise.*

Later, Zoë was never certain how she ended up on her back, with Mercer's imposing weight pressing her into the softness. But in that moment of perfect madness, it felt right; a part of herself she dared not deny.

Mercer lay with one hard, heavy thigh between her own, his chest fully over hers, and what should have felt crushing and oppressive felt anything but. This was no young man's seduction. There was no teasing in Mercer's touch. Just utter masculine certainty. That she was his. That he wanted her. His mouth moved over her, his tongue languorously thrusting as one hand roamed expertly over her left breast.

In response, she rose against him and felt the firm ridge of his manhood press intimately against the joining of her thighs. On a deep groan, his thumb hooked beneath the bodice of her gown, and drew it firmly, inexorably, down, taking her chemise with it. The cool night air breezed over her breast, and Zoë knew beyond a doubt that it was bare.

"Zoë," he whispered, his mouth sliding along her jaw. *"Zoë."*

Lower and lower, down the length of her neck his lips slid, his teeth nipping lightly at her flesh. Along her collarbone, his tongue trailed a faint ribbon of heat, drawing out her need like a fine, taut thread. And then his lips closed over her nipple, causing her to cry out and arch hard against him. Her head was spinning with sensation. It was too much to bear, those long, clever fingers and insistent mouth. That rigid weight, so demanding between her legs.

Dear heaven, *this* was the sort of man they should have warned her about! Not Robin. Not even Brent. This man was dangerous. She knew it with the whole of her being. Knew she had to have him—to somehow be joined to him—or she would die of the longing.

Again he urged his hips against her, creating a wondrous sensation that went shuddering through her. She kissed him more deeply, one hand going round his neck, her fingers sliding up into the soft, thick hair at the nape of his neck. "Mercer," she whispered against his mouth. *"Please.* I want—"

He captured her mouth with his again, and she felt the cool breeze of her skirts slithering up. And then the warmth of his hand was on the inside of her thigh, sliding higher, touching her most intimately. His mouth crushed hers, possessed her, and still she couldn't get enough. Her every fiber seemed to tremble as his clever fingers found the opening of her drawers.

She should have been ashamed, but instead she yearned to melt against him. To crawl inside him. Yearned for him to touch her and set free the clamoring beast inside.

And then he did. One finger slid deep between her thighs, rubbing her lightly. *"Ahh,"* she softly cried, the words muffled against his cheek.

Her breath came in small, soft pants now. Her hips lifted against his hand. Hungrily, she let her own hand stroke lower, shaping the hard muscles of his buttock with her palm as she urged him against her.

Again and again, he eased his rigid erection against

her thigh, still stroking her. He returned his mouth to her breast, teasing lightly at her nipple with the tip of his tongue. He made a soft, choking sound, and touched her again, two fingers stroking deep, rubbing her. Beneath him, she writhed, and he shifted his weight, holding her captive with the thick muscles of his thigh even as he urged her legs wider. Suckling her breast, he probed deeper, one finger easing inside her while his thumb stroked and his breath roughening almost savagely.

She cried out again, a soft, thready sound of need. He shushed her gently, thrusting and stroking more rhythmically as she began to tremble. The room about her dimmed, and there was only him. Only Mercer, still touching her, his breath soft on her breast. His body heavy and demanding atop hers.

And then he stroked again, once—twice—and Zoë shattered. The room came apart in a kaleidoscope of splintering glass. In his arms, she shuddered and rocked, pleasure surging like a warm, gushing stream. It was bliss almost unendurable. Like nothing she'd ever experienced before.

When she came back to herself, still floating on a wave of bliss, it was to see that his head was bowed, his forehead set lightly to her breast. She waited for him to speak, or to do *something*. But what? For a girl who knew a good deal more than she should about lovemaking, Zoë felt suddenly ignorant.

"Mercer . . . ?" she whispered.

For a long moment, there was nothing but the sound of his breath drawing roughly through his chest. "Tell me, Zoë," he finally rasped, his embrace tightening fiercely, "tell me if Robin can make you feel like that."

"Oh, Mercer," she whispered. "I . . . I don't think this is about Robin anymore."

"Just tell me," he choked, lifting his head to look up at her. His eyes were soft and filled with something like sorrow. "Has he?"

"No." She shook her head. "What you make me feel is—"

Her words were cut off by the sound of a door slamming somewhere nearby. Zoë jerked at the sound, alarm shooting through her.

On a vile curse, Mercer sat up, dragging her up with him.

"Mercer—?"

"Dress yourself," he said hoarsely, turning away.

Heavy footsteps thudded nearer. A servant? *Her father?*

Panicked, Zoë sat upright, hastily yanking up her bodice and jerking down her hems. She bit her lip until she tasted blood. Then the steps passed by and continued down the corridor.

Zoë sagged with relief.

His back to her, Mercer sat on the edge of the chaise. His broad shoulders were rigid as a slab of stone beneath this coat, his elbows on his knees, his head in his hands.

"Mercer?" She set a light hand on his arm.

For an instant, he trembled beneath her touch. "Zoë," he managed, "please just make yourself presentable, and go."

"Mercer, no, we should—"

"Please just *go*," he barked. "Go to your room. Go to bed. For God's sake, just *get out*."

She drew back, confused. "I beg your pardon," she

answered, suddenly angry. "Is that it, then? You simply wished to make a point? That I am . . . what? No better than I should be?"

Abruptly, he stood. For a long moment, he stared out into the darkened forecourt, one hand set at his waist, the other at the back of his neck. She could feel him still thrumming with emotion.

"The point is," he said quietly, "that we are damned lucky Robin didn't ride home early and see us through this window."

Zoë was left reeling. Now *he* was worried about Robin? And this had meant nothing to him? He had driven her near mad with pleasure . . . simply because he could? Simply to punish her?

Well, if she had wanted to humiliate herself—not to mention her future husband—she had certainly accomplished that.

Shame washed over Zoë, settling sickly in the pit of her belly. On a sob of anguish, she fisted up her skirts in one hand, then jerked to her feet and ran from the room.

Chapter Nine

IN WHICH LADY KILDERMORE
BEGINS TO SCHEME.

"How long have we been here, my dear?" asked Mercer's mother over breakfast one morning. "Upon my word, it is shocking how one loses track of time in the country."

"Three weeks Wednesday, I believe."

And a long three weeks it had been, too. Mercer turned from the window, his mother's delicate coffee cup held in his hand. He had refused to sit down and take breakfast—he hadn't, in fact, had an appetite in days.

"We have seen so little of you this past week," Lady Kildermore remarked, deftly carving up a rasher of bacon. "Not even for dinner. Indeed, you're away from daylight until well past dark."

Mercer had no answer for that. Instead, he returned his gaze to the window, staring out at the stable wing, and alongside it, the immaculately tended parterre. He could no longer admire its perfect shape and symmetry without remembering Zoë's first day at Greythorpe. Of how he'd very nearly kissed her there in broad daylight. And his weakness had but portended worse to come. He swallowed hard, set the coffee down, and braced his hands wide upon the windowsill.

For almost a week now, shame and desire had warred in his heart. How long, he wondered, had he imagined his self-control would survive with Zoë beneath his roof? Always he'd known—on some deep, metaphysical level—that she was like a flame to him. Something elusive and beautiful, but never to be touched. Something that would set him afire, and leave him in ashes. And now it had.

"My dear?"

He turned to see his mother pensively stirring her coffee. Despite the turmoil that raged inside, Mercer kept his voice emotionless. "I told you, Mamma, when you insisted upon this trip that I would not be available to you," he said. "I haven't time for dinner parties and pleasantries."

"No, no, I quite understand," she murmured. "But Sir William is coming to dine tonight, and wishes to discuss the autumn hunt. Kindly make an effort to be here."

For a moment, he held his breath, wishing himself to the devil. But he couldn't avoid Zoë forever. "Very well," he said tightly. "Tonight, then."

"Lovely," said his mother. "Now tell me, my dear, how do you think your brother goes on?"

"Much the same, ma'am." His voice was cool, but his guard went up. "Why do you ask?"

Jonet set down her spoon with a little *click*. "Oh, no reason."

And that, thought Mercer, *was a bald-faced lie.*

His mother didn't so much as crook an eyebrow without a reason. On this particular summer morn, they were alone together—Mercer, his mother, and Charles Donaldson, who was quietly sorting the post—in her private sitting room where the countess preferred to take her breakfast. Mercer's stepfather was out for his customary morning ride, the hour being not yet seven, and the rest of the household was just beginning to stir.

Jonet was a sociable creature by nature, but Mercer knew that this time was reserved for conducting the business of the day, and for private meetings with her children. Today it was Mercer's turn to be summoned to the inner sanctum, for age and prosperity, he'd learned, did not exempt a man from the occasional dressing-down or, more likely still, an interrogation. Moreover, his mother had a terrible tendency to know things she oughtn't.

Oh, he would not quarrel with her—even his mother dared not press him. But there were questions he would not answer, not even to himself. Nor could he even look his brother in the eye, not that Robin any longer noticed or cared. As to Zoë, on those rare occasions when their paths had crossed, she simply averted her gaze, and left the room as soon as he entered it.

Indeed, for nearly a week, Mercer had successfully avoided everyone. It had not been difficult. Matters in the surrounding villages grew daily more dire, and soon there would be the harvest to get in.

"Sit, sit, the both of you." Jonet motioned impatiently to the empty chairs.

And so they sat, the three of them—the countess, the marquess, and the butler—making an odd trio. And yet not so odd, all the same.

Jonet was liberally buttering a piece of toast. She seemed able to eat anything, and had borne six children without gaining a pound, so far as Mercer could see.

"What news, my dear, of the Vicomtesse de Chéraute?"

she asked innocently, dipping a knife into her jam pot. "Anything?"

"Just her letters," said Mercer. "The usual thing. She seems to go on well enough."

Jonet looked at Donaldson. "Charlie?" she asked. "Your runner still watches her?"

"Aye, follows her from pillar tae post, an' back again," he said in his low voice. "And there's been anither package from your chap Kemble."

"Oh, God." Mercer exhaled slowly. "What this time?"

Donaldson cut him a pitying look. "An emerald and diamond parure," said the butler. "And no' mere baubles."

"And what is that to cost me, I wonder?" Mercer muttered.

"Whate'er your Mr. Kemble says," warned Donaldson. "We're a wee bit at his mercy, us being here, and her runnin' loose aboot London."

"I thank you, Charlie," he said. "I really do. But it's a sad sight what a man must pay for his sins."

Donaldson's long face looked mournful. "Think of it, lad, as an investment. In your future."

"In your *freedom*," Mercer's mother corrected. She stabbed her knife in his direction. "And think of it, too, my boy, when you are tempted to give your brother one of your notorious tongue lashings. It remains to be seen, quite honestly, which of you has made the bigger soss of it."

Donaldson almost snorted with laughter, then quickly covered it with a cough.

Oh, you don't know the half of it, thought Mercer. But he said, a little grimly, "Thank you both for your wise counsel."

"You are welcome." Jonet nibbled away the rest of the toast, then dusted off her fingers. "Charlie, pass Stuart that old newspaper I've laid out on the sofa."

"Newspaper?" said Mercer.

"Yes, it came over on the Calais packet yesterday," she went on, "but I just got round to reading it. Take it to your study, my boy, and turn to page twelve. If you've kept up your French, you will find there, I venture, something of grave interest."

Donaldson passed him the folded paper.

"What news from France would interest me?" asked Mercer, looking at it.

His mother flashed a wintry smile. "I fear there's been an accident in the Comte de Chéraute's family," she said. "His uncle and two cousins. Lost at sea off the coast of Algiers, and thought likely dead."

Mercer gave a low whistle and stared down at the paper. "Good Lord! The old *duc*?"

"Indeed," said his mother. "I'd laugh if it weren't such a tragedy. But then, Claire mightn't think it quite so disastrous, *hmm*?"

Mercer's gaze flicked up to catch his mother's. He knew precisely where she was going with this. "If *le comte* discovers she carries my child, it shan't matter what she thinks. He will ask the French courts to set aside the child, and he will disavow her."

His mother lifted one delicate shoulder beneath the ivory silk of her dressing gown. "And if she is not with child?"

Mercer drew in a deep, pensive breath. "I cannot say," he answered. "Chéraute isn't happy with his wife just now."

Again, the countess smiled. "Ah, but your Claire is very clever, my dear boy," she murmured. "Now, you are going back to Fromley today, I collect? And your father is to accompany you?"

Mercer's face fell. "Yes, the rector has died," he murmured, laying aside the paper. "Papa is going to call upon the curate, to see what needs the congregation may have."

"*Tch, tch!*" said his mother. "In our modern world, with every imaginable convenience, that a man should go unvaccinated! What can he have been thinking?"

"Well, he isn't thinking at all now," said Mercer sadly, pushing back his chair. "Charlie, you will put Mr. Kemble's package in the safe, won't you? And Mamma"— Here, he bent to kiss her—"have a splendid day."

"All my days are splendid," she said serenely. "But please, wait."

Donaldson, too, had risen. Jonet turned to him. "Charlie," she said sweetly. "Miss Armstrong is next on my list."

With a dreadful, sinking sensation, Mercer paced back to the window and stared blindly out. "I need to go, Mamma," he said when the door thumped shut. "Father will soon be ready."

"Nonsense," she said sweetly. "There would have been hoofbeats ere now. My hearing, you know, is shockingly acute."

He turned, and cocked one hip upon the sill. "Very well, then," he murmured. "What is it you wished to say to me that cannot be said in front of Charlie?"

A bland expression came over his mother's face. "Why, nothing at all, my love," she said. "I merely wished to hear how the tenant farmers go on. Mrs. Fitch—is she still quite ill?"

"Quite as ill as she was when last we discussed it," said Mercer, "which was yesterday afternoon, I believe?"

"Was it indeed?" His mother began to neaten the pleats of her silk dressing gown.

"Mamma, you know she has been poorly for years," Mercer went on. "I very much fear she will not throw off the smallpox."

"Yes, and those four children! Whatever shall become of them?"

"Like so many I've already seen, it will be a tragedy," he quietly acknowledged. "But this one will strike close to home."

His mother's affection for the Fitch family notwithstanding, they were a further five minutes into the conversation when Mercer acknowledged defeat. His mother was stalling him—but to what end? She asked little she did not already know; plans for the harvest, how the roof repairs were going. All the most mundane of topics. Then abruptly, she stood.

"Well, run along now, my dear," she said, rising to ring the bellpull. "I know you have much to do."

Mercer bowed, and took his leave.

Zoë was in the schoolroom bouncing her brother Callum on her knee, and taking breakfast with Valerie, Arabella, and the rest of the Amherst girls, when Mr. Donaldson found her there.

"To Lady Kildermore?" she repeated.

Donaldson bowed. "Aye, miss. When you've had your breakfast, o' course."

"Thank you, I'm quite finished." Laying aside her napkin, Zoë rose at once, Callum balanced on her hip. "I shall see myself down."

"Oh, Zoë, no!" said Davinia in her wheedling voice. "You said you would walk with Val and me to the village!"

Zoë kissed Callum, and handed him to his nurse, then set a hand atop the girl's head. "And so I shall, Dav," she promised, trying to hide her sudden unease. "But this afternoon, all right? You know one cannot gainsay your mother."

Davinia's lip came out, but she said no more. All of them, at one time or another, had been called to Jonet's breakfast table. Now Zoë was summoned.

Her heart beating rather too rapidly, she hastened down one floor to her bedchamber so that she might tidy her hair and check her nose for smuts. Before breakfast, she'd been playing horse with Callum, romping about in the nursery floor while he clung to her back, egged on by Freya Amherst, who'd thought it all a great joke.

Callum's happy cries always cheered Zoë. Indeed, she had been spending larger and larger parts of her day in the children's wing of late, for it seemed the only place her heart could find a measure of peace. With the children, she could be herself. They neither pitied her, nor avoided her. They simply loved her—little Callum especially.

At least someone did. Robin had begun to spend his afternoons in the village tavern, coming home only for dinner—and often foxed, though Zoë harbored some hope no one noticed it save her. As if to compensate for his absence, his parents had become overly effusive.

With her own family, Zoë fared little better. Evie had begun to cluck and coo and smooth Zoë's hair as she'd not done since Zoë was ten, while her father was looking more hollow-eyed with each passing day, and the little telltale muscle in his left cheek was starting to twitch every time he saw Robin. A bad sign, that—and one which Robin would do well to heed.

As to Mercer, the man simply made her tremble with outrage every time she laid eyes upon him, which was rarely. On a huff of frustration, Zoë leaned over her dressing table and stared at her image in the mirror. What was it about her that made men think she could be had for the taking? Oh, she knew that in the past, she'd been too flirtatious, and even a little wild. But not with Mercer. In all the years she'd known him, Zoë had never so much as winked at the man. Tormented him, yes. Been ever aware of him, yes; for Mercer was the sort of man who, upon entering a room, possessed it—and the attention of every female in it, too.

Perhaps that was it, she thought, straightening up. Perhaps Mercer was just jealous of his brother? Absently, she plucked a pair of pearl earbobs from the porcelain dish on the table, and considered it.

No, she thought, that made no sense. There was nothing to be jealous of, save perhaps for Robin's charm. But men, in her experience, did not envy charm, or even beauty. Wealth, strength, power—those things men might kill for—and all of them Mercer already possessed in abundance. And as to beauty, that, too, he had in spades, though it was not the classic beauty that Robin possessed. It was a rugged, almost savage beauty, and one saw it in his eyes. Felt it in the lithe strength of his body and in the power of his touch.

Unable to hold her own gaze in the glass, Zoë looked down at the dish. She felt heat and color spring to her cheeks. For the truth was, while she'd never winked at Mercer, she had rarely ever stopped thinking about him. And then there had been that *one* little instance, all those years ago . . .

Her hands shaking a little, Zoë jerked the first earbob from her ear and hurled it back into the dish. Oh, why must life be so confusing? Things had seemed so much simpler in London. There, she'd understood, for good or ill, precisely who she was and what people thought of her.

Here at Greythorpe, she scarcely knew herself any longer. She was supposed to be Robin's affianced bride. Instead, she'd behaved indecently with his brother— allowed him to do things to her that even now could make her blush with shame and confusion. Things that left her lying awake and feverish in her bed night after night. Things she'd never done—or even contemplated doing—with Robin. And she remembered every delicious one of them, too.

But the guilt she felt was crushing, and with every passing day, she dreaded more and more her coming marriage. More and more she felt the wrongness of it, and the dread had become like a sickening fear in the pit of her stomach. Yet she could see no way out of it.

And now she had been summoned to Jonet's chambers . . .

* * *

Mercer opened his mother's door just as a footman came in to clear away the breakfast tray. Nodding good morning, he turned and set a brisk pace toward his study. He felt as if he were fleeing an interrogation, yet his mother had asked him almost nothing. He could not have guessed matters were about to grow worse.

He had but turned the first corner into the narrower passageway that connected Jonet's wing to the main house when he saw her. Zoë swished round the last turn of the east staircase wearing a morning gown of deepest burgundy, her mass of dark curls drawn up into a soft, casual arrangement that fell down her neck and brushed lightly at her cheeks.

He jerked to a halt, his stomach bottoming out like some green lad's. But her mind, obviously, was elsewhere.

"Zoë," he said softly.

Her head jerked up just before she bumped into him.

"Zoë," he said again, the word coming roughly. "We should talk about—"

"No." Her voice was clipped. "We shouldn't."

She dodged left, then right as if to pass him, but he caught her by the shoulders and held firm.

"Don't—!" she barked, raising her shoulders as if to throw him off. "Just . . . don't touch me. I cannot think straight, Mercer, when your hands are on me."

But he followed her back a pace, still gripping her. "Zoë, just look at me," he demanded.

"Why?" she snapped.

Why?

It was a bloody good question. "Because," he rasped. "I need to know . . . I just need to know you are all right."

"As opposed to what?" she said caustically. "Prostrate with grief? Angry at having been used, then thrust aside? As if it were *my* fault?"

He hung his head and exhaled slowly. "Zoë, you are . . . you are my brother's fiancée."

"And you think I've forgotten that?" she whispered. "You think I am not ashamed of myself? No matter how he has hurt me, Robin does not deserve what I let you do."

"*Has* he hurt you?" Mercer's head jerked up. "Zoë, *look* at me!"

At that, she turned her incisive gaze to his, and pinned him with it. "You keep barking that at me as if I am yours to command. I grow exceedingly weary of it."

"You are not mine," he said. And never had he felt the truth of his own words more acutely.

"No, I'm not, and much joy does it give the both of us, I daresay," she muttered. "But sometimes, Mercer, it feels as if you have been bossing me around the whole of my life."

Against his will, his grip on her tightened. "And sometimes it seems that you have been vexing me the whole of mine," he returned.

"And that is my fault?" she softly cried. "What have *I* ever done to you?"

You have maddened me, he wanted to say.

But her eyes were blazing with fire, and suddenly, he yearned to crush her mouth beneath his again. To force his tongue into her mouth. To take what he so desperately wanted—slake the lust he'd bottled up and hidden from himself for years on end—and damn the consequences.

He had the power to do it, too. He was a man who generally got what he wanted, one way or another. But this was Zoë, and she was as wild and as dangerous as ever. Moreover, he had no excuse this time; not concern, not anger, not even so much as the bottle of wine he'd had at dinner that awful night—as if there was any justification for what he'd done. Zoë just *was*. And yes, she maddened him. As always.

He let his hungry gaze drift over her. As a child, Zoë's hair had been lighter, but now was nearly black. And her eyes—he had never been perfectly sure what color they were. Like her mood, Zoë's eyes were as changeable as the earth itself, and could seemingly alter with the breeze. But she was beautiful—just achingly beautiful.

"God's truth, but you are a torment," he whispered. "And I think perhaps you don't even know it."

"Oh, what nonsense!" she said, trying to elbow past him. "Just get out of my way."

He held her firm. "Zoë," he said hoarsely, "I wanted to tell you . . . that I shall be at dinner tonight."

She widened her eyes, and went still. "So?" she said. "Come to dinner. It is your house. For pity's sake, Mercer, do not mistake me for some faint-hearted female who'll swoon in your lordly presence. I am angry, yes. At the both of us. But you have not broken me. I am not bowed by you. I accept responsibility for my sins, and I suggest you do the same. Save the words *vex* and *torment* for your pretty vicomtesse. You may have better need of them."

The thought of Claire jerked Mercer back to reality. The dark shadow of the damage she might yet do Zoë— and possibly his child—still hung over him. Indeed, until he had the whip hand on his mistress—until he had the truth—there was nothing he could offer Zoë.

But who was he deluding? He had nothing Zoë wanted. And she was spoken for now. It was too late.

Mercer dropped his hands and let her go. "I beg your pardon," he said stiffly. "I have clearly overestimated the distress I may have caused you."

"Clearly," she said, lifting her nose, "you have."

Then, with one last parting glance over her shoulder, Zoë picked up her skirts and swished round him, as if he were a pile of steaming manure in the street. And she looked as flushed with color and fury as he felt drained and empty.

Less than ten minutes after her summons, Zoë found herself entering Jonet's sitting room, shaken and yet seething with an indignation which somehow stiffened her resolve. The breakfast service was being swept away by one of the footmen, and in moments, only a silver tray holding a coffee service remained.

Zoë forced herself to be calm, and looked about. She had handled Mercer well enough; now she must manage his mother. The countess's sitting room was a large chamber with a high ceiling of white Etruscan medallions on a blue background, and walls which were hung with shimmering ice-blue silk. The room held a sitting area, a desk, and the large mahogany table at which the countess now sat.

"Zoë, my dear!" said Jonet brightly. "Do sit, child. Will you have coffee?"

"Yes, thank you, ma'am," she said, curtseying. Though

Jonet had long been a part of her life, Zoë was mindful that the woman was now to be her mother-in-law.

They made small talk about the sultry weather as Jonet poured and offered the coffee. "Well, I shall come straight to the point, my dear," she said, after refilling her own cup. "My son—my elder son—informed me some days past that you were asking questions."

"Questions, ma'am?"

Jonet put her cup down, her gaze drifting over Zoë's face. "You look like your mother, my dear," she said musingly, "though you have the Scots in you, too. It is the eyes, I think. And the willfulness."

Zoë let her gaze drop to her clasped hands. "I do not mean to be willful," she said.

"Oh, child, 'tis a compliment!" said Jonet lightly. "In life, sometimes only the willful survive. And in times past, sometimes only strong families survived. That's why we care about our clan, Zoë, is it not? And everyone in it?"

"You have always cared about me," said Zoë honestly.

"That I have, child," said Jonet musingly. "Though I did not think on it nearly so much until my father died."

"And then you became Countess of Kildermore," said Zoë, her voice solemn. "You became the head of the family."

Slowly Jonet shook her head. "Perhaps, but it was something else, too," she answered.

Across the table, Zoë watched her. She had the oddest sense that Jonet wished to say something—and wished to say it with more than just words. "I see," she murmured. "Am I to know what it was?"

Jonet was fiddling pensively with the handle of her

coffee cup. "Aye, I should like to tell you," she finally said, "for soon you'll be not just my cousin, but my daughter. You see, when my father died, he told me something important—a sort of secret—one which made me think, in broader terms, about our family and my duty to it."

"What sort of secret?" asked Zoë, holding Jonet's gaze.

"Ah, child, if I told you that, it would no longer be a secret."

"No, I daresay not," Zoë agreed.

"But tell you I shall," Jonet continued, leaning nearer, "if I have your promise."

"Yes, of course," said Zoë. "What sort of promise?"

Jonet reached across the table to cover Zoë's hand with her own, warmer one. "Promise me that you are going to marry my son," she answered. "Promise me, Zoë, on your Armstrong blood."

Zoë held her gaze unblinkingly for a time. *Was* she going to marry Robin? After what she had done in the library? Her face flushed with heat. But the truth was, she had little choice.

"Our marriage is decided, is it not?" she finally said.

"Is it?" asked Jonet pointedly.

"Indeed." Zoë swallowed hard. "I—I promise."

Jonet gave a muted smile. "Good, then," she answered. "For the secret is about my father, the old earl of Kildermore, who was a wicked old rip. And it is something we do not speak of outside this family, do you understand me?"

"Yes, ma'am." Zoë felt her eyes widen. "Quite."

Jonet relaxed into her chair. "My mother, you know, was an Armstrong," she began, much in the tone of an ancient storyteller. "She was descended from the third Marquess of Rannoch, and was your great aunt."

"Yes, Papa told me."

Jonet smiled almost dotingly. "In the last century, the Armstrongs wished a union with the Camerons, and Mother was sent to be Kildermore's bride. The marriage was a misery, and I the only child. The only *legitimate* child."

"There were others?" asked Zoë, not surprised.

"Two, so far as I know," she said. "Before I was even born, our laundry maid bore a son—forced on her, or so it was whispered. The boy was my playmate as a child, and strange as it sounds, we were very close. We still are, for he is now my butler."

Her butler?

"Mr. Donaldson?" Zoë managed.

Jonet's smile turned inward. "Yes, Charlie," she said. "When my husband Henry was killed, I sent for him at Kildermore. Because I was frightened. And because I knew I could trust him implicitly. If it sometimes seems he wields a little more power than any servant might— well, that is why. And that will never change. You need to know this, because you, too, will be a part of our household."

Zoë swallowed hard. "Who else knows?"

Lightly, Jonet shrugged. "It is a poorly kept secret," she said. "I think a great many of the servants know, because most came down from Kildermore with Charlie. But my father's second son, now that one is a very grave secret indeed. One I did not know until my father lay dying, for he'd done a terrible thing—a thing he hid."

"And did he confess?" Zoë whispered. "Because of guilt?"

Slowly she nodded. "Because of guilt, yes," she said. "And perhaps because he no longer trusted Henry to take care of me. My first marriage, you may have heard, was not a happy one. For a time, there was even some scandal attached to my name."

"I never heard of any," Zoë whispered.

Jonet's eyes danced with laughter. "Then you must be deaf, child," she answered. "Or a very good liar. Indeed, a great many people speculate, as I am well aware, that Robin is not Henry's child."

Zoë felt her blush deepen. "It has never mattered to me," she said, dropping her gaze to her lap. "I love Robin all the same."

"I know, Zoë, that you do," said his mother solemnly. "And I thank you for that. But Robin *is* Henry's son, not Lord Delacourt's. The latter would be impossible, you see. Delacourt is also my brother."

Zoë felt her eyes widen further, if such a thing were possible. She could utter not one word. She knew the wealthy, dashing Lord Delacourt—everyone did. And, as Jonet said, it was widely believed he had once been Jonet's lover. Indeed, upon the previous Lord Mercer's death, there had been a terrible scandal, and some very ugly speculation, too.

"So Robin is not . . . ?" she murmured.

Jonet shook her head. "Robin is his nephew," she said. "That is why, you see, they resemble one another so strongly. They are very like my father, both in coloring and temperament—ah, yes, so very handsome and charming. That is why, you understand, it must never,

ever be spoken of outside this family. Not even to your parents, my dear. It would blight the name of Delacourt's late mother, who was a fine and good lady, and who suffered terribly at my father's hands."

"So Delacourt—he is not . . ." Zoë uttered. ". . . not his father's—"

"His father's child? Not technically." Jonet smiled reassuringly. "The previous Lord Delacourt knew this. He married his wife whilst she carried my father's child, and he had his own reasons for doing so. But that is neither here nor there. What matters is that we take care of our own, Zoë, no matter how they came to be amongst us. Do you understand?"

"Yes." She swallowed hard. "So that is why you came to me. When I was small."

"It was," she said softly, "for blood is always—*always*—thicker than water, Zoë. If you take nothing else from this room today, take that, for it is what we swear by in this family. Our family had a duty to you. And when you were old enough, I gave you our protection to every extent I could."

At that, Zoë dropped her head and felt the sting of shame yet again. "Yet I have repaid your kindness very poorly, I fear," she said into the floor. "I have caused Robin to be stuck in this betrothal, and . . . and I fear he is not happy."

Jonet tossed her hand, the jewels on her fingers winking in the morning sun. "Oh, I would not greatly trouble myself over Robin," she said evenly. "Such matters have a way of working themselves out, I have found. Besides, Robin never takes anything too seriously for very long.

Now Stuart—ah, he is another matter altogether. There is not an ounce of frivolity in him."

Zoë couldn't argue with that. "No, I daresay not," she murmured.

"Alas, Stuart takes everything to heart." Jonet lifted the pot and began to refresh their coffee. "The burden of duty was thrust upon him almost from the cradle. Indeed, when his father was killed, he became the Marquess of Mercer at just nine years of age. It has weighed him down in a way few can understand. It has made him grave. And careful—too careful, I sometimes think—especially in matters of the heart."

Warmth flooded Zoë's face again. "Was he not in love with the Vicomtesse de Chéraute?" she whispered. "Everyone said it was a great romance."

Jonet laughed richly. "Oh, it was a great infatuation, perhaps," she conceded, putting the pot down. "For a month or two, at least. But we all of us have a way of showing our colors—and pretty quickly, too. My son is a deeply passionate man, but never has he been a fool. He knows lust for what it is."

Jonet's plain speech was a little shocking. "Still," Zoë murmured, "I am sorry they have quarreled."

"Are you?" Jonet asked a little sharply.

"Well, yes," she answered. "For he told me . . . he told me she claims to carry his child."

"Did he?" Jonet lightly lifted one eyebrow. "And how do you feel about that?"

"I—why, I think it hardly matters how I feel."

"Indulge me," said Jonet firmly.

Zoë opened her mouth, then shut it again. "Well, I am

sorry for the child," she finally answered. "Who would know better than I? Lord Mercer must take the babe and raise it himself. Indeed, that is what he says he means to do, and I believe he would be right."

Jonet relaxed into her chair with a satisfied smile. "In any case, it is but a charade, I daresay," she remarked, lifting her hand regally. "All will be revealed soon enough."

For a long moment, Zoë looked down at her lap. Her fingers were entwined, and nearly bloodless. "Has Lord Mercer . . . that is to say, has he truly broken with her? Permanently?"

Jonet's smile merely deepened. "Ah, *that*," she purred, "is a question you should best ask my son." She pushed back her chair and stood, signaling that the interview was over. "Well," she said brightly, "now that dreadful topic is finished, I have some good news."

"Yes?" Zoë's eyes widened as she came to her feet. "What is it?"

"We are to have guests for dinner," she explained as they strolled toward the door. "Sir William is coming to dine again. And the Wares. Then tomorrow, well, let us just say he and I have contrived a way to get Robin out of bed perhaps a little earlier."

"I can't think what," said Zoë a little ruefully.

"Sir William shot a fox last night preying on his hens," she said. "He has decided to lay a dragline, and take his pups out in preparation for the season."

A drag hunt, Zoë knew, was sometimes used to test a new foxhound's ability to scent. The dead fox would be used to lay down a trail.

"I thought we might go along, for there won't be a

great many gates," Jonet went on, drawing open the door. "I know you sit a horse as prettily as anyone."

"I am fond of riding, indeed," Zoë admitted. But she had always longed to go with the men; to go sailing over fences and gates with impunity. A sidesaddle, however, would not permit such antics, and though she was not above it, even Zoë dared not don breeches in such a social setting.

Jonet waved her hand toward the stables. "Stuart keeps several fine hunters," she said. "Ask him to help you choose one."

Zoë felt herself blush. "Thank you, ma'am," she said quietly. "But I have no preference in horses."

Jonet's eyes lit with wry humor. "Do you not?" she murmured. "Well, then. Shall I see you at dinner?

It was half past two by the time the three young ladies set off on their stroll to the village, accompanied by Miss Adler. Zoë started off in haste, seething with nervous energy. A narrow but pretty footpath wound them through the wood and over a log bridge; a shortcut, Davinia assured her, to the heart of Lower Thorpe.

Both girls were full of idle chatter, and somehow Zoë slowed her pace, and forced herself into the spirit of things. Walking arm in arm with Davinia where the path permitted it, they laughingly exchanged what gossip Miss Adler would allow. Robin's sister, Zoë discovered, fancied herself in love with the eldest of the vicar's sons, Edward Ware, who was nonetheless about ten years too old for her. This, however, did not prevent the girls from swooning at every mention of his name.

As they approached the village green, they passed the

post office, and beside it, the infamous Rose and Crown. Zoë could not help but look over her shoulder at the tavern as they went by. The place looked a little shabby, and she could not but wonder what attraction it held for Robin that he should wish to spend the better part of his days—and his nights—there.

But she had come to be a good companion to the two younger ladies whilst Miss Adler performed her errands, so she looked away and tried not to think of it. At the mercantile, they went in to purchase shoelaces, but came out with Davinia's pockets full of peppermints. They visited the hatmaker, where they bought a new hat ribbon for Valerie, and the linen draper's, where Miss Adler picked up a packet of lace for Jonet.

Soon they turned round and set off in the direction of home again. At the post office, however, Miss Adler went in to mail a letter. In the yard of the Rose and Crown adjacent, a young ostler stood holding a large bay horse that looked familiar. Almost at once, the taproom door flew open, and a familiar, barrel-shaped gentleman trundled out, his stubbled gray hair unmistakable.

"Sir William!" Davinia rushed into the yard with unseemly haste, Valerie in tow.

Left with no alternative, Zoë followed.

The squire had already swung into the saddle. "Good afternoon, Lady Davinia, Lady Valerie." He looked down, then his expression seemed to stiffen ever so slightly. "Ah, and Miss Armstrong! How do you do?"

"Quite well, sir," said Zoë, bobbing. "I hope Lady Shankling is w—"

"Sir William, is it true?" Davinia burst out. "Are you to have a hunt tomorrow? Might I ride out to watch?"

The squire laughed. "Oh, we shall have something like a hunt, minx," he said charitably. "As to your going, you must ask your mamma about that."

Davinia's face fell. Zoë smiled up at him. "I understand we shall have the pleasure of your company at dinner?"

"You shall indeed," said Sir William, his beefy hands reining his horse toward the high street. "Now hurry along home, my dears. I feel a rain coming in off the Channel."

Zoë looked up at the cloudless blue sky.

"We must wait for Miss Adler," said Davinia.

Something strange passed over the squire's face. "Ah, well. Then I give you all good afternoon." With that, the squire touched his crop to his hat brim, and spurred his horse away.

Davinia turned round, and kicked a stone from the tavern's yard. "Mamma shall never let me go," she said on an aggrieved sigh. "And I have a new habit, too."

"Come along, Dav," Zoë whispered. "Miss Adler might scold us for standing in a tavern yard."

Just then, the taproom door creaked again, and swung open to a peal of feminine laughter. To Zoë's shock, Robin came backing out with what could only be described as a leer plastered on his face, and his cravat half unwound.

"Now let that be a lesson, ye cheeky bugger!" A round, buxom blonde followed, seizing hold of his neck-cloth and jerking as if to drag him back inside.

"Aww, Jemmie, love, you're breaking my heart!" Robin shouted good-naturedly. "You weren't near so shy last night!"

At that, the girl pealed with laughter again, drew his head to hers with the cravat, then smacked a kiss soundly upon his lips.

"Ooh, that's Jemima," said Davinia in a scandalized whisper. "Cook says she's got round heels."

"Round heels?" Valerie blinked innocently. "Doesn't everyone?"

Davinia shrugged. "Cook wrinkled her nose when she said it."

Jemima was still whispering in Robin's ear. Zoë watched, arms crossed, as he laughed again, then turned away from them as if heading toward the rear stables. Just then, the young ostler returned leading a second mount.

Suddenly, Zoë had had enough. "Good afternoon," she said rather loudly. "Fancy meeting you here."

Robin staggered round, goggling at the three of them. "That you, P.K.?" he said, his brow furrowing. His tall, black knee boots were dusty, his coat rumpled as if he'd slept in it.

"Hullo, Robin." She sashayed boldly across the yard. "On your way home, are you?"

He looked at her, blinking a little rapidly. "Aye, to have a bath before dinner."

Zoë leaned into him and sniffed. "I would advise it, yes," she said in a low undertone. "Smells as if Jemmie favors eau de bar towel to me."

"Hullo, Robin." Davinia sidled up to him. "I've got peppermints. Would you like one?"

"Peppermints?" Robin took the reins from the ostler, and pressed a coin into his hand. "Oh. Indeed."

Just then, footsteps crunched in the gravel behind them. "Good afternoon, Lord Robert," said Miss Adler stiffly. "Girls, come along, if you please! This is not the sort of place ladies linger."

Zoë turned round. "Lord Robert has offered to take me up before him," she announced. "We shall take the carriage road, and see you at the house."

"At the house?" Miss Adler blanched. "Well. I am not perfectly—"

"We are betrothed," Zoë lightly interjected. "I am sure it's quite all right."

Miss Adler inclined her head, her mouth tight with disapproval. "As you wish, Miss Armstrong."

With a chary glance over his shoulder, Robin led the horse to a mounting block. "Your petticoats are going to show," he warned, offering his hand.

Zoë hopped effortlessly up. "Frankly, Robin," she said in a dark undertone, "I should rather ride naked through the village than suffer the humiliation of a tavern maid kissing my betrothed in front of half the population— and I rather imagine that isn't the half of what's been seen inside."

Eyes narrowing, Robin hurled himself up and squeezed in behind. "Oh, well done, Zoë," he said quietly. "One would almost imagine you're jealous."

With that, he tapped the horse's flanks and sent it bolting from the inn yard. Within minutes they had turned into Greythorpe's carriage drive and were passing beneath the elaborate gates with the rearing black lion.

"Set me down," Zoë demanded as soon as they were beyond sight of the road.

On a sigh, Robin drew up on the grassy verge. Zoë leapt to the ground, landing neatly.

"I would have helped you," he complained, looking down at her. "Zoë, I'm not an ass."

"That remains to be seen," she answered, trembling with rage.

Robin rolled his eyes. "I have to come down for a trimming, don't I?"

Zoë stabbed her finger at the ground. "This *minute.*"

Robin threw his booted leg over the saddle, dismounted, then draped his reins over a tree branch.

"How *dare* you!" she began the instant he turned round. "How *dare* you kiss that—that *whore* in front of everyone?"

"It wasn't everyone," Robin countered.

"No," she retorted, pacing along the verge. "No, it was your fourteen-year-old sister!" She thrust her arms into the air with each syllable. "And Valerie! And Sir William!"

At that, Robin blanched. "He *told* you?"

"No, he told me a rain was coming in off the Channel," Zoë shouted, setting her hands on her hips. "Because he felt sorry for me. And I tell you, Robin, *I will not have it.* You can ignore me, and you can avoid me, but if you dare to make people feel sorry for me, I swear to God you'll regret it the rest of your days."

Robert lifted his chin, a flash of sudden anger in his eye. "I don't know what's more disturbing, Zoë," he returned. "The fact that you, of all people, are throwing barbs at me over a flirtation. Or the fact that you don't really care if I *am* bedding that girl."

Zoë's eyes flared wide. "I beg your pardon?"

"Oh, just admit it, Zoë. You don't give a tinker's damn

if I slept with a score of barmaids," he said accusingly. "You care only that other people know. Can't you see, Zoë, what that says?"

"It says that I still have a measure of pride left to me!" she spat. "It says that I am tired of everyone looking at me with pity in their eyes!"

"Oh, well then, let's talk about your flirting with the Ware boys!" He stabbed a finger in her direction. "Let's talk about Jim Shankling, and how you let him stare halfway down your cleavage at dinner last Wednesday."

"Why, how dare you!"

"Oh, no, wait!" Robin sneered. "I have it now! Let's talk about you and my brother!"

At that, Zoë faltered back a step. Her breath seized.

"No?" Robin lifted both brows enquiringly. "Cat got your tongue, Zoë?"

But Zoë could only stand there, trembling. In her rage at the tavern yard, she had forgotten. Forgotten that she was the greatest sinner of them all. That Robin might have swived half a dozen tavern wenches and it would not equal the sin of what she had permitted. She had betrayed him with his own brother.

And he knew.

"Aye, miss, you've not got so much to say now." Eyes narrow, Robin threw his arms over his chest. "Do you think I stay so drunk I can't see how he watches you? How his eyes follow you from one room to the next?"

"I . . . I don't know," she managed. "D-Do they?"

"They always have." He jerked his chin derisively. "Oh, aye, Zoë, I know he lusts after you, but he's so poker-arsed, he can't even admit it. Worse, he has Claire to deal with, and all his money and all his power can't shut that bitch up if she decides to drag your name through the mud."

"Robin," Zoë uttered. "Robin, what are you saying?"

"I'm saying that mayhap the old boy would have half a mind to marry you himself if it wasn't too late," he spat. "But if he dares do it now, Claire will haul that bairn off to France, and make sure all Mayfair hears he's marrying his brother's leavings."

"*Leavings?*" she shrieked. "Why, you—you *ass!*"

Something inside her exploded then. She flew at him with her fists, pummeling him; his chest, his shoulders. Half mad, she flailed at Robin until her hair came down and his hat tumbled into the grass. Somehow, he caught her fists in his, and drew them tight to his chest.

"Whoa, whoa up here, Powder Keg!"

"Damn you, don't call me that," she shrieked, still jerking. "I'm sick to death of it! Do you hear me?" To her shame, tears sprang to her eyes.

"Zoë, Zoë," he soothed, drawing her to him. "Dash it, just *stop!*"

She fell against him on a wrenching sob. Misery surged, stripping away the strength and the anger which mere moments ago had sustained her.

Dear God, how had she managed to lower herself so thoroughly? She had lain with her betrothed's brother. Now she had *hit* him. And she was so heartsick she wished the earth would crack and swallow her whole.

Gently, Robin set her away, studying her warily. His face had actually gone pale. "Zoë, what the devil has happened?" he whispered, his voice mystified. "This . . . this isn't *us*. This isn't what we are to one another."

"Robin, I—I am not—" She drew in a ragged breath, and stepped back a pace. "I am *not* your leavings."

He shook his head. "I didn't say you were," he answered. "I'm just saying that's what Claire will make it out to be. That's how it will look when she's finished. Stu knows it. So do I. So we go on, all of us, just as we are. Whether any of us likes it or not."

"Robin." She stepped forward, clutching her hands. "Oh, Robin. Are we going to survive? *Are* we?"

He would not hold her gaze, but instead shoved a hand through his already disordered locks. "I don't know," he finally rasped. "How does one define *survive*?"

"I—I cannot say," she whispered. "I don't know. I—I don't understand anything anymore, least of all, you."

He walked away then, and snatched his reins from the tree branch. "We have to go," he said, his voice devoid of emotion. "They will be expecting us at the house."

Zoë backed away, shaking her head. "No, I—I cannot," she said. "Not yet. You go. I shall walk."

He stared at her for a long moment. "Zoë, it's three miles."

"I—I don't care." Her entire body seemed to be shaking inside. "Go. Just . . . leave me."

His face tightened with some inscrutable emotion. Anger? Frustration? She hardly knew—and she hardly cared. In that moment, she wanted only to escape him. To flee from his all-seeing eyes, and the truths he told.

With one last dark glance, Robin shoved his boot into his stirrup, threw himself into the saddle, and tapped his horse's flanks. Zoë watched him go, the horse's hooves tossing up bits of dirt and grass, until at last they vanished around the next turn. An almost overwhelming fatigue shuddered through her then.

What had she let her life come to? Zoë had believed life was hard in London, had believed herself the most injured and put-upon of God's creatures. She had spent, she suddenly realized, the whole of her life angry at fate, never thinking of all the good in her life. Indeed, she had been wicked and —as Trudy sometimes said—spoiled.

So what if she was a bastard? At least she was a rich man's much-loved bastard. There were far worse fates in life. And suddenly—there, in the middle of a road that quite honestly led to nowhere—Zoë realized that she had been wrong. That perhaps she should have listened to her father, and humbled herself to marry Sir Edgar Haverfield. What was the disdain of one's mother-in-law to this? The ruin of a good friendship. The unalloyed misery of someone you loved. And the awful ache for a man who scarcely spared you a thought, other than to rail at you, or to kiss you senseless just to prove you were wicked.

For an instant she considered giving in to the misery, and simply flinging herself into the grass for a long, hard bawl. But what good would that do? Plainly, histrionics were getting her nowhere. And the humiliation of seeing Robin kissing his Jemmie would be but compounded times ten were she to return to Greythorpe with bleary eyes and tear-stained cheeks.

So Zoë extracted her handkerchief, blew her nose, then stabbed the pins back into her hair, scraping her scalp almost brutally. That done, she set her shoulders stiffly back and set off. And as she strode, she tried not to think of what Robin had alleged.

It likely meant nothing, anyway. There had always been a certain degree of sibling rivalry between Robin and his brother. Mercer had never desired her—not in the way Robin implied.

But what Robin did not overestimate, she feared, was the Vicomtesse de Chéraute and her spite. Indeed, wasn't that the very thing which had got Zoë into this mess? As she had said to Phaedra, it was just damnable luck Mercer's jilted mistress had been the one who—

"Ouch!"

Zoë found herself hurtling forward on a frightful jerk. Somehow, she caught herself before falling ignominiously onto the carriage road face-first, but when she set her left foot down, something did not feel quite right. She lifted her skirts, then turned her half boot to look.

Drat. A missing heel!

She looked back down the path and saw the chunk of black leather hanging off a bit of stone which protruded up from the roadbed. Cursing under her breath, Zoë hobbled back and snatched it.

The next three miles were walked at a limp, the left hems of her skirts trailing in the dirt, one leg now being half an inch shorter. Zoë cursed the whole of the journey, dredging up every vile word she'd ever heard—some of which she scarcely knew the meaning of, until at last the towering stone portico of Greythorpe came into view.

Jerking free her bonnet strings as she went, Zoë hobbled up the steps just as a footman swept open the massive door to admit her.

"Thank you," she said sweetly. "Can you tell me where I might find Mr. Donaldson?"

The footman bowed. "In the butler's office, miss,"

he said. "Down the stairs and to your right, if you please."

Zoë went down into the servants' quarters to smell the beginnings of dinner already wafting through the wide, airy passageways. Here and there, servants in white pinafores or elegant livery went to and fro, carrying trays, baskets, even piles of snowy linen. Just along the passageway, Mr. Donaldson's door stood open. Zoë pecked on the doorframe and went in.

The servant stood at a tall, mahogany butler's desk, the fall of which was down, revealing row upon row of tidy letter slots and compartments. A heart-shaped box of black leather lay open upon the green baize surface, and Donaldson turned from it, his face alighting with what was almost a smile.

"Miss Armstrong!" he said. "Gude day tae ye. How may I help?"

With a rueful smile, Zoë lifted her hand. The filthy boot heel sat in the center of her palm, the bare nails still protruding.

"Ah!" he said softly.

"You did say *anything*," Zoë teased. "I'm very sorry to trouble you, but I haven't another pair of boots with me."

At that, Donaldson did smile, his dark eyes dancing. "Let's just fetch a hammer, shall we?"

"Oh, thank you," she said. "Can you fix it?"

"Oh, aye," he said. "Weel enough tae get you a few weeks' wear."

With that, he vanished through a second door and into the depths of the servants' quarters. To distract herself, Zoë roamed about the room, which was expensively furnished, yet bare to the point of asceticism. As she drifted past the open desk, however, the heart-shaped box caught her eye. Zoë turned to look, her breath instantly catching.

The box lay open on gold hinges, and nestled inside on a white velvet bed was a diamond and emerald parure the likes of which Zoë had rarely seen. Gold-foiled emeralds the size of her thumbnail were surrounded in lacy gold cannetille and hung from diamond stud ear-bobs. The necklace consisted of a row of nine graduated stones, the largest the size of a robin's egg. An equally elaborate brooch and a pair of matching cuff bracelets completed the ensemble.

Zoë let out her breath on a sigh. Her love of beautiful things, she supposed, was yet another of her many shortcomings. This set looked to be at least a hundred years old, and had obviously cost someone a fortune. A tiny white tag dangled from the necklace, the cramped copperplate almost too small to read.

Impulsively, Zoë picked it up and turned it to the window. It held but one word: *Chéraute*

Zoë dropped it as if the paper had burst into flame.

So Mercer and his mistress had managed to reconcile—or if they had not, such an exquisite gift would likely do the trick. Zoë went to the window, and stared out unseeingly. Her hands, she realized, were inexplicably shaking.

Good Lord, it was just jewelry. It was just *Mercer*.

She should be glad. Mercer had plenty of money, and the happier he kept Claire, the easier life would be for all of them. But when Donaldson returned, Zoë was still standing by the window, and chewing pensively at her thumbnail, a frightful habit of Phaedra's, and one for which Zoë had so often scolded her.

She dropped her hand, and turned to smile at the butler. "Any luck?"

"Oh, aye," said Donaldson, swinging a slender cobbler's hammer. "Now let's see what can be done aboot that heel, hmm?"

Coincidence, as Zoë well knew, could sometimes be disconcerting. An hour later, she was dressing for dinner when a hard, imperious knock sounded upon her door. Almost at once, the thought of Mercer shot through her mind, and a shameful anticipation curled up in her belly.

"I'll get it, miss." Trudy laid down Zoë's hairbrush and went to the door. "Oh! Good evening, my lord."

Zoë turned in some surprise as another marquess altogether entered the room, a thin red box in his hand.

"Ah, you have my favorite dinner gown laid out," said her father, his eyes warm. "The red silk becomes you, minx."

"Papa!" Zoë rushed to give him a swift hug. "What is wrong?"

He shrugged, lifting his massive shoulders, a strange, uncertain gesture for a man so large and inherently confident. "Do I need a reason to spend a quiet moment with my eldest?"

Zoë laughed, and drew him to the edge of the mattress. "No," she said lightly, "but I daresay you have one."

He sat down beside her, dwarfing the narrow, four-poster bed. Trudy discreetly withdrew.

Rannoch sighed, and looked down at the box he'd carried in. "I'm sorry, lass," he said quietly. "Something's gone all cock-up round here, hasn't it? I'm not sure what."

"What do you mean, Papa?"

Again, the shrug. "There's an uneasy feeling in this house," he murmured. "Young Robert's behavior leaves much to be desired. And yet we are all of us a little at fault, are we not? Me, perhaps, for being stubborn, and you for being—well, just what I brought you up to be, I daresay. I just wish . . . I wish things hadn't come to this."

Zoë set both hands on his arm. "Papa, whatever has gone wrong, 'tis no one's fault but mine," she said. "And you brought me up well. Indeed, you've given me everything—and sometimes I think I've given you naught but trouble."

"No, never say that." He turned and held her gaze almost pleadingly. "But is it going to be all right, lass?" he whispered. "Just . . . tell me. You must know I could never bear to see you unhappy."

Zoë wanted to flinch, the question was so similar to the one she'd put to Robin mere hours past. Instead, she forced herself to smile. "It is going to be all right, Papa," she answered, vowing she would make it so.

Yes, somehow, she would be a good wife. She would shut out the fantasies of Robin's brother, and stop the little lurch that rose from the pit of her belly every time she glimpsed his hooded eyes and lazy, cynical smile. By sheer force of will—and hers was infamous—Zoë would sever that awful yearning she felt for Mercer's touch.

"I promise, Papa." Lightly, she kissed his cheek so that he would not see the tears that sprang to her eyes. "I will make this work."

His mouth turned up into a rare smile. "Ah, I'm glad, lass," he said. "I'd thought perhaps . . . but there, I've misjudged matters, eh? Listen, love, your mother and I have something. Something we wish you to have. We'd thought to give it to you on your betrothal, but . . ."

But her betrothal had been no cause for celebration.

Her father did not need to say it aloud. And this—well, it was obviously a peace offering of sorts. He laid the red case in her lap.

Zoë placed her hand over it, and felt the warmth of her father's touch emanating from the leather. How long and how hard he'd gripped it was anyone's guess. She wanted, suddenly, to sob, and she wasn't sure why.

"What is it?" she managed, staring down at it.

"Ah, just open it, lass," he whispered.

The case closed with a tiny gold hasp. Zoë flicked it loose with her thumbnail, and gently lifted the lid. At once, she gasped. A collar of bloodred rubies winked up at her, each fringed in fine gold cannetille, just like the vicomtesse's parure. Indeed, this necklace, though it was alone, was quite the equal in terms of weight and ornamentation. And it was glorious.

"Oh, Papa, it is beautiful," she breathed.

"I knew you'd like it," he said, though it was clear in his tone he hadn't been sure at all. "You always were my little dark-haired raven, so fond of any bright, shiny bauble. And I've always loved that about you."

The tears welled nearer the surface, and Zoë forced them down again. Today of all days, for him to give her such a thing! But oh, how very pretty it was. "I think perhaps I am a little shallow," she confessed with a faint laugh. "Indeed, I do love it. Papa, I will treasure it always. Do you wish me to wear it tonight?"

"Oh, it's too elegant, I daresay, for our informal country dinners," he acknowledged. "But your mother and I wished you to have it all the same. Because we love you, Zoë, and want more than anything that you should be happy in your marriage."

"Thank you, Papa," she said.

"It's not new, by the way," he murmured, drawing a finger along the fiery stones. It was my mother's."

"Oh!" Zoë looked down and blinked back tears. "Then Evie should have it."

"Oh, no, lass, she's too fair," said her father. "She wants you to have it, just as I do. Red is your color. You'll do it proud."

Zoë wanted to say that she didn't deserve it; that she'd dishonored him and her future husband, and in a dozen little ways. But as if reading her mind, Rannoch gently closed the box, and folded her hand over it.

"There," he said quietly. "'Tis done. Now kiss me, and hurry on down. We can't keep our hosts waiting."

But Zoë's newfound sense of humility was not to last long. When she arrived in the grand parlor, she was shocked to find Lord Mercer holding court by the hearth, and looking every inch the rich young nobleman as Sir William, his son, and the Wares appeared to curry his favor. Zoë turned away, too late, as a little shiver of sensual awareness ran through her.

Dear heaven, for all the calm she was able to elicit, Mercer might as well have run his hand up her thigh again! She thought of the promise she'd just made her father, and felt vaguely ill in the pit of her belly. Oh, surely, surely she was not falling in love with that infernal man? Surely the fickle-hearted Zoë Armstrong could govern her passions a little better than this?

Looking across the room, Zoë forced herself to smile, and joined Lady Shankling, who was soon extolling the virtues of fine needlework, a topic sure to damp down one's lust. But despite the dull conversation around her, Zoë could still sense a strange, heavy stillness in the room. Indeed, all her senses seemed too fully aware. The smell of the sea drifted through the French windows on air that felt damp as it breezed over her warm skin. And contrary to her best efforts, Zoë's eyes kept straying to the hearth. To the lean, broad-shouldered form who stood there, one elbow propped with an almost studied ease upon the mantelpiece, one slender, long-fingered hand languidly gesturing to his rapt audience.

She had once believed Robin the embodiment of masculinity, Zoë recalled, glancing surreptitiously over one shoulder. But by contrast, he now seemed merely clever and handsome. His brother was not clever. Instead, he was incisive; almost coldly so. He was not handsome; he was striking in a raw, overtly male way. And it now seemed to Zoë as if *this*—the taut, barely leashed energy of a man who held rigid control of himself—yes, *this* was the embodiment of what a man should be.

Mercer knew it, too. Or acted as if he did.

All their talk, Zoë observed, was of tomorrow's hunt. As the largest landowner by far, Mercer must give his blessing before the hounds and horses traversed Greythorpe's lands. Zoë watched across her wineglass as the crowd of gentlemen soon burst into a round of laughter and back slapping. An agreement had been reached, then. Even Robin had joined them, a glass of Madeira in hand as he halfheartedly participated in a discussion of which gates must be kept closed, and which horses might best be taken out.

"In any case, I daresay I dropped a stitch," Lady Shankling was complaining. "For as soon as I held it up, the vexatious thing raveled out! All my hard work! Have you ever, Miss Armstrong?"

Zoë turned, and tried to pretend she'd been listening. "No, no," she murmured. "Never." Which was perfectly true, she considered, since *stitch* and *work* were scarcely in her lexicon.

Lady Shankling pursed her lips, as if her needlework had personally insulted her. "Well, I am utterly *resolved* to finish it!" she declared, "for you simply *must* have it for your trousseau. Lord Robert, you know, has ever been a favorite of ours—and so very kind to our Jim."

But inexplicably, Zoë still watched Mercer from one corner of her eye. As he so often did, he wore unrelieved black, save for his dove gray waistcoat. Tonight, his wardrobe was ornamented by a fob and watch chain, along with a heavy gold signet ring worn on the last finger of his left hand, which glinted in a shaft of late-day sun as he lifted his hand to drink.

But Lady Shankling, she realized, was still awaiting a response.

"Ma'am, you are kindness itself," she managed. "Were they close as boys? Mr. Shankling and Robert, I mean?"

"Oh, indeed!" she trilled. "And Lord Mercer, too, of course." Then she leaned nearer, and dropped her voice suggestively. "Though I must say, Mercer is rather hard

232 ～▭ LIZ CARLYLE

to know, is he not? So stern and so reserved, even as a young man—not of course, that anyone can blame him. Such wealth, I always say, is a burden unto itself."

"Tell me, ma'am," Zoë murmured aside, "does no one hereabouts find him arrogant?"

"Mercer?" she said, her brows going up. "Oh, heavens, no! Arrogance is a tool of the weak. Mercer is sure of himself, but I think it is not at all the same thing."

Zoë pondered that for a minute. For a twittering featherbrain, Lady Shankling made a certain amount of sense. Just then, a low rumble sounded beyond the open windows.

"Oh, dear," murmured Lady Shankling.

Zoë turned to the window. "Sir William's storm," she murmured, almost to herself. "It is coming, after all."

"Indeed," said his wife. "I must tell him we dare not tarry after dinner."

As the lady turned and started toward her husband, Zoë saw Robin stand and take another glass of wine from the footman. He caught it awkwardly, listing a little starboard as he tried to sit back down. His gaze was glassy, his face devoid of any emotion save a strange, sideways sneer.

Fleetingly, Zoë closed her eyes. Oh, dear.

When she opened them again, Donaldson was standing in the doorway, signaling dinner was ready. Perhaps, for once, she should try to encourage Robin to go up to bed afterward. The evening would soon be over.

To her disapprobation, however, Jonet directed that Zoë was to go in on Mercer's arm, which was odd. By rank, it should have been Evangeline. But then, they had stood on little ceremony when dining at Grey-thorpe thus far.

With a strange, fluttering sensation in the pit of her stomach, Zoë turned to find Mercer, only to discover he was already observing her from his usual position by the hearth, his elbow still propped languidly upon the mantelpiece, the wineglass still in his hand. Without breaking eye contact, he lifted the glass in a mocking salute, drained it, then set it aside with a faint *chink*.

There was nothing to do save brazen it out. Zoë smiled, crossed the room, and let her hand slide round his arm. A very solid, very large arm—which might as well have been bare skin, given the frisson of desire that shot down her spine. As if to emphasize it, there came an accompanying crack of lightning, faint but unmistakable, followed by another low rumble of thunder.

Zoë exhaled sharply, and wondered if God had seen the wicked thought that had just run through her mind.

Mercer merely worsened matters by leaning nearer, his heat and scent tantalizing her in the thick summer air. "I did not ask for this," he murmured as they strolled from the room. "If you wish, I shall see it does not happen again."

She lifted her chin, and cut a glance up at him. "Why, how very silly you are, my lord," she said haughtily.

"Am I?" His dark gaze swept over her. "Alas, you may be right."

And those were the last words Mercer spoke to Zoë throughout the meal, save for "kindly pass the salt," though she sat at his elbow, a position in which conversation between them would ordinarily have been de rigueur.

As if by mutual agreement, they politely ignored one another. Instead there was much casual banter all round the table, and when that slowed, Zoë entertained herself by conversing with the youngest Mr. Ware, Francis, who wished to talk of nothing save the next day's hunt, in which Sir William had asked him to whip in, whilst his elder brother Edward took charge of the dragline.

"I do wish you could join me," he said as the final course was cleared. "Lady Kildermore assures me you are more than up to the task."

Zoë blushed. "I rather think Sir William is not apt to want a woman whipping in his hounds, even if I could."

"Oh, no, I daresay not." Vaguely deflated, Mr. Ware relaxed into his chair. "Did you know a Frenchman has invented a leaping saddle for ladies? That would be grand, wouldn't it?"

Zoë's eyes widened. "It would be better than sneaking out in boots and breeches," she murmured, making Mr. Ware grin. "Where might one get such a contraption?"

"I do not know," he confessed, "but for you, Miss Armstrong, I shall endeavor to find out."

To her right, she could feel the intensity of Mercer's eyes upon them, but she did not give him the satisfaction of turning.

"Miss Armstrong?" said Mrs. Ware from farther down the table. "I do beg your pardon, but Lady Rannoch was just explaining that you and Lord Robert were distant cousins. I did not realize."

Zoë brightened her smile. "Indeed, we have known one another from childhood," she answered, casting what she hoped appeared to be a fond gaze upon her fiancé, who was, regrettably, eating little and drinking more wine than could possibly be wise.

"So you are marrying a good friend," remarked the Reverend Mr. Ware. "Truly, there can be no better foundation for a marriage."

"Oh, Robin might have been Zoë's playmate," said Jonet in a teasing tone, "but Stuart served as her paladin. He had to be forever at hand to extract Zoë from whatever mischief she and Robin got themselves into."

Mrs. Ware laughed lightly. "That does sound rather like Mercer," she remarked. "Do you care to expound upon these adventures, my lord?"

Mercer's mouth twitched humorlessly. "Actually, no," he said. "But my mother, I collect, is about to."

All eyes turned to Jonet, whose gaze was alight with an unholy glee. "Well, the first instance I recall," she began, "was in Brook Street. Zoë and Robin hid themselves in the schoolroom cupboard, and accidentally pushed the key out from the other side."

"Oh, my!" trilled Lady Shankling.

"Oh my, indeed." Jonet dropped her voice. "Our collie Scoundrel promptly nibbled it up. Stuart had to pick the lock with one of my hairpins to save Robin from a thrashing."

Mercer's eyes widened. "Ah, knew about that, did you?"

His mother paused for a heartbeat. "My dear boy, I know everything," she said in an odd, faintly ambiguous tone. "I am, after all, your mother."

At that, all the ladies chuckled, and the odd tension melted. Or perhaps Zoë had imagined it?

"Then there was the tale of Zoë and the pig," Mr.

Amherst continued amidst the laughter. "Now, *that* happened at Elmwood and what a to-do it was!"

"Oh, no!" On a laugh, Zoë let her face fall into her hands. "Sir, you really are too cruel!"

"Lud, not the sow story!" Evangeline rolled her eyes.

Jonet began to laugh. "No, no, this one is too rich to be given up!" she declared. "Zoë, you see, decided she wished a newborn piglet for her toy cradle. So she and Robin slipped into the pigsty to fetch one."

"A suckling sow?" Sir William groaned. "Oh, this cannot have ended well!"

"No, it ended in tears," Jonet agreed. "And a vast deal of laundry."

Mr. Amherst set an elbow on the table, and leaned forward. "Stuart, you see, had to rescue Zoë from the corner in which the sow had trapped her," he put in. "But first, he had to persuade her—by force, as I recollect—to let go the squalling piglet. Then he shoved her out, headfirst through the slats."

"My dear girl!" Sir William chided. "The two of you might have been killed!"

Zoë was already blushing. "Frightfully stupid, was I not?" she admitted, glancing down the table at Robin. But her betrothed seemed disengaged from the conversation, and was still drinking his wine. Suddenly, he shoved the glass away, and cleared his throat.

"Here, I have a heroic tale for you," he interjected. "Stu thrashed the devil out of me one year at Christmas for kissing Zoë beneath the mistletoe. Fancied himself her knight in shining armor, I reckon."

An uncomfortable pause ensued. Mercer's jaw gave a little twitch. "She was *fourteen,* for pity's sake."

"And I was seventeen." Indolently, Robin lifted both shoulders. "Did it really warrant a blacked eye and a bloody nose?"

Somehow, Zoë managed to laugh. "Well, at the very least, it convinced you to make an honest woman of me," she remarked, "so I daresay I should thank him."

At that, everyone at the table laughed. Everyone save Robin, who instead shot Zoë a sullen, sidelong glance.

"And then," said Jonet a little loudly, "there was the time Zoë pretended to drown in Elmwood's lake. To this day, I don't think Stuart has ever really got over that one."

A sudden hush fell across the table. All eyes returned to the countess.

"You were what, my dear?" Jonet glanced down the table at Zoë. "Fifteen? Sixteen?"

"Almost sixteen," Evangeline put in.

"And they decided, I gather," said Jonet, "that it would be a great joke if Zoë fell out of the boat whilst Robin and Frederica rowed off without her."

"Mamma, really," said Mercer darkly. "I think you should hold your tongue."

Jonet held up a hand. "No, no, it is quite a funny story, though I got it secondhand," she said. "Apparently Zoë flailed about quite convincingly, so Stuart leapt in to save her wearing his new gold pocket watch. It was the July he turned twenty-one, and we'd just given it to him. I don't think he has ever quite forgiven her for it. Indeed, he has behaved a little oddly with Zoë ever since."

"Mamma, what nonsense," Mercer gruffly admonished.

Zoë dropped her chin. "Nonetheless, I am still

ashamed of that trick," she said quietly. "It was badly done of me."

Evangeline looked down the table in some sympathy. "Well, the pocket watch was not lost in vain," she remarked. "Zoë, I collect, did not fully appreciate the amount of water a lady's skirts and stockings would take on. What began as a joke rather terrified her. We are all quite lucky Lord Mercer jumped in when he did."

"Oh, my!" Lady Shankling pressed a hand to her chest. "Lord Robert, did you not go back for her?"

He set away his wine a little awkwardly. "I've never worn petticoats in my life," he said coolly. "I thought it all a part of her ruse."

"Indeed, Robin and Freddie rowed away to a little island on the other side, unknowing," said Jonet. "By the time I found her, Zoë was in the boathouse, wrapped in a blanket, and shivering in Stuart's lap. Between the two of them, I don't know who was the more distraught."

Just then, yet another crack of lightning sounded, this one a little nearer. Lady Shankling gave a shriek. "There it is again!" she said, the plume on her hat bobbing. "Sir William, I think we ought not linger, and start home before full dark."

"Yes, yes, my pet." Sir William stood. "Miss Armstrong, you have been very good to permit us to make sport of you tonight."

"Not at all." Zoë lifted her chin in specious pride. "My exploits are legendary."

Sir William laughed, then bowed to his host. "Mercer, my apologies, if you will indulge us?"

"By all means." Mercer lifted a regal hand in the

direction of the footmen, his gold signet ring catching the candlelight. Without further instruction, a servant dashed off to fetch the Shanklings' carriage. Almost at once, the Wares, too, decided to depart.

"There will be mud," said Mrs. Ware. "And Edward must be up very early tomorrow."

"Yes, all the better to get a good night's rest, eh, Miss Armstrong?" Francis Ware smiled down at her.

"Quite so," murmured Mercer, his gaze running over Zoë. "All the better, indeed."

Five minutes later, all of the guests had gone, and another unnatural stillness fell across the room. Zoë looked down the table at Robin and sharply cleared her throat. He did not so much as spare her a glance.

"Well!" said Mr. Amherst a little too cheerfully. "This is convenient. Why do we not forgo our port, and have the coffee brought to the table, now that our guests are gone? We should all turn in a little early, too."

"Certainly," said Mercer coolly. This time, Zoë noticed, he did not even need to lift his hand. As if by magic, the tray was borne in, and set down in front of Jonet.

Zoë's father was watching his cousin pour. As she passed a cup to him, Rannoch spoke for nearly the first time that evening, his gaze turning to rest upon Robin.

"It occurs to me," he said quietly, "that we have all been here some weeks now. Perhaps it is time we began to lay some plans for this wedding?"

"I have been thinking the very same," said Mr. Amherst. "The sugar, Jonet, if you please."

"Yes, of course." She passed it, then turned to hand a cup of coffee down to Robin. "Your stepfather and I were wondering, my dear, if you and Zoë mightn't wish him to perform the ceremony? It is not unheard of, you know, for a father to serve in such a way."

Lifting one shoulder, Robin took the cup. "Yes, I daresay."

As if it were a signal, the footman swooped in to snatch up the half-full wineglass. Robin watched it go a little sorrowfully.

Jonet's smile seemed to dim. "Zoë, my dear," she said, turning to smile at her, "would you like that? Or would you prefer to be married from home, at St. Mary Magdalene? A bride's wish must take precedence, of course."

Zoë searched for the right words. "I just want Robin to be happy with our choice," she finally said, forcing her gaze from the tablecloth. "He will be my husband. I will defer to him."

"Robin?" said his mother.

Robin's face held no emotion. "I have no opinion," he said, thrusting a spoon into his coffee. "One will do as well as the other, won't it?"

"Certainly," said Cole, a little too swiftly. "And I was thinking, also, that we might hold the wedding here, in the peace and quiet of Lower Thorpe. It's been an age since a Rowland was wed in the parish church. If you are agreed, Ware could call the banns on Sunday." He touched his napkin delicately to his lips; then, in the awkward silence, looked more pointedly at his son. "Robin? What say you, my boy?"

"Fine," Robin snapped, setting down his spoon with a clatter. "Whatever you wish, Papa. Pray just plan it, and have done."

Rannoch's expression was like a gathering storm. He

set one elbow on the table, and leaned across a little menacing. "Recollect, if you will, sir, that you *asked* for my daughter's hand in marriage," he said darkly. "I hope it is not too much to expect that you be civil about it."

A deathly silence fell across the table. Suddenly, Robin jerked from his chair. "Good God, I said I wanted to marry her, didn't I?" He hurled his napkin onto the empty seat. "Must I now dance a jig over it? Kindly excuse me. I am going out."

Zoë set her glass down awkwardly, very nearly tipping it over. "Robin, wait!" she cried after him. "Where are you going?"

Robin did not turn round. "Back to the Crown," he snapped, "to get drunk."

"Oh, I'll be damned," Rannoch growled, shoving back his chair. "Rowland, it is time you and I had a long talk."

"Elliot, *please*—!" Evangeline cried.

But Rannoch was shoving up his sleeves as he went, hard on Robert's heels. Zoë set a tremulous hand to her mouth, fear rising like bile in her throat. They vanished from the room, their heels ringing across the marble as they strode, voices already raised in a clamorous argument.

Jonet rose, and pressed her fingertips to her lips. "Oh, Cole," she said, her voice shaking, "I think that you should go after them. Rannoch is like to kill him—justifiably, perhaps."

Mr. Amherst, too, had risen, and was watching the empty corridor with disapprobation. Somewhere in the house a door slammed, and then another. Abruptly, Mr. Amherst sat back down and cut a sympathetic glance at his wife. "I think, my dear, that we had best let Robert extract himself from this quagmire of his own making," he said softly. "If they are to be a family, he and Rannoch must learn how to make their own peace."

"Well, yes," said Jonet unsteadily. "I daresay. Evangeline?"

Evangeline shot an assessing look at Zoë, pity sketching over her face. "Yes, I do think Cole is right, Zoë," she murmured. "Robert is just tired. You mustn't think he . . . that he . . ." Her words fell weakly away.

But Zoë was shaking now, on the verge of true tears. "Think *what,* Evie?" she answered, jerking awkwardly to her feet. "That Robin hates me? That that I have ruined his life? Well, I have, haven't I? He is perfectly wretched now. You may all be angry at him, but I cannot be! Because this—all of it—is my fault!"

Jonet moved as if to take her hand. "Oh, Zoë, my dear chi—"

"No!" said Zoë, her gaze moving from one to the other as she backed away. "Stop calling me child! All of you! This was what you wanted—every one of you— and now, by God, you shall have it. But what of *me?* This has cost *me* my dearest friend! Can none of you can see that?"

On a sob, she turned and hastened toward the door, Evangeline catching her by the shoulder as she went. "Zoë!"

"I'm sorry, but I want to find Robin," she said, her voice breaking on his name.

"He has gone out," said Evangeline quietly.

"Then I shall go for a walk!" Zoë could not get her breath. The walls, the worried faces, the expectations—

it was all closing in on her. "Just . . . leave us alone. All of you, please just leave us alone."

And Zoë was to have at least half her wish. She rushed from the dining room and down the grand staircase in a choking panic, only to find herself quite utterly alone in the great hall below. All but blinded by her tears, she went out the back into the parterre, the slam of the door behind her reverberating through the house again as if it were an empty mausoleum.

Chapter Ten

LORD MERCER'S
DARK AND STORMY NIGHT.

Lord Mercer stood in his shirtsleeves by the windows of his study, looking out into a night made impenetrable by the rain that lashed at the glass. Spatter struck intermittently, like handfuls of rice skittering across a kitchen floor—an improvement of sorts, for an hour past, it had sounded like gravel flung full force.

But now the storm without was quieting, moving inland toward Town, where it would become a soft summer rain. But the storm within—ah, that would not be so easily quieted, he feared. Still staring at the window, he pulled the stopper from his decanter of cognac, and unthinkingly poured a glass. A glass which would not wash down the anger and frustration he was feeling. Anger at himself. Frustration with his brother.

Wherever Robin and Zoë had gone, he prayed they were dry, at the very least. Perhaps they had slipped back into the house unseen; Robin was ever the resourceful one. Perhaps even now they were reconciling. Embracing. Sharing another of their fevered kisses . . .

He did not realize he was biting the inside of his cheek until he tasted blood. Good God, what an imagination he had developed! Robin fancied himself in love with Mrs. Wilfred—that much was painfully apparent. The damned fool had sooner wallow in his newfound misery than to rise and behold the exquisite treasure fate had tossed into his path.

At that, Mercer grunted aloud, then tossed back half the brandy, savoring the slow burn down the back of his throat.

When had he come to think of *Zoë* and *treasure* in the same breath? *Tribulation,* perhaps. *Trouble. Trial. Termagant. Tease.* Lord, he could go on. But her betrothal to Robin had shaken him to his core. And tonight, he had ached for her. His parents' teasing had risen from affection, and out of the comfort they felt with her. And Zoë had borne it well, outwardly at least. But Robin's words had been the last straw, and none of them, he now realized, had grasped quite how raw Zoë was just now. How fraught with doubt.

He did know. He had seen it in her eyes days ago. And instead of consoling her, he had seduced her.

That thought required the rest of the brandy. He tossed it back just as his mother cleared her throat behind him. He looked up at her watery reflection in the black window glass.

His mother still sat bent over his desk, her attention focused upon the letter he'd given her to read some five minutes past, Bonnie and Mischief asleep at her feet. They were alone together for a few private moments, she already in her dressing gown, and Mercer's coat and cravat long since tossed aside.

"So . . . you still believe she will turn up here?" Jonet murmured, tilting the paper to the light.

"Aye, she will," he answered. "I am a gambler myself—when I must be."

His mother made a *hmph*ing sound. "So I've been

told," she remarked, tossing the letter aside, and setting her fingertips to her temples. "But this letter—oh, my dear, Claire sounds so very bitter."

Mercer still observed his mother in the glass. Her hair was down in a long, heavy braid, black against the ivory of her silk dressing gown. Though she looked far younger than her years tonight, he knew she was disconcertingly astute—thus, no doubt, his reluctance to turn and face her.

"That letter was written before the *duc*'s accident came to light," he said, lazily swirling the brandy in his glass. "By now she will have seen the newspapers. And she will have written to her contacts in France to see how Chéraute's wind blows."

"And to ensure no survivors have washed ashore," Jonet caustically added.

"Aye, that, too," he said dryly. "And when she is sure—when all her jewelry is gone, and she is utterly bankrupt from her gaming—then she will come to me. I have only to wait."

His mother sighed. "Doubtless you are correct," she conceded. "But I do sometimes fear, my boy, that you have ice water in your veins."

He wished to God she were right. Ice water would be a bloody sight better than the rash, feverish blood that had been coursing through him these last few weeks.

"I saw, by the by, your latest trinkets in Charlie's safe," his mother continued. "You are running Mr. Kemble off his legs. By now he must be on speaking terms with every pawnbroker and jeweler in London."

"He already was," said Mercer sardonically.

"Well, he is buying up your freedom at a very great cost indeed."

"It may not quite be my freedom," he remarked. "Not if she is with child. But then, she may be just a liar."

"What do you think?" His mother turned to look at him.

For the thousandth time, he pondered it. "She lies," he finally said. "I feel it in my bones. But this is a child I gamble on, not a turn of the cards."

His mother sighed again, more deeply. "Oh, what a damnable coil this is!"

He smiled faintly. "Papa would chide you for that."

But his mother was lost in thought. "Still, Stuart, when she has run through everything she owns, what is to keep her from simply taking another wealthy lover? There must be a few who can afford her intrigues."

Mercer gave a bitter bark of laughter. "She forestalled that option, I fear, when she suggested she was with child," he answered. "No one will want her just now—a circumstance I rather doubt she considered before tossing her little tidbit to the *ton*'s slavering gossip hounds."

"Oh." His mother's mouth twisted. "You are quite right, of course."

"Don't fash yourself, Mamma," he said, borrowing one of Charlie's favorite words. "I will handle it."

"You are always so confident."

"In this, one cannot afford to be otherwise," he murmured.

"Well," she said with some asperity, "I hope you do not lose what you truly want in the process."

He gave a vague smile. "Really, Mamma," he answered, "what more could I possibly want?"

He heard the rustle of fabric as she left the desk, then felt the silk gown against his waistcoat. Jonet set her arms about him from behind, and laid her cheek against his back. "Very well, keep your secrets," she murmured. "I must go to bed. You should go, too."

"I cannot sleep," he confessed. "I shall wait up until I'm sure they are safe."

"Robin and Zoë?" she said. "Still playing the guardian angel?"

Mercer felt his hand clench around the brandy glass. "I'm going to play the avenging angel if Robin can't soon get his head out of his arse," he said grimly. "Zoë deserves—"

He jerked to a halt, unsure he could complete the sentence.

"Zoë deserves a man who can love her unreservedly," his mother finished.

"Someone who can get a grip on the little hellion, you mean," he gritted.

"Someone who can appreciate her blithe spirit, and not be cowed by it," his mother corrected.

"Whatever you call it," he said grimly, "Robin doesn't appear to be up to the job." Then he craned his head, and looked back at her. "What was all that about tonight, by the way?"

"What?" She lifted her head, eyes widening.

"Oh, don't come the innocent with me, Mamma," he answered. "You are ill suited for it. At dinner tonight— that drum roll of Zoë's stunts. I am not at all sure she appreciated it, by the way."

"Oh, she will forgive me," said his mother, dropping her embrace. "But Zoë is not nearly so embarrassed by her stunts as you seem to think she should be, my dear." Then she reached round to lightly kiss his cheek. "Well, good night, my dear."

For a moment, he toyed with asking her to stay. Or asking, perhaps, for her advice.

But about what? Zoë was not for him; he'd always known that. Together they were like flame to oil. All he could do, perhaps, was persuade Robin to be worthy of her. An honorable sentiment, indeed—and one which had begun to make him sick to his stomach.

God's truth, but he had no wish to be alone this evening, looking out into this black, black night, and wondering where they were. Or what he could have done differently, perhaps years ago.

Instead, as he had for most of his life, he kept his counsel and said nothing. Not to Zoë. Not to his mother. Nor to anyone else. He had ruthlessly crushed his every instinct, warning himself that in any other direction lay madness where Zoë was concerned. What would truly be madness now would be to reverse course when they were all so nearly cast upon the shoals.

So he turned and set his arms about his mother. "Good night, old thing," he murmured, setting his lips atop her head before releasing her.

Jonet's tread was barely audible as she left him to go out into the great hall and up the stairs. But on his next breath, Mercer heard the front door creak inward on its massive hinges. The footman on duty was addressing someone in an urgent tone.

Hastily, he dragged a hand through his hair, and went

out to see what was the matter, the dogs on his heels, claws softly tapping on the marble.

To his surprise, Robin stood there dripping, still in his dinner attire. The footman was lifting his sodden coat away.

"Robin?" he said, hastening across the great hall. "Robin, where is Zoë?"

Robin looked at him blankly. "In bed, I daresay," he answered, his words slurred. "What, must I account for her whereabouts before I've even wed the chit?"

Just then, his mother called down. Mercer looked up to see her leaning over the balustrade, her heavy braid swinging over her shoulder. "Robin? Is that you?"

"Aye, Mamma," he grumbled. "Go to bed."

"Is Zoë not with you?" Jonet's voice was sharp.

"Why should she be?" Robin was shaking the damp from his hat.

Mercer circled round, and yanked the hat from his hand. "What, you have not seen her?" he demanded. "She went out looking for you, you fool."

Robin looked up blankly. Mercer gave up, thrust the hat at the footman, and headed for the stairs.

"Wait, Stuart, where are you going?" asked his mother as he pushed past her.

"To fetch Zoë's cloak," he returned. "Someone has to find her before she dies like a drowned rat in this downpour."

"Rain's over." Robin's voice echoed up, emotionless. "Moon's come out."

Mercer stopped, and glanced down from the landing to see that his brother had gone into the study, and was headed straight for the brandy decanter.

"Take the dogs to bed," he ordered, speaking to his mother over his shoulder. "I'll find her."

"Yes, of course."

Mercer went at once to Zoë's room where her maid looked at him blankly, and shook her head. A quick interrogation of the servants determined that no one had seen her leave the house, or return to it. But left she had. Mercer remembered hearing a door slam.

Outside, he went to the stables. No horses were missing. The veranda along the parterre yielded nothing. He walked round to the front of the house, and looked out the carriage drive. The moon had indeed come out, casting the road in deep shadow. But two hours ago, it would have been pitch black. No one—not even Zoë—would have been fool enough to go that way.

Only the path to the summerhouse was lit at night, and that only nominally, by the sconces along the west wing terrace. Mercer crossed the parterre, his strides long, and dashed up the terraced lawns to the carriageway under the west wing. As he'd done the afternoon of Zoë's arrival, he hastened down the hill, this time not in knee boots and breeches, but in his dinner attire. Heedless, he cut through the tall grass that whipped wetly about his trousers, soaking him to the knees.

There was an irrational fear in his throat and a tightness in his chest that made no sense. The night was warm, the air still thick with moisture. They were in the middle of rural Sussex. Where ever Zoë had gone, she was perfectly safe.

Except that he'd never seen her in such a state before. Never seen that look of madness in her eyes; like some wild, fey thing caught in a trap. She had gone in search of Robin—and she had not found him. Not that Robin had been in any shape to have been of much use to her. But what would her state of mind now be?

Below he could see the long stretch of water, silvery in the nascent moonlight. As he neared the foot of the hill, he could see the summerhouse. He reached it in a few swift strides and yanked open the door.

"Zoë!" he shouted, vaulting over the threshold.

He passed swiftly through the cottage and out the other side. Then, beyond the shadowy racks of rowboats, he saw her. She stood on the planked dock, her back to him. She had not heard him—or was, perhaps, incapable of it in her distress. She stood perched on the very edge, her arms uplifted in the moonlight like some pagan goddess, a thin white robe billowing round her in the breeze.

Her shift. She had stripped down to her shift.

She was going in.

"Zoë!" he shouted. "No!"

And then she sprang like a cat, and was gone with scarcely a splash.

"Zoë!" Inwardly cursing, Mercer strode swiftly between the racks. Jerking to a halt at the edge of the planks, he looked out across the glasslike surface. Nothing. Not so much as a bubble. He set his hands on his hips and scanned the shore, or what he could see of it in the gloom.

Surely she was all right? This was madness, yes. But Zoë was a strong swimmer.

She was also distraught. She could have hit her head. A thousand little tragedies began to play out in Mercer's mind, and still she did not surface. Stripping off his shirt and waistcoat as one, Mercer hurled them aside. Then, kicking off his slippers, he hit the water like a knife.

He dove straight down into the impenetrable blackness. Nothing. Just a great, dark void. For long, timeless moments, he swam, feeling with his arms and his legs for something—*anything*—panic propelling him deeper. He reminded himself how often he'd seen Zoë swim; how indefatigable she was. But these thoughts were meaningless against the reality—that she'd leapt in an eternity ago, and had not reappeared. Or so it felt. And when he could hold his breath no longer, he plunged to the surface and came up gasping, shaking the hair from his eyes.

Again, he dove down, kicking out hard with his legs, going as deep as his breath would allow, flailing about almost desperately. Nothing. He surfaced, breathed, and went down for a third time. And again and again, until exhaustion and the lack of oxygen began to wear away the panic.

This was insanity. She had come up. His lungs about to burst, this time, Mercer surfaced and began to tread water, looking desperately about.

And then he saw her. Just a faraway smear of white, floating on the surface, almost indistinguishable in the shadow of a tree. With strong, certain strokes, he swam out a good fifty yards.

Zoë lay flat on her back, arms outstretched like an angel, rocking on the waves of his wake, the thin shift plastered to her skin.

"Zoë," he said, sliding an arm beneath her. "Good God. You scared the life out of me."

She turned her head just a fraction and looked at him with eyes that were unseeing. "It is so quiet out h-here," she whispered, beginning to shiver. "I just want . . . to be quiet."

"Zoë," he said, fighting down the terror that still choked him. "The water is cold. Let me take you back."

Still treading, Mercer tried to draw her to him, but she pulled up her knees and pushed out of the shadows. "No," she said, sinking up to her chin. "Leave me. Just . . . leave me alone. I want to float." Her voice was hollow. Defeated.

"Zoë, you are in a sort of shock," he pleaded, sidling up to her. "Just give me your hand. Let me take you back. Please, love. It's so cold. You're freezing."

She blinked, her expression almost childlike, the moonlight limning one side of her face. "I just wanted to f-feel the water," she murmured. "To feel it all around me. It's so quiet here."

"It is quiet on the dock, love," he said in a soothing voice. "Come on. I shall put one arm beneath you. And we'll go back. I have blankets. On the dock."

This time when he approached her, she did not fight him, but let him slide an arm beneath hers, and draw her back against him. Stroking backward with the other arm, he drew her gently toward the dock, certain that at any moment she might bolt, and sink back into the black void below. She skimmed along the water, weightless and ethereal, but it felt like an interminable journey.

Minutes later he had her out of the water, but she was shaking violently. Somehow he persuaded her into the cottage, then threw up the lid of an old sea chest kept handy by the hearth. Inside were a dozen old blankets used for picnics and the like. Mercer jerked out the topmost and wrapped it tight about her, then drew her into his embrace.

In his arms, Zoë jerked and shivered almost uncontrollably. Dimly, he understood that her distress was as mental as it was physical. It was as if she could not stop trembling; as if everything inside her was collapsing inward, shaking her to her core.

He held her tight for what felt like hours, shushing her with words he was later unable to remember. He knew only that she felt so frail against him, and he was inexplicably terrified. Terrified of losing her. Terrified of hurting her.

At last, the shaking began to ease. Reluctantly, Mercer returned to the chest, and tossed out a pile of dry blankets on the floor. Unwrapping the wet one, he flung it aside, wrapped Zoë in another, heavier blanket.

"Don't make me," she whispered. "Don't make me go back."

Mercer set his hand to her cheek, wishing he could see her eyes. "You don't have to," he answered. "We'll stay here for a time."

She made a sound—a sort of sob of relief—then gave another bone-deep shiver. After a moment, he let go of her long enough to light the fire that the servants kept laid in the hearth. It was little more than dry twigs, really, but enough to give the impression of warmth. Soon it was crackling to life, the yellow flames licking voraciously up the kindling. After pitching on a log, he sat down in front of the fire, and pulled Zoë onto his lap.

With one finger, he tucked a damp curl behind her ear and watched the dancing flames cast light and shadow over her fine-boned face. How otherworldly it felt to hold her tonight. Zoë's presence in his life was much like a fire; sometimes a soft glow burning in the background, sometimes a raging inferno. But never had he seen her like this.

It was as if something inside her had finally shattered under the weight. As if the laughing, devil-may-care husk had been stripped away, laying bare the small and tender heart of her. So he crooned softly, and rocked her in his embrace, because he did not know what else to do.

It was not the first time he'd held her so, he remembered, pressing his lips to the top of her head. As his mother had so recently recounted, the last time Zoë had nearly drowned herself, he'd pulled her onto his lap like this, his arms about her, her head against his shoulder. But on that occasion, she'd had nothing more than a fright—a fright that had quickly turned to something else.

In the end, however, it had been he who had come away frightened. Frightened by the intensity of need that went shuddering through him when he kissed her. Frightened of what might well have occurred had his mother not turned up. At the age of one-and-twenty— and a man of significant experience—never had he touched a woman who set him afire like Zoë.

This time, however, it was as if she did not care enough to be frightened. This time she was . . . well, he did not know what she was. Mercer's chest tightened suddenly, almost painfully, his heart breaking just a little. On impulse, he whispered her name, then kissed her again, pressing his lips to her wet hair.

To his dismay, the shaking resumed at once, becoming an almost spasmodic jerk. As if to steady herself, Zoë set one ice-cold hand against his shoulder, then turned her face into him. Her breath was warm, stirring the soft hair on his chest. Stirring something else, too. But when he looked down, he realized that Zoë was no longer shivering.

She was crying.

The sudden tightening in his groin relented at once. Tenderly, he crooked his head and set his lips to the pale skin of her temple. "Zoë, Zoë," he shushed, "Oh, Zoë, I have you, love. It's all right."

"No," she sobbed, her words muffled against his bare chest. "It isn't. Oh, Mercer, it's awful, and it will never be right again!"

And though her sobs tore at him, something like relief surged through Mercer. She had come back to herself. She had come back to *him.*

"It will be all right," he whispered, cradling her head to his shoulder. "Zoë, somehow, I'll make it so. I promise you."

"Oh, Mercer!" she sobbed. "I—I *cannot* marry him. I *cannot.*"

To that, Mercer said nothing. He was beyond trying to persuade anyone—least of all himself—that this marriage was wise. It wasn't. It would irreparably ruin all their lives—his included, he now acknowledged. He was going to have to intercede somehow; to speak to Rannoch. To find a way out of this mess—a way to neutralize Claire, save Robin from himself, and yes, make Zoë happy again.

"Zoë," he said firmly. "Love, look at me."

She shook her head, her damp curls scrubbing the hair on his chest. "Everyone expects me to live with Robin for the rest of my life," she wailed. "But I should rather l-live in Scotland w-w-with the *sheep*—!"

"With the sheep?" he echoed, tipping up her chin.

"Oh, I am so sorry," she whispered, her gaze sorrowful. "Oh, Mercer, I am so sorry for everything. Please, please, just don't scold me. I know I deserve it—but please, not tonight. I couldn't bear it."

He shook his head, and felt something hot and urgent pressing at the backs of his eyes. Was that what she'd come to expect of him? That he would scold her?

Of course it was. He thought back to the day she'd arrived at Greythorpe; of how cold, almost condescending, he'd been toward her. How he'd seethed inside with a hundred ugly emotions—foremost amongst them jealousy.

To his shame, one small tear leaked out, quickly dashed away by the back of his hand. God's truth, just how long had he burned for Zoë, while taking his frustrations out on her? How long had he been secretly envious of his own brother—and every other man with whom she flirted—yet unwilling to step up and lay his own heart on the line? How long had he meant to go on pretending what he felt toward her was a sense of duty?

The fact that she likely wouldn't have had him served up on a silver platter did not lessen his cowardice one whit. It made it worse. With her slender, still shaking body pressed so near to his, Mercer felt suddenly petty; a little cruel, even.

He set his lips against her cold forehead. "I am sorry, too, Zoë," he murmured, his chest tightening. "I have nothing to scold you for. I wish . . . I wish things were different. For all of us."

She swallowed hard as she looked up at him, the slender muscles in her throat working. "You are scowling," she whispered, blinking back tears. "Always, you seem to be scowling at me. But I'm not sure, Mercer, that I mind it anymore. I know I've been nothing but trouble."

"Zoë, I'm not—" He cut his eyes away, and shook his head.

"What?" She made a sound; a weak laugh, perhaps. "Not angry with me?"

"No," he whispered.

I am angry with myself, he silently added. *Angry with myself for wanting you. Angry I didn't see the truth sooner. Angry I've let it come to this.*

Still trembling, Zoë shifted her weight as if to go.

"No," he said, tightening his grip. "Zoë, I . . ."

She held his gaze in the firelight, her eyes wide and limpid. "What, Mercer?" she whispered. "Just say it."

He couldn't say it. Couldn't find the words. When it came to Zoë, the whole of his life had been like this—a tangled-up enigma of emotions. His notorious dispassion failed him, leaving him irritable and a little disoriented. What he felt for Zoë was something more than lust. More than frustration. And it was not remotely akin to familial affection.

No, the truth—the truth he'd tried to deny all these years—had cut through him like a lightning strike the instant he'd seen Zoë in this brother's embrace that terrible night in Brook Street. It had stunned him. Driven the breath from his lungs, and almost unmanning him even as he had striven to keep himself from throttling Robin dead with his bare hands.

Yes, God help him, he was in love with Zoë Armstrong, and refusing to say it—even inside the confines of his own head—made it no less the truth. Worse, he had not *fallen* in love with her. He simply . . . loved her. And for the life of him, he could not say when or how or even why it had happened, but only that it was so.

But she was still looking at him, her eyes reflecting the firelight, her long, velvety lashes tipped with tears. "It is true, isn't it?" she whispered. "What your mother said tonight."

"About what, Zoë?" drawing her tighter against him.

"That it was you," she answered. "Always."

"Always . . . me?"

"Who saved me from myself," she whispered. "You were there, even when I was too pigheaded to know I needed you . . . like tonight, I daresay."

He said nothing, but instead let his gaze roam over her small, heart-shaped face and high cheekbones. The too-sharp chin that looked so perfect, and the round, wide eyes that usually seemed to look at the world with childlike mischief. Then her throat; that long, milky column that was all womanly grace and smooth turns. And when he bent his head and set his lips to it, everything in the world seemed to turn instantly right side up again.

"Zoë," he murmured, bending tightly over her. "Oh, Zoë. I thought I'd lost you."

Her hand slid beneath his cheek, turning his face to hers. "And I thought I wanted to be lost," she whispered. "But perhaps . . . perhaps I don't now."

Her lashes looked almost impossibly long in the flickering light; her bow-shaped mouth faintly tremulous. And so he kissed her, gently at first, setting his mouth to hers in a soft, tender gesture meant to comfort and to reassure.

Without opening her eyes, Zoë sighed and kissed him back.

He could stop at this, Mercer told himself, even as his tongue played lightly over her lips. It was just a kiss of comfort. Of reassurance. Except that it wasn't—and he knew it when Zoë's hands came up to cradle his face. Her thumbs stroked lightly over his cheeks, and as if he had willed it, she opened her mouth beneath this.

Perhaps she had tempted a hundred men just so, leaving them stuttering and disoriented. Mercer no longer cared. He stroked his way slowly into her mouth, sliding his tongue sinuously along hers. On another sigh, she returned the gesture, making tiny, tentative forays into his mouth. He told himself it was what she wanted— what she needed—and deepened the kiss, his fingers threading into the hair at her temples. And then he was not so much *holding* her as he was drawing her into him. Over and over he kissed her, slanting his lips over hers, reveling in the spicy-sweet taste of her mouth.

One hand curling into the hair at the back of his head, she clung to him as her other hand roamed restlessly over his back. She was warming now, her dizzying scent of jasmine and citrus rising to tease at his nostrils. He had always thought it a seductive perfume, but perhaps it was not. Perhaps it was just *her.*

Oh, for so long he had wanted this, denying it even to himself. But tonight, Zoë needed him—and she admitted it. Perhaps that was all it took to shove him over the edge. For her to simply say it, with her words, and with her touch.

Somehow he forced himself to slow, to pull away despite her whimpered protest. He looked into her eyes, at the heat and need that simmered there. Slowly he eased her down onto her back. "Zoë," he rasped, bending over her, "do you want this?

She reached for him and closed her eyes. "I *need* this," she whispered. "I need *you.*"

Raw desire shuddered through him then. He crawled over her, the damp fabric of his trousers dragging up one side of her wet shift. He kissed her again, this time sensually, slowly thrusting, forcing her head back into the softness of the blankets. This was happening, and this time, he was going to let it.

Lust throbbed in his groin with every beat of his heart. Zoë was no green girl; he'd always known that. But this . . . this was dangerous. He lifted his mouth to say so—to warn her—sliding his hand round her cheek as he did so.

But with her lashes lowered, Zoë turned her face to his hand and kissed it.

"Don't pull away from me this time," she whispered. "Just . . . don't."

Too roughly, he pulled her to him and kissed her deep, showing her what he intended with his tongue as his hands shaped her body. Zoë kissed him back, her skin afire now despite the shift that clung wetly to her breasts and her belly, all but baring her to his gaze. Her nipples were hard, her areolas dusky beneath the fabric.

This time he slid both hands up her face, plunging his fingers into her damp hair, stilling her to his thrusts. But it was he who was in danger of drowning now; he who floated on a pool of desire, his will gone as weak as his body was hard.

He felt Zoë begin to tremble again, but this time with

need. "Mercer, I know what I want," she whispered. "Please."

Dimly Mercer considered that a decent man would walk away. This was too close. Perhaps it even went beyond tenderness or caring. But he wanted her too badly, and in the end, his honor lay in ashes. For once in his life, he simply didn't allow himself to think logically—or even to think at all—which was precisely what he'd always feared when it came to Zoë.

She kissed him back with abandon, her hands sliding up his body as she sighed. He wondered vaguely if this was how she kissed Robin; if this was how her body felt beneath his brother's. But the thought was so horrific, he shut it out by sheer force of will.

This was not about Robin. This time Zoë was in *his* arms. And it felt as if she meant to drive him insane, her hands urgent and demanding as they stroked him. One slender finger slid beneath the waist of his wet trousers, skimming lightly and making him shiver like an anxious stallion. Her other hand went to the small of his back, then lower, to roam restively over his buttock, caressing. Urging.

Yes, he knew what she needed. And to Zoë's credit, she denied him nothing, opening her mouth to taste him deeply. Her kisses, at first tentative, soon became a practiced siren's song, drawing him ever deeper. Again their tongues tangled, and the simmering heat began to pool between his legs, his cock going rock-hard against her thigh.

For an instant, he tried again to think. To be sure. But Zoë's body rose to his, tempting and perfect. So small and soft and sweetly round. As if she sensed his hesitation, Zoë coaxed him, sliding her tongue provocatively along his, her hands warm and certain on his body.

"Mercer." With lips soft as silk, Zoë drew him, sliding one leg up his own, then hooking her knee over his, binding them together in the most intimate of ways. And when she tore her mouth from his, it was to whisper his name in his ear.

"Mercer," she whispered, one hand slipping loose a trouser button. "Let me forget. Just for tonight. Give me something that will make me forget."

He didn't answer; he had not the words to say *yes,* nor the strength to say *no.* Instead, his mouth captured hers, and he kissed her again, one hand going to her breast. And in that moment, it seemed as if the impossible was possible. As if Zoë had been made for his touch, and that duty and responsibility and yes, even honor meant nothing.

He pressed her back into the softness of the blanket and let the firelight set her skin aglow. Zoë was so small, so delicate, and always he had thought her perfection. But beside her he felt almost dangerously large. He rolled a little away so that he did not crush her, and slowly inched up her drying shift.

Zoë made a little sound of pleasure, and lifted her hips. He did not stop, but drew it up and up, then lifted her to him, and gently pulled it over her head. Her arms went up, surrendering herself to him, and the white cotton breezed away leaving her naked before his eyes. And even in his heated dreams, she had not been so lovely.

"Zoë," he managed to whisper. "Oh. You are . . . exquisite."

She lowered her lashes, then trailed her finger along the waist of his trousers again.

Gently, he laid her down and rolled to one side so that the firelight might play across her skin. Her breasts were full and round, the pink-brown centers sweetly peaked, begging for his mouth. Below that, her ribs turned beautifully to a slender waist above hips that flared wide, and far more lushly than he would have expected.

With Zoë watching him, wide-eyed in the firelight, Mercer set his hand between her breasts and let himself feel the beat of her heart beneath his palm. He closed his eyes and felt the life and the strength pulsing through her. Yes, always, to him, Zoë had exemplified those words.

And when he opened his eyes, he drew one finger down and down; along her breastbone, down that sweetly rounded belly, then lower, to the thatch of dark hair between her legs. She gave a little moan of pleasure, then tugged more impatiently at the waist of his trousers.

"These are damp," she whispered. "Take them off."

He obliged her uneasily. He stood and turned his back, then one by one released the buttons at the fall. He shucked them off, trousers and drawers, and tossed them onto a chair.

"Turn around," she said.

"Zoë, I—"

"I'm not afraid." Her voice was soft, but determined. "I wish to see you."

Mercer hung his head, pinching hard at the bridge of his nose. He wanted her, and he was so bloody tired of fighting it.

"Turn around," she said again. "Lie with me, Mercer."

Zoë sensed it the instant he gave in. Mercer lifted his head, and turned slowly in the firelight, the sleek muscles of his thighs glowing golden in the firelight. And when he stood fully naked before her, Zoë felt her eyes widen but she did not make a sound, save for a hum of pleasure in the back of her throat.

But she wanted to gasp.

Zoë had thought she knew what naked men looked like. In years past, she'd seen glimpses of Robin—and even Mercer—swimming in their drawers. She'd seen Grecian sculptures, Renaissance paintings, and even giggled over a few naughty books. But nothing could have prepared her for the raw strength which radiated from this man.

She held out her hand, and he came down beside her, the muscle of his thigh bulging as he knelt. "Zoë, are you sure?"

It was a question that certainly required no answer now. "You are . . . so *male*," she whispered. "Always, I thought you beautiful, but . . ."

Her word falling uselessly away, Zoë let her eyes take him in; the broad chest, layered in muscle. The lean waist and impossibly flat belly. Arms, she well knew, that could cradle a woman, even carry her when necessary. His was a man's body, all hard planes and inherent power.

Mercer came down over her, covering her mouth with his. He kissed her again, long enough to still her, then his lips slid down her face, down her throat, his breath hot on her flesh until he reached her breast. On a groan, his mouth closed over it, suckling it firmly into the heat of his mouth. The sensation was indescribable.

That delicious, now-familiar thread of heat came spiraling up from her belly, then it went lower, drawing at her very center and leaving her craving more.

She cried out when his teeth clamped gently on her nipple. His other hand slid lower, easing between her legs. His clever hand found her most secret place, sending her head back into the softness of the blankets, and her hips arching up. Oh, she was wicked—and doubtless he would remind her later. But in this moment, she did not care. In this moment, her every secret longing coalesced. This was ruin, and she craved it. She craved *him*. And to have him—to have him on her, inside her—whatever the price, she would pay it.

Mercer touched her, drawing at her nipple, laving and sucking until the pleasure bowed her up inside. Drew her taut. Drove her mad. And when she thought she would die—when she felt that sweet light edge near—he stopped and rose over her on arms that were sculpted with muscle. His head bowed, his dark hair nearly dry now, Mercer set his tongue between her breasts and traced a line of sweet, hot fire down her chest and over her belly. At her navel, he paused, lightly rimming it with the tip of his tongue until she shuddered, then he moved lower.

She gasped when he set his hands along her thighs. His fingers dark against her pale skin, Mercer urged her legs apart, then put his tongue where his hand had been. Zoë cried out, and for an instant it was as if she came up out of her body, her hands fisting in the old blankets, wrenching with all her strength.

With his thumbs, he opened her flesh, and drew the tip of his tongue over her very center. She felt her face flame with the intimacy of it, but his touch bound her to his command.

Incapable now of refusing him anything, Zoë began to tremble anew, losing herself with every stroke until her every fiber seemed drawn taut enough to snap. One long-fingered hand set warm and flat across her womb, Mercer eased first one finger, and then a second, inside her. He began slowly to thrust, and to tease lightly with his tongue.

Oh, she wanted . . . she wanted and she ached and it felt as if she might fly apart at any moment. "I want you." The rasp sounded foreign, not her voice at all. "Mercer, *for God's sake*. I want you to—to be inside me."

Then he touched her one last, perfect time, flicking his tongue across her very core, and a blinding pleasure shuddered through her. Wave after wave washed over her, shot through her, and left her limp in his hands.

When the waves subsided, Zoë opened her eyes, gasping, to see Mercer braced over her, his strong arms set wide. He looked wild in the firelight, like some feral creature lost in a world she could not comprehend. His eyes had gone hot, like molten gold, and his manhood was pressing into her softness, a thick shaft of hard, silken flesh.

Acting on instinct, she drew up one leg and felt him nudge inside. It felt alarmingly large. He apparently agreed. As tiny bead of sweat rolled down his throat, Mercer closed his eyes.

"Zoë." He spoke through clenched teeth. "Zoë, are you a virgin?"

She seemed unable to think. "What?"

"Are you . . . *a virgin*?" He gritted out the words.

For an instant, she couldn't breathe. If he hesitated, she would die. "No, don't stop," she choked, her hands going to his trembling arms. "Do not *dare*. Just—"

He did.

"Aah!" The sound ripped from his throat.

Zoë cried out at once, the pain sudden and sharp. The weight of him filled her, hard and invasive, pulling her flesh beyond bearing. She could hear her own breath. Her own heartbeat. She held herself still until the pain became a throb, then passed entirely.

"Zoë—?"

The one, small word sounded as if he'd dragged it up from the pit of his belly.

"Y-yes?"

"Zoë, you said . . . you were *not* . . . a virgin."

Tentatively, she rocked her hips, rather relieved to realize that it did fit after all—and rather nicely.

"Zoë!" He his head, his hazel eyes burning into her. "Answer me."

"Yes, well, what I meant was—no, *don't stop,*" she said softly. "Indeed, I think that's what I did say—I could tell, you see, what you were thinking."

"Ah." The word was soft. "And what am I thinking now?"

She rocked her hips again. He gave a grunt of pleasure and closed his eyes.

"I don't know," she murmured. "But I'm not a virgin now, so it really doesn't matter, does it?"

His eyes snapped open, softening. "Zoë, I could have been gentle."

She let her hands slide down his back, curled her fingers into the taut, lean muscles of his buttocks, and moved her hips invitingly. "What is a little physical pain?" she murmured. "Come, 'tis over."

To her shock, he drew back, and deepened the thrust on a groan, his taut arms trembling.

"*Yes,*" she whispered.

Watching the flat muscles of his belly work, Zoë lifted herself against him and felt the merest hint of pleasure. Mercer's size, she suddenly realized, had its advantages. His body filled hers, stretched her almost impossibly, creating a sweet, exquisite friction as he pushed into her.

"*Oh . . .*" she said again, closing her eyes.

Mercer set a rhythm, moving inside her as if he performed the most delicate of dances. As if he knew just how and where to pleasure her. Soon there was no memory of pain, but only of this, his perfect strokes sliding deep, holding her captive, tormenting her with just a hint of pleasure to come.

Zoë lifted one leg higher, sliding it along his as she tilted her hips into that tantalizing place where their bodies joined. She met him and matched him, stroke for stroke. Instinctively, she began to rise to him, both with her body, and with something more. Her heart, she feared. And as she watched him—the virile intensity of his body, the hard, beautiful planes of his face—she realized just who he was. Not just Mercer, but the one person who had always, always been there for her. Even when she didn't think she needed him.

But oh, she needed him now. Needed something she could scarce give name to. Lifting herself higher, Zoë dragged her body hard against his. The intensity inside her was building again, as if unslaked. She wanted, oh, she wanted. Wanted him. She tried to tell him so, pleading with words that made no sense, and then with her mouth, tangling her tongue with his, begging him.

Mercer understood, shifting his angle ever so perfectly. The little bead of sweat had become a dozen, pooling at the base of his throat. His hard face was a mask of intensity, the breath sawing in and out of his chest. The sounds of their passion filled the night, their sweat-slick bodies sliding sinuously against one another until at last the pleasure drove her to the very edge.

His eyes flew open. Locked with hers. "Zoë," he rasped. "Zoë, you are mine."

Those hazel-gold eyes commanded her; captured hers and held her in thrall. He said it again. And again. Until a piece of her heart broke away, and the world shattered again, more intense than anything she'd dreamed possible.

Dimly, she heard Mercer cry out, a raw sound of male satisfaction. Felt the surge of his seed filling her. Caught the murmured words that fell from his lips like a psalm as wave after wave of pure, molten joy surged through her, bringing with it the fleeting sense that life was perfect. That he was perfect. That she was loved.

Long moments later, Mercer set his forehead to hers, his male scent surrounding her. Comforting her. "Oh, my God." His voice was an awed whisper. "Zoë, are you all right?"

She closed her eyes. "I am . . . perfect," she whispered. "Thank you."

After that, time held little meaning. Their bodies still

joined, Mercer pulled what was left of the pins from her damp hair and buried his face in it. He ran his hands through it. He kissed her—her throat, her nose, the warm pulse point beneath her ear. Then he set his cheek to hers and exhaled slowly. For a man so large and so solemn, it was a joyous, almost exuberant act.

Deeply, she sighed.

"Did I hurt you?" he whispered against her ear. "Oh, God, Zoë. If I had known—"

"Mercer, I'm not *that* wicked," she said on a laugh. "Knowing a bit about how it's done is one thing, but . . ."

He lifted his head. "Zoë, I never meant to suggest you—" He broke off awkwardly, his face heating in the firelight. "But you . . . and Robin. I just wasn't sure . . ."

She closed her eyes, and shook her head. "Don't let's ruin it," she begged. "Oh, please. I don't want that."

"I'm sorry," he said softly, brushing his faintly stubbled cheek over hers. "What do you want, love? Tell me."

"Hold me," she murmured. "Just . . . hold me and let me pretend, Mercer, just for a little while, that my life is not one great, monstrous mess."

And so he rolled back up on his elbow, scrabbled about for another blanket, and tossed it smoothly over them. Once on his side, he pulled Zoë into his embrace, settling her back against the wall of his chest, and enfolding her in his body.

Enervated and sated by Mercer's lovemaking, she began to drift. It had been sheer and utter bliss. He had given her what she needed; consolation, ecstasy, and joy—and taken her to heights she had never expected, or ever dreamed of. And this, she decided—this being nestled like something precious in his arms, surrounded in his warmth and his scent—was in some ways the best part of all.

Yet even in sleep, Zoë did not delude herself. The next few days were certain to bring all manner of trials, and terrible truths that would have to be faced. Still, she would at least have this one remembrance to comfort her. This one perfect memory of lying in Mercer's strong arms.

Zoë was not perfectly certain how long she drowsed, but when she awoke, her shift was hanging by a roaring fire, the room was warm, and Mercer sat in a chair, his elbows on his wide-set knees.

Zoë rolled over, and stretched. "What are you doing?" she murmured, smiling up at him.

"Watching you sleep," he said, a ghost of sadness sketching over his face. "Zoë, you are so beautiful. Always, you have been beautiful to me."

Zoë laughed, and held out her arms. "Then come back," she suggested, "and make love to me again."

He shook his head, his eyes again solemn, but he did rise and lie down with her. "This is too new, love." Propped on one elbow, he traced a fingertip along the lines of her face. "You are too tender. I would be a brute."

"As you wish," she said lightly.

But he kissed her again, then slowly urged her onto her back. And he did make love to her—with his mouth, and with his hands, and with an unerring gentleness she could never have expected from a man so large and so commanding. He suckled her breasts, threaded his hands through her hair, and murmured his soft, crooning words against her belly. Then he set his mouth to that special place, and sent her world spinning into the light again.

When Zoë again lay sated and grateful, she slept. But she knew instinctively that Mercer did not. Instead, his eyes were upon her, watchful and guarded—as they had ever been, she realized, for all the years she had known him.

Chapter Eleven

THE HUNTING
PARTY.

*M*ercer awoke to the clanging of a bell some-where in the haze inside his head. Rolling up to a sitting position, he dragged both hands through his hair, then looked about in the gloom, awareness slowly returning. Beside him, Zoë drowsed, a warm, surprisingly reassuring presence.

Mercer had enjoyed all manner of pleasant sensations with the many women he'd bedded, but a sense of reassurance had never been amongst them. How very odd—and how very comforting—it felt. In sleep, Zoë looked disconcertingly small and young, her exhalations steady, one fist curled into the hem of their blanket—the blanket which, even now, held their commingled scent and warmth. He drew it in, and for a moment allowed himself the unalloyed delight of watching her, a little taken aback by the pleasure it brought him. But the bell sounded again, muffled yet real.

He had neither the time nor the inclination to reflect further on what had just happened; his well-ordered life turning upside down might as well have been a regular occurrence, no more thought did he spare it. He was a practical man. It was done. And—to paraphrase George Kemble's favorite phrase—*après ça, le déluge.*

So let the deluge rain down upon their heads. The

nearing dawn—and the sorting out of Zoë's increasingly complicated life—were his immediate concerns. Gently, he slid away from her and padded barefoot through the boat room onto the dock beyond. As he'd feared, the moon was fast fading, its luminescent glow upon the water now just a faint, rippling shimmer.

To his far right, from the distant hillside, the clanking came again. Mercer peered into the gloom at a large, lumbering shape. He exhaled with relief. A cow, instinctively wandering toward the barn for milking, perhaps.

He returned to the untidy pile of blankets, and pulled on the drawers he'd tossed out to dry while Zoë slept. Then he poked up the fire so that he might better see her face. That done, he lay back down beside her, and slowly kissed her awake.

She stirred, and gave that taut, fisted stretch again—like a cat unfurling itself from a sunny spot— her mouth curving into that slow, mischievous smile that always tempted him despite himself. Her curls were spread out like a curtain of black silk across the old wool blanket, and he could not resist twining one about his finger.

"Good morning, Mercer," she murmured. "You are looking very well satisfied."

It was a little disconcerting, really, just *how* satisfied he was. And how languid and happy and resigned to his fate he felt. He was a man who was always at peace with who and what he was. He was confident, often even content. But happy? That fleeting emotion seemed more a memory of childhood. But rather than try to explain that to Zoë, he merely smiled, then kissed her again, slowly and thoroughly.

Ah, this, he thought, lifting his lips from hers, *this is the stuff of happiness.*

And if, in order to have it, some of the peace and contentment was to leave his life—and with Zoë, it would—then he was beginning to think it more than a fair trade.

"You'd better dress, love," he whispered against her cheek. "It must be after five."

"Oh," she said with a little start. "Do you think we've been missed?"

Mercer had already considered that. Only Zoë's maid and his mother were apt to be aware of their absence—and his mother, well, he had a strange suspicion she would keep her own counsel, and trust him to deal with *le déluge.*

Zoë swiftly assured him of Trudy's discretion, then her lip came out just a fraction. "But I had better go now, hadn't I?" she added, her voice sad. "Back to real life—and to dealing with Robert and Papa."

Mercer set a hand over her heart and felt it beat against his palm. "Zoë," he said, closing his eyes. "You will tell him today. Robin, I mean."

He felt her turn toward him. "Tell him?" she whispered. "About . . . this?"

"That you cannot marry him," Mercer paused to thread his fingers lightly through her hair. "Not now, Zoë. Not after this. But you knew that, didn't you?"

Zoë closed her eyes and let herself feel Mercer's fingers stroke her scalp. This had been a wonderful, magical night, but now there was a stubborn resolve in his voice that gave her pause. She should not have been surprised.

"Mercer, I couldn't marry Robin before," she

answered. "I cannot marry him, period. But let's not make it about *this*."

"*This* is all that matters now." His hand slid round her face, clasping it firmly. "Zoë, this is everything."

Zoë sensed what was in his mind. "*This* was something beautiful," she whispered. "We made love, and oh, Mercer. I thank you for that. You saved me—not from the water, but from something worse—utter despair. But I did not do this for any other reason save that I wanted you."

"Zoë, what are you saying?" he murmured.

Her eyes searched his face. "I cannot open another door, Mercer, until I close the last," she said quietly. "I know what you are thinking. Do not say it, I beg you. Do not make our lives any more complicated than they already are."

"Complicated? What is complicated about this?"

She let her gaze sweep over him, dubious. "Mercer, listen to yourself," she chided. "You are supposed to be the very definition of cool, hard-nosed logic."

"And I begin to think it has served me ill," he returned.

She stroked the tips of her fingers down his face, then along that stubborn, stubbled jaw. "I've things to settle with my father and with Robin, yes," she murmured. "You have Claire—and do not tell me that your relationship with her is over. I know it isn't."

Mercer cut his gaze away. "It may never be," he said. "Not entirely—and you, of all people, know why. But I want you to tell Robin it is over, Zoë. I want you to tell him today."

"Mercer, you have spent almost the whole of your life annoyed with me," she said softly. "Am I to believe that after one night of passion, all that has changed?"

"It wasn't annoyance, Zoë," he said, his voice softening. "And yes, all that has changed—and yet nothing has."

Zoë rolled up onto her elbow, and kissed him. "I will tell Robin," she said, "and I will make him very happy in doing so. But first I owe my father the respect of telling him, and that will be a long and painful discussion, I fear."

"But you'll tell him why, Zoë," said Mercer. "This isn't over. There are things to settle, aye, I'll give you that. But we are bound now."

She shook her head slowly. "You are not bound to me," she softly answered. "It isn't like that, Mercer. I am still the same person I ever was. I am still just Rannoch's bastard daughter. And this time, you cannot simply save me from my folly with one of your heroic gestures."

"Folly?" he said, his voice tightening. "You think this was folly?"

She cut her eyes away. "A very pleasant sort of folly, perhaps," she amended. "And yes, perhaps it is even something more. Time will tell, won't it?"

"Zoë," he said warningly.

Mercer's expression was grim, and Zoë realized she should have expected this—a noble sacrifice, and his implacable insistence on having his way. But in this, she could not give in. Mercer would regret, she feared, any commitment he made to her now. Oh, never had he looked down on her, precisely. But never had she believed herself worthy of him, and perhaps, when the heat of passion had faded, Mercer would not believe it, either. Perhaps he would go back to thinking her no more than a flirtatious little hellion.

"Yes, I will tell my father that I refuse to marry

Robert," she finally said. "And he may well put me over his knee for it, or ship me off to Perthshire. But this time, I will not back down. As to *this* . . . well, let us see where life leads us."

Mercer cut a swift glance toward the window, his scowl deepening. "I haven't time to argue with you just now, dash it," he muttered. Then he kissed her again, and hauled her to her feet. "Come along. Let's get you dressed and into the house unseen."

"Yes, my lord and master," she answered, smiling slyly.

His dark gaze held hers but a heartbeat. "Oh, I will master you, my girl," he said grimly. "One way or another—daunting task though it may be."

"Will you indeed?" she murmured. "I think I should rather like to see you try."

Then, lowering her lashes, Zoë leaned into him, twined her hands round his neck, and returned the kiss more thoroughly. And once begun, it was very hard to pull away. Even now, sated and once again sane, Zoë discovered the infernal man could still make her knees go weak.

This morning Mercer smelled of warm, sleepy male, and the hint of beard he'd worn last night was a dark bristle this morning, shadowing his stern jaw and making him look just a little more ruthless than usual. The awful truth was, she realized, she was head over heels in love with him. In love with his strength and his honor—and yes, even his stubbornness.

Perhaps she had always been. Perhaps that was why his disapproval had always stung, and she had taken such pleasure in goading him. But what she felt for him now was no girlish infatuation. It was need which was rapidly deepening, becoming all-encompassing, and impossible to ignore. And yet she meant to keep that her secret—at least until he got over his old-fashioned notions of chivalry—for the future loomed up before them, uncertain and troubling.

Just then a sharp sound splintered the air—a high-pitched *yip-yip-yip* beyond the lake. Zoë leapt away, her hand to her heart, but Mercer drew her back at once.

"'Tis nothing, love," he soothed, his breath warming her temple. "Just a fox, looking for his mate."

"Oh," she whispered. Then, more loudly, "Oh, *no!*"

Mercer set her a little away and looked down, his harsh, dark eyebrows snapping together.

"Sir William's foxhunt!" she whispered. "Blast! We'd better hurry!"

Trudy said not a word when Zoë slipped inside her bedchamber still wearing last night's dinner dress, which was at least dry, thanks to Mercer.

"Go head, Tru!" said Zoë, flinging herself across the bed. "Let fly! Just please, *please* ring for my bathwater whilst you scold—extra hot, if you please."

"Lord," huffed Trudy as she wearily yanked the bell. "I haven't the heart to scold, miss."

Only then did Zoë realize she was lying upon a bed of lumps. She rolled over, patting it tentatively. "You stuffed pillows under the counterpane!" she said, tugging the topmost out in her fist.

Trudy came to the edge of the bed, wringing her hands. "I thought you wouldn't wish anyone to know, miss, that you was out," she said quietly. "I slept on the cot beside, and her ladyship—Lady Rannoch—popped 'er head in round midnight. And then Lord Robert came round—in a terrible state, 'e were, and I made 'im go away again. But I kept quiet, miss, and never let on. Was that right?"

Oh, it was a bad sign when Trudy started dropping her h's. It meant Zoë had pushed her too far. Again. Zoë leapt up and kissed her cheek. "Bless you, Trudy," she said, beginning to unbutton her gown. "I'm sorry to be so wicked. Truly I am."

The maid gave a brittle smile. "You aren't wicked, miss, precisely," she answered. "Just . . . a little wayward— and Lord knows you've a good heart."

"But wayward, *hmm*?" It was a bit of an improvement, Zoë decided, over wicked. "Well, whatever one calls it, I know I've been a trial to you, but I'm thinking of mending my ways. Truly, I am. Now quick, help me get out of this. Have you my black habit to hand?"

Two hours later, Zoë was riding swiftly through Lower Thorpe mounted on a prancing, long-legged gray. Mercer had presented Zoë with the gelding in the forecourt after breakfast, leaning almost inappropriately near as he pressed the reins into her gloved hand.

For an instant, his eyes had flashed, and something hot and knowing had passed between them, sending a rush of heat down her throat. "My mother assures me you know how to manage large, headstrong beasts," he murmured, his eyes suggestive. "I begin to think she may be right. But *do not* make me regret this, Zoë. Zephyr is a handful."

Zoë had managed to smile sweetly. "A great many large, headstrong beasts are, I believe," she murmured.

"Indeed, in some respects, a good deal more than a *handful*."

It had been Mercer's turn to blush.

Now Zoë rode alongside her father at a more sedate pace, Mercer having led them off the main road and onto a broad bridle path. They were situated just behind Mercer and his mother, giving Zoë an unobstructed view of his broad back and shoulders. The gentlemen had dressed today in hunting pinks, Mercer pairing his with tall black boots, their brown tops turned down, and breeches that molded snugly to his powerful thighs. But the long red coat, regrettably, fell well below his cantle, and blocked his very fine arse from Zoë's view.

She sighed a little dejectedly, and settled her gaze instead on the view to her right. They were edging nearer the Channel again, riding along a high, green ridge—a shortcut, Jonet had said, to Stony Manor, Sir William's seat, where the hounds would await. Soon the narrow lane was following the cliffs, sometimes edging breathtakingly near. Zoë looked down at the water, and the undulating ribbon of beach, her head spinning a little.

In addition to Zoë and her father, Greythorpe's party consisted of only the die-hard riders: Mercer and his mother; Mr. Amherst, a former cavalry officer who practically lived in the saddle, and Arabella, who had clearly inherited her parents' love of riding. Robin brought up the rear on a horse she had not seen before, a snorting black stallion who looked like the devil, and was, in fact, called Lucifer.

Zoë would ordinarily have accounted it a victory to see Robin up so bright and early. Yet in this case, she rather feared by the look of him that he mightn't have been to bed at all. The more she thought on this, the more it troubled her.

"I am going to fall back," she said aside to her father, "and ride with Robin."

Her father nodded, but there was no mistaking the banked wrath in his eyes. He was quite obviously still angry with Robin, and Zoë dared not ask him what, if anything, had transpired last night between them.

She pulled Zephyr up on the verge, then waved Arabella and her father past. Riding in front with Jonet, Mercer turned round in his saddle and cut a glance back at Zoë, a flash of irritation in his eyes.

Zoë smiled; then, with a light tap of her heel, moved back into the roadway and drew up alongside Robin. As if taking exception to Lucifer, Zoë's horse jerked, side-stepped for a few paces, then settled uneasily in, tossing his head.

Robin cut a dark look down at him and grunted. "Even your mount doesn't like me."

"Never mind him," she chided. "Robin, have you had any sleep?"

He lifted one shoulder. "Why? Does it matter?"

She looked askance at him. Could she but smell his breath, she was half afraid of what she might find. Oh, this really would not do! Robin could not go on like this; drunk, depressed, and almost desperate.

"I am not at all sure you should be riding, old thing," she murmured. "Turn round and go home. I shan't mind."

"No, I daresay you wouldn't," he said bitterly.

"And what is that supposed to—" Her words fell away as she saw for the first time the dark bruise just visible above the brilliant white edge of his shirt collar. Her mouth must have fallen agape.

"What?" he demanded, shooting a glance at her.

"Is that—" Zoë crooked her head, confused. "That bruise on your neck," she whispered. "Did my father— Good Lord, Robin, did Papa try to *throttle* you?"

At that, Robin looked away, his face coloring furiously. "No, it was . . . an accident," he said. "Never mind what."

Zoë cast an anxious look up ahead at the back of her father's shoulders, and slowed her mount. "Never mind?" she echoed incredulously. "I'm worried my father tried to kill you, and you say *'never mind'*?"

She saw Robin stiffen, saw his hands on the reins contract almost spasmodically. "Perhaps I should ask *you* what happened last night?" he said under his breath. "Tell me, Zoë, did Stu manage to find you? Did he rescue you yet again?"

Zoë jerked her gaze away. "I'm not sure it's any of your business," she said, suddenly suspicious what the bruise was. "And how dare you change the subject, anyway?"

"Oh, the *subject*!" Robin rolled his eyes. "The *subject*, Zoë, is always my heroic brother! I swear to God, that's all anyone ever talks about anymore. Sir Galahad to the rescue, saving Zoë from one of Robin's bollixed-up escapades!"

"Robin." Angrily, Zoë jerked her horse nearer, causing Lucifer's head to toss in disapproval. "No one has *ever* blamed you for my stunts—*ever*. If anything, 'tis the other way round."

"Aye, well, there's blame enough for the both of us,

I daresay." His whispered words were bitter. "Tell me, Zoë, who did Trudy hope to fool with your old pillow trick anyway?"

For an instant, Zoë was stricken. How on earth had he known?

Because he knew her. Because he knew every ruse, wile, and hoax in her vast and well-honed repertoire—indeed, he'd taught her most of them. And the pillows-under-the-counterpane trick was the very least of it.

Robin's face was a mask of agony now, his eyes laced with unfathomable pain. And the worst of it was, it had nothing to do with Mercer. She knew it instinctively. Robin was killing himself with grief, and that grief was sending him down a path of inevitable self-destruction. And she had set it all in motion.

"Robin, listen to me," she said quietly. "We must talk. I know about Mrs. Wilfred. And I think she is why—"

"Oh, save your breath to cool your porridge," Robin cut in. "Maria doesn't give a twopenny damn for me."

"But I think you are in love with her," Zoë whispered.

A look passed over his visage then; something both dark and hopeless. "What of it?" His voice was unsteady. "She has forbidden me ever to contact her again. Indeed, it is the only thing she has ever asked of me, so I shall honor it. And Maria is no longer a topic I will discuss with you, Zoë."

"Robin, it isn't just Mrs. Wilfred," she whispered. Zoë gathered her reins in one hand, and tried to reach for him, but he nudged away. "Please, Robin. Don't shut me out. We are best friends."

He shook his head, and turned his face away, leaving Zoë with the most dreadful suspicion he was blinking back tears. "Listen, Zoë," he rasped when he turned back around, "I don't care if you were with my brother or not. And this bruise"—Here, he rammed a finger under his shirt collar and yanked it savagely down—"for this you can thank Jemima. She got a bit out of hand last night. Not that I took any pleasure in it."

The bruise, Zoë realized, was just a small passion mark. "Robin, I don't care to hear this," she murmured, cutting an uneasy glance at Jonet.

"Don't you?" His eyes were dark with pain, his voice rising, causing heads to turn. "Well, you can listen anyway. To say her talents were wasted is an understatement of epic proportion. That's why I came home early. I thought, you see, that I owed my bride-to-be an apology."

"Keep your voice down," said Zoë quietly. "Yes, you owe me an apology, just as I owe you—"

But it was too late. Jonet had wheeled her mount around and was headed toward Robin.

"Ride up ahead and open Sir William's gate," she snapped, her eyes flashing, "since you seem to have plenty of wind."

"Aye, madam." With a bitter smile, Robin tugged at his hat brim as if he were a servant, then spurred Lucifer hard. Zephyr again took exception, and went dancing sideways, tossing his head angrily. Thank God the path had turned from the coastline and up a steep, wooded lane. Lucifer bolted through the middle of the riders, brushing past Arabella almost dangerously, and sending her horse skittering off the path.

Jonet's eyes glittered with rage. Tapping her mount, she surged through and set off after him, her crop held tight as if she meant to use it. Humiliated, it took all of

Zoë's will to settle the gray back down. By the time they reached the gate, he was stepping neatly again, but his ears were still back, his eyes uneasy. Robin stood holding the gate open, but Jonet had vanished.

Soon they were riding past a stone stable block, and beside it a vast kennel, the hounds barking and bounding madly about. Zoë could hear even more racket beyond; the sharp barks of dogs eager to be off. The farm lane turned sharply, zigzagging round a low, ornamental fence dividing a strip of lawn from the pasture. Up ahead, Zoë could see a lushly landscaped garden surrounding a pretty manor house.

In the graveled carriageway Sir William and a dozen mostly red-coated riders milled about, leading their mounts. Amidst them was the huntsman and a pair of helpers, awash to their thighs in leggy young foxhounds whose black-and-tan markings gleamed in the sunshine.

"Good morning, good morning!" Sir William led his mount forward to greet them, one hand raised. "Young Edward has an hour's start on us, so I think we're almost ready to see what these pups can do."

Jonet had dismounted, and was looking over the dogs with Francis Ware. Lady Shankling was crossing the lawn, clearly not dressed for riding. Mercer rode through, and he and Mr. Amherst also dismounted, bowing politely to their hostess.

Just then, Robin caught up with them, bringing the big black horse up too fast, and halting in a skitter of gravel, almost as if he wished to give offense. And it worked. Zephyr chose that moment to wheel nervously about, pawing at the carriageway. Then, as if to emphasize his distress, the horse reared a few feet, then set himself down again, snorting and shaking his head.

Despite the sidesaddle, Zoë hung on and reined him back around to face Robin, but Zephyr was growing edgy, clearly sensing the tide of emotion. "Shush, laddie, shush," she crooned, slicking a hand along his withers.

She returned her gaze to Robin, but at that very moment, Francis Ware edged nearer on a broad-chested hunter. "One might think your horse is itching for a race, Miss Armstrong," he shouted over the din of the hounds. "Perhaps that black beast of Lord Robert's will oblige you?"

Zoë laughed. "Ah, Mr. Ware, you have learned my propensity for leading poor Robin astray," she called back, trying to diffuse the tension. "Alas, I'm riding side-saddle today."

Anger flashed across Robin's face. "God damn it, I've had enough of this," he gritted, cutting Lucifer around. "I think I *shall* leave. Go flirt with Ware—or try Stuart again."

Zoë reined around to follow him. "Robin, what has got into you?" she said, keeping her voice down. "Ware was just teasing me."

His lips thinned. "No, he's dredging up last night's dinner conversation, and I'm sick of hearing about Stuart's heroics."

"No one mentioned anyone's heroics, Robin."

"They don't have to," he gritted. "And if I am going to have to marry you, Zoë, my brother is off limits, do you hear?" he whispered. "And don't say you weren't with him last night. I *know* it. I sense it."

Zoë began to tremble. "And what if I was?" she hissed. "What if he was there for me when you were not?"

"Then marry *him*," Robin snapped. "Oh, wait! I forgot about good old Claire! Wouldn't she brew up a right stinking scandal broth with that!"

"Robin, you are drunk," she whispered. "Do hush, or let us go home together."

"Why don't you just try and catch me?" Then he raised his voice, and lifted his crop. "Come on, then! Let's go, by God!"

Zoë did not grasp his intent until Robin's crop came down with a sharp *crack!* and sent his mount bolting back down the farm lane. For an instant she watched, mouth open. Zephyr reared beneath her again. As he reached the turn, Robin did not cut his horse away from the ornamental fence. Instead, cracking his whip again, he went sailing over it.

Good Lord, Robin was apt to kill himself!

Zoë's eyes swept the crowd. No one else save Francis was mounted—or watching. Unthinkingly, she tapped Zephyr's flanks hard. The big horse surged. Robin took the next fence with equal abandon, clearing it easily. The gate, however—

Dear God. Did he remember the gate?

Or was he so distraught he mightn't? The big gray rolled beneath her, emotion propelling them both. They were coming up on the low fence, hooves pounding. Zoë had to decide. Acting on instinct, she tucked herself low, and let the big gray fly. They sailed over as one, her knee hooked hard. In a few bounds, the second was upon her. Somehow Zoë clung on, cursing her sidesaddle to hell.

She could not possibly take the farm gate—but then, no one could.

Zoë tapped Zephyr's flanks hard, leaned over his withers and sent the beast flying. It was no use. Robin was barreling back down the hill. The big black was at a flat-out run.

"Robin!" she cried. "Robin, *the gate*!"

He did not hear. Her heart in her throat, Zoë followed. The gray thundered on, every muscle pumping in unison. They drove into the turn. Robin was ten lengths ahead now. The gate rose up, tall and impervious. Robin did not falter. "*Stop!*" she screamed. "*Stop*, you cannot take it!"

Lucifer thought otherwise. Robin spurred him again, and the great beast leapt, sailing high and clear, Robin's red coattails flying out behind.

Then, at the last instant, something went horribly wrong. A snag—the merest fraction of a hoof. A frightful crack rent the air, splintering wood. Lucifer's hip twisted. The horse touched down awkwardly, pitching Robin headlong. After that, everything happened in a flash. There was a tangle of legs and hooves. The horse flew over Robin, pummeling him. Robin's limbs flailed about like a tangle of rags.

"*Robin—!*"

Blind with terror, Zoë drew the gray up sharp and went hurtling from the saddle. Beyond the gate, Lucifer was pounding down the farm track, reins flying free. Robin lay in a lifeless heap. One leg was twisted beneath him, his arms outstretched. Zoë could see red. *Red, red, everywhere.* Clawing at the gate, she fell to her knees.

Moments later, a tide of red coats came surging round her. Someone was still screaming.

"Miss Armstrong! Miss Armstrong!" A gloved hand touched her mouth. The screaming stopped.

"We must open the gate, child." Strong, stout arms came round her, picked her up. Dragged her back, ripping her hands from the gate. Francis Ware jerked frantically at the latch.

Zoë looked up into Sir William's eyes, and saw the horror there. The gate swung wide on squalling hinges. The red coats went surging through, and half the dogs with them, barking madly. Everything came as if through a fog, her knees knocking.

"Get a cart!"

"Blankets, Jim! Quick!"

" 'E's losing a lot er blood, sir. Give me yer neckcloth."

And then Jonet was on her knees in the dirt, her black-gloved hand clamped over her mouth as she bent over Robin. Sir William let Zoë go.

Mercer loomed up beside her, still clutching his crop, trembling. "You just had to egg him on, didn't you?" he rasped.

Zoë opened her mouth to speak, to defend herself, but nothing came out.

And it little mattered. Robin lay dying. Mercer had strode on past. He pushed through the crowd, then slowly knelt at his brother's side. Then, bowing his head, he set his thumb and forefinger against his eyes, his face twisting with grief.

Zoë watched him, and began to pray.

Chapter Twelve

A QUIET VIGIL.

*I*t was full dark that evening before Jonet left Robin's bedside, her head down, her every motion speaking of a bone-deep sorrow. They were gathered across the hall in a small gentlemen's reading parlor; Zoë and her parents, Sir William and the Wares, along with Donaldson and Mr. Amherst, both of whom had been in and out of Robin's room all afternoon.

Mr. Amherst and Zoë's father went at once to Jonet's side, taking her arms, for she appeared near collapse.

"Is there any change, my dear?" Amherst asked. "Anything at all?"

But Jonet merely shook her head, and sank into a chair. "Stuart is with him now," she said, her voice almost inaudible. "Robin appears insensible, but ... but Dr. Bevins is not certain. He wishes to speak with me out here."

Evangeline, whose hand had covered Zoë's all afternoon, gave her fingers a comforting squeeze. Drawing it away, Zoë rose and went to kneel by her cousin's chair. "Oh, Jonet, I am so sorry," she said, her voice catching on a sob. "I thought only to stop him. Not to drive him on. Truly, *truly*, I did not."

Jonet covered Zoë's hand with her own where it lay upon the chair arm. "It was a terrible tragedy, child," she managed. "You are no more to blame than any of us. Robin is just—" Here, she turned to her husband, her face crumpling. "Oh, God, Cole, he is just so headstrong!"

On that, a pitiful whimper escaped her lips, and her hand flew to her mouth. Mr. Amherst knelt to settle an arm round her shoulder and she looked at him with fathomless sorrow in her eyes.

"It is all right, Zoë," he murmured, looking not at her, but at his wife. "No one blames you for this."

"Mercer does." Zoë rose, her head hanging. "He thinks I pushed Robin."

Francis Ware jerked from his seat. "This is all my fault," he uttered, his gaze flying to Jonet's. "My lady, truly, I was just teasing them. But Robin—why, he just exploded, and I . . . well, I froze."

Jonet lifted her watery gaze. "Oh, Francis, please do not—"

But at that moment, the bedchamber door opened again. Zoë could see Mercer, still standing rigidly by Robin's bed, hands clasped behind his back, his head bowed, just as he'd stood the whole of the afternoon.

The doctor came out, a battered brown satchel in hand, his face a mask of grief and fatigue.

"Any news, Bevins?" asked Amherst, rising anxiously. "Any . . . sign of consciousness?"

The doctor shook his head. "No, sir," he answered. "But it may be God's mercy. Lord Mercer has helped me restore the dislocated hip. Still, if he wakes—"

"*If* he wakes?" Jonet cried.

Amherst pulled her close.

"If he wakes, my lady," the doctor continued quietly, "then the pain will be severe. Indeed, he shan't be able to walk for a time. As to the arm, I think it fractured, but not badly, for which we must thank God. But bruises are forming, and by tomorrow . . . well, I fear you must prepare yourself, Lady Kildermore. Lord Robert is going to look a fright."

"But bruises . . ." she uttered. "Bruises will heal, will they not?"

The doctor slowly nodded. "One hopes," he murmured. "But internally . . . there is no knowing. Organs may well be ruptured, and if that be the case . . . well, we shall know before the night is out, I daresay."

"If he is going to wake up, Bevins," asked Amherst stridently, "how long will it be?"

But it was clear from the doctor's expression that he had grave doubts. Another sickening wave of grief rolled over Zoë, and she sank back into her chair. She was trembling uncontrollably again.

"There is no knowing, I'm afraid," the doctor hedged. "Lord Robert has taken a terrible blow to the head, and it appears one hoof caught him full in the face. The resultant gash, well, it is quite deep. But I have sutured it as best I can, and the bleeding has stopped."

"Is there a danger of infection?" Amherst demanded. "Will he take a fever?"

Fever, Zoë knew, was a soldier's greatest fear. Men who survived their injuries on the battlefield died, more often than not, from the raging infection that set in after.

A look of weary resignation sketched over the doctor's face. "In truth, sir, infection is the least of our worries," he finally answered. "But facial lacerations—even deep ones—are not prone to infection like, say, a saber wound or a gunshot."

"Thank God," said Amherst, his shoulders relaxing.

"I have left you a tincture of laudanum, Lady Kildermore, should Lord Robert begin to stir," said the doctor. "I have explained to your nurse how it must be given."

"She knows," said Jonet swiftly. "Nanna is very skilled."

"Yes." Bevins smiled faintly. "She has gone down to prepare some poultices which she believes will help."

"Will they?" asked Jonet, one hand going to her throat.

"They cannot hurt," said the doctor quietly. "At this point, I will take all the help I can get."

With that, the doctor left, advising he would return the following morning unless there was a change in the night. With solemn words and sympathetic gestures, Sir William and the Wares soon followed suit. Jonet implored the rest of them to go down to dinner, then returned to Robin's bedside.

Zoë went reluctantly, swamped with grief, and feeling that it was wrong of her to go; that she should have stayed, and done . . . something. But what? And for whom?

Mercer clearly did not want her there. When he had deigned to glance at her, his message could not have been clearer. They were a family. And she was not part of it. He had not leaned upon her, nor turned to her in even the smallest way. And she did not blame him. This was her fault; all of it. Francis Ware could say what he wished, but Zoë knew the truth.

Her every action—and seemingly every breath she'd drawn—since that awful night in Brook Street had sent all of them recklessly careening toward this tragedy.

Now the only thing that mattered to any of them was Robin, and he lay near death, his body as broken as his heart. Even if he woke, would he wish to live? She must do all she could, Zoë realized, to ensure it.

"I beg you will excuse me," she said to her parents at the top of the stairs. "I find I have no appetite."

Evangeline set an arm about her shoulders. "Come, my dear, just bear us company."

Zoë shook her head. "No," she said softly. "No, I have something I must do. Something . . . pressing."

Her parents exchanged odd glances, then Evangeline slipped her arm away. Zoë's father gave her a swift, hard embrace. "Good night, then, lass," he murmured. "We must hope for a better tomorrow."

Zoë returned to the shadowy silence of her bedchamber, lay down upon the bed, and let the darkness fall around her as her tears came slow and steady. After the rush of grief began to wane, she gathered her thoughts carefully, sorting out what she knew must be done from the blind panic that earlier had raged.

When this was settled in her own mind—when she had a plan—Zoë rose, washed her face in cold water, then went to her desk to light a candle. After drawing a sheet of letter paper from the drawer, she dipped her pen into her ink pot, and began to expiate her sins.

"No one is up yet, miss," Trudy fumed the next morning. "There's no breakfast laid out, nor even the draperies drawn!"

Zoë had slept little, passing much of the night curled in a ball again, sobbing her heart out as Trudy lay beside her. Now she stood looking through her window at the wood that was slowly materializing from the gloom, while Trudy did up the buttons of her oldest, plainest morning gown.

Seen in the edging light of dawn, sobbing seemed an exercise in futility; a self-indulgence that did nothing to help Robin, nor to comfort his family. It did not begin to make amends for what she had done. It made not one step toward repairing her friendship with Mercer. Instead, it served only to redden her nose and swell her eyes, for Zoë was not one of those women who cried prettily.

Now, with her hands clenched and her stomach in a knot, she was nonetheless resolved. "I cannot sleep," she said. "And I cannot wait. I am going to Robin's room."

"It mightn't be thought seemly, miss," Trudy warned, pushing the last button through. "Her ladyship will be most put out with me for letting you go."

Zoë set a hand on Trudy's shoulder. "You cannot stop me, Trudy," she said quietly. "And my mother will know that. Besides, I think we are all quite beyond worrying about my reputation."

Trudy had the good grace not to answer that. Instead, she lowered her gaze and stepped aside.

Zoë paused long enough to seize the letter from her writing desk, then pressed it into Trudy's hands. "I need you to post this for me," she said, rummaging for some coins. "Do not ask Papa to frank it, but take it to the village yourself. Will you do that for me, Tru?"

Trudy glanced down at Zoë's hastily scratched direction. "Oh, miss," she said quietly. "What on earth have you done?"

"Just never you mind," said Zoë, handing her some

coins. "Then, when I get caught, you can claim ignorance."

"Oh, miss," said Trudy again. "I think you are making a mistake."

"No, I am setting one to rights," Zoë muttered, "insofar as I can."

With that, she hastened out into the corridor, only to discover that someone was indeed awake. To her shock, her parents stood near the foot of the stairs, their heads bent in quiet conversation.

Zoë hastened toward them, her heart in her throat. "Papa!" she whispered. "Evie! Oh, please, do not say—"

Her father gathered her to his side. "Robert has lived the night," he said quietly. "He is unchanged."

"But he lives." Zoë swallowed hard and looked up at her stepmother. "That is something, isn't it? We must thank God."

Evangeline's face was uncharacteristically drawn, her eyes brimming with sympathy. "My dear, you have not slept," she murmured, stroking a hand down Zoë's cheek.

There was nothing to say to that. "You were coming to my room," said Zoë. "Why?"

Her parents exchanged awkward glances. Rannoch cleared this throat. "Your mother and I have decided we should leave today," he said. "We are in the way here. Ask Trudy to pack your things."

"Papa, no!" Zoë pulled away. "No, how can you even think of going when Robin is so ill?"

"It is because Robin is ill," he said gently. "Jonet has her hands full. As much as she cares for us, she does not need a houseful of guests just now."

Evangeline leaned nearer. "Zoë, I think it best."

"No, we cannot go!" Zoë cried. "Not until Robin wakes up. I—why, I have to talk to him. I must see that he is going to be well again."

"Zoë," said her stepmother softly, "it is quite possible that Robin is not going to wake up."

"I won't believe that!" she cried. "And you—why, you mustn't even think it! Really, Evie, I believe you don't know Robin at all. He is strong. He will get well."

"But he mightn't, lass, and I fear that is what the doctor was trying to tell Jonet last night," Rannoch gently countered. "Young Robert is badly hurt, and even should he wake, he might never be the man he was. Do you understand me, Zoë?"

She had gone cold, as if her blood had ceased to circulate. But now was not the time to show weakness. "I understand," she whispered, stepping back a pace. "I understand that you are trying to help Jonet, and protect me, and I thank you. But I am not a child anymore, Papa. I am a woman grown. And I am still Robin's fiancée. What would it say to the world if I go running back to London now, and leave him here to die?"

Again, a strange look passed between her parents. "We are underfoot, Zoë," her father pressed. "So long as the six of us and all our servants remain, Jonet will feel the obligation of hospitality."

"You are quite right," Zoë murmured, her gaze turned suddenly inward. "Of course you are. You must go. I shall stay. Trudy will stay with me."

"Oh, Zoë," said her stepmother, "I do not think—"

"No." Zoë set her head at a stubborn angle. "After

Robin wakes up—after he is up and about again—then, why, you can send a carriage back for me."

At that, Evangeline and her father exchanged assessing glances. A strange look passed over Rannoch's face, then one of his big shoulders lifted ever so lightly. And Zoë knew that she had won—won at least this small victory.

Her father dragged a hand through his thick, dark hair. "It is up to Jonet, then," he said quietly. "If she can make use of you . . . then it is up to her."

Zoë rushed down the stairs and along the twisting corridors to Robin's room, relief surging through her. He was alive. She had truly feared the worst upon seeing her parents by the stairs, and her guilt had been fleetingly forgotten as the grief had rushed in. *But he was alive.* Whatever she had done, whatever she had caused, at least Robin yet drew breath.

At Robin's door, she paused to give only the slightest of knocks, then went in without hesitation. Mercer sat by the bed in his shirtsleeves, his elbows propped upon his knees as he leaned forward, hands clasped. Attired in a cream-colored dressing gown, Jonet lay next to Robin on the bed, her hands folded beneath her cheek, her gaze fixed upon his battered face.

Both turned upon hearing her enter. Instinctively the gentleman, Mercer rose, his visage etched with exhaustion. In the lamplight, his face was shadowed with black stubble, his eyes swollen and shot with red. They lit upon her face, inscrutable yet tinged with grief. His tall riding boots, she saw, lay tossed in a corner, his red coat flung across a chair. And as she stood there at the foot of Robin's bed, her hands gripped tightly before her, Zoë had the most dreadful feeling that if she did not say something—if she let this awful silence linger—things would never be right between them again.

Oh, she had no hope of salvaging whatever they had begun that night in the summerhouse. But his affection, however distant, and his regard, whatever might be left of it—oh, those things she would not lightly surrender. For without them, her heart would surely, surely break.

So she went round the corner of the bed, and set a hand on his arm. "You are a good brother," she said quietly. "You *are*. And you have been here all night, with no rest, and not even a mouthful of food. But Mercer, no man—not even one such as you—can long go on like this."

He sighed, the air shuddering out of his lungs. "I have no appetite," he said, his voice raspy as if from disuse. "Nor can I leave him."

Zoë let her hand slide down his arm to take his hand. He did not flinch, nor strike out at her as she had feared he might. He was beaten. Emotionally exhausted.

"You *must* go," she said. "You must rest. And you must do it for Robin's sake. For he will need all of your strength in the days ahead. You'll do him no good if you collapse."

Mercer opened his mouth, shook his head, then closed it again.

"Then at least sit back down," Zoë softly ordered.

To her shock, Mercer did so.

Jonet lifted her head. "She is right, my dear," she said quietly. "Robin has lived this night. He can live another.

And another. And I will need you as much as Robin does."

And still he remained, unmoved. But Zoë had not been thrown out on her ear as she deserved, which gave her hope. She edged nearer. "How is his breathing?" she whispered. "Is it steady?"

Jonet gave a faint nod, her long hair scrubbing on the pillow. Then, ever so lightly, she brushed the back of her hand down Robin's face—the half that was not laid open by a horrific gash from temple to jaw.

"My poor, beautiful boy!" she whispered. "He will never be beautiful again, will he? Even his beloved Mrs. Wilfred will not want him now."

Zoë felt herself tremble with sudden anger. "Then Mrs. Wilfred is not worthy of the grief she has caused him," she returned, her voice hoarse with emotion. "If a scar and a few bruises are all it takes to dissuade her affections, better he should know it now. Better never to be loved at all, I should say, than to be loved by someone so inconstant."

She bit off the last of her words, a little shocked by her vehemence. Even Mercer's eyes had widened with surprise. And it wasn't just a few bruises. Robin's face, his throat, his hands; every bit of visible flesh was purpling now. Moreover, it was entirely likely Mrs. Wilfred *was* inconstant; doubtless Robin, like most men of Zoë's acquaintance, chose his lovers with his eyes, not his heart.

But Jonet had sat up a little abruptly on the bed, it having dawned on her precisely what she'd suggested. "Forgive me, Zoë," she murmured, setting a shaking hand to her forehead. "I . . . I was not thinking."

"Because you are tired, and because it does not signify," said Zoë quietly. "Truly, Jonet. I know Robin loves her. His feelings have become all too apparent, have they not? And if she no longer loves him—sadly, I fear you'll be proved right in that regard—then I am sorry for it. Deeply sorry. If I had known . . . but there—if wishes were horses, beggars would ride, wouldn't they?"

Jonet's gaze passed to Mercer, but he said nothing.

Just then, the door opened again, and Jonet's elderly nurse came in carrying a tray with two big bowls and a pile of linen strips.

Out of deference, Zoë gave a little bob. "Good morning, Nanna," she said. "Have you brought some of your special concoctions?"

"Aye, Miss Zoë, 'tis fresh comfrey," said the old woman. "And arnica for the swelling."

Jonet cut the nurse a look of affection. "Nanna has been at it much of the night," she said, "with her compresses and poultices."

"Aye, and my prayers," said Nanna.

"Just now he needs them," said Mercer, dragging a hand through his hair. "Bevins will be back at nine. Perhaps . . . Perhaps he will offer us a little more hope."

"Och, laddie, there's always hope," the old woman grumbled, her black, raisinlike eyes suddenly flashing. "And doctors—*hmph!*—they don't know owt but how tae come in here an' fash your poor mither. Death's door, 'pon my soul!"

The old woman was bustling about the room now, pouring out hot water, setting out her bowls, and generally taking charge of the room like a sergeant major, though Zoë knew she had to be near eighty. Indeed,

Nanna had been old for as long as Zoë had known her. Once she had been as round as she was tall, but age had stripped the flesh from her bones and gnarled her fingers with rheumatism.

Still, she was a comfort to Jonet. One could see it in the faint lift of Jonet's shoulders. She had risen and gone to the window, which was cast now in a cold, gray light, and for a moment, she seemed to let her attention wander, as if Nanna's presence lessened her fear.

"I wonder if the children slept?" she murmured. "They were so distraught last night."

"Shall I go and check on them, ma'am?" Zoë offered.

Jonet shook her head. "Cole is with them. He will not have left their sides."

"No, no, to be sure."

"We might have a little more rain, thank God," Jonet murmured absently, pulling back the drapery. "But the roads will grow muddy by afternoon."

Zoë edged nearer. "My parents are leaving this morning," she said quietly.

"Aye, Rannoch suggested as much last night." Jonet turned from the window with a sad smile, the ashen light casting her face in muted shadow. "I am sorry, child. This has been a tragedy no one could have foreseen."

"Jonet, I am not a child," said Zoë softly. "If I ever was . . . well, I am not now."

Jonet smiled faintly. "No, you are not," she agreed. "I sometimes forget that."

Zoë leaned nearer, and took Jonet's hand. "As to leaving Greythorpe," she said, "I don't mean to go with them. I mean to stay, and be of help to you. Truly, I am not as useless as some people think me."

Behind her, she heard Mercer's chair creak. Heard his soft footfalls approach. "Zoë, there is no need for you to watch this," he said, his voice low and still raspy. "It does no good."

She turned around, and looked him in the eyes. "No good for whom?" she said. "I can sit with Robin and apply poultices—Nanna can show me how. And I am his fiancée." Zoë returned her gaze to Jonet. "Until Robin wakes up and says otherwise, I am still his fiancée, am I not? So I wish to help."

Surprisingly, Jonet's gaze flew to her son. Mercer had crossed the room to the door.

"Zoë," he said darkly, "I wish to see you outside."

Well, there was to be no avoiding it. Perhaps Mercer had every right to rail at her, but Zoë meant to stand her ground.

"Of course," she said.

Cutting one last look at Jonet, Zoë picked up her skirts and crossed the room, swishing past him and into the corridor. Mercer closed the door with an ominous *thud*. He took her arm a little too roughly, and hauled her across the passageway into the parlor.

"Zoë, what in hell's name are you talking about?" He towered over her in his stocking feet, his hands set stubbornly upon his narrow hips. With his dark stubble, flashing eyes, and tousled hair, he looked thoroughly disreputable—and faintly dangerous.

Zoë lifted her chin, but her voice was gentle. "Mercer, I am not just a useless ornament to hang upon a gentleman's arm," she said. "I am not stupid. And I *am* still Robin's fiancée. And yes, I know, too, that in a roundabout way, this is all my fault."

Again, he dragged a hand through his hair, leaving Zoë to wonder if he was soon to wear a path through it. "Zoë, it's just . . . just that you cannot stay here."

There was no fight left in Zoë, just steely determination. "It is your house, Mercer," she said quietly. "There is no question of that. You may throw me out, and my baggage behind me if you wish, but that is what it will take."

In three strides, he closed the distance between them, and set a firm hand on her arm. "Do not put words in my mouth, Zoë," he gritted, his bloodshot eyes flashing. "I never said I would throw you out. I never said that."

"Then I mean to stay," she said calmly. "Unless my presence here causes you—or your mother—insufferable pain, then I mean to stay. And you may continue to blame me for all of this if you wish. None of that matters to me now."

Mercer felt the earth suddenly sliding from beneath his feet; felt the fatigue dragging him down into that abysmal black hole of guilt and fear he kept crawling his way out of. *None of that mattered?* And just where did he fall? Did *he* matter? Worse, how could he even wonder such a thing when his brother lay near death?

Little more than a day ago, Mercer's life had seemed impossibly complicated, yet at once rich with promise. Now it felt like a series of unbearable tragedies. No, he did not want Zoë here. And no, he couldn't bear to see her go, either. *Did* he blame her? Or did he simply blame himself? Assuredly he was shutting her out—to punish himself, perhaps. It scarcely mattered. Zoë clearly meant to put up a fight, but what was she fighting for? For him? Or for Robin?

Christ, he couldn't think about all this just now. As his mother said, Robin had lived the night. He could live another, and another after that. In the meantime, it fell to Mercer to be strong, to get all of them through this. To think not of himself, or of the distant future, but only of Robin's tomorrow.

And now here was Zoë, offering up herself; claiming that she was still engaged—engaged to a man who would be lucky to live to see another day, let alone rise from his bed a whole and healthy man. Was that why she now clung desperately to a betrothal that, mere hours ago, she had vowed to forswear? Was it pure guilt?

Slowly, he released her arm, horrified to see the harsh red marks beneath his fingers. "Zoë, I am sorry," he managed. "Robin does not love you. Not like that."

"Mercer, I know that," she said, dipping her head as if to catch his gaze. "And I accept it. But I cannot cast him aside now, nor would you wish me to. I would be no better than what I called Mrs. Wilfred, would I?"

She was right. He dragged his hand through his hair again, and began to pace the parlor. The sun was fully up now, the house beginning to come to life with the sound of draperies being drawn and the clatter of breakfast trays being carried up by his army of servants. Everything was normal. And yet nothing was. His heart was breaking all over again, and he wasn't sure why.

Zoë caught his arm, and forced him round to face her. "Mercer, you need to rest," she said firmly. "Go to your room, try to eat something, then go to sleep. Do you hear me? When the doctor arrives, I will wake you. I promise."

He exhaled slowly, perhaps a bit of the grief going out

of him. Inexplicably, he trusted her. "And you . . . you will not leave him?"

She shook her head solemnly, her gaze locked with his. "I will not leave him," she said. "So long as Robin needs me, I will not leave him."

And that, thought Mercer, *was just what he was afraid of. . . .*

Chapter Thirteen

IN WHICH NANNA
TAKES CHARGE.

$\mathcal{I}$n the end, however, Dr. Bevins was of little further use to anyone, though he came and went over the following days with the best of intentions, and an appropriately solemn demeanor. According to modern medical knowledge, Robin would either wake, or he would not. He would either live, or he would die. Nothing more was known, and thus the matter of his recovery was placed—at Jonet's insistence—into Nanna's capable hands.

No other servant, save for Charlie Donaldson, was permitted into Robin's room. Jonet was schooled in crisis and—when it came to protecting her children—steeped in mistrust. Perhaps it was the clannish Scot in her, or perhaps the treachery which had once surrounded her family. Whatever it was, over a period of several days, it fell to Zoë's advantage, and the household fell into a strained pattern. Zoë and Nanna sat with Robin during the day, whilst Mercer and his mother stayed at night, alternating in shifts by his bedside. Mr. Amherst worked with Dr. Bevins in dealing with the smallpox that still raged, and spent the rest of his time consoling his wife and daughters.

Zoë shut out any thought of the future by looking no further than the next day, and by keeping herself as busy as was humanly possible. It was not hard. In addition to routine care, there were countless heaps of comfrey to be ground, linen to be cut, willow bark to be steeped, and bandages to be changed—and so she did.

If anyone thought it improper that an unwed female should tend a sickbed, they made no mention of it. Certainly Nanna did not; the finer points of rank and sex and decorum were refreshingly beyond the old woman's grasp. Like the practical woman she was, Nanna expected whoever was at hand to serve.

Twice a day, Nanna would go into the stillroom belowstairs to stir and grind and brew all manner of concoctions. When Donaldson was available, Zoë began to go along. Under Nanna's tutelage, Zoë learned to boil barley water, and how to properly sieve a beef tea. Then she learned how to put all of it down Robin's throat without choking him—the latter involving a great many pillows, and a vast deal of patience.

On the fourth evening following Robin's accident, she was trickling a stout chicken broth into his cheek when Lord Mercer came into the room almost two hours earlier than usual. He came to stand at the other side of the bed near the window.

"No change?" he asked hollowly.

Zoë shook her head. "But he is resting comfortably."

It was how they began every conversation nowadays, though Zoë wondered how long a man could go on thus, broken and insensible, with no nutrition to speak of. She had not the heart to muse upon it aloud. Instead, as she spooned the broth, Zoë watched Mercer as he glanced toward the darkening window. His eyes were tired, his broad shoulders slumped. During their weeks at Greythorpe, amidst all the difficulties thrust upon him, he had neglected to cut his thick brown hair and it now lay softly over his collar.

As he had done for the last two evenings, Mercer began to strip down to his shirtsleeves almost absently, tossing his coat and even his waistcoat over a chair, just as any gentleman might do in the privacy of his own rooms. As if theirs was the most intimate of acquaintances.

And in a way, it was. Could one be any more intimate than they had been together? The memory of it was ever with her—even throughout these awful days—tucked away in a secret place. Even now she wished to go to him, hold him, and tell him that all would be well. Zoë forced her eyes away, shame flooding over her. Robin lay half dead—her fault, in part—and she thought only of comforting his brother.

And yet a part of her was not just sorry for Robin, but angry with him, too. One way or another, Zoë meant to get him well again, she vowed. She would massage his muscles and pour broth down his throat until one of them keeled over from the effort. And as soon as he was recovered, she meant to slap him a cracking good blow across his cheek—the uninjured one, of course—for putting all of them through this. She was desperately sorry he'd lost his Mrs. Wilfred, but one could never give up hope. Robin was a better man than that.

As if sensing her frustration, Mercer turned from the window, his jaw lifted, one finger tugging at the knot of his neckcloth to loosen it. "Why don't you go?" he murmured. "I am here for the evening. Have a decent dinner instead of a tray."

WICKED ALL DAY 313

Zoë looked up to see something that might have been gratitude in his eyes. And she was grateful, too—grateful he did not claim this wasn't her cross to bear. It was, and she grieved for Robin as deeply as anyone.

But Mercer was still looking at her, and offering her yet another olive branch. "Thank you," she said, swiftly lowering her gaze. "Let me just get the rest of this broth into him, and see what further Nanna wishes done."

Mercer leaned a little over the bed. "Might I help?"

Zoë flicked a quick look up from the bowl. "You can draw down the bedcovers," she suggested, "and move his legs a bit."

Mercer did so, cutting an odd look in her direction. Robin's legs were long and well formed, and completely bare beneath his nightshirt.

"Just lift them up in turn," she instructed matter-of-factly. "Bend the knee, and flex the ankles. Nanna says it will keep him from going stiff, but mind the right hip."

Mercer lifted the left leg a little gingerly. "Do you do this?" he asked as he rolled the ankle round.

Zoë shrugged. "Nanna hasn't the strength," she answered, "though she doesn't wish anyone to know it. Donaldson helps."

"But Charlie is . . . well, he is a man."

Zoë dropped the spoon into the bowl with a clatter. "And this is about . . . what, precisely?" she asked, cutting a sharp glance up at him. "Propriety? My delicate sensibilities?—for I assure you, Mercer, I haven't an ounce of the latter, and could scarce care less about the former."

Mercer laid Robin's leg down. "I know that, Zoë," he

said softly. "It's just that his legs are a dead weight. You don't seem strong enough."

"Oh, I am strong enough," she said in a firm, low undertone. "I sometimes think, Mercer, that you do not grasp just how strong I am."

Mercer said no more, but came round the bed to stand beside her, and lifted the right leg, this time very carefully. "Shall I move his good arm, then?" he asked when he had gingerly worked it.

"Move anything that isn't broken," Zoë advised. "Then rub up the blood in his muscles—those which are not bruised. Anything to keep the blood moving."

Mercer worked in silence for a time, observing as Zoë leaned over his brother, tending him with a touch which was unerringly gentle. Watching her small, slender hands, now a little raw from working in the stillroom, he wondered if he really knew her at all.

What did she feel for Robin? Devotion, certainly. She proved it, day after day. But had there ever been anything like romantic love on her part? Or was it no more than Robin had claimed—an abiding friendship, and a flirtation that had got out of hand?

But he would not ask. Not now.

Over the years, Mercer had come to believe many things about Zoë—that she was spoiled and a little vain. That she was too flirtatious, too beautiful for her own good, and more effervescent than was strictly decorous. But she seemed none of those things now. And perhaps she never had been, or perhaps he had magnified her faults to justify keeping his distance from something he sensed was a danger to his peace of mind.

Well, he hadn't any peace of mind now. And so long as

he loved Zoë, he never would. He accepted that. But true to her word, Zoë had stayed by Robin's side nearly her every waking moment. Nonetheless, when he entered the room, he could sense the wariness in her.

She claimed he did not know her strength, and perhaps she was right. Perhaps that which he'd always taken for recalcitrance was instead tenacity. Or perhaps Zoë had simply grown up when he wasn't looking. And if he did not know her strength, she most assuredly did not know his weakness. No one did.

Between his shoulders and his stepfather's, the whole of his family's world was propped up. Mercer did not permit himself so much as a tear—not until his mother slept and the household lay in silence. It was then that the almost crippling sense of loss would come over him. He cried for his brother; for the vigorous and happy young man he'd been. And perhaps he cried, too, for what he'd almost had—for the thing, now feared lost, which he'd sworn he never wanted.

He did not realize he had stopped working until he felt Zoë's gaze upon him, intent and unflinching.

"Do not imagine, Mercer, that I cannot know how you feel." She held the bowl again in the palm of her hand, the tiny spoon aloft. "You are a man who commands nearly everyone and everything around you, and yet you cannot control what must surely be a near unbearable pain."

For an instant, her remarks felt as incisive as a razor's blade, and so near the truth he had to bite back his sharp words of denial. Instead, he let his gaze trail down Robin's limp form. "What is my unbearable pain to my brother's?" he finally said. "Tell me, Zoë. I am alive, and walking about on two legs whilst he . . . he may never be."

She set the bowl aside, and wiped her hands on her smock. "You cannot blame yourself," she said. "I am sorry, Mercer—more sorry than I can say—for everything I've done to bring Robin to this terrible place. But I did not cause him to bolt on that horse, nor did you. He was drunk—too drunk to be on horseback—and apparently I was the only person who saw it."

Mercer seized hold of the footboard, his fingers curling hard against the wood. "Zoë, just . . . *don't.*"

But she had risen, and come round the bed beside him. "And I will tell you what else I am not sorry for," she said, her voice low and tremulous. "I am not sorry I gave myself to you."

"Zoë, please . . ."

He closed his eyes, and prayed she did not touch him. It had been hell to come here half a dozen times a day to watch his brother withering before his very eyes, and beside his limp and broken body, the woman whose embrace and comfort he yearned for.

Her voice was as gentle as her touch. "You may be sorry, and if so, I accept that as a penance I must pay," she went on, her small hand cool against his cheek. "But I am not sorry. I will never be sorry. *We* are not what caused Robin to get hurt."

"Zoë, I don't know." He steeled himself to her touch, his voice sounding choked and foreign, even to him. "I don't know what's happened to any of us. I know only that my brother lies half dead, and that I cannot bear the thought of losing him."

"It is not your fault," she said again. "It is mine, but only in that I caused him to be betrothed to me when he loved another."

Mercer drew away. "Christ, Zoë, how did we bollix this up so badly?" he said, lifting his hands in an expansive, impotent gesture. "If Robin loved Maria so much, why was he making love to you?"

"Because he is young," said Zoë. "Because he is young, and like most handsome young men, he is too brash, and because I tempted him. But I never would have done it, Mercer, had I known his heart was engaged."

"How can we any of us know such things?" said Mercer hollowly. "If he does not know himself—not until it is too late—how can we be expected to know what is in his heart?"

And then it struck him that the same could be said of him. He remembered the blind rage which had struck him upon seeing Zoë in his brother's embrace—then the almost overwhelming surge of pain, and the sense of having discovered a deep and enduring truth but an instant too late. He had practically suggested as much to Robin at the time, putting his own feelings into his brother's mouth, praying to save Zoë from her father's wrath.

Always a part of him had loved Zoë. He accepted that now. But he had been too proud—perhaps even too cowardly—to admit it, even to himself. And in that, was his sin any worse than Robin's?

"Zoë, I do not blame you," he managed to say. "I spoke out of grief and guilt that day."

"Thank you," she said quietly.

Just then, Nanna pushed backward through the door, carrying another steaming bowl wrapped in a towel. Zoë returned to her chair.

"Gude day to ye, lad." Nanna nodded at Mercer as she passed. "Young Robert's bruises are yellowing, did ye notice?"

"That is a good thing, Nanna, isn't it?" Mercer went to the side of the bed and resumed his work.

"Oh, aye." The old nurse set her bowl down on the night table and began to unwrap it.

"Nanna, do you need me further?" Zoë leaned forward to dab lightly at Robin's mouth with a napkin.

"No, there's nae mair tae be done," said the old woman. "Awa' w'ye, lass."

"Thank you, let me just—" Zoë's words fell away, her gaze focused upon Robin's face.

"What?" said Mercer, putting Robin's foot down.

Zoë leaned across the bed. "Look," she whispered. "His eyes."

"What about them?" Mercer set his hand on the back of her chair and bent closer.

"They're darting about." Zoë's voice was a whisper. "As if he dreams."

"Weel!" The old nurse had gone to the other side of the bed. "A verra gude omen, that."

"Look!" cried Zoë. "There—did you see? Just for an instant."

"I saw nothing," Mercer whispered.

Zoë set the bowl down abruptly, and leapt up, her head almost striking beneath Mercer's chin. "Oh, terribly sorry!" Zoë slid past him. "Here, sit down and look closely."

But Mercer had already sunk into her chair and was bent forward, transfixed.

"Och, he'll wake soon, laddie, sair and ill as an auld bear, but on the mend," said the old woman, coming round to pat his shoulder. "Dinna fash yourself."

Mercer reached up without taking his eyes from Robin's, and caught her hand in his. "I pray you are right, Nanna," he murmured, giving it a squeeze.

But Zoë had already gone to the door. "Mercer," she said, her hand on the knob.

"Yes?" He turned to see her blinking back tears.

"*If* he wakes up," she said, her voice unsteady and a little threatening, "then *you* will wake *me*. No matter the time. Do you understand?"

"Aye, then." He nodded solemnly. "I understand."

Zoë closed the door and exhaled a long, shuddering breath. For an instant, she leaned back against the door, her palms pressed flat to the smooth, cool wood.

Dear heaven, was it possible?

Despite her words of encouragement to herself and everyone else, Zoë was not sure that deep down she had believed Robin would wake. Suddenly elated, exhausted, and overwrought all at once, Zoë realized there was no possibility of rest just now. What she needed was time to think. What she needed was a long walk.

That decided, Zoë hastened down the corridor to fetch her shawl. When she reached her bedchamber, Trudy followed her in with a stack of clean laundry.

"I am going to have a walk out to the cliffs before the light fades," said Zoë, after telling her about Robin's eyes. "I don't know how long I shall be. Please have your dinner, Tru, then take the evening off."

"Very well, but have a care, miss." Trudy smiled and began to tuck the clothes away. "You mustn't set so much as a foot down the cliffs."

"No, I shan't be so foolish, Tru. Thank you." Zoë tossed her shawl about her shoulders and made her way through the corridors to the great hall. At the top of the steps, however, she felt a stiff breeze sweep up. Peering over the balustrade, she saw that both the massive front doors stood open. Footmen were carrying out hampers and bundles and loading them into a light, well-sprung chaise.

Below, Mr. Amherst stood on the grand portico, his shoulders slumped as he spoke to Mr. Ware and Dr. Bevins. Even from a distance, Zoë could see their faces were etched with grief. Hastening down the staircase, she reached the door just as the two callers started back down the front steps. Below, Dr. Bevins's gig waited in a shaft of low afternoon light.

Zoë hesitated, her hand on the wide oak doorframe. "I beg your pardon," she said, leaning out. "Has something happened?"

"Ah, Zoë, my dear!" Mr. Amherst bestirred himself as if from a dream. "Yes, I fear Mr. Fitch's wife has passed."

Zoë felt a stab of sudden grief. "Oh, dear! In that cottage west of the home farm?" she murmured. "Arabella pointed it out to me."

Mr. Amherst managed a sad smile. "Yes, tragedy is all around us," he murmured. "Fitch has four children, and none above fourteen, I daresay. I'm off to see to the family in Stuart's stead. Perhaps there is something . . . something we can do to help."

Zoë hesitated but a moment, then stepped onto the

portico. "Would you like an extra pair of hands?" she asked. "I . . . well, I have nothing pressing to do."

Mr. Amherst winced. "It is a hard business, Zoë," he said. "The family is quite broken up."

Crossing her arms over her chest, Zoë tilted her head toward the waiting chaise. "Have you supper in those hampers?" she asked. "At the very least, I can see the children fed, can I not, whilst you speak with Mr. Fitch?"

Mr. Amherst smiled, and offered her his arm. "I should be glad of your company."

Soon they were on their way, rattling along a series of narrow country lanes and farm roads that had begun to feel pleasantly familiar to Zoë.

"Thank you for bringing me," she said after they had traveled for some miles. "I keep finding myself at loose ends these days." Then she told him what Nanna had said about Robin's eyes.

"Praise God," said Amherst under his breath. "Perhaps in time, something good will come of all this."

Zoë glanced at him with a twisted smile. "I can't think what," she said honestly. "Robin will be scarred, at the very least. And I am sure he will suffer great pain."

Amherst lifted both broad shoulders. "Sometimes the Lord tries our strength, Zoë," he said quietly. "As hard as it may be for us to comprehend, he sometimes finds it necessary to fire us in the forge of tribulation like a piece of Sheffield steel. And in that way—much like the steel—we become more perfect, not less. Our scars become not a disfigurement, but a badge of earthly triumph."

Zoë stared at the farm track with its strip of grass down the center, and pondered Mr. Amherst's philosophy. Even as a child, she had taken comfort in the calm certainty of his convictions—both religious and secular—and it was a gift he had seemingly passed to his eldest stepson. Indeed, in many ways, Mercer was more like his stepfather than his mother. Cole Amherst was a clean, cool breeze to Jonet's fire. Perhaps that was why they seemed so happy.

"I am sure, sir, that you are right," she finally said. "You always are. I just wish I had your faith."

"Oh, you have it," said Mr. Amherst softly. "And I think, Zoë, that you are finding it. Perhaps Robin's accident is your forge, too?"

Zoë found herself unexpectedly blinking back tears. "Oh, pray do not, Mr. Amherst," she murmured, cutting her eyes toward the hedgerow. "Do not make me arrive at poor Mr. Fitch's already a watering pot."

"No, no, I shan't, child," he murmured. Swiftly, he gathered the reins in one hand, and settled and arm around her shoulders, pulling her to him. "I am sorry. This has all been so very hard for you."

Yes, and I have made it harder than it had to be, she thought, allowing herself the comfort of his shoulder for a moment. But she did not say the words aloud. After a time, she lifted her head and he let her go, cutting her an almost doting glance.

"You have changed, Zoë," he mused. "Oh, that vivacity of yours is quite intact, but there is something . . . something I cannot quite put my finger on."

Zoë stared at a point far in the distance. "I have grown up," she said, her voice hollow.

"Oh, I do hope not." Mr. Amherst broke into a broad grin. "Nothing *quite* so dire as that. But you are more settled. I believe you have learned what it is you want out of life."

Yes, she had learned what she wanted—she wanted something she could not have—and the knowledge made every little trial and tragedy which had come before it pale to nothing. "I have learned to accept life as it is, Mr. Amherst," she said quietly, "instead of railing against it, but my learning has cost Robin dear indeed."

"That simply is not true, my dear," he said quietly. "It simply is not."

But they had little more time to discuss it. The Fitch cottage was coming into view. Soon there would be a very real tragedy to be dealt with—something far worse than a poor little rich girl feeling sorry for herself.

Zoë dashed one hand at the corner of her eye, and turned round to pick up the first hamper.

Mercer sat stiffly by his brother's bed as night began to fall across Greythorpe. Ordinarily, this was his favorite time of day, when the day's work was done and a man could be at ease in his own home, a little tired from his efforts, yet confident that all was right with the world.

But all was not right with his world, though outwardly, one would not have known it. Through the open window, he could hear the soft *hoo-hoo-hoo* of a dove calling its last. The low of a distant cow. Slowly, and in a blaze of red glory, the sun sank below the trees, its last shaft falling from Robin's windowsill as Charlie came in to draw the draperies.

"Will ye be all right, lad?" he asked as he passed.

Mercer nodded. What else was there to say? The truth?

Charlie cast an eye at the more or less uneaten supper he'd carried in earlier. "Shall I bring us a whisky, then?"

Mercer shook his head.

"Verra weel, then. Ring if you change your mind." Charlie swept away the tray again, closing the door behind with an echo that sounded hollow in the stillness of the house. Soon even the brisk footsteps of servants going about their evening's duties had faded away, and the dove had given over to the distant call of an owl deep within the wood. The moon rose, clear and nearly full.

Mercer shifted in his chair, unable to rest. He dragged off his boots, and tossed them into the corner. It did not help. He could think only of Robin, and of Zoë; of how he'd watched them together this afternoon. Her gentleness. Her near ruthless determination. And now, according to Charlie, she'd gone over to the Fitches' with his stepfather.

No, perhaps he did not know her strength at all.

Until today, they had spoken not a word about what had passed between them that night in the summerhouse; about the promises implied, or the expectations unmet. Of the future. How could they, when Robin mightn't have one? Even were Robin to recover, he would never be the same. His extraordinary beauty was marred, if not lost altogether. If he lived, he would walk with a limp, at least for a time. If he walked at all. Just as his mother had said, Maria Wilfred would not likely look twice at Robin now.

And Zoë—what were her intentions? If he lived, would she go through with this mistake of a marriage out of guilt? How could she not? And how could he bear it? Would she tell Robin the truth?

Dear God, he had bedded his brother's betrothed wife.

Robin would never forgive him—nor should he. And yet Mercer did not regret it. He dropped his head into his hands, realizing that that was the most disturbing thing. Were he given the choice—those fleeting hours with Zoë in his arms, versus his brother's untarnished devotion— he would have chosen Zoë, in an act of utter selfishness. An act not worthy of the man he'd believed himself.

On a swell of grief, Mercer got up and went to the other side of the bed. He lay down beside his brother, stretched out his legs, and threaded his fingers through Robin's colder, thinner ones until their hands were clasped palm to palm. Then, staring up at the ornate plasterwork ceiling, Mercer let the darkness fall all around them, and with it the memories. They came out to wink at him like stars on a clear, cold night; recollections of whispered secrets and midnight fears. Of adventures both rash and imprudent, and punishments equally shared. Never had they truly quarreled, or so it seemed to him now. Never had they failed to stand by one another.

He tightened his grip, and gave Robin's hand another squeeze. They had often slept thus as boys, particularly in those awful months following their father's death. Even as they had grown up, the two of them had remained inordinately close, and yet very separate. Mercer could not remember ever having begrudged Robin his looks or his charm or his vast circle of friends. And, so far as he knew, Robin had never envied Mercer's wealth or his titles, or his ability to find contentment in solitude. How could they? They were two sides of one coin.

Mercer was not sure how long he slept thus, or if he even slept at all. But slowly, his memories of a happy childhood began to blur into a darker, more other-worldly haze. He dreamed of Elmwood; of warm, fresh-cut grass, and of running barefoot till his lungs nearly burst, Robin on his heels.

After a time, he realized he still clutched Robin's hand, but when he looked down, he realized he was dragging Robin up through a gaping black hole. Then the void shifted, and became something else. *The trap-door. In the hayloft.*

He was gripping his brother's smaller, sweatier hand and trying like the devil to heft him up past a splintering rung. Beneath Robin's dangling feet, the packed-earth floor swirled in a cascade of gold-brown hay that caught the afternoon light as it fell. Terror leapt in his breast, and Mercer tightened his grip, only to feel Robin's relax.

Mercer opened his mouth to cry out, to beg Robin to hang on. But his scream was soundless, and he came awake on an awful surge of terror, only to find that Robin had tightened his grip again, and now held his hand quite firmly.

"If you"—came a weak rasp—*"if you . . . are in my bed, you'd best be . . . blonde and buxom."*

Mercer sat bolt upright. "Robin—?"

His brother gave grunt of pain, his hand clutching at Mercer. "Good God," he managed, "you've a damned hairy wrist!"

"Robin?" Mercer set both hands gingerly on his good arm. "You are awake?"

"Am I?" his brother wheezed. "Oh, Lord . . . head . . . hurts."

Mercer bolted from the bed. With hands that shook, he found his coat and fumbled for his matches. Somehow he got the lamp lit. He turned the wick high to see his brother's swollen visage looking up at him, eyes wincing against the light.

"Stu . . . ?" he muttered, his lips barely forming the word. "Wha' the . . . devil?"

"You came a cropper on Lucifer." Mercer settled himself on the edge of the bed, and leaned over his brother, setting one hand on his shoulder. "Do you remember? The day of the hunt?"

Robin tried to shake his head, wincing against the pain. "Good God," he rasped again. "I hurt, Stu. I hurt . . . all over. Where . . . we?"

"At Greythorpe," said Mercer. "In your room at Greythorpe. We came down several weeks past. Do you remember?"

Something passed over his brother's visage then, a look that was at once plaintive and withering. "Christ," he croaked. "*Zoë?*"

Mercer lifted himself a little away. "Yes, Zoë," he murmured.

Robin's tongue came out to lick his dry lips. "Devil take it," he managed. "Where is she? Gone?"

"Asleep in her bed, I daresay," Mercer managed. "Look, Robin, let's not talk of that now. Let me get you some water. You're hurt, old man, and pretty badly."

"Bloody well right." Robin lifted one corner of his mouth, a twisted parody of a smile, but it made him wince. He lifted a trembling hand, and lightly fingered the gash along his face. "Oh, God. Am I . . . marred? Crippled?"

"Probably not the latter." Mercer saw no point in lying. "But you're going to look rather dangerous and dashing once that gash heals."

Robin grunted. "I'll live, eh?"

Mercer nodded. "You are going to live," he said firmly. "I shall make sure of it."

Robin shifted uncomfortably. "Always were . . . a sadistic bastard," he whispered. "Gawd, my head hurts. What happened?"

"You let Lucifer take Sir William's farm gate," Mercer said again. "Zoë—she was behind you. Trying to stop you, I daresay. But I thought . . . I thought you were racing. I was wrong."

Some of the haze seemed to clear from Robin's eyes. "Aye, she . . . she was shouting," he muttered as if to himself. "Wasn't she?"

"Look, just lie still," said Mercer. "I'm going to ring Charlie to bring Mamma. She's been worried sick for days now."

"Days?" Robin's brow furrowed, then abruptly, he caught Mercer's wrist in a grip that was surprisingly strong. "Wait, Stu. What about . . . Zoë? She all right?"

Mercer let his weight relax onto the bed again. "Perfectly well, aye."

"Listen, Stu." Robin's eyes, still dazed, held his. "If . . . If I turn up my toes, tell Zoë—"

Mercer laid his hand over his brother's. "You are not dying on me, old boy," he gritted. "Stop suggesting it."

"Feels like I might," Robin croaked. "And if . . . if I do, you must tell Zoë . . ."

Mercer relented. "Tell Zoë what?"

"That I love her." He paused to swallow, his eyes narrowing against the pain. "I do. Dashed fond of her. You . . . You know that, right? And don't blame her." His eyes fell shut. "Promise you won't blame her."

"I shan't," said Mercer. "But this is foolishness. Here, let me ring for Mamma."

But Robin tightened his grip. "Wait, Stu . . ."

"Yes?"

"Stu, if I live . . . God, Stu. How am I going to marry her? I'm . . . I'm no good for Zoë. If I died, mightn't it be as well?"

"Hell, no, it won't be." Mercer set a firm hand on Robin's arm. "Don't speak of dying again, old man. Or as soon as you're up and about, I'll make you wish you had, do you hear?"

Robin's eyes rolled back wearily. "Aye, I hear. I-I'm sorry. But you see it, don't you? That I'm no good for her?"

Mercer looked away, unable to hold his brother's gaze. "That is between the two of you," he managed. "A gentleman may not cry off. And she . . . well, she might not. The guilt—seeing you here like this—it has been awful for her. Can't you understand that?"

Robin exhaled tremulously, and made no answer.

"You can offer to release her, Rob," Mercer continued. "Perhaps you can even tell her how you feel. But I am not sure I understand Zoë anymore. Indeed, I begin to wonder if I ever did. Still, I believe . . . I believe that you should try."

But even as he said it, Mercer wondering if he were giving Robin the right advice, or simply acting in his own interests. And Zoë—would she stand her ground, believing that Robin needed her now—or worse, that Mercer did not need her at all?

"Can't . . . try," Robin grunted, turning his gaze to the wall. "Claire. Keep forgetting . . . Claire."

"I can manage Claire," Mercer said, hoping he spoke the truth. "I have taken steps." Then he seized his brother's hand again. "But we aren't going to speak of that now, Rob. I'm going to send for Mamma, all right?"

But his brother's glassy gaze was still focused on the wall. That all too familiar look of despair was once more plain upon his face, and his hand had again gone limp.

Chapter Fourteen

IN WHICH OUR HEROINE
HAS AN ADVENTURE.

Zoë woke shortly before midnight, or more accurately, she hurled back the bedcovers in frustration, for she'd scarcely slept at all. After a slow journey home in the dark from the Fitch cottage, Zoë had skipped dinner out of exhaustion, in favor of a hot bath, to no avail. Sleep still danced just beyond her grasp. She could think only of Robin—wondering if or when he might wake—and of Mr. Fitch's bewildered children, just beginning to mourn the loss of a mother. And, if she were honest, she thought of Mercer, and of what she longed for. No matter how she tried to devote herself to others, it seemed her own selfish need kept breaking through.

Frustrated, she climbed from the bed and went to the window to draw back the heavy velvet drapery. Through the undulating glass, she looked out across the lawns to the soft white light which spilled through the trees beyond, then threw up the sash. The summer breeze lifted at her hair, now loose about her shoulders. Above, a three-quarter moon sat high in a cloudless sky, tempting her.

Why not be just a little foolish? A moonlit walk scarcely qualified as high jinks by Zoë's standards. Besides, life could be so very short; poor Mrs. Fitch's passing was a stark reminder of that. Hastily, she threw off her night rail, and dressed in her simplest cotton gown. Eschewing stockings altogether, Zoë shoved her feet into a pair of soft leather slippers, and tossed a light shawl about her shoulders.

Downstairs, the great hall lay in silence, but the rear doors were easily unlocked, and all along the veranda, sconces still burned. She crossed the parterre, circling round the massive fountain, then climbed up the most distant terrace to the wild stretch of land that opened up to the rear of the house. Here a fence and stile separated Greythorpe's vast manicured lawns from the swath of pasture and, farther along, the coastal footpath.

Zoë hitched up her skirt and stepped lightly up, turned, then dropped down into the taller grass on the other side. Away from the sheltering walls of the house, the sounds of a summer night closed in around her; the song of field crickets, the sough of the wind, and below it something that sounded like the distant *shush-shush-shush* of the sea.

Heedless of her skirts, Zoë hastened along the path, easily discernible in the moonlight, until, some distance farther, she reached the cliffs. It was here that Mercer had forbidden her to go without him, and the instant Zoë stepped out onto the high, chalk ledge, she realized why. The land spun away almost dizzyingly, dropping away in a steep tumble of scrub and chalk and jutting cliffs to the shifting ocean below.

Suitably intimidated by the danger—and, though it was lowering to admit, by Mercer's implacability—Zoë sat down upon a stone outcropping at the very top, and let her legs dangle. Here the view was breathtaking, made more so by the sheen of the moon upon the water. The tide was going out, exposing a long, curving strand of beach below, and beyond it, nothing but the glistening, shifting ocean as far as the eye could see.

Zoë was not perfectly sure how long she sat there, mesmerized by the beauty of the scene, and hoping it would fleetingly crowd out her troubles, but eventually she became aware of heavy footsteps, and the unmistakable sound of grass whipping against leather. Her every sense leapt at once to awareness; her certainty so keen she needn't even turn round to know the source of the strong, vibrant force now standing behind her.

She held up a hand. "I did not go down," she said. "I did not step one foot farther than you see me."

Mercer said nothing, but instead sat down beside her, and threw his long, booted legs over the ledge, still in his shirtsleeves, as if he'd left the house in some haste. "Zoë," he said, his voice edged with excitement. "Zoë, he is awake."

Eyes wide, Zoë turned, relief surging. "Robin . . . ?" She flung herself into his arms, almost toppling them both off the ledge. "Oh, please, please, Mercer, tell me he is well!" she cried, the words muffled against his wide chest.

"He is all right, I think." Zoë could feel him sagging with relief even as his arms came around her, safe and strong, his warm scent of cologne and tobacco settling over her. Then he shocked her by setting his cheek to her shoulder. "He is in pain," he whispered. "A little vague still. And his mood—well, he is alive, Zoë. And just now, that is all I ask."

"Oh, thank heaven!" Zoë murmured. "I should go to him. But your mother—?"

Mercer lifted his head and gave a weary half smile. "Aye, just now he is awash in Mamma's tender ministrations, and I rather doubt she will leave his side tonight."

"I . . . I shan't intrude on her joy, then," Zoë said, her arms slipping away. "I shall see him tomorrow."

Mercer felt the loss of Zoë's embrace keenly, and caught her hand at the last moment. Would it ever be this way, he wondered? Was he destined to spend the rest of his life hoping for just a little piece of her?

He hoped not. Prayed not. For a little piece of Zoë would never be enough to fill up that gaping hole of longing she had already left in his heart. And so he clung to her hand as he clung to hope. "I promised I would wake you," he said, entwining his fingers with hers. "But your room was empty."

He did not mention the night rail, tossed so casually across the unmade bed, or the fact that he'd fought the urge to caress it, to pick it up and bury his face in her scent—a fight he'd lost.

"How did you find me?" she whispered.

"I was crossing back through the gallery," he said, "and looked out to see someone climbing over the stile on the ridge."

"And you could not pass up the opportunity to chide me, I am sure," said Zoë on a laugh. "Oh, but first, do tell me how is he! Does he know where he is? Is the pain unbearable? Does he remember?"

Mercer stared out across the Channel. "Yes, no, and a little," he answered. "And I did not come out here, Zoë, to chide you."

"Did he say anything?" Doubtless Zoë was suppressing the urge to hasten back to the house. "Mercer, did he . . . mention me at all?"

He hesitated, cursing himself for his own weakness. Of course she was concerned for Robin, just as he was. And yet Mercer could not escape the suspicion that a better man than he would have sent her rushing to Robin's side, rather than indulging in a spate of jealousy.

"What do you wish me to say, Zoë?" he whispered. "What is it that you hope for?"

They sat again sat side by side. He felt her shrug, her shawl brushing his shirtsleeve. "I don't know," she confessed. "I just don't wish Robin to be angry with me. Or to . . . to blame me."

"He does not," said Mercer.

Withdrawing her hand, Zoë drew her knees to her chest and wrapped her arms round them, her expression pensive. Perched upon the rocks in the clear, white moonlight, she looked so small and ethereal. Almost childlike.

But Zoë, he realized, had not been a child to him in a great many years. She had been his heart. His soul. And it frightened him how thoroughly he'd been able to shut that knowledge away. Had he become so hard and so dour that he had forgotten how to seize life? How to let himself go? Or had he ever known? Perhaps there was something to be learned from Robin after all.

"So," she said quietly. "What happens next, I wonder?"

Somehow, he looked at her and smiled. He lifted his hand and pointed at the sea. "Next," he said quietly, "we go down there."

Her dark, perfect eyebrows went up. "To the Channel?" she said sharply. *"Tonight?"*

He shrugged. "I cannot sleep," he said. "Nor can you, obviously. And I promised to take you. Perhaps tonight is a night, Zoë, to celebrate life, and not think quite so much."

Her eyes widened, and her mouth curled up into an almost mischievous smile. "What a relief that sounds. Can you find the way?"

"In the pitch dark," he said confidently. "But instead, we've a nearly full moon. Yes, I can take you down, if you will go behind me, and do just as I say—a singular notion, to be sure, but I will trust you this once."

Zoë clambered to her feet, her eyes shining in the moonlight.

He took her hand, and led her along the cliff to a deep cleft in the rocks. "Just here," he said. Then he yanked his shirttails loose. "Now, lean into me, and grab hold of my shirt from behind—and if you slip, don't panic, but just hang on to me. I shall catch you."

Zoë was staring over the precipice.

"I won't go over, Zoë," he said, chucking her lightly under the chin. "Nor will I let you."

She lifted her gaze to his. "No," she said, her voice unwavering. "No, I am quite sure you will not. You—and Papa, too—can always be counted on to keep me safe. I see that now."

He watched her for a long moment in the moonlight. Here, at the top of the cliffs, her long, unruly curls seemed to lift and toss on the rising breeze like a soft dark cloud. "Your hair is so lovely down," he murmured. "I had not seen it like that for an age. Not until—"

Until that fateful night they'd made love in the summerhouse. The night that had changed his life so inexorably, and thrown it into utter disarray.

Zoë laughed. "And your hair has grown far long," she returned. "You've begun to look a trifle uncivilized of late."

He had felt a little uncivilized, too, he thought, his gaze taking her in. He managed to smile. "So," he said, turning to descend. "Off we go."

It was not the first time he'd gone down in the dark; he knew the hills of Greythorpe like a hefted Highland sheep. This particular descent was simply a matter of knowing where the best trail lay, amidst the brambles and ledges. And while it was by no means the dramatic chalk sheers of Dover or Beachy Head, it was dangerous if one did not know which rocks were loose, and which cliffs to tuck under.

Deftly, he inched between the outcroppings and the mounds of coastal scrub, Zoë clinging to his shirt, so close he could feel her warmth. The ocean breeze whipped his hair back, and occasionally into his face, when he paused in a particularly treacherous spot to glance back. But never did Zoë look frightened. Instead she slunk carefully along the ledges like a clever kitten, smiling, with her hand fisted in his loose linen shirt. No fainthearted female, she. Zoë was always up for a lark, and perhaps it was time he simply gave in to it?

He pondered it for a few yards, wondering if the flood of euphoria he'd felt at Robin's awakening had simply gone to his head. But in his heart, he feared that what he felt had shockingly little to do with his brother. He was *happy*—and Zoë made him so.

Suddenly the wind buffeted back against a cliff, and Mercer turned his head, only to be teased with a hint of the seductive jasmine scent that rose from Zoë's skin and hair, and seemed to be the very essence of her. He turned round reluctantly and pressed on, but the scent remained with him like a memory.

Two-thirds down the path, Mercer led her up onto perhaps the most dangerous point—an outcropping of rock with minimal footing and no scrub to catch hold of. Instinctively, he glanced back to reassure himself, only to see Zoë lift her face to the moonlight like some pagan goddess.

"Mercer, it is so beautiful here!" she whispered, one arm thrown out. "So natural and so . . . *untamed*."

Untamed. It was an apt description, perhaps. Mercer let his eyes drink her in—the wild dark hair tossing in the wind, the thin muslin gown whipping round her slender form, and the look of exultation upon her face—and felt himself slip over the precipice. A precipice made not of stone or of earth, but of a man's hopes and intentions. And in that moment, he knew.

Zoë was his.

She had always been his, and he was going to take her. And it almost did not matter how or why, or even who got hurt in the process. Zoë was his, and it was always meant to be. And if she insisted on trying to throw herself away on Robin, he would simply stop it. If they had to face down gossip or censure, they simply would. If he had to throttle Claire to keep her quiet—well, he would not quite do that. Not to the mother of his child. But he was beginning to feel quite thoroughly, ruthlessly selfish.

He realized suddenly that he had stopped atop the rock outcropping. On impulse, he turned and drew Zoë to him. Her eyes flaring with surprise, she let go of his shirt, and came against him. He lowered his mouth to hers, and kissed her without hesitation. Molding his lips to hers, sweet and pillow-soft, Mercer tasted her thoroughly, giving her no chance to protest.

But Zoë wasn't protesting. She was kissing him back a little desperately, her hands skating beneath his billowing shirt and up his bare back. He stroked his tongue inside her mouth, and she flattened her breasts against him, her nails digging into the muscles that layered his shoulder blades in one heady, dizzying moment. Mercer felt the wind whipping round them, and the crashing surf beyond, as something wild and unbidden rose within him. He deepened the kiss and felt himself come oddly alive with it. And yet he was not himself at all, not the man he knew—but perhaps the man he could be.

They came apart, gasping, still clinging to one another. Zoë's eyes were wide, her mouth still wet and swollen from his kiss. And then Mercer did the strangest thing—and a dangerous thing, too. He swept Zoë completely off her toes and twirled her around in his arms, right at the cliff's edge, as the sea crashed and glistened beneath them.

"Oh!" she shrieked when he set her down again. "Oh, Mercer, have you quite lost your mind?"

But her eyes were dancing, and she was laughing as she clung to him. Yes, he'd lost his mind—or at the very least, Zoë would soon have him well on the road to Bedlam. But he no longer cared. "Come on," he said, grabbing her hand. "Let's go swimming."

"Swimming?" she shrieked as he hauled her off the precipice.

The rest of the path was clearer; more sand than rock, with the scrub and bramble falling away as they neared the sea. At the last, he half dragged, then half carried Zoë the rest of the way down as she whooped with laughter. They reached the wide stretch of sand, both of them gasping, both of them laughing.

"Why, we've become perfectly giddy," she said, leaning forward to set her hands on her thighs. "It must be the relief."

"Or the moonlight?" he suggested, grinning. Then he reached down and stripped his shirt over his head. "Come on. The water will be refreshing."

"The water will be cold, you fool," Zoë answered. But she straightened up, and began to unfasten her buttons.

Mercer wasn't laughing anymore. "Here," he said, his voice coming out husky. "Let me."

He made short work of them, then watched as Zoë shrugged the gown off her narrow shoulders and shimmied it off her hips. The fabric slithered down her small, shapely length to form a puddle of pink muslin on the sand. She stepped out of it wearing nothing but her shift, then turned round.

Mercer picked up the gown and shook off the sand as Zoë kicked away her shoes, then cleverly shucked her drawers without even lifting her shift.

"One gets the impression you've done this sort of thing before," he murmured. "And where are your stockings, by the way?"

"I'm not going back up that hill in damp drawers," she said, turning around. "And yes, I've done it hundreds of times—at least a dozen of them with you. And no, I haven't any stockings, for I hadn't any intention of socializing on my midnight escapade."

"Is that what you were looking for, Zoë?" he murmured, eyeing her. "A midnight escapade?"

That she did not answer, but Zoë's eyes were still shining as he carried their clothes to a stone outcropping. The natural rock formation jutted toward the sea, then curved round like a misshapen comma, winnowing away to form a sheltered nook beneath the cliffs. *Robin's fort,* he had always called it, where, as boys, they'd often fought off imaginary French invaders, though in truth it was no more than two or three feet at its highest.

But this was not about Robin. This was about the moment he was trying to seize. He was trying to learn how to embrace the whirlwind that was Zoë, to ride out the emotional storms the woman engendered. Carefully he laid Zoë's things across the highest stone, then tossed his shirt atop them. Mercer sat down, dragged off his boots and shucked everything save his drawers. Then, on impulse, he caught Zoë up in his arms, and headed into the surf as she squirmed.

"Oh!" she cried, her hands going to her face when the first wave hit.

Mercer shivered and plunged onward until the water reached his chest and Zoë was floating. On a laugh, she paddled backward into the deep. A wave came crashing over, and ever game, Zoë turned and swam into it with strong, determined strokes. He laughed and shot after her. Soon they had ventured beyond the break into calmer waters.

"The tide is going dead low," he said when they stopped to tread water. "But it won't last."

Zoë giggled, and sank beneath the shimmering surface. In a moment of panic, Mercer dove beneath, found her, and dragged her up again. She came up spurting water and laughing as she clung to him, her hands going round his neck.

"You f-fainthearted hen," she said. "C-Come on, let's get our b-blood moving."

Given the heaviness tugging at his groin, Mercer figured his blood was already moving a little too well, but when Zoë released his neck and stroked away, he followed her. They swam for some distance alongside one another, parallel to the coast, through the cool, smooth water, then doubled back and swam it again. In the moonlight, the coast was shadowed in gloom, but never far away.

After they had exhausted themselves, Mercer dragged Zoë back into chest-deep water, balancing her in his arms. Her mouth curved with a faint, simmering smile as she coasted backward, just inches from his grasp, her hair floating free in the water. His limbs felt weighed down with a sweet lethargy, and he began to long to curl himself around her, and warm her with the heat of his body. To make love to her until she cried out with pleasure. To sleep in her arms until sunrise.

It was not to be, it seemed.

"Mercer," she said quietly, "what are we really doing here?"

It was a question he'd been avoiding since sitting down beside her atop the cliffs. "Living," he said simply. "Living for the moment. For now, Zoë, it is enough."

She came back to him then, and circled her arms round his neck. "Is it?" she murmured, her eyes falling shut. "Just for tonight . . . is it enough for you?" Then she twined one leg round his waist, and kissed him, hot and open-mouthed.

He returned the kiss, one hand sliding beneath her derrière to lightly balance her in the water as his other arm went round her, holding her to him. She floated in his embrace, still kissing him until his head began to spin and even the cold water was not enough to dissuade his cock. It rose through the water, tenting his drawers and teasing lightly at Zoë's bottom.

At that, her eyes opened wide in the moonlight, then slowly she kissed her way along his jaw. "It's rising," she whispered against his ear.

"Umm," he murmured. "Noticed that, did you?"

She drew back with her irrepressible grin. "The *tide,* you lecher," she said. "The tide is rising. The surf will knock us over soon."

"Ah." He waded another few feet toward shore and reluctantly released her.

Zoë slid down his length, her eyes closed like a cat being stroked. But when the contact was over, she began to shiver a little. He took her by the hand and led her from the water. They had emerged a few yards farther down the beach. "Come on," she cried. "Let's run back!"

And she did, hitching up her shift like a true hoyden, exposing her small, slender legs as she went pelting along the coarse sand beach. He watched her for a minute, shaking his head at the absurdity of it. Then, on second thought, he bolted after her.

Zoë hadn't a chance. He was better than a foot taller, most of it in his legs. He caught up with her well before she reached the rocks and snatched her up again. They fell into the sand, laughing like the children they had once been.

And then they weren't laughing at all, but looking into one another's eyes. Though much of her face lay in darkness, her back to the moon, he could feel her gaze upon him, strong and steady. He resisted the urge to kiss her again, and instead set his hand to her heart.

"Are you cold?" he whispered.

"Y-Yes," she chattered.

He rose and held out his hand. "Come, I'll build us a fire."

Farther up the beach, Mercer situated her in the lee of his boyhood fort. It took but a few moments of padding barefoot up and down the beach to gather enough driftwood and old bracken to make a decent conflagration. He pushed out a shallow pit in the sand, laid it up, then rummaged in the pockets of his breeches, grateful to find the vesta he'd left there.

In a few minutes, the fire was roaring. Zoë sat and reclined against the flat of the biggest rock, as if it were a giant pile of pillows, and he joined her there, grateful to feel the warmth that still radiated from the stones.

"This is like a time out of place," she murmured, gazing into the fire. "Like a thing that isn't really happening."

"What do you mean?"

"As though tomorrow we mightn't remember it at

all," she said, her voice a little wistful, "or if we do, it will be as a dream."

"This isn't a dream to me," he managed, rolling toward her on his elbow.

He could see her face full in the firelight now, the soft dark curls springing dry around her heart-shaped face, and that fine-boned nose that was perhaps a little too strong, and yet looked perfect on her. Her lips were full and impish, her chin as wonderfully sharp as her personality. She was a dark, sloe-eyed beauty, his Zoë—and yet she wasn't really his at all. He wondered, in truth, if any man could ever possess her.

Certainly he meant to try. Even if it meant madness.

He rolled nearer, and brushed his lips over her temple. "Zoë, I want to make love to you."

She turned her face into his. "And I want you," she answered, her expression almost raw with honestly. "I begin to think . . . well, that perhaps I always have. That it was always you."

"Always me," he murmured, setting his lips to her cheek. "And not Robin?"

She gave a thready laugh. "It was never Robin," she said. "Robin is my friend. You have always seemed . . . too perfect. Too unattainable for someone like me."

"Trust me," he said, his lips sliding down to her throat. "I have never been perfect. And I am very, very attainable just now. *Especially* for you."

"And no questions asked?" she whispered. "Just for tonight, and then we . . . we go back to real life?"

In that moment, Mercer would have sold his soul to the devil just for the chance to lie her back in the warm sand and thrust himself inside her. So he kissed her, his mouth hot and hungry on hers. "Perhaps this is real life?" he murmured when he lifted his lips away. "Perhaps this is all it boils down to, Zoë?"

"I wish," she said. Then she kissed him back.

He let his hands roam over her, touching and caressing his fill as they kissed. Her breasts were small and perfect through the thin, wet fabric; just enough to fill a man's hands and fuel his fantasies. Her throat—God, he'd always loved her throat, so long and so white. And then there were her arms, thin and yet strong. Somehow, amidst all the heat and longing, Mercer managed to tug Zoë's wet shift away. His drawers soon followed.

He drew back, knelt in the sand, and looked at her. Zoë was still reclined against the flat of the big rock, one arm behind her head as the golden firelight flowed over her, warming her bare, flawless skin. Her tangle of curls was fanned out across the rock, already half dry, her body warm and inviting.

"What?" she said, almost laughing.

"You are so beautiful," he whispered. "So perfect."

"Only because you want something from me, Mercer." Her face broke into an impish, knowing smile. "You never thought me anything near perfect before."

"No, you are not perfect," he rasped. "Not like that. You are spoiled and heedless and vain—and kind and good and full of life. And you madden me. But you are what I want, Zoë. I've given up fighting it. And I would not change you one iota."

Mercer surprised even himself with the truth he spoke. And while Zoë's eyes were still wide with the shock of it, he bent, and kissed one of her knees, then on impulse, settled himself between them. "I thought men generally lied to women to get what they wanted," said Zoë on a giggle.

He shook his head, and set one hand on the sweet swell of her belly, right over her womb, a little shaken by the dreams that went spinning through his mind. Dreams of waking to Zoë in his bed. Of Zoë, round with his child. "I never will lie to you," he said, looking up at her. "Besides, I should rather give *you* what you want."

He shifted his weight lower, and set his mouth where his hand had been. "I have to taste you," he said, the words thick. "Let me, Zoë."

"Y-Yes," she said uncertainly.

He knelt between her legs now, undaunted by the coarse sand. His hands going to her breasts, Mercer drew his mouth down her belly almost worshipfully, feeling her skin shiver against his touch.

"Just lie back," he ordered. "Close your eyes."

"Umm," she purred when his lips touched her belly.

Mercer went slowly, knowing full well this was still new to her. This time he vowed to take his time; to bring her to climax in a slow, perfect spiral of desire. He urged her legs a little wider still, and touched her lightly with his tongue.

"Umm," she said again, more vibration than sound.

He stroked her again, a little deeper, then brushed a finger teasingly through her folds. Already she was wet and welcoming. Slowly, so slowly, he stoked her passion until she was shaking, until her hands clutched at his shoulders, and her nails dug into the muscles of his back. He eased the tip of a finger inside her silken sheath and felt it draw taut and eager, inviting him deeper. After a time, Zoë's trembling deepened to a bone-deep shudder, her hips rising to his mouth, her words of need nothing but soft, sweet cries in the night, thrilling him.

Zoë came apart beneath him as the ocean crashed and his body shafted with a need driven higher by the sounds of her passion. And when she was still again, he kissed his way quietly along the softness of her inner thigh, then shifted back onto his knees to see her lying, languid and sated against the rock. Hastily, he yanked his shirt from the rock and tossed it out on the sand.

"Lie down," he ordered.

Her eyes opened slowly, her mouth curling up at one corner when she saw the jutting hardness that rose up between them. "No," she said softly. "Trade places with me."

"Zoë," he said warningly.

She came onto her knees, seized his shoulders, and kissed him deeply. "Mercer," she said insistently, lifting her mouth away, "I shan't swoon and tell you how good you are, because you've been told a thousand times, I'm sure. But if you think turning my knees to jelly makes me your slave, perhaps you've chosen the wrong girl to tumble?"

"Dash it, Zoë, this isn't a 'tumble,' " he snapped. "I need you. I need you so badly I—"

"Then trade places with me," she said again, shifting away.

With one last, longing look at the shirt, he did as she asked, reclining against the stone. Zoë tucked herself under his arm, curled one leg over his, and set her small, warm hand to the muscles of his chest. "What's that Nanna always says?" she murmured, stroking the soft hair that trailed down to his belly, then lower. "Something about sauce for the goose being sauce for the gander?"

"Zoë, I don't think—"

His breath seized when she touched him.

"Zoë, I—"

Her small, clever hand encircled him, stroking down, pulling his heated flesh with it until the head of his cock swelled near to bursting. She did it again, working up and down again, her hand fisted tight.

"Umm!" It was more of a grunt than a word. "Zoë, I think—"

Her lips touched his belly, causing his thought to melt away.

"And I think," she murmured, her words vibrating against his shivering flesh, "that you should stop thinking."

She shifted, lifting herself over his left leg and settling herself on her belly between his knees. Both her hands were on him now, urgent and wicked, the beautiful swell of her buttocks like warm ivory in the flickering firelight. And when she bent nearer, her damp, curling hair brushed along his thighs, making his skin prickle with sensual awareness. It was as if every inch of his flesh had sprung vibrantly to life, anticipating what he knew was to come.

And he would not stop her. He wasn't even sure he could. Zoë was a force of nature, and though her motions were experimental, she seemed perfectly aware what she was about. She set one arm on his right thigh as if holding him down, then touched her tongue to the sensitive head of his cock. He jerked and gasped, but already she'd settled her mouth over him, tugging him gently into her warmth.

Oh, he'd had women do this a hundred times over, but in Zoë's small, inexpert hands, the experience was like nothing he'd ever felt. After a few strokes, she stopped, the ocean breeze cooling his wet, burning flesh.

"Am I doing this right?" she murmured.

Was she doing it right?

He made a sound, nothing remotely resembling the King's English. Zoë, thank God, took it as a *yes,* and resumed her seductive attentions. She drew him deep, suckling and stroking, her wicked little tongue flicking back and forth over his tip. Mercer's head went back against the rock, his eyes squeezing shut with sensual agony, his limbs rigid with desire as his ballocks seized warningly.

With her womanly intuition Zoë sensed it, one hand going down to cradle his sac. "You are too close," she murmured, releasing him. She was right. Mercer dared not open his eyes, half afraid her wicked smile might send him over the edge.

Zoë responded by drawing the tip of her tongue down the underside of his shaft, all the way down. Then she lightly touched the flesh below, brushing him through the soft hair.

"Zoë!" he choked.

"May I not do this?" she whispered. "Is it . . . all right?"

"Yes," he managed.

One hand still lightly fisting his cock, she teased at his sac with the other, her tongue playing delicately down the seam. "My goodness, Mercer," she murmured, "you have got sand in some interesting places."

"Have I indeed?" He gave a weak laugh as she teased even more intimately with her tongue. *Oh, you are . . . very, very clever . . .*

And wicked. Just as wicked—and as wonderful—as he'd always feared . . .

"You like this?" Zoë sounded inordinately pleased, and repeated the process. Her hand kept easing along his length, drawing his flesh taut as her tongue played temptingly below. His cock began to throb, the pulse deep in his groin and in his brain. He felt his vision cloud, felt himself losing contact with time and place.

His hand came down, lashing about her wrist. "Stop!" he choked, his other hand fisting in her mass of unruly curls. "Come. Up. Here."

She must have heard the urgency in his voice. Slowly, she slicked her hand back up his length and released him. He pulled her again, half dragging her up his length. She tumbled onto him in a cloud of jasmine—her essence, not the perfumer's—and set those hot, clever hands to his chest.

He opened his eyes and held her gaze. Zoë's eyes simmered with desire.

"Set your knees wide," he demanded. *"Now,* for God's sake."

She did as he ordered, her soft nest of curls teasing at his swollen head. With his hand, he guided himself through her desire-slick flesh, and thrust home. "Oh, God!" he choked. "Oh, *God,* Zoë."

Instinctively, she set her hands on his shoulders, and sank down to take him.

"*Ohhh,*" she sighed when he was fully inside her.

He drew a deep, shuddering breath and prayed for strength. He set his hands on her hipbones, and lifted her up just an inch, trailing the tip of his tongue over one of her pert, rosebud nipples as she rose. She was exquisite. Perfect. And he was lost to her. "Zoë, we were meant . . . to . . . to—"

He surrendered, unable to form coherent thought. Never had a woman affected him so, and she likely knew it, the minx. Zoë sighed and sank down again, taking him deep. Mercer lowered one hand, stroking it over the top of her thigh, then lower. He caught her breast in his mouth, suckled her until she cried out, then found the center of her aching and touched her lightly.

She whimpered and rose up again, urgent and eager against him. Her rhythm was perfect; her every instinct flawless. Zoë knew how to love him; knew it as if God had made her for this very act of joy and of reverence. She moved hungrily again, and Mercer began to lift his hips, driving himself up to meet her; touching her, suckling her nipples into his mouth as she rode him. He reminded himself that this time he mustn't spill himself inside her, that he would not lay that risk upon her slender shoulders, but the promise was soon forgotten in the searing heat.

They came together in a sweet, blinding fury; a surging of need and love that drove them both over the edge. Zoë cried out, murmuring his name over and over, and when he came back to the real world—to the crash of the turning tide, the sand and the stone, and Zoë's arms round his neck, he buried his face against her throat and tried not to weep with the joy of it.

This, he realized, was what he had so long feared. Being utterly lost in her. Helpless to control himself or deny her, in even the smallest of ways. She was a vixen. A siren. He had always known it. And now, he simply did not care.

Long moments later, they lay before the fire, Zoë on her back, finally making use of his shirt. He kissed her again, long and lingeringly, then settled himself beside her.

"Zoë, you are so beautiful," he murmured, drawing a finger down her breastbone. "Always, I have thought you beautiful."

"And a little wicked," she added, smiling. "Admit it, Mercer. You have ever been wary of me."

He looked away. "Perhaps because I knew what a danger you were to my heart," he murmured. "Even to my very sanity."

She lifted her head. "Oh, balderdash!" she said on a laugh. "You are always so in control—of yourself, and of everything around you."

"I cannot control you." Mercer dragged a hand through his hair. "I can't even control myself when I'm with you. It's like a madness coursing through my blood. But Zoë, we do have to talk. About this. About . . . everything."

She stiffened beneath him. "Not now," she softly pleaded. "Oh, Mercer, I . . . I am so weak just now. When you touch me, I can't think straight. Let us just savor this night. Let us celebrate life—Robin's life, and ours. Let us be grateful we all have one another."

"Damn it, Zoë, I want you," he said, his voice a little too harsh. "I want you for myself, can't you see? I love my brother, but . . . but what I feel for you is not the same."

Her eyes softened. "And what I feel for you—well, it is most imprudent," she whispered. "Oh, Mercer. Will you make me say it?"

"Zoë, I love you." He set his hand to her cheek. "Do you love me?"

She looked away and swallowed, her throat working sinuously.

"Zoë," he demanded, *"do you love me?"*

"Of course I do," she whispered. "I always have."

"Not like that," he snapped. "Do you love me as a woman loves a man? Can you make love like that, and *not* love me? Because I cannot think it possible."

By the glow of the fire he saw the tears spring to her eyes, and cursed himself. "I don't get to love you like that," she whispered. "I don't get to choose. I never have. Particularly not now, when life is in such disarray. And I am not for you, Mercer. You've always known that, because—"

"Zoë, hush," he said softly.

"—because if I were, why, you would not have kept your distance for so long, don't you see? When this is all over—when Robin is well, and I am gone from this place, you will think of these weeks as . . . as what I said before. A time out of place. A thing which was not real. And you will be relieved to have escaped me."

He speared his fingers into her hair, and turned her face back to his. "This is very, very real, Zoë." His voice was low and unsteady. "What I feel for you is real, and it is strong, and I will not share you. Not with anyone, in any way. And I do not know, Zoë, precisely what is the right thing to do now. But all I can see here is you, throwing yourself away on yet another man who—"

"Who what?"

"Who does not love you," he said quietly. "And whom you do not love. Not like that, Zoë."

"I love Robin with all my heart," she said fervently. "But no, Mercer. You know I don't love him like that. But I'll be damned if I'll shame him on what might yet be his deathbed."

"Zoë, I would never ask that of you."

"Then what are you asking?" Her gaze was faintly accusing. "Are you asking me to be your wife? Because you will have to. I cannot humiliate Papa by being anything less. And I am not the wife for you."

"Of course you are the wife for me," he choked. "Of course that is what I am asking. Good God, how can you think otherwise?"

She looked away as if ashamed. "I have learnt the hard way, Mercer, what my place in society is," she said firmly. "And I know, yes, that Robin does not want me. You are right. He never did. He is not going to marry me, and I am not going to hold him to his vow. Not after what . . . what you and I have been together."

"So what do you mean to do?"

"Once he is well, I should cry off as soon as it can be decently done, and if he tries to make himself out some sort of martyr—if he insists—then . . . well, I am going to have to tell him the truth. And then you will hate me all the more."

"Then I will tell him," said Mercer. "I want you, Zoë. I will do what I must."

"You have other fires to tend," she answered. "And I . . . well, I am practically ruined already. And it might—"

"It might what?" he demanded.

Zoë would not look at him. "It might get far worse."

"Worse?" he rasped. "What do you mean? Zoë, what is it you aren't telling me?"

For a moment, she chewed at her lip. "Nothing," she finally whispered. "Nothing I wish to talk about. It doesn't matter. And it certainly doesn't help the fact that that you could be made a laughingstock, Mercer, if you married me."

"I don't give a damn what others think," he said grimly.

But he knew as soon as the words left his mouth that he lied. He cared about Zoë; about her happiness, and her good name. For himself, it mattered so little, but he would not see her shamed.

All she had done that awful night in Brook Street, he now believed, was to cling to Robin out of pain. She had been so worn down by society's subtle scorn—told time and again, in the politest, most delicate of ways, that she wasn't good enough—until Zoë had begun to think herself worthy of nothing better. Jilting Robin to marry him now would provide society with a se'night of scandalmongering at worst. That was easily weathered. But anything more?

He did not know.

"I will manage Claire, if that is all that worries you," he said again, his voice softer. "Zoë, I promise you."

"How?" Zoë gently challenged. "With money? Perhaps. But that is like paying blackmail, and something you do not wish to start, particularly if she carries your child."

"She does not," he answered, his voice firm.

"You cannot know that. Not yet."

"I know her every move," he answered. "She goes on just as she always has. She is neither ill, nor weak, nor has she gained so much as a pound. She stays out gaming all hours of the night and day, and has nearly bankrupted herself. No woman with a child in her womb would go on so."

"She still wishes to be reconciled?" asked Zoë. "You still provide for her?"

Mercer hesitated too long. "I provide for her, yes."

"And she is so very beautiful. One can see how she might tempt you." Suddenly, Zoë cupped her hand round his cheek. "Oh, Mercer, please do let us drop this! I shall begin to feel perfectly shrewish."

"A little jealous, dare I hope?"

In the firelight, she rolled her eyes. "God, you are so arrogant," she answered. "Besides, it mightn't be just Claire that haunts us. We can't go any further just now, you and I. My life is a mess, and so is yours. I just need time to see how everything settles out."

He held her gaze, his heart suddenly bursting with desire for her, and half afraid that he could never make her love him as he loved her. He hated her hesitance, and didn't understand it, either. But that was Zoë, stubborn to a fault. And he was being selfish.

"What do you want right now, then?" he asked. "What is it, Zoë, that would make you happy? Just for tonight. Just for now—since we must live our lives doled out in dribs and drabs?"

Her arms twined round his neck, and pulled his body over to hers. "Make love to me again," she begged, her eyes soft and shining. "Make love to me, and take my breath away, Mercer, as only you can do. Just for tonight. Just for now."

And so he did, for—as he'd always feared—already he had become addicted to her. And any little taste of Zoë was better than none.

Chapter Fifteen
∼

IN WHICH BONNIE
DEMURS.

"I tell you, Mamma, I do not want it!" Lord Robert hurled the piece of toast back onto his plate, jostling his silverware and making one of the footmen jump.

Zoë lifted her gaze from the small breakfast table, and shot Jonet a sympathetic look. "It is bread, my dear," his mother cajoled. "You need to eat."

"I'll eat what I can bloody well feed myself." Robin's voice was tinged with pain, both physical and emotional. "A man doesn't wish his mother buttering his toast for him."

Cole Amherst laid his knife down very firmly, as if he feared he might use it. "Robert, I know your leg and your arm pain you, but I must insist you be civil to your mother."

Robin hung his head. "You are quite right, sir. Forgive me."

He spoke as if he meant it. Indeed, he sounded lately perfectly horrified with himself, and with his outbursts. It had been thus for nearly a week. As Robin's body healed, his emotions came more and more to the surface; the residual effects of the concussion, Dr. Bevins said. Robin had been coming down to dine for three days now, looking stronger with each passing day. And yet he was no happier.

Nor was Zoë. The scar on Robin's face, at least, was healing. The scar on her heart was not. It had been pure heartbreak, sitting alongside Mercer at breakfast, longing for his touch even as she worried about Robin. Indeed, she was *tired* of worrying about Robin, and yet she could not escape the knowledge that she, in part, had brought him to this awful point.

As to Mercer, he had resumed his pattern of absence at luncheon and dinner. The outbreak of smallpox had waned, but other estate matters consumed him. His temper, too, was short. His dark, barely veiled glances at Zoë still simmered with heat, and with something more. With thwarted desire, she thought, and he was not a man who long tolerated being thwarted.

This morning, however, he had not even come down to breakfast, and there was an odd edge in the room; looks exchanged between Jonet and her husband with an unease which went beyond their concern for Robin. Stranger still, neither had commented upon Mercer's absence.

Perhaps it had something to do with the visitors who had arrived in the night. During a bout of insomnia around midnight, Zoë had roamed into the library only to espy an expensive traveling coach in the forecourt below, surrounded by outriders and servants, with a loaded fourgon behind. And yet nothing had been said this morning. The callers, whomever they were, apparently had business with Mercer, and not the family.

Suddenly, Mr. Amherst stood, lifting one eyebrow in his wife's direction. "My dear, I shall see you at dinner," he said. "I've letters to write, then I'm off to Fromley to oversee preparations for the new rector."

"Sir," said Zoë, almost rising, "is there something I might help with?"

"Oh, we can always use help," he said with a weak smile. "The office in particular needs a good turning-out. The rector left his bookshelves and paperwork in a shambles—but that's dusty work, my dear."

"Well, I can sort out books and papers as well as any-one, can I not?" said Zoë. "And later, perhaps you might set me down near the Fitches? I have a book for the chil-dren."

Mr. Amherst smiled his wide, golden-god smile, lighting up the room. "Nothing would give my more pleasure, my dear. Shall we meet downstairs at eleven?"

Abruptly, Robin shoved back his chair. "I shall walk back up with you, Papa," he said. "Ladies, your pardon. I find I've little appetite." As he rose, one of the servants hastened forward with his cane. "Thank you," he said, hitching his sling firmly against his chest. Then, bearing much of his weight on the cane, Robin lurched toward the door.

But when he reached it, he seized hold of the knob and turned, his expression pale, leaving the gash down his face all the more prominent. "I'm sorry," he said out of nowhere. "For everything. I realize I'm not fit com-pany for any of you just now. So I've been thinking—and I've decided—well, that it might be best if I just went away for a time."

"Went *away*?" his mother echoed.

"I mean to move into the summerhouse for a few weeks," he went on. "I just . . . I just need the peace and quiet. And when I'm a little better—when I can ride again—I mean to go up to Kildermore for a time."

"Well," Jonet murmured. "It seems you've quite made up your mind."

Robin turned his gaze on Zoë. "We ought to marry before I leave, I daresay," he said quietly. "But you needn't go to Scotland, old thing. I know you dislike it."

A silence fell over the room then. Robin said no more, and his stepfather followed him out, his expression one of frustration. But when the door had closed softly behind them, Jonet motioned to the footmen. "Leave us, please."

They disappeared through a service door cut discreetly into the wainscoting. Jonet let her hands fall into her lap. "Oh, he is so desperately unhappy! Zoë, my dear, I am sorry."

Zoë set her shoulders back. "Indeed, I wished to speak with you about that, ma'am," she said quietly. "I think I'm going to have to tell Robin that . . . well, that I mean to cry off." She dropped her head, and fisted her hands in her napkin. "I am so sorry, Jonet. I know I promised you I would marry him."

"Well, no," said Jonet, "that is not quite what you promised."

"And people will say, I know, that I am cruel," Zoë went on, missing her point. "It will be whispered I've cast Robin aside because he . . . he is not perfect. But to me, he is the same person he ever was. He is Robin, and I adore him. And yet, it is clear neither of us will ever love one another in that way."

"Oh, Zoë," she murmured. "You are certain?"

"Yes, quite." Zoë felt her throat tighten. "Indeed,

I think I no longer care what the gossips have to say about me. I just wish Robin's life to be right again. And I wish . . . oh, Jonet, I just wish us all to be happy! And I fear we never shall be."

Jonet surprised her then by reaching over to cover Zoë's hand with her own. "Oh, my dear, this has become more difficult than even I imagined," she said. "You have every right to hold Robin's feet to the fire. Indeed, he will marry you tomorrow if you but ask him to."

"I know he will," said Zoë stridently. "Indeed, he will do anything I ask. That's what got us both into this awful mess. But I am watching my oldest friend destroyed, and I cannot bear it."

Jonet squeezed her hand, a look of sympathy sketching over her beautiful, flawless face. "My dear, it is he who has destroyed himself," she said. "I am afraid, Zoë, that Robin has made the one mistake which dashing young blades ought never make: he has fallen in love with his mistress."

"And that is the thing I cannot fix," Zoë whispered.

Jonet fell back into her chair. "Perhaps when he is free to do so, he will return to her and plead his case," she said, her gaze suddenly far away. "But as I've said, she mightn't have him now. He will wear that scar forever, and quite possibly the limp, too."

"He will not go to her," Zoë whispered. "He has sworn to her he will never trouble her again, and I know Robin. He shan't. Perhaps that's why he is going to Scotland. So that he will not be tempted. And Mrs. Wilfred—she will not return to him. She truly meant it when she turned him off."

"You sound quite certain of that last, my dear," she murmured.

Zoë could not hold her gaze. "Yes, quite certain," she whispered. "You must not ask me why."

"Lud, child, what have you done?" Jonet clucked, her eyes sweeping down Zoë's face.

Something unutterably stupid, thought Zoë. As if being caught *en dishabille* with Robin wasn't enough, she had driven the nails into her coffin of ruination, and should Mercer ever hear of it . . .

"Your father will be angry enough you've refused Robert," Jonet continued. "I pray you've not done something even more impetuous."

Zoë did not look up. "I have done what I thought best for everyone," she said. "I beg you, ma'am, ask me no more. I wrote Papa yesterday for the carriage, so I shall be returning to London shortly."

Jonet looked unhappy. "What will your father say when you tell him?"

"He will banish me to his estate in Perthshire," said Zoë evenly. "And I have decided there are worse fates in life. Indeed, it occurs to me there is much good I could do there if I but put my mind to it."

"And what of my son? Where does that leave him?"

Zoë looked at her blankly. "I am persuaded a marriage to me would but compound Robin's misery."

A faint smile curved one corner of Jonet's mouth. "Actually, I meant my other son."

Zoë felt the blood rush to her face. It was as Robin had always said: his mother saw too much. "Mercer has always felt an exaggerated sense of responsibility toward me, I fear," she murmured, jerking awkwardly from her chair. "My being here—his having to witness my distress over Robin—has merely awakened his natural sense of chivalry. If he has suggested otherwise . . . well, he is confused."

Lightly, Jonet laughed. "Oh, Stuart is the sort of man who is rarely confused about anything, my dear," she answered. "And no, he has said nothing to me. But there, I must leave that between the two of you, I daresay."

"You have always been most kind to me, Jonet," she said. "Kinder perhaps than I deserve. So you may be sure I will do nothing else which might bring scandal down upon your family. I hope we understand one another?"

At that, Jonet laughed. "Oh, child, this family has overcome scandal before," she said. "You forget that half the *ton* once believed I murdered my husband."

"But at least it was a proper marriage," said Zoë, dropping her chin. "And you were blameless. You brought no embarrassment to your family."

"Indeed, it was a very proper marriage," said Jonet. "And a perfectly miserable one. Now my second—ah, that, as you see, was a love match! The wicked marchioness married her handsome army captain—a man of God, no less. What do you think people said about that?"

Zoë tried to smile. "Nonetheless, you shan't have any more idle gossip on my account."

"Thank you, Zoë." Humor lit Jonet's eyes. "Your heart, I daresay, is in the right place."

Zoë went at once to the door, then paused, her hand already upon the knob. "Jonet," she said, turning round, "might I ask whose carriage that was that came in the night?"

Jonet dabbed at her mouth with her napkin as if stalling for time. "The traveling coach, do you mean?" she murmured. "That was one of Stuart's. From London."

For a moment, Zoë did not comprehend. "I did not recognize it," she said. "It was unmarked."

Jonet folded the napkin and rose. "I believe it is a carriage he keeps at his house in Fitzrovia."

Suddenly, the truth dawned. "The Vicomtesse de Chéraute?" Zoë whispered. "He . . . He was expecting her?"

Jonet came toward the door. "I'm afraid you'll have to ask him about that," she said quietly. "But I rather doubt she will stay here very long."

Zoë felt her color rush up. "Why, it is none of my business, I'm sure," she managed. "As I said, I shall be gone soon."

Jonet closed the distance between them. "Zoë, our home will ever be yours," she said, setting a hand on her shoulder. "Do what you must, of course. But regardless of Claire's presence, you need not leave Greythorpe until you feel ready to face your papa."

At last Zoë lifted her gaze. "Thank you, ma'am," she said. "But trust me, I am quite ready to face Papa. Indeed, I am finally ready, I hope, to deal with whatever life brings."

"My lord?"

The Marquess of Mercer barely glanced up from the piles of account books and correspondence stacked neatly across his wide, mahogany desk. "What is it, Page?" he asked, slashing his signature across the next document.

The waiting footman stepped over his threshold. "Mr. Donaldson said to enquire as to whether you'd like your breakfast served here?"

Mercer realized the man was carrying a tray. "Ah, thank you, yes." He set away his ink pot, and motioned for the tray to be put down on one corner of the desk. "What did Donaldson send up?"

"Your usual, sir." The footman whipped off the domed lid. "Coffee, black. Three eggs, one rare beef-steak, black pudding, and tomatoes. Ah—and the kipper. Will there be anything else, sir?"

Looking up from the next letter, Mercer motioned him away. "No, that's excellent, Page. Thank you." He picked up the plate containing the kipper, and set it down under Bonnie's nose.

The collie came awake, sprang up, and dug in with a swift *snap-snap* of her teeth. As she ate, Mercer stroked a hand down her silky black head. This was the time of day he and Bonnie always spent together; the time when Mischief, younger and more spry, preferred to go out of doors, and Bonnie preferred to laze in the sun or, when there was one, by the fire.

"My lord?" The servant was lingering uneasily.

Mercer looked up from the floor. "Yes, Page?"

"The lady who came last night? She has arisen, sir, and is already strolling along the veranda in a bit of a temper. I believe she wishes to see you as soon as may be."

Mercer grunted. "Does she now?" he muttered, pushing aside his ledger, and replacing it with his warm breakfast plate. "Let her cool her heels awhile. Patience is a virtue."

"Certainly, sir." The footman closed the door.

Mercer ate with relish, skimming through his remaining correspondence as he did so. He had known, of course, that Claire would turn up eventually. His instincts with regard to her had become unfailing during their long, memorable year together. He wondered yet again what he'd seen in her. She was beautiful, yes, but so was an ice storm—and both were treacherous.

Bonnie finished her morning kipper, licked her chops, then crossed the room to a broad beam of morning sun, flopping down with a satisfied grunt.

"Well, what do you advise, old girl?" he asked, looking at the dog. "Shall I let her wear a furrow in the veranda? Or put her out of her misery?"

But Bonnie wisely refused to get involved in such a contretemps. She had never quite taken to Claire—which should have been Mercer's first clue that her beauty was only skin deep. After a sigh, he dispatched his breakfast, then finished his ledgers, and just before the clock struck eleven, rang for Page to show Claire in. He would be civil, he vowed, so long as she was—at least until he discovered what he so desperately wished to know. After that, well, it was up to Claire.

She sailed into the study, her golden hair piled high, wearing a morning gown of pale yellow silk flounced and beribboned in purest white. If the wait had tried her patience, Claire wisely gave no sign of it. Her face was fixed in a welcoming smile, her eyes artificially bright. It was an expression he knew well.

"Mercer, *mon trésor!*" she cried, floating toward him. "How very handsome you look!"

He had risen and stepped round his desk. "Good

morning, Claire." He offered his cheeks to be kissed in the French fashion. "I trust you slept well?"

"Oh, *oui!*" One hand still cupped his face, her other set lightly upon his chest as she leaned into him. "This pure country air, Mercer, *c'est très magnifique!*"

He bent his lips to her ear. "What a pretty little liar you are, my dear," he murmured. "You abhor the country."

She gave her light, tinkling laugh, as if he were the cleverest man on earth.

Having had enough of the specious pleasantry, Mercer stepped back and motioned Page to shut the door. Too late, he saw the small figure who had paused in the center of the great hall, a wicker basket hooked over her arm. *Bloody hell,* he thought as the door swung shut. *Just what I needed.*

But Claire was swanning around the room, taking it all in as Bonnie eyed her warily. "So this is the place from which the great Lord Mercer commands his universe!" She spun round, her bottom lip coming out. "I cannot believe, *mon cœur,* after all we meant to one another, you never invited me here!"

Mercer cocked one hip on his desk and leaned back, his arms braced to either side. "Let us get down to business, Claire," he said. "What brings you to Greythorpe? And with every piece of baggage you own, it would appear?"

Her gaze dropped, and again the lip came out. "But that frightful man said that I might call upon you if I needed your help."

"What frightful man?" asked Mercer quietly.

"Why, the one you sent to the house!" she cried, her

chin coming up. "The slender man with the evil eyes—the one who brought me my sapphire *broche*. He—why, he said it was a gift from you."

"Ah, *that* man," said Mercer dryly. "You lost the pin at Crockford's, I believe?"

"*Oui,*" she said softly. "But I do not know how it was you came to have it."

"You have, in point of fact, lost all your jewels," Mercer added, still propped languidly on his desk. "Or perhaps I should say *Chéraute*'s jewels?"

"The *broche* was mine!" Petulance sketched over Claire's lovely face, then quickly vanished. "All the sapphires were mine, *mon chéri*. The necklace, the bracelets, and the rings. They were never Chéraute's." Here she paused to give an affected sniff. "And I miss them so very desperately. Mercer, you cannot know how difficult this has been for me!"

"But you sold all of them," said Mercer flatly. "Or gamed them away outright."

"*Oui,* I have been so very bad." Again, her eyelids swept down, a look of childlike contrition.

"And now you cannot go home without them, can you?" Mercer folded his arms over his chest. "A dukedom awaits—your husband's new châteaux, his wealth, his vineyards, that idyllic little island off the coast of Spain—and let us not forget your new title and your place at court. And none of this can you avail yourself of unless you go home and obtain his forgiveness."

Claire hung her head even further. "That man—the one with eyes like ice—he said you would help me, that perhaps you even *have* my jewels?" She set her hands prayerfully together. "I know, Mercer, that you would never fail to rescue your poor, poor Claire!"

Mercer let his arms drop. "You forget something, my dear," he said coldly. "You forget the one thing that really matters to me."

"*Oui?*" She batted her eyes innocently. "And that would be?"

He stalked toward her, and laid his hand very firmly over her belly. "This, Claire," he whispered. "My child."

"Oh, *mon Dieu!*" she cried, falling back a step. "Oh, Mercer! Such bad luck! The child, it is lost."

"It is *lost?*" He followed her, making her flinch. "What do you mean, *it is lost?* Claire, one loses a hairpin. Not a child."

"It is lost!" she cried, fear flaring in her eyes. "These things, they happen!"

"I think you lie, Claire," he growled.

"*Non, non!*" She shook her head wildly.

He pressed her nearly to the wall. "Now mark me well, my dear," he said, his voice lethally quiet. "I mean to have that evil man with the eyes like ice search out every back-alley abortionist from Kensington to Stepney, and so help me God, if one of them so much as knows the color of your hair, I'll make you rue the day you laid eyes on me."

"Already I rue it!" she cried.

"As do I," he roared, leaning in until she hitched up against the wainscoting. "So tell me, Claire, did you miscarry? Or did you get rid of it? Or did it never exist? And think carefully—think very carefully about your châteaux and your island and your fine French court before you answer me, because I have the power to ruin you."

Her gaze flicked up, swift and wary. "It never was," she whispered. "I—I was heartbroken, Mercer, certainly. But I was late. Such things, they happen, *oui*?"

He turned his back and walked away, telling himself he should be relieved. That it was *over.* And yet he could not escape the awful truth; that a little part of him had hoped for it, even if it convoluted his already complicated life, and bound him to her, this woman whom he did not like and would never trust. He *wanted* that child, yes—if it existed. But he *dreamt* of a child with unruly dark curls, a too-sharp chin, and oddly colored eyes. Yes, patience was indeed a virtue.

He collected himself, and turned around. "I shan't even bother, Claire, to ask how long you've known this," he said, hands clasped rigidly behind his back. "I will hope and pray, in fact, that you aren't the outright liar I suspect. And I will do this, Claire, because I mean to move on with my life, and I want you out of it. Congratulate me, my dear. I am getting married."

She drew back as if he had slapped her. "Married!" she said. "To whom? *Mon Dieu,* you have been stuck here in the country with your cows and your pigs and your—your—*merde* for weeks! Who can you possibly mean to marry?"

"My brother's fiancée, though he does not know it yet," said Mercer coolly. "Nor does she. But trust me, Claire. That is what is going to happen."

Claire could not suppress the merriment that sprang to her eyes. "Oh, *mon chéri,* you mean to marry the girl with the green-and-gold garters?" she cried. "To steal your own brother's bride? Really, Mercer, I always said you were cold. Nothing stands in your way, does it?"

"Certainly you will not," he said grimly.

"Just give me my jewels," she snapped, "if you really have them."

"Oh, I have them, my dear," he said. "I have become very skilled at getting you out of hock—one way or another." With that, Mercer went to his desk and unlocked the drawer that Charlie had secured but a few hours earlier. Withdrawing the heart-shaped box, he snapped it open and thrust it at her.

"Oh, *mon Dieu,* my parure!" Her eyes widened as she stared at the huge emeralds. "Oh, please, please, Mercer!" She reached for it. "You must give it back to me!"

Mercer snapped it shut again. "In due time," he said, "perhaps."

"But Mercer, I . . . I cannot return to Chéraute without it!" she cried, her hand thrust plaintively out. "And you—why, *you* do not want me! I thought you meant to help me! That is what your vile, mean-spirited man claimed. Did he lie to me?"

"Mr. Kemble?" Mercer murmured. "He does tend to lie when it suits him, yes. And he's so very good at it, too, do you not think, Claire? After all, it takes one to know one."

"Mon Dieu, it is true!" Tears were welling as she spat out the words. " 'Merciless Mercer!' For that is what they call you behind your back, *mon chéri!* I vow, you love that—that—*dog* better than you ever loved me!" She thrust an accusing finger at Bonnie.

But Mercer had opened the box again, and was studying the allegedly priceless emeralds. "I knew, Claire, when you gambled the parure away that you were desperate indeed," he said. "They are the crown jewels of *les vicomtes de* Chéraute, are they not?"

"Oui," she hissed. Tears had sprung to her eyes.

"I almost wish I could have watched you this last fortnight, pacing the floor, tearing at your hair, and wondering how you were to extract yourself from this nasty little trap of your own making," he murmured. "Knowing the riches and the honors that await you, if only you could persuade your husband to take you back. No, you cannot return to France without his jewels, can you, my dear—particularly not *this*."

"Non." She sounded defeated, her slender shoulders rolling inward. *"Non,* I dare not go without them. You are too cruel."

Mercer shut the box and tossed it on his desk as he passed. Claire made a faint, whimpering sound. As if relenting, he turned, picked it up, and thrust it at her. "Do not stamp your little feet with delight quite yet, my dear," he murmured, returning to his desk.

Claire clasped the case to her bosom, and collapsed into a chair.

Mercer sat down, steepled his fingers, and looked across the desk at her. "I took the liberty of having my jeweler make a copy of the real parure," he said quietly. "Chéraute's remaining jewels will be on your dressing table when you return to your bedchamber, and you may have them as a token of my former esteem. But *your* parure is in my safe. I am keeping it, you see, as my insurance policy."

She looked at him, horrified. "Insurance policy?"

she echoed. "I do not know what this thing is, *insurance policy.*"

Mercer planted both hands upon the desk, and leaned far, far over it. "It ensures, my dear, that you have not lied to me about my child," he said. "And it ensures your continued good behavior for . . . oh, a few years, at least."

"I . . . why, I do not know what you mean!" she fumed.

"It means that I shall have you watched, Claire, every minute of every day," he said. "Indeed, I will put a spy beneath Chéraute's very roof. I will bribe his bloody footmen if I must."

Her empty hand fisted. "Oh, but this abominable!"

"And if you swell with child in the coming weeks," he went on, coming round the desk, "or if you spread so much as one vile scrap of gossip about my wife-to-be, then I will make sure Chéraute learns that his duchess has duped him with a box full of pinchbeck and paste. Do I make myself clear?"

"*Nique ta mère!*" she snarled, her beautiful lips twisting to something hideous and ugly.

At that, Bonnie rose from her sunbeam, snarling.

"*Tut, tut,* Claire!" Mercer caught her chin in his hand. "I think Bonnie speaks French. Now, your vile mouth aside, have we a bargain here? Or no?"

For an instant, she quivered with indignation. "What choice have I?" she finally snapped.

"Excellent." He released her chin. "Now, in a few years, when age and marriage have mellowed me, and you have proven yourself a good little duchess, then I will send you the original. In the meantime, I suggest you do nothing to cause Chéraute suspicion. I particularly suggest you give up gaming."

Claire licked her lips uncertainly. "And my sapphires, *mon chéri*?" she asked. "Am I to have them back?"

"No, as it happens." He hitched his hip back onto his desk. "Kemble has found a buyer for the lot—a rich American who will pay twice what the stones are worth, because he has more money than sense. And it will cover a mere fraction, Claire, of what I have spent cleaning up after you these past weeks."

"But—But—what shall I tell Chéraute!" she burst out.

"You will tell him, my dear, that you sold them," said Mercer quietly, "in order to live. After all, you had a house to let and servants to pay."

Her pale brow furrowed. "But I lived in your house!" she said. "And I did not pay . . ."

Then realization slowly dawned in her eyes. Mercer smiled. "Trust me, Claire, it will go a damned sight easier for you if you play the repentant wife, not the cast-off mistress."

Her eyes flared wide with rage. "Cast off?" she cried, leaping up. *"Cast off?* Why, how dare you!" And then she drew back and slapped him. Again.

Mercer remained impervious, his hip still cocked against his desk as color bloomed up Claire's cheeks.

"Well," said Mercer quietly, "this has grown tiresome, my dear. If you leave tomorrow at dawn, I daresay you'll just make the afternoon packet to Calais."

In an odd, melancholy mood, Zoë took the shortcut through the wood as she walked home from the Fitches late that afternoon. On one hand, she was oddly satisfied to have exhausted herself with a day spent sorting and dusting the vestry, and happy to have spent an hour reading to the younger children. But in every quiet moment, this morning's vision of Mercer in the vicomtesse's embrace kept coming back to torment her.

Of course, it likely meant nothing, she told herself as her feet shuffled softly through last year's dead leaves. Mercer did not love the woman, of that Zoë was certain. And yet . . .

And yet she had come to Greythorpe. She wanted Mercer back, and had made little secret of that fact. In a few months' time, she might well bear Mercer a child. Unthinkingly, Zoë set a hand over her womb. It was a gesture, she knew, of hope, and sometimes even of grief—and one she had so often seen from Phaedra in the two years it had taken her to conceive. And though Zoë had never felt the urge herself—not until this moment—she was enough of a woman to know what it meant.

She stopped abruptly, and jerked her hand away. Good God, was she ten times a fool? Above, the summer wind soughed through the branches, sending sunlight and shadow shifting across the path before her, as changeable and as uncertain as her future.

That night on the beach—in Mercer's arms—seemed unreal to her now. His declaration of love felt suddenly like a chimera, as if a stiff breeze might blow it away. She realized now that she had spent most of her life admiring Mercer from afar, sometimes even deliberately tormenting him, just for a few moments of his attention. And always he had been a strong, stern, and yes, a reassuring presence in her life. But never had he felt attainable. Not to her.

But here, so far away from London, so caught up in her desire for him, and so fraught with worry for Robin, Zoë had let her keen grasp of reality slip away. And somehow, she had managed to consign the Vicomtesse de Chéraute to the rubbish bin of forgotten jealousies. But that, perhaps, had been most unwise. The vicomtesse was tall and fair and quite stunningly beautiful, like an ice princess or a fairy queen.

Perhaps when he was back in London—when his ice princess had swollen large with his child, and impending motherhood had softened her—yes, perhaps then Mercer might feel a resurgence of what had surely once been a deep affection, if not love. Was it possible? Zoë remembered again the vicomtesse's lips brushing softly along his cheek, and her light, carefree laugh, and for the first time in a great many years, Zoë felt suddenly naïve in the ways of the world.

It was not a feeling she embraced. Instead, Zoë almost resented her heart—and Mercer—for leaving her so weak-kneed and vulnerable.

She picked up her pace toward the house, and forced away the horrid sense of helplessness. She was not vulnerable; she knew better. She was not helpless, for she had learned long ago to look out for herself. She resolved instead to think of poor Mr. Fitch, who had at last left the chair by his wife's empty bed and returned to the fields. In his hard and simple world, the harvest waited for neither life nor death, and there had been one last cutting of hay to get in.

And she thought, too, of Mary, the eldest of the two girls, who was learning to keep the house tidy, and the younger ones who were in turn taking on new responsibilities. Such were the harsh lessons of life for them, and by comparison, Zoë reminded herself, she had no problems at all.

Having left the youngest looking over a picture book she had purchased in the village, Zoë had given her pledge to return on the morrow with Mr. Amherst. Now she had a notion of taking Trudy along, and giving the kitchens a good scrubbing before she left Greythorpe. Heaven knew she'd no talent for cleaning, but after today the idea of doing something hard and physical oddly appealed to her. How very strange she had become. Perhaps it was time she, too, returned to London.

Having left the footpath through the wood for Greythorpe's manicured side garden, Zoë rounded the corner of the house to see a wagon at the foot of the grand staircase, and footmen loading it with furniture. Jonet stood at the top of the steps on the portico, her hands clasped. Untying her bonnet as she went, Zoë wove round the men and dashed up.

"There was no furniture upstairs," said Jonet hollowly. She looked not at Zoë, but at the mattress that was being hefted atop the heap. "In the summerhouse, I mean. Really, Zoë, what can he be thinking?"

He was thinking that he wanted to escape, thought Zoë. She set a gentle hand on Jonet's arm. "Do you know, I think perhaps I understand," she murmured. "Has he gone, then?"

Jonet pressed her lips together and nodded, as though Robin had removed to the West Indies instead of a cottage a quarter-mile away. "Come, we should go inside," Zoë said, urging Jonet toward the door.

"Yes, of course," said Jonet a little sorrowfully. "Miss Adler is expecting me in the schoolroom."

"Look, I shall pop down and make sure he has everything he needs," Zoë reassured her. "And I . . . well, I have something to tell him, don't I?"

Jonet nodded, and squeezed her hand. But on the threshold, they ran squarely into Lord Mercer, who had obviously been watching them from the shadows of the great hall, his hands set at his hips, his coat pushed back from his lean waist. He flicked a concerned glance at his mother, but the heat of his gaze settled on Zoë.

Jonet, too, noticed. "Good afternoon, my dear," she murmured, drifting toward the stairs. "Well, I must go on, I daresay, to the children who actually need me."

But Mercer was still watching Zoë. "You are going down there?" he demanded. "Why?"

Zoë stood unflinchingly. "Because I just told your mother I would," she answered, "and because we have unfinished business, Robin and I."

She moved as if to leave again, but Mercer caught her arm almost possessively, heedless of the servants passing to and fro. "Zoë," he rasped, "I have to see you. Alone."

"But you have a houseguest, have you not?" Her temper inexplicably spiked. "I suggest you attend to your business, Mercer, as I mean to tend to mine."

But Mercer did not release her arm. He towered over her as he always did, a dark, indomitable presence, but this time his mood felt strained and oddly unpredictable. They stood so close Zoë could detect the warmth which radiated from his body, and the clean, seductive scent of his shaving soap. "What do you mean to do?" he demanded.

His commanding eyes won out. "What I must do," she said, dropping her gaze. "What I promised you I would do. I keep my word, Mercer. Above all things, I keep my word."

"And I keep mine." His voice was low and certain.

His hand still gripped her arm. She looked up again and saw not disapproval or scorn in his eyes, but a tenderness that shocked her. "I know that, Mercer," she finally said. "No one has ever doubted your honor. Certainly not I."

For a moment, the air about them was charged with electricity. Then at last, he released her arm. "Go, then," he said quietly. "But if you think, Zoë, that you and Robin have unfinished business . . ."

Inexplicably, Mercer let his words fade away.

Her heart suddenly tight in her chest, Zoë turned round and went back down the stairs, barely dodging two footmen lifting part of a bed frame onto the wagon. Still carrying her bonnet, the ribbons streaming out behind, she hastened along the west wing and down the hill. The ducks were out, gliding along the water in formation, the smaller ones now half the size of their mothers, a beautiful sight. Zoë focused on that, and on the difficult task before her.

On the narrow stone stoop of the summerhouse, she paused to knock, and on hearing nothing, lifted the latch and stepped guardedly inside. She had deliberately avoided coming back here since that fateful night with Mercer. Perhaps she had been wary of letting herself remember the depth and the intensity of what had happened. Of what she might learn about herself, and her need for him.

She strolled slowly through the shadowy stillness, her steps echoing in the near empty room. As she had known she would be, Zoë was assailed by a thousand memories, her skin all but prickling with a sudden, sensual awareness. And yet it was a feeling that went beyond the sensual, to something far deeper. Far more primitive. Her eyes went at once to the hearth; to the worn wool rug where Mercer had laid her down, damp and shivering and so full of despair, she had been broken inside.

The scent of cold soot and bayberry still tinged the air. Even the scent of his bare skin came back to her, warm and faintly musky. And for a moment, she could all but see him, sitting in the old ladder-back chair, elbows on his knees, regarding her steadily through his solemn eyes as she'd woken, lethargic from his lovemaking.

Even then she had known that Mercer was wondering just what he'd got himself into. Oh, he wanted her. Perhaps he always had. But he did not *want* to want her— and to Zoë, that made all the difference in the world. No matter how he might desire her, she would forever be an inconvenience to Mercer, a man who was as controlled and self-disciplined as she was capricious.

But this was about Robin, she reminded herself, forcing her gaze from the hearth. Already, in their hurt and confusion, they had caused enough harm. To their families. To one another. She would not cause more. She turned and went through the door to her right, into a tidy kitchen and dining room, but even they were empty.

Zoë returned to the back door, opened it and looked out through the gloom of the boat shed. Through the shadows, she saw Robin on the dock beyond. He stood at the railing, leaning on it as if to rest his lame leg. His mahogany hair lifted lightly on the breeze, and his face was turned toward the hills. Though his face had grown thinner in illness, and the scar was a stark testament to tragedy, Robin still looked strikingly handsome

She tossed her hat onto an upturned rowboat, then went through. "Hullo," she murmured, joining him at the railing. "May I pay a social call? I shan't stay but a moment."

He gave a snort of laugher, and hung his head. "There's no escaping the lot of you, is there?"

"Wretch!" she said, pretending to elbow him lightly in the ribs.

"Ow, Zoë! I'm a wounded man."

"Yes, you are, aren't you?" she murmured. "And I'm sorry for it. Truly."

They fell into silence then, both of them looking out over the water. "It's so soothing down here," she murmured. "In a way, I rather envy you."

"Getting a trifle hot up on the hill, is it?" he asked ruefully. "I had to get out, old thing. Sorry."

Zoë shrugged. "Your parents are kind to me," she said absently. "The water in the lake—where does it originate?"

Robin lifted his good arm, and pointed north. "There's a chalybeate spring up there," he said, "plus all the water that leaches through the chalk."

"Mr. Stokely taught us about chalybeate in chemistry class," Zoë said, twirling a loose curl about her finger. "It's made of iron, manganese, calcium, and magnesium."

"All that, eh?"

Zoë tossed her hand airily. "Just filled with useless information, am I not?"

At that, Robin looked round, narrowing his eyes

against the August sun. "You're smart, Zoë," he said. "That's what you are, though you pretend not to be. You have a fine education—one most men cannot brag of."

Again, she lifted one shoulder. "And what good has it done me, I wonder?" she mused. "Anyway, did you know they used to prescribe chalybeate waters for the insane? Stokie told me."

This time, he did laugh. "Think we need to take the cure, do you?"

She turned her face to his and smiled. "I think it quite likely," she answered. Then she set her hand on his arm. "Come, let's at least dangle our feet in the water. Can you get down?"

"Aye, if I brace myself on that column."

Taking his cane in hand, Robin limped over to the open spot where the boats tied up, then set his shoulder to the wood. "Does your leg hurt terribly?" she asked, watching.

Robin laughed as he eased himself down. "Well, I don't want to cast up my accounts now when I get out of bed," he answered. "But aye, it hurts. Still, I've got to keep moving, Bevins says, or it will wither or freeze up or some equally dire thing. Thought I might start swimming down here now that my arm's feeling better. Get the weight off the leg, you know, and work the muscles."

Zoë joined him, stripping off her shoes and stockings, then dipping her legs in the water. Robin was a little slower, but he soon had his trouser hems rolled to his knees. She was pleased to hear him speak of a future, and relieved to hear him imply he wished to get well again. For a while, she'd feared he mightn't.

Robin reached inside his coat. "Cheroot?" he asked.

Zoë shook her head. "No," she said glumly. "I seem to have lost my taste for them."

He laughed, his hand falling. The cool water swirled round Zoë's ankles, soothing her weary feet. Robin lazily circled his good leg, his eyes focused somewhere in the depths of the water. She thought of the many times they had sat thus at Elmwood's millpond, and of the comfort two friends could find in utter silence. She did not know what the future held for her beyond this place; beyond this incredibly painful and amazingly beautiful summer. But even if her dreams of Mercer were never met, or if Robin never found it in his heart to fully forgive her, Zoë prayed at the very least she might salvage their friendship.

She drew in a deep, ragged breath. "Robin," she finally said, "I am not going to marry you."

He cut a sidelong glance at her. "Can't say as I blame you, old thing," he said. "But Rannoch will have a different view, I daresay. We'd best just do it, Zoë, and get it over with. It will be all right."

She clucked her tongue. "Listen to you!" she said. *"Get it over with?* Robin, we both deserve better than that."

He narrowed his eyes and looked into the sun again. "Aye, well, I don't," he said quietly. "And what I want, I'll never have anyway. So I'll marry you, Zoë, if you like. Or not—if you can stand the heat."

"No, I am resolved." Then she covered his hand with hers where it lay flat upon the weathered boards. "But I love you, Robin," she went on. "You were my first friend, and my truest. Always, I will value your friendship. But I will not marry you. And it has nothing to do, by the way, with your injuries."

"Aw, Zoë, I know that!" he said. "It has to do with me being a cad and an arse and a womanizing bast—"

"Stop!" She slapped a hand over his mouth. "We'll be here all night if you start apologizing for your sins."

He smiled through her fingers, looking perhaps a little like the old Robin.

She dropped her hand, and for a time, the companionable silence flooded in again, broken only by the warbling of a bird amongst the trees that edged the water. Zoë felt her shoulder brush against Robin's, and thought about the many times she'd kissed him. Of how very much she'd enjoyed it—not the doing of it, so much, but the wickedness of it; the perverse pleasure of being just as naughty as everyone seemed to expect. And with someone as gleefully sinful as herself.

But now she knew what a real kiss was, God help her—a kiss between two passionate adults, with all their barriers down. Now she knew what it felt like to have that raw, incessant yearning simmering in the pit of one's belly, ready to twist like a kindled flame from womb to breast at the slightest touch. Of how it felt to have one's heart leap at a mere glimpse of one's beloved. The joy of fully joining one's body with his.

Perhaps had she never known those things, she could have married Robin and been happy. Perhaps the girlish hero-worship she'd so long nurtured for Mercer would have slowly faded into familial affection. God knew it would have been easier than what she sometimes felt now. But it was too late for her, as it was too late for Robin. They were bound, at least in heart, to others now.

"I'm sorry," she said again. "Robin, I am so sorry for what I caused."

"Zoë, don't be daft," he said, lifting his bad leg just a fraction. "You did not cause this."

"Not that." She closed her eyes and shook her head. "Mrs. Wilfred. You might never have lost her, Robin, were it not for me."

"And I might never have known what she meant to me, either," he whispered. "Perhaps, Zoë, you have given me that? Perhaps that is what I needed to learn."

"Nonetheless, when all of this is said and done, I will still remember that I caused my oldest, dearest friend to lose what he most loved. That, I suppose, is what I really came down here to tell you."

He looked away, his throat working up and down. "She is gone, isn't she?" he whispered.

Zoë glanced down at her feet, faintly greenish-brown beneath the shimmering water. "I fear so, Robin," she finally said. "If I could bring her back to you I would, but I—"

"You? How could you bring her back?" He shook his head. "I am the one who drove her away."

"You are too hard on yourself," Zoë murmured. "But I do think, Robin, that she . . . well, that she has moved on in some fashion."

She sensed he was blinking back tears. "God, Zoë, if you could have seen it!" he choked. "That woman cut me off clean and quick as a razor's blade—but I deserved it. For what I did to her, aye, I deserved it."

She squeezed his hand. "Robin, you can tell me about it."

"No!" he said sharply. Then he gentled his tone. "No, Zoë. I thank you. But I begin to find much to admire in my brother's silent stoicism."

"Well, should you change your mind, I am still your friend," she whispered. "And I—I wanted to tell you, too, that . . . that some of the things you accused me of? They weren't entirely unfounded. We have neither of us behaved especially well, I fear. It has not been just you. Not entirely. It would be unfair of me to let you go on thinking that."

Abruptly, he turned to look at her, his eyes sharp and clear and filled with an ache she understood too well. "Zoë, I just don't want to know," he said wearily. "And I can't think why he's invited that bitch Claire, with all else that's gone on here."

"Perhaps he did not invite her?"

Robin shook his head. "He had to have done," he muttered. "She would not dare show up at his estate uninvited. She knows better. No, I think perhaps old Stu has lost his mind. So my offer stands to marry you, Zoë. Just in case. But spare me the details, all right?"

It was her turn to look away. "Very well," she said. "But I won't be marrying you, Robin. No matter what."

He shrugged, and said no more.

"Well," she said after a time, "one cannot very well practice stoicism and self-flagellation if guests keep barging in." She lifted her feet from the water and scooted back onto the planking. "I had best go back up. And I sent to London, Robin, for Papa's carriage. I expect I shall be gone by week's end."

He turned to face her, his expression oddly wistful. "Well, old thing," he said, "I'm sorry for how this has all turned out."

"Me, too, Robin." She reached out and caught his hand.

He managed to smile. "Well, come, then, my girl, and give your poor, slighted beau one last kiss," he said. "For auld lang syne, and all that, eh?"

"For auld lang syne, then," she whispered. Then Zoë set her hands atop his shoulders, and settled her lips lightly over his for one infinitesimal moment. But when she drew away, he clutched at her, the other hand still cupped round her cheek.

"Robin, what?"

He searched her eyes with his for a moment. "Go on, Zoë," he finally said, his face more honest than ever she'd seen it. "Go to Stuart if you want him. And put up a kicking, screaming catfight if that Frenchie's got her claws in him again. My money's on you, old girl. Go and be happy."

Go and be happy?

Given what she had seen this morning, it seemed an almost impossible task. And then there was that damning letter—that impulsive, accursed letter—which had altered Robin's fate not one whit, but had likely sealed Zoë's. Given all that, his entreaty now seemed almost laughable. But Zoë was far from laughing.

Swiftly, she kissed him again, then bounded to her feet, snatching up her shoes and stockings as she went. She plunged back through the shadowy, memory-filled cottage, then dashed out barefooted into the late afternoon sun, already blinking back tears.

Chapter Sixteen

IN WHICH
ALL IS REVEALED.

Zoë rode out the following morning with Mr. Amherst and Trudy, her mood much cast down. They took with them a haunch of venison and a half-bushel of parsnips for the Fitches, along with two cakes of strong lye soap, a bucket of good, clean sand, and a jug of Cook's best vinegar. It would all be sorely needed, for the Fitches' kitchen did not look to have seen a proper scrubbing since poor Mrs. Fitch's health had weakened months—or perhaps years—ago.

As the open gig lurched along an especially rutted stretch of farm lane, Zoë held on to the seat, scarcely seeing the trees that bowed over both sides to form the verdant canopy overhead. Instead, she thought of Mercer, and of his notable absence in the house.

As with breakfast and luncheon, neither he nor the vicomtesse had come down to dinner the previous evening. Zoë had been a little shaken at the stab of jealousy she'd felt at the notion of the pair dining privately together.

Then Jonet had commented—somewhat deliberately, Zoë thought—that Mrs. Ware and her daughter had gone up to London for the week. Mercer had thus been invited to enjoy a bachelor's evening of roast beef, brandy, and cards with the Ware gentlemen. As to the

Vicomtesse de Chéraute, she apparently kept Town hours, and declared herself unable to dine before nine o'clock. Accordingly, a late tray had been taken up to the lady's rooms—a guest suite, Trudy had gossiped, very near Lord Mercer's own.

Zoë did not know what to make of it all. And in truth, it was none of her business. She, of all people, understood Mercer's need to maintain an amiable relationship with the lady—at least for a time.

"Penny for your thoughts, my dear?"

Zoë's head jerked up. Mr. Amherst was smiling down at her, his brown eyes crinkling at their corners. Somehow, she managed to smile. "I was just wondering, honestly, when we might expect the Vicomtesse de Chéraute to go away," she confessed. "Frightfully small-minded of me, is it not?"

Mr. Amherst laughed, and guided the horses into a sharp bend. "Well, I am reliably informed the lady is gone," he continued. "She apparently left for Dover well before daybreak, and with any luck at all, she and her wagonload of luggage will soon be on a fast boat back to France."

Zoë looked up in surprise. "She has gone back to France?"

"And not a moment too soon, according to my wife," said Mr. Amherst.

"My heavens," said Zoë. "Would I be very unchristian, sir, if I said I hope she means to *stay* in France?"

Mr. Amherst chuckled again. "I have had the same hope myself," he answered. "Ah, look up ahead. Is that not young Andrew Fitch come to meet us?"

Zoë exchanged a swift look with Trudy. There would

be no more gossip today. Mr. Amherst slowed the carriage, and Trudy reached down to hand Andrew up.

"Which coat, sir?" Harding, Lord Mercer's valet, held up two, a charcoal and a black.

"The black, of course," Mercer snapped, lifting his chin to make the last, most delicate turn in his cravat. The valet turned away with a faintly injured sniff.

Though the day had turned bright and lovely, and he had finally got rid of Claire, Mercer's mood was still a foul one, for reasons he could not quite put his finger on. Nonetheless, only a small-minded man would take his frustrations out on a servant—and a very good servant, at that.

"I do beg your pardon, Harding," he said conciliatorily. "The black will do nicely. Thank you."

The problem, he realized, was not Claire, though her visit had most assuredly left a bad taste in his mouth. The problem was Zoë, and this odd, frustrating impasse they had reached. She had been holding herself a little apart from him since that night on the beach. And yesterday morning—the look on her face as she'd watched Claire kiss him—did not bode well.

Now Zoë had made her peace with Robin, or so his mother reported. She had broken her engagement, and she had sent for her father's carriage. He was relieved by the first, and oddly rankled by the last. Why Zoë had felt such a thing necessary when she must have known Mercer would have been better pleased to send her home in one of his carriages, he could not say.

Yes, he could say. He realized it as Harding held out the coat. She had done it in order to avoid an argument.

To keep him from demanding she stay. And perhaps to avoid the slightly intimate act of arriving at her father's door in a carriage belonging not to her betrothed, but to another man.

Vaguely irritated, Mercer shoved his arms into the coat sleeves, settled it over his shoulders, then turned round to see himself in the cheval glass, and was reminded yet again that he was by no means his brother. It struck him suddenly, and with a newfound significance.

Yes, he was a striking man; most would say even a distinguished man. And in his severely elegant attire, even Mercer would admit he looked every inch the rich, powerful young aristocrat. But he had not his brother's beauty, nor perhaps even his physical grace.

Mercer studied himself with his usual cold objectivity, his gaze taking in his height and his build, nearly identical to his late father's, or so he was often told. He was taller and darker than Robin, too. His nose was strong. His jaw too harsh, and unless he shaved twice a day, shadowed with dark beard. And where Robin's eyes had always held laughter, Mercer's were hooded, and yes, a little cold. There was nothing of the light-spirited, laughing rogue in him—but then, there wasn't much of it left in Robin now, either.

A little saddened, Mercer turned away from the mirror.

"Tell Donaldson I expect to be about two hours with the Lord Early and his justice of the peace," he said, drawing on his driving gloves. "They've a farmer in gaol over there—a sort of boundary dispute gone wrong, I collect—and hope to resolve it before the autumn assizes."

"Very good, sir." Harding handed him his elegant black top hat.

Mercer tucked it and his crop beneath his arm, and went out and down the stairs to find his phaeton waiting in the forecourt with a pair under the pole just as he'd ordered—his favorites, too; a spirited set of matched blacks which were fast as blazes, and quite perfectly suited to his snappish mood.

He set off in some haste, driving toward Lower Thorpe perhaps a little faster than was wise. But even as he pushed his horses, Mercer was still ruminating over Zoë, and wondering how he might manage a private moment. He wanted to talk about Claire; to explain to Zoë just what she'd seen, and to tell her about the child. There had been too much confusion between them already. Too many things assumed and misinterpreted, particularly on his part. Perhaps he was only now beginning to truly understand Zoë. Certainly he had begun to understand himself—and he was done with denying the inevitable. He was hopelessly in love with her, and always had been. He was going to have her or die trying, and whatever madness and mayhem came of it would simply be dealt with.

Newly resolved, he cut the pair into the last turn and was descending the slight hill toward Greythorpe's rather ostentatious black and gold gateposts when he saw something that jerked him from his reverie. It was a slight, almost fragile-looking creature—a woman, carrying a portmanteau half as large as she, and clearly trudging toward Greythorpe. She appeared to be dressed simply, but with just enough elegance to rule out her being a servant. A gently bred female, then. But without a carriage, or even so much as a horse.

Curious, Mercer drew the pair up just inside the gate, the horses tossing their glossy black heads and snorting with disapproval. He held them nonetheless, and watched in silence as the woman approached. She had seen him; of that there could be no doubt. And yet she did not so much as lift her head until she was but a few yards distant, and then only when he more or less forced her to do so.

"Good afternoon," he called in his most authoritative voice. "Might I ask if you are lost?"

The woman lifted her chin then, and he was struck by a startlingly green gaze in a face that appeared far too thin, and at once vaguely familiar. She dropped the portmanteau like a dead weight, and curtsied on the grassy verge as formally as any countess might.

"My lord," she said quietly. "You do not remember me."

He peered down from his lofty perch, his crop tucked neatly beneath his arm. "Good Lord!" he said at last. "It is Mrs. Wilfred, is it not?"

"Yes." Again, she lifted her gaze to his.

Hastily, Mercer bounded down, his heart thudding oddly in his chest, his brain grappling for an explanation. But it would seem her presence could hold but one meaning.

"My dear woman," he said, sweeping off his hat. "Where is your carriage? However did you come to be here?"

Her expression was stark, and wracked with dread.

"I . . . I do not own a carriage," she whispered. "I came by mail coach."

"Mail coach?" He took her hand. "My God—yet you are all of a piece, I pray?"

But she did not smile, and instead, squeezed his fingers, her other hand going to his wrist, clutching at him. "Oh, my lord, just tell me!" she whispered. "Just tell me I have not come too late?"

"Too late?" He looked at her in puzzlement. "Too late for what?"

"Lord Robert," she choked. "Does he live?"

Some of Mercer's confusion cleared. "Oh, yes, yes, set yourself at ease, ma'am," he urged, gently extracting his hand from her grasp. "My brother was badly injured, and for a time we did indeed fear for his life. But he is up and about again, if not altogether well."

What little color the lady's face possessed drained away. "Oh!" she cried, her hand going tremulously to her mouth. "Oh, thank God!"

Tears sprang to her eyes, and Mercer wisely seized her arm then, as it was clear the lady's legs were about to collapse beneath her. "My dear Mrs. Wilfred," he said. "I cannot think you entirely well yourself."

"No, no," she protested, even as she bore her weight onto his arm. "It is just that I have not slept. These many days of travel, they have quite exhausted me, I fear."

"But it cannot have taken you above a day to come from London by mail coach," he said. "Come, get up into my carriage. Let me take you to the house."

"Oh, thank you, but I did not come from London," she said as he helped her up. "I had gone to my father in Yorkshire, you see, when the letter came."

"The letter?" Mercer hefted up her portmanteau, and wedged it into the phaeton. "I'm sorry. I was given to understand that you and my brother had parted company."

"Oh, indeed, we have done." Her misery appeared to deepen. "But the letter—it was from his fiancée, Miss Armstrong. And I was not at home to get it." This last was said tearfully, her words winnowing away on a little sob.

Mercer turned the horses round, and headed them back up the hill. "Pray let me understand this," he said. *"Miss Armstrong* wrote to you?"

But Mrs. Wilfred's face had flamed beet-red. "Yes, but perhaps I ought not have said?" she whispered. "Indeed, it was quite the bravest thing to do. She told me of Robert's accident, and said that I must come to him at once; that even as I read the letter that Robin might . . . *might be gone!*" She twisted her hands, wringing upon a lace handkerchief she'd extracted from a pocket. "But the letter lay in my drawing room unread, until at last someone took it in mind to send it on to me in Yorkshire, and . . . and oh, God, I came as quickly as I could! And thinking quite the whole time that Lord Robert might already be . . ."

"Dead?" supplied Lord Mercer. "Rest assured, ma'am, that danger is past. But I wonder, have you that letter to hand?"

Mrs. Wilfred's fingers brushed her reticule. "Yes, indeed. It has not left me for a moment since it reached me three days past. But please, my lord, do tell me how Robert goes on?"

Mercer spent the next few minutes telling her in great

detail precisely what had happened to Robin while gloss-
ing over some of the less flattering details of the accident,
and all the while wondering what Zoë had done, and
why. What could she possibly have said to make Mrs.
Wilfred fly down from Yorkshire like a madwoman to
see the man she had forsworn?—and forsworn quite fervently, according to Robin.

They reached the house in quite good time, the footmen flowing back down the curving staircase to greet
them. "We have a guest, Page," he said. "This is Mrs.
Wilfred. Her portmanteau is in the carriage. Kindly
bring us tea—strong tea—in my study, and have Donaldson prepare her a chamber in the west wing. And
leave the horses standing, if you please."

They went up the stairs together, Mrs. Wilfred clinging a little less weakly to Mercer's arm. At every turn, she
looked about the house in silent awe, taking in the vast,
pillared portico, the marbled great hall with its towering
columns, and even the gilded opulence of his study. Mercer never noticed any of it, having lived with it all of his
life, but perhaps to Mrs. Wilfred it was all rather much.

The lady had not been at all sure of her welcome here,
he rather feared as he watched her. And indeed, even
given her fatigue, she did look a little frayed about the
edges. Clearly Robin had spent shamelessly little on the
woman's wardrobe. Then Mercer suddenly remembered
that the lady had firmly eschewed his every offer of sup-
port. Whatever the woman wore upon her back, it had
been put there by her husband, or by her father—and
Mercer thought the better of her for it.

When they reached his desk, he bade Mrs. Wilfred
be seated, his gaze taking in the plain muslin gown, and

the sturdy brown boots, a little worn. Her shawl was of the most ordinary sort possible, and her chip bonnet little better than that which Mercer's own housekeeper might have worn. And yet none of that—not even the stone of weight she had so obviously lost—could entirely dim the lady's fair beauty.

He did not sit opposite her at the desk, but instead took the seat beside her, and took her hand in his. "Mrs. Wilfred, I must ask again—have you been ill?"

She tore her gaze from his, and looked away, her lower lip trembling ever so faintly. "In a manner of speaking, perhaps," she said quietly. "That is why I went to my family in Yorkshire, you see. I had hoped that away from London, I should feel my old self again."

But the truth was easily read upon her face. Robin had broken her heart, very nearly destroying her in the process. And that, Mercer thought sadly, made two of them, for Robin had been bent on destroying himself as well. Mercer only prayed he and Zoë could escape being fate's next such victims.

"My lord?" she said, her voice trembling. "Where is Lord Robert? Might I see him?"

"Yes, of course, but he is not here," Mercer answered, recalled to the present. "He, too, has not been himself."

"So Miss Armstrong declared," Mrs. Wilfred whispered.

"Did she indeed?" he murmured. "I confess, you quite pique my curiosity, ma'am. My brother, by the way, has moved into our summerhouse. I shall take you there myself once we've got some tea to buck you up a bit. But just now, if you please, I should very much like to see that letter."

Again, her hand went tellingly to her reticule. "Oh, I do not know," she said uncertainly. "I am not sure Miss Armstrong would wish—"

He laid his hand over hers. Mercer disliked taking advantage of her fatigue, and of his power to turn her away, but in his concern for Zoë, he was not above it. "The letter, Mrs. Wilfred," he said firmly but gently. "I'm afraid I must insist. I am quite sure Miss Armstrong will not mind. In fact, I suspect I can tell you precisely what it says without having so much as glanced at it. I begin to think—somewhat to my surprise—that I know Miss Armstrong rather well."

Mrs. Wilfred had gone a little pale. "Do you?"

He nodded. "I daresay she told you that it was you whom Robin loved, and not her?" he quietly suggested. "And that even before the accident, my brother had been grief-stricken at losing you, and that he declared his undying regret for having caused you pain?"

Slowly, she nodded.

"I thought as much." Mercer released her hand. "And I suspect she told you that Robin was simply acting the gentleman by offering to marry her? That he was merely saving her from her father's wrath?"

"*Yes!*" Mrs. Wilfred seemed to collapse inward with relief. "Yes, that is just what she said!"

Mercer watched her warily for a moment. He was developing a deep, uneasy feeling about this letter. "Very forthcoming, our Miss Armstrong," he murmured. "And what else, pray, did she admit to?"

The lady cut her gaze away. "She admitted that she behaved scandalously," Mrs. Wilfred whispered. "And that everything which happened to cause their betrothal was entirely her fault, and none of his. She said that she had thrown herself at Robert. That she had, in fact, seduced him."

At that, Mercer hissed quietly through his teeth. "Mrs. Wilfred," he said, "I really must have that letter."

"Yes." She opened her eyes. "Yes, all right."

Slowly she extracted and unfolded it, then laid it in his hands as if it were her most precious possession—which it likely was.

Mercer read the letter with great care, taking in every word of Zoë's scratchy, haphazard penmanship. The letter had quite obviously been written in a feverish spate of emotion, and with a stark and sincere belief that Robin lay near death. But it was the last two paragraphs that took Mercer's breath away.

> So yes, I simply seduced Robin against his will, and when we were caught, I cried, and begged him to marry me. It was a perfectly wretched thing to do—I see that now—to trap a gentleman into marriage when he had made it plain where his heart lay.
>
> And now I am giving you, Maria, all this in my own hand. You may ruin me with it, if you are vindictive. Indeed, post it in the *Times*, if it pleases you, for it is about what I deserve. Or instead, you may hasten to Robin's side, knowing that, if he lives, he will never be the man he once was. He will be scarred and he will be crippled and he will still be beautiful to me. We must now see if he is still beautiful to you.

Good God. Mercer realized his hand was shaking ever so slightly. He rested it on his knee.

This was it. This was the thing which Zoë had hinted at that night on the beach. The reason for her hesitance toward him, perhaps, or a part of it. The little idiot had nailed herself to the cross to free Robin from his sins. And she had done it weeks ago, without knowing Mrs. Wilfred, or what she might do with this bloody letter. As to himself, he had been intent on silencing Claire, never knowing what danger lay in another direction.

He refolded the paper, and spoke with suppressed emotion. "Miss Armstrong has given herself quite utterly into your hands, Mrs. Wilfred," he said quietly. "You have the power to ruin her with this."

But Mrs. Wilfred was already shaking her head. "Vengeance is of no use to me," she said. "But please, just tell me, Lord Mercer—is it the truth? *Is* it?"

Mercer winced. "The truth?" he said rhetorically. "The truth is hard to discern, ma'am. Let us just say that there is a great deal of truth in it."

"But she overstates matters, does she not?" Mrs. Wilfred gave her handkerchief another twist, but her voice was calm. "He cannot have been as innocent as she says. But there, it does not matter, does it? It matters only that Robert is still alive."

"He is still alive," said Mercer. "And what Miss Armstrong does not exaggerate, Mrs. Wilfred, is my brother's devotion to you, or his regret at having treated you so shabbily. In Robin's defense, I believe he fell quite head over heels in love with you, without even grasping what had happened to him."

"Do you?" she asked.

"I find that is often the case when it comes to falling in love," said Mercer ruefully. "One often does not know for sure until it is too late. But another thing Miss Armstrong does not exaggerate is the depth of my brother's injuries. I fear he was quite badly damaged." He paused to look pointedly at her. "He is scarred, literally and figuratively. Do you understand me, Mrs. Wilfred?"

She looked at him as if he were a fool. "Yes, but what is any of that to me?" she cried. "It matters only that Robert is alive. Who gives a fig for what a man looks like?"

"You have not seen him," Mercer warned.

"I do not need to see him," she said, her voice low and certain. "I love him. I always have. I lied when I told him that day that I did not."

Lord Mercer held up a staying hand. "Mrs. Wilfred," he protested, "I beg you will not rush into anything. For your own sake."

At that, something akin to humor passed over her thin, lovely face. "Oh, Lord Mercer, pray do not think me a fool," she whispered. "Do not imagine for one moment that I mean to fling myself at your brother, declare my undying devotion to him, and believe every little tarradiddle Miss Armstrong has told me."

Mercer leaned back, and tapped the letter pensively upon his chair arm. "No?"

She gently shook her head. "No, for I know your brother for what he is," she answered. "He is vain, rich, and far too used to having whatever he wishes. I rather doubt that any injury will much change that. And yet . . . and yet, I am not ashamed to admit how much I love him. How desperately afraid I have been for him. I gather that surprises you?"

"It does indeed," he admitted, studying her.

She gave him a smile so vague Rembrandt himself might have painted it. "Lord Mercer, if ever you fall in love, I pray you will not require the object of your affections to be perfect," she said quietly. "For you will be sorely disappointed. Indeed, you may find, as I have done, that one does not get to choose whom one loves, or even their very nature."

At that, Mercer shifted a little uncomfortably in his chair.

But Mrs. Wilfred was still speaking. "Indeed, Lord Mercer, I have been heartsick over your brother these many weeks," she said. "Still, you must not mistake me. I regret nothing I have done. Lord Robert has treated me shabbily—and yes, I have let him. But that is at an end now."

"And yet you have come here," said Mercer. "I do not understand."

"I have come to reassure myself that he is all right," she said quietly. "Because I love him more than life itself. And yet I cannot know what the future holds for us. But I know what it does not hold. I am done being Lord Robert's doormat—his mistress, if you will. When he is well again, and we are all finished feeling sorry for him, then Robert must decide what he feels for me. Perhaps he will choose to court me—properly, and publicly, as I deserve. Or perhaps we will remain simply devoted friends. Or, indeed, he may decide I am too far beneath him—and there are many who would say he is quite right."

"No, ma'am," said Mercer. "I am sure there are not."

Finally, she laughed quite wholeheartedly. "Oh, Lord Mercer, you surely cannot be as naïve as all that!" Then, after a long, silent moment, she swept to her feet, suddenly almost regal in her posture. "Please, sir. I do not wish for tea. Please, will you take me to your brother now? I fear my recitation of his many failings has made me quite long to see him."

Mercer, too, had risen. "To be sure, ma'am," he said, offering his arm. "It would be my honor to drive you down. But I am afraid I must keep your letter. I think it best it be returned to Miss Armstrong."

The lady's gaze fell to the folded paper in his hand. "Yes, of course," she said at last. "Just take me to Robert now. I do not need the letter anymore."

But when he drew open the door for her, Mrs. Wilfred turned, and glanced back at him. "Might I gather, sir, that *you* do not resent my coming here?" she asked, her voice quiet. "And that you truly do not think me too far beneath your brother?"

Mercer studied her intently for a moment. "On the contrary, my dear," he finally said. "I am quite sure, in fact, that where my brother's recovery is concerned, you will prove just what the doctor ordered."

It was early afternoon by the time Lord Mercer set off for the Fitches, having first dropped Mrs. Wilfred at the summerhouse. He had watched from a distance as Robin drew open the door, then dropped his cane and embraced her, burying his face in her neck. The poor devil had looked very much as if he were weeping.

Mercer had driven away in haste. The pair of them would be sooner mended, he suspected, than would Robin's injured leg. And he was happy for his brother. Truly, deeply happy. Contrary to first impressions, Mrs.

Wilfred seemed woman enough to put Robin to the rack, should it prove necessary.

But the lady's damning letter still burned in Mercer's pocket, and a dozen unanswered questions burned in his heart. He drove the horses hard wherever he could make time. What a heedless little fool Zoë had been to send such a confession—and what a pack of lies it had been, too.

And yet Mercer had to admire her for it. If these past weeks with Zoë had taught him anything, it had taught him that sometimes Zoë's faults were often her greatest strengths. That heedlessness could be just another word for courage. That her flirtatiousness was just another sort of vivacity, a part of her rich, infectious love of life. And all of it was a part of why he loved her. He admitted it now.

He had believed that in marrying Zoë he would be taking on a life of eternal frustration and chaos—not that loving her wasn't worth the sacrifice. But now he realized that Zoë might instead bring light into his solitary and sometimes grim existence. That her audacity and joie de vivre were precisely what his life needed.

Perhaps there was a reason why opposites attracted? Perhaps, as with his mother and stepfather, two very different halves could indeed make a whole, and provide for a richer, fuller life that was better for having been lived together?

Still, that letter could have been Zoë's ruination. Mercer wanted her to know he had it. That she was safe. And after that, he meant to demand some answers of his own—answers which would not be put off again. A sense of urgency drove him, the big blacks eating up the carriage drive. There was the oddest feeling in the pit of his belly; like a faint hint of butterflies.

Butterflies! He hadn't felt such a lowering thing since . . . oh, his first day at Eaton, most likely. He slowed the carriage to turn onto Fitch's farm road and carried on, fretting until at last he saw the final bend. At the little cottage, the doors and windows stood wide, and in the side garden beyond a tidy hedgerow, he could see chickens pecking about in the grass, and three children screeching with delight as a fourth stumbled about blindfolded in the dappled sunshine.

Mercer drew his glossy black phaeton alongside his stepfather's low-slung chaise, the back of which now held an empty hamper and a bucket. He leapt down just as the eldest Fitch boy pushed through the gate and tugged at his forelock.

"My lord," he said, his eyes humbly downcast. "Afternoon to you, sir."

"Ah, young Andrew, is it?" Mercer smiled. "How tall you have grown these past months. I was so very sorry, lad, to hear about your mother."

The boy maintained a respectful distance, but he did look up. "Thank you, m'lord."

"I was looking for my father," Mercer went on casually. "Is he here?"

Andrew Fitch pointed at a footpath dotted with pecking chickens. "'E walked out to the churchyard with Pa, sir."

Ah, they had gone to Mrs. Fitch's grave. His stepfather was ever thoughtful about such things, and deeply pious, too, in his pragmatic sort of way. The thought made Mercer swallow hard, and narrow his eyes against the sunlight.

"Yes, I see," he murmured. "And Miss Armstrong? She came with Mr. Amherst, did she not?"

The lad jerked his head toward the small cottage, and the open front door. "Still in the kitchen with Miss Trudy, sir," he said respectfully. "Shall I fetch 'er for you?"

Mercer eyed the open door. "Thank you, Andrew, just tie up my horses," he ordered, tossing the lad a shilling. "I shall fetch the lady myself."

As Andrew went about his task, Mercer strolled up the worn path that lay in afternoon shade. At the open door, he tucked his hat beneath his arm as he bent low beneath the vine-covered lintel. Inside the cool, shadowy depths of the stone cottage, his eyes adjusted to the light as he listened with one ear to the murmur of feminine conversation that echoed from the rear of the house.

Mercer lingered for a moment in the narrow, white-washed parlor. It was clean but simply furnished, its hearth well blackened with age. Atop the rough-hewn mantel, someone had perched a small crock filled with a surprisingly elegant arrangement of wildflowers; betony and daisies and spiky golden shafts of ladies' bedstraw, all tied up with a wide, yellow ribbon.

He knew instinctively that it was Zoë's work, and crossed to the hearth to touch the ribbon. Pure silk, as fine and delicate as Zoë's skin. He wondered what it meant that she had been drawn to this humble place, and to these people who had suffered such a devastating loss. Perhaps it was because she had lost her own mother too young. Or perhaps she had found a measure of peace here that she could not find at Greythorpe. The notion saddened him.

Just then, amongst the female chatter, there came a sharp *crack!*—like the sound of wood striking the same. Mercer strolled through the parlor as the women broke into a spirited quarrel, something about Zoë's ineptitude with a broom. The notion of Zoë wielding a broom made him chuckle, but when he reached the door that opened onto the sunlit kitchen, he peeked in to see that indeed she was sweeping, and rather vigorously at that.

"Now, get well up in that corner, mind!" Zoë's maid, Trudy, was bent over the kitchen table, scrubbing it hard with a wad of wet rag. "Aye, shove it in like that, scrub it round good and proper, then sweep it all out again."

Zoë was hunched over in one corner, her dark, unruly mass of hair caught up in a white cap which sat well askew. "Who knew sand could be so bloody useful!" she complained, shoving the bristles round. "I swear, Tru, I hope I never see another grain of it so long as I live. This is vile."

"Aye, but 'twill bring up the grime like a house afire," said Trudy as Zoë ducked beneath a hanging cupboard. "Lud, miss! Mind your head!"

Too late.

"Ow! Bloody hell!" Zoë stepped away, rubbing hard at the top of her head as she glowered at the offending corner. "Trudy!"

"Don't *Trudy* me," said the maid evenly. "Reckon this was your crackbrain notion."

"Quite literally," said Zoë, wincing as she rubbed her head.

"Oh, aye, Christian charity, indeed!" Trudy grumbled, still scrubbing. "Suddenly you're just brimful of it—when afore today, you'd not so much as rinsed your own chamber pot."

At that, Mercer burst into a great guffaw of laughter, causing both women to jerk round, and sending Zoë's white cap flopping over one eye.

"Mercer!" Her tone was almost accusing, her cheeks flaming bright pink. "Must you go about like that, sneaking up on innocent, working folk?"

At that, he laughed again and tossed his hat onto a chair. "Ah, Zoë, even Trudy knows you are not innocent—and from her expression, not much of the latter, either."

Trudy dunked her rag into her bucket of water. "Now to be fair, sir, she's proved a dab hand," said the maid, wringing it out again. "What she lacks in experience she makes up for in grit, I reckon."

"That's right," said Zoë, puffing upward on a tendril of hair which was teasing at her nose. "And I can curse like the lowliest swabbie, too, when it's warranted—which it is. I swear, Mercer, did you ever scrub a wooden floor? You cannot imagine the odd places sand gets stuck."

"Oh, I have a little experience with sand stuck in odd places," he answered evenly. "Perhaps you will recall it?"

"What are—" Then her eyes rounded.

Mercer's grin was carefully muted. "Come, Zoë, put down your broom," he ordered. "I wish you to ride back to Greythorpe with me."

"What? Now?"

Trudy cut her a strange look. "Go on with you, miss," she said. "We're almost done here. I'll gather up the last buckets, and be off with Mr. Amherst within the hour."

But Zoë was watching him warily, her eyes laced with suspicion. "I started this," she said. "I need to finish it."

"We *have* finished it," Trudy protested, scrubbing her way across the kitchen table again. "Or all but."

Mercer braced his hands on the back of the old ladder-back chair, leaning over it. "I came to tell you, my dear, about an interesting letter I received this morning."

"Indeed?" Zoë set her broom down sharply. "From whom?"

Mercer lifted one shoulder. "Into the carriage, my girl," he said firmly. "And then I shall tell you all—and trust me, *this* letter you will wish to see. It is truly shocking."

"All right, you win," Zoë grumbled, already cramming her cap into her pocket. "Tru, leave the vinegar, the soap, and one of those buckets behind. I shall see you at the house."

Mercer picked up his hat, and offered Zoë his arm. And as he turned, he was almost—*almost*—certain he saw Trudy wink at him.

Zoë set about her wheedling as soon as he'd handed her up into the carriage and forced her to let him examine the bump on her head. The skin wasn't broken, and the swelling was minimal. Reassured, Mercer turned the carriage round and set off again. But to Zoë's mounting frustration, he made nothing but small talk about the weather until he had retraced his route back to the carriage drive.

"I beg your pardon," she finally said, "but if I'd wished to hear another dull discourse about the mud and rain of Sussex, I could have spent the afternoon with your brother."

He cut her an odd, sidelong look. "Got that bad, did it?"

Zoë said nothing, but merely rolled her eyes and threw her arms over her chest, causing her dark curls to bounce. Shrugging, Mercer continued on for another mile, then turned the horses from the main road and into the little wood which ran along Greythorpe's highest ridge.

Zoë was fairly vibrating with impatience now. "Mercer, where on earth are we going?" she complained. "There is no track at all here. You are going to get the carriage stuck."

"I know the way," he said calmly. "There is an old track here if one knows where to look."

"Well, then, do you mean ever to tell me about this 'shocking letter'?" she said hotly. "Or is this all a ruse? I begin to believe you mean to drive me out into the wilds of Sussex and simply leave me to starve. At least I would never frustrate you again."

At that, he threw back his head and laughed again. "Oh, you are far too clever for that, my dear," he said. "By the time you'd trekked home with your hair full of leaves and twigs, you'd have learned to skin squirrels and make fire with a pair of dry sticks. Then you'd likely garrote me with a bit of braided vine or some equally lethal device."

Zoë sniffed. "What nonsense!"

"Oh, I never underestimate your talent," said Mercer evenly. "After all, just today you learned how to wield a broom and rinse out a chamber pot."

"Oh, for pity's sake!" she grumbled. "I could just smack Tru for that! And we only cleaned the kitchen.

It is not precisely Newtonian physics." Suddenly, she turned a little on the seat. "Is that a clearing up ahead?" Zoë pointed at the wide swath of sunlight cutting through the trees.

"It is indeed." Abruptly, he drew the horses to a halt.

"Where are we?" asked Zoë. "Why are we here? Really, Mercer! How shall you turn the carriage round for all these trees?"

Mercer made her no answer, but instead turned on the seat, and gathered her to him. She squirmed for a mere moment, then settled against him with a sharp sigh.

"I swear, Zoë," he murmured against her cheek, "do you never stop talking?"

"Yes," she said, "once I get my way."

"Hmm," he said. Then Mercer kissed her, thoroughly and languidly, with one arm about her waist, and the other hand set at the back of her head, his fingers spearing into the warmth of her hair. Her hands twined round his neck, and she sighed again. Mercer deepened the kiss, tangling his tongue with hers, then thrusting slowly inside her mouth.

When they came apart, Zoë's eyes were wide.

"Now," he said quietly, "I have had *my* way."

"My goodness, Mercer," she said breathlessly, her lips still wet from his kiss. "Is *that* what you drove me out here for?"

"In part." His eyes fell half shut, and too tempted to do otherwise, he kissed her again, this time allowing his hands to roam. For a moment, he lost himself in her, and thought only of what she had looked like naked in the firelight on the beach. On the night he had realized he simply could not live without her.

Perhaps it was time he told her so?

"Zoë," he rasped, lifting his mouth a little away. "Zoë, I cannot live without you—and I'm not going to. Do you understand?"

Her eyes holding his, she set a hand to the rough stubble of his cheek. "Oh, Mercer!" she said softly. "What has happened? *Tell* me."

"Everything has happened." He set her a little away, and grasped her slender shoulders. "Zoë, I have got rid of Claire, once and for all. And there was no child, just as I said. She will never trouble you again, I give you my word."

Zoë gave a bemused smile. "Heavens, did you push her off the cliff?"

"No, better than that," he said. "I packed her off to Dover this morning."

"I did hear that," she admitted. "But the other—are you quite sure? She was not *enceinte,* after all?"

He shook his head. "It was a lie from the outset, I suspect," he answered. "Though she won't quite admit to that. Still, she has returned to France. To her husband."

"To her husband? Will he have her?"

Mercer smiled grimly. "Oh, Claire has certain talents," he murmured. "She'll persuade him—and I have given her every incentive to do so."

"Not the cliff, then, just ordinary blackmail?" Zoë grinned. "Good Lord, Mercer. You really are as cold as they say."

"Zoë, that poor woman was going to be your ruin," he said softly. "And I have done nothing she did not deserve."

At that, Zoë's smile faded abruptly. "Perhaps not,"

she murmured. "But I rather fear I can manage to ruin myself without Claire's help. Indeed, I . . . I fear I have already done so."

Mercer kissed her again, just the merest brush of his lips, and when he came away, he realized Zoë's eyes had misted with tears. "Zoë!" he softly admonished. "Let us have no more talk of anyone's ruin. Here, read this."

Slowly, she took the letter. "Oh!" she cried when her eyes alit on the scrawled address.

"Zoë," he said again, his voice gentle. "Oh, my dear girl. Whatever were you thinking?"

Zoë stared at the fold of paper, unable to believe her eyes. But there was no mistaking what it was. How on earth had Mercer got hold of it? Then it occurred to her there could be but one way. Her hands had had begun to shake.

"Oh, Mercer!" Her eyes flew to his, beseeching. "Oh, can it be? She has come at last?"

"She has come," he said quietly.

Abruptly, she turned on the seat. A kaleidoscope of thought and emotion had been twirling in her head ever since Mercer had set his lips to hers. And this—good Lord, *this*. It was a miracle.

"Oh, please," she begged, blinking rapidly. "Please tell me she has forgiven him! Tell me she loves him still. She must do, mustn't she? To come all the way from London?"

"She loves him still," he answered, smiling down at her. "And in time, yes, I think she will forgive him. But she came from Yorkshire—by mail coach, no less. That is why, you see, she was so long in getting here. You had come to despair that she never would, had you not? I wish, Zoë, you had confided in me."

Zoë's gaze fell again to the letter. "But you would have scolded me," she said, smoothing the wrinkles from the paper as if it were precious. "You know, Mercer, that you would have done. I can never do anything to suit you."

He made a soft, clucking sound beneath his tongue. "Zoë!" he said softly. "Am I truly that much of an ogre to you? Even after all we have been to one another?"

She made a sound, something between a laugh and a sob. "Yes!" she declared. "You are the strictest, sternest man alive! I have never been able to please you."

"Now that, my dear girl, is most assuredly *not* true," he said. "You please me too well. Ah, Zoë, what is to become of us?"

"I do not know," she confessed. "Just tell me what you have done to poor Mrs. Wilfred?"

"I drove her down to the summerhouse before coming after you," he said. "I handed her down, and left her there in Robin's arms."

"And she was not put off by his scar?" Zoë demanded.

"I fancy not," he said, grinning. "The lady was kissing him rather ardently—on his lips, and then all over his face."

"Oh!" said Zoë breathlessly. "And so she will marry him, do you think?"

"Oh, I think Robin will soon ask her to marry him, for he has learned his lesson," said Mercer. "But as to the lady, *she* has a piece of Sheffield steel where her spine should be. I am not sure Robin was aware of that when he fell in love with her."

"Oh, but we do not choose," Zoë whispered. "We do not choose, Mercer, who we love."

He took her hand and kissed it. "Do you know, my love, someone very wise recently told me the same thing."

"And it's true," she went on. "We simply fall. We fall in love. Sometimes headlong, as Robin did. And sometimes so slowly we barely know it is happening."

"Aye, that's how it was for me." His voice had roughened.

She cut a strange, sidelong glance at him. "Which?"

"Both," he answered. "Slowly at first, but in an agonizing little trickle I tried to hold back—and then all at once, in a crashing, inexorable cascade, rather like a dam bursting."

"How romantic," she said dryly.

He surprised her then by cupping her face in one hand. "I'll tell you what is romantic," he said, holding her gaze quite steadily. "*This* is romantic." And then he tightened his arm about her, and drew Zoë fully against him, kissing her again with exquisite sweetness. And when he was done, he took up the reins and clicked to his horses.

The carriage lurched into motion. "Where are we going?" she asked breathlessly.

"I'll show you."

He drove but a few yards farther, squarely toward the patch of sunlight. They were mounting the last little rise along the ridgeline, she realized, to a place where the trees had been quite obviously cut away, perhaps to afford a view.

And what a view it was! They broke out into pure summer sunshine and mounted the peak, and suddenly all the majesty of Greythorpe came into view, spreading out on the opposite hill, its massive stone wings folded back like an elegant bird of prey, the columns of the portico soaring almost pewterlike in the afternoon sun.

"My God," Zoë murmured. "What a vantage point! Better, even, than the carriage drive."

"It is magnificent, is it not?" Mercer narrowed his eyes against the sun. "My grandfather had an ornamental temple built here to enjoy the view. It isn't used much nowadays."

Zoë craned her neck to peer over the horses' heads. Just over the rise, cut into the hillside, she could see a round, copper roof, and beneath it, six marble pillars, miniatures of those along Greythorpe's front façade. All the affluence and power of the marquesses of Mercer were symbolically laid out before her, the house and the immaculately landscaped grounds an architectural testament to the family's supremacy. If Zoë's first glimpse of Greythorpe had been stunning, this one rendered her near speechless, and brought home to her once again the yawning chasm of disparity between Mercer's status and her own.

Mercer had leapt down, and was now holding his hands up to Zoë. After one last look at the house, she rose. Mercer caught her round the waist, lowering her from the high phaeton as if she were weightless. Then he kissed her lightly on the lips.

"Come," he said, catching her hand.

He led her over the rise and down a set of wide, white steps to the marble folly. She stepped inside, and went immediately to the stone balustrade that seemed to hang out over the valley, overlooking not just Greythorpe, but even the lake and the summerhouse, too.

Mercer joined her there, a warm, comforting, almost larger-than-life presence at her side. Always he had seemed thus to her. Zoë thought again of how very long she had known him—even relied upon him, sometimes, to save her from herself. Even to herself, she had never really admitted just how much she had counted upon him. Or how very much she had loved him—loved him from afar, knowing as she did that he was not for her. And now the future rose up before her, seeming as uncertain to her as Greythorpe seemed indomitable.

Mercer caught her hand in his, palm to palm as they stood beside one another, then he lifted her knuckles to his lips. "Marry me, Zoë." His voice was low and demanding. "Marry me, and be mistress of all this. Marry me, and make all this truly, truly perfect."

She squeezed his hand. "Mercer, don't rush—"

"*Marry* me, Zoë," he interjected. "Don't quarrel. Don't argue. Don't offer up another dozen excuses why we cannot be together. I mean to marry you. It will be a good deal easier, love, if you just say yes. Otherwise . . ."

She cut a sidelong look up at his profile, harsh against the brilliant blue sky. "Otherwise—?"

Still gazing into the distance, he gave a muted smile. "Well, there is always Gretna Green," he said quietly. "I could simply kidnap you, and haul you away."

"Hoo!" she said dismissively. "The great Lord Mercer? Lowering himself to kidnap a bride? I think not."

At that, his head snapped round, his eyes seizing hers. "No?" he interposed. "You *love* me, Zoë. Your kisses say it. Your body says it. Yes, *you* said it—once or twice, I seem to recall. And God knows I love you. And I am going to have you."

"Oh!" The word held a wealth of exasperation. "Are you indeed?"

He simply nodded. "Yes," he said quietly. "And yes— if you persist in being foolish, then I will haul you off in my carriage, and have the job done the old-fashioned way—the *Scots* way. Indeed, it seems rather fitting, now I think on it."

"Mercer," she said quietly. "Are you quite, quite sure you wish to do this? You know me too well. You know what I am. I shall drive you utterly mad inside a month."

"The latter may well be true," he acknowledged. "I shall take my chances. But the rest of it? Did I know you? Before this summer, I mean? I think, perhaps, that I did not. Indeed, perhaps I did not fully know you until I read that damned fool letter. What were you thinking, by the way?"

"Only that I was responsible for Robin's unhappiness," she whispered.

"And now you would be responsible for mine?" he said quietly.

There was such sorrow in those eight little words. Zoë inhaled a ragged breath. "Mercer," she whispered, "would you truly be unhappy?"

"Truly," he answered. "For too long I have taken your presence in my life for granted. And then, when I was faced with your marrying someone else, even Robin . . . it shocked me how wrong it felt. And I knew then, Zoë, that what I had always felt for you . . . oh, it was so much more than familial love. The thought of losing you . . . Christ, it sucked the breath—no, the life—right out of me."

Zoë's fingers flew to her mouth. "I never knew," she

whispered, her voice almost inaudible. "Oh, Mercer. I never knew. I just thought you were angry."

"And I was. At myself." Then he turned fully to look at her, his solemn eyes almost pleading, his stern face breathtakingly beautiful to her. "You, Zoë, are what I need. You complete me. You make me . . . whole, somehow. Without you, I think that I am too dour and too driven and too . . . oh, I do not know. Too obstinate, perhaps, for my own good? But with you, I am happy. Even when you madden me and frustrate me, I am still happy."

But Zoë could not speak. Her fingertips were still pressed to her lips—her suddenly wobbly lips—and the hot, urgent press of tears was burning behind her eyes. And then one leaked out, running not elegantly down her cheek, but awkwardly, meandering toward her nose.

Mercer looked down at her with a muted smile, and stroked the ball of his thumb beneath her eye. "Zoë, we are indelibly linked, you and I," he said quietly. "There is no escaping this. Not for either of us. Now, *will* you marry me? For God's sake, woman, just say *yes*."

"*Yes.*"

The word seemed to explode, unbidden, from her lips. And then Zoë's arms went round him as she buried her face against his neck. "Yes, Mercer. I will marry you, and make your life a living madhouse."

He pressed his lips into her hair. "Ah, Zoë, you know what the Stoic philosophers said," he murmured. "There's no great genius without some touch of madness—and you and I together . . . ah, love—now *that* is pure genius."

True love
is timeless with historical romances from Pocket Books!

A Malory novel

Johanna Lindsey

NO CHOICE BUT SEDUCTION

He'd stop at nothing to make her love him.
But should she surrender to his bold charms?

Liz Carlyle

Tempted All Night

When deception meets desire, even the most
careful lady can be swayed by a scoundrel....

Julia London

HIGHLAND SCANDAL

Which is a London rakehell more likely to survive—
a hanging, or a handfasting to a spirited Highland lass?

Jane Feather

A HUSBAND'S WICKED WAYS

When a spymaster proposes marriage as a cover,
a lovely young woman discovers the danger—and
delight—of risking everything for love.

Available wherever books are sold or at www.simonandschuster.com

POCKET BOOKS
A Division of Simon & Schuster
A CBS COMPANY

POCKET STAR BOOKS
A Division of Simon & Schuster
A CBS COMPANY

20472

Delve into a *passion* from the *past* with a *romance* from *Pocket Books!*

LIZ CARLYLE
Never Romance a Rake
Love is always a gamble....But never romance a rake!

JULIA LONDON
The Book of Scandal
Will royal gossip reignite her husband's passion for her?

KARIN TABKE
Master of Surrender
The Blood Sword Legacy
A mercenary knight is bound by a blood oath to reclaim his
legacy—and the body of the one woman he desires.

KATHLEEN GIVENS
Rivals for the Crown
The fierce struggle for Scotland's throne leads
two women to courageous new destinies...

**Available wherever books are sold
or at www.simonandschuster.com.**

19096